REBIRTH IN ACADI

Rebirth in Acadi

A novel

by

SUSAN SWANSON

Adelaide Books
New York / Lisbon
2021

REBIRTH IN ACADI
A novel
By Susan Swanson

Cover design © 2021 Adelaide Books

Published by Adelaide Books, New York / Lisbon
adelaidebooks.org

Editor-in-Chief
Stevan V. Nikolic

For any information, please address Adelaide Books
at info@adelaidebooks.org
or write to:
Adelaide Books
244 Fifth Ave. Suite D27
New York, NY, 10001

ISBN: 978-1-954351-38-7

Printed in the United States of America

For my grandson, Christopher Swanson,

who has encouraged my writing.

Contents

Chapter One   *Severing the Lifeline*   **13**

Chapter Two   *Camaraderie*   **16**

Chapter Three   *Losing Everything*   **22**

Chapter Four   *Kindred Soul*   **27**

Chapter Five   *A Gamble*   **37**

Chapter Six   *Mr Lombard and the Museum*   **43**

Chapter Seven   *Storage Unit*   **58**

Chapter Eight   *What Can I Say?*   **63**

Chapter Nine   *Low Bid*   **81**

Chapter Ten   *You See What I Mean?*   **84**

Chapter Eleven   *Finger to Lips*   **89**

Chapter Twelve   *So Many Questions*   **94**

Chapter Thirteen   *No One Will Ever Know*   **97**

Chapter Fourteen   *Bound by a Sad Truth*   **101**

Chapter Fifteen   *She Could Be Reasonable*   **105**

Chapter Sixteen   *C and B*   **114**

Chapter Seventeen   *Lord, Do I Trust My Eyes?*   **118**

Chapter Eighteen   *Not an Ordinary Joe in the Bunch*   **126**

Chapter Nineteen   *Vernon, You Just Don't Know*   **130**

Chapter Twenty   *Not Your Typical Easy-Going Broad*   **134**

Chapter Twenty-One   *Tacit Blackmail*   **137**

Chapter Twenty-Two   *Memories*   **139**

Chapter Twenty-Three   *Matching Monogram*   **143**

Chapter Twenty-Four   *The Attic*   **157**

Chapter Twenty-Five   *Looking at Things Rationally*   **163**

Chapter Twenty-Six   *Greedy*   **168**

Chapter Twenty-Seven   *Mama*   **171**

Chapter Twenty-Eight   *Friday Evening*   **177**

Chapter Twenty-Nine   *FTD and Flowers*   **180**

Chapter Thirty   *Looking Quite Fine*   **182**

Chapter Thirty-One   *An Interesting Lunch*   **187**

Chapter Thirty-Two   *What Do You Think
She's up to Now?*   **196**

Chapter Thirty-Three   *A Solid House*   **199**

Chapter Thirty-Four   *Better Get Your Camera*   **200**

Chapter Thirty-Five   *He Just Didn't Understand*   **204**

Chapter Thirty-Six   *Retribution*   **208**

Chapter Thirty-Seven   *You Actually Could
Live with Yourself?*   **211**

Chapter Thirty-Eight   *A Fine Kettle of Fish*   **214**

Chapter Thirty-Nine   *You're Sure They're Lazy?*   **219**

Chapter Forty   *Making Friends*   **221**

Chapter Forty-One   *Impatience*   **224**

Chapter Forty-Two   *Two Babies?*   **225**

Chapter Forty-Three   *Empty Space*   **230**

Chapter Forty-Four   *AK-47*   **238**

Chapter Forty-Five *Spicy Facts* **241**

Chapter Forty-Six *Elusive Worm* **242**

Chapter Forty-Seven *Stone-Cold Dead* **244**

Chapter Forty-Eight *Daylilies and Hummingbirds* **248**

Chapter Forty-Nine *Botherin' the Boss* **251**

Chapter Fifty *Curling Fog* **256**

Chapter Fifty-One *I'm Coming In* **259**

Chapter Fifty-Two *We Should Have Known* **264**

Chapter Fifty-Three *Margaret, I Love You* **266**

Chapter Fifty-Four *I Been Feedin' 'Em* **272**

Chapter Fifty-Five *Holy Joes* **275**

Chapter Fifty-Six *Another Try* **280**

Chapter Fifty-Seven *The Battle* **285**

Chapter Fifty-Eight *Dinner* **292**

Chapter Fifty-Nine *Bradley* **298**

Chapter Sixty *If You Want To Talk* **304**

Chapter Sixty-One *Not Funny, Louise* **309**

Chapter Sixty-Two *Mother* **313**

Chapter Sixty-Three *The Straight Story* **319**

Chapter Sixty-Four *Tending to Business* **325**

Chapter Sixty-Five *So Nice of You* **330**

Chapter Sixty-Six *An Adoption* **335**

Chapter Sixty-Seven *On to Something* **342**

Chapter Sixty-Eight *Bang-Up Job* **349**

Chapter Sixty-Nine *Trees and Birds* **358**

Chapter Seventy *A Medal* **362**

Chapter Seventy-One *Get Off It* **367**

Chapter Seventy-Two *Filthy Blood* **371**

Chapter Seventy-Three *A Fine Idea* **373**

Chapter Seventy-Four *The Gathering* **379**

About the Author **383**

Chapter One

Severing the Lifeline

The thought of what her mother would do after she'd read the note brought tears to Elizabeth's eyes, a response a lot like when as a child she'd imagined her mother's reaction if she died. Back then, she'd reveled in the thought of how her own tragic end would affect others. Thinking about it now, she wasn't sure why it had given her such pleasure, but suspected it was the fancied drama of it that made her ache with something akin to satisfaction. Now, picturing her mother alone in her stuffy house with the humming fridge, lifeless answering machine, and a bedroom closet cleared of all but old shoes, ragged shirts, and dust balls, Elizabeth felt no satisfaction. This drama was real and it hurt. Her most revered relative would be alone. The house dark and empty when she got home from work. But for the cleared-out closet and fewer cosmetics and hair accessories crowding bathroom shelves – and the gouge Elizabeth had made in the bedroom door frame as she struggled with a jam-packed suitcase – everything would look the same as when her mother left for work that morning. At least her mother had that. But it was scant compensation for what Elizabeth knew to be true: that her unexpected departure would leave her parent with, at the least, a heavy heart. And when she walked in that evening and realized her daughter was gone, she'd be at wit's end, rattling about, room to room, trying to figure out what to do, maybe even thinking of calling Rebecca and Mary. On the other hand, that wasn't likely. She wouldn't want to bother them. They were, after all, busy with their own lives. Besides, they'd learn soon enough. Come Sunday they'd be around for chicken stew, cherry pie, and *60 Minutes*.

As far as tonight? Locked doors, shades drawn, lights off, early to bed. The realization that her life was changed, likely forever, and that the only way to deal with it was to put one foot in front of the other was something her mother probably hadn't even considered yet. But she would soon enough.

As for Elizabeth, she had considered it. She'd thought it through. She knew how life-changing – and problematic – her decision was. And she'd gone back and forth. Was this really what she wanted? Did she have what it took to carry it out – willpower, backbone – or would she come crawling back like a fenced dog who'd broken out but gotten hungry? As well, was this the way to make the break? What if she'd done it gradually, leaving but keeping in touch for a time while pretending the arrangement wasn't meant to turn into a total split. If she'd done it that way she could've set the stage for a whole new identity at the same time she held onto the lifeline to her mother and Brackenville, New York.

Yet, doing it like that would've led to problems with the name change. Especially once she'd reached journey's end in Louisiana. One slip and her plan could well be down the drain. All her dreaming and planning gone south, and simply because she'd compromised. The simple truth was that there was too much at stake to let something like compromise mess things up. Which meant that the only way to go about it was full speed, just as planned: complete break with Brackenville and the mother she loved. At least for the moment it had to be that way. Maybe someday, when she'd either moved several notches up in the social scale or simply decided she didn't care anymore, she'd "come out" and, if it came to that, take her licks. But that would be in the distant future, if ever.

She'd thought about it long and hard. This dream of freeing herself from an identity that made life nearly unbearable had been simmering for years. From the beginning, she'd even known where she'd go when she made her break. It would be Louisiana, where her superstar antebellum forebears, Albert and Charlotte Bancroft, had left their mark. She could start anew there while at the same time learning what had happened with them. Ever since Grandpa first told her their weird story she'd wanted to know the rest — the details of the duel that cost Albert his life, why that duel went on beyond accepted limits, why Charlotte hadn't gone to him as he lay dying.

Ironic as it was, she'd hide her identity and history while pursuing it. What was just as ironic was that she'd be patterning herself after a father she'd never known who, she supposed, was also living in sweet, light-skinned obscurity. Like him, she'd fade from memory, perhaps never to be heard from again. Or not, depending on uncertainties. What was certain at this point was that in the year 1993 Louise Dennis — formerly Elizabeth Bancroft — was headed to the quaint Louisiana river town of Acadi to take a stab at a new life.

Chapter Two

Camaraderie

As he leaned against a redwood cabinet in his kitchen Pierre couldn't keep his eyes off Louise, now concentrating on slicing a Mardi Gras king cake. No one on this planet did such wonderful justice to short skirts. Shapely, tanned – her legs were first class. But that wasn't all that set off sparks. Wavy dark hair, huge hazel eyes framed by long black lashes, tempting mouth, olive skin – really, there was little about her that wasn't totally cool. She knew how to make the most of it too. Simplicity. Never flashy. Letting the bod speak for itself. Skimpy skirts, tiny jackets, stiletto heels that gave a guy the hots. It was truly insane that foster homes had turned out such quality.

As for himself, at six feet with square shoulders, slender hips, melting brown eyes, and dark curly hair that wouldn't stop, what was there to say? And the two of them together? Primo. Head turners. Louisiana River Road's version of Adonis and Aphrodite. Plus a few years, of course, which –

His Greek goddess was speaking. "This has been in the freezer since before we went skiing. Hope it's not stale." A quick sniff of one of the wedges she'd cut from the twisted circle of baked dough seemed to set her mind at ease. "You know, it's not half bad," she said, sounding like a northerner sampling a crawfish tail for the first time. "Still smells like almonds."

He reached over and brushed colored sugar from the tip of her pretty little nose, and she laughed. "Knowing our guests," he told her, "I don't think they'd be able to tell the difference."

She rolled her eyes and began arranging the wedges on a plate. When she'd finished, she got the cups, spoons, napkins, and walnut tray out of the "serving center," where she also pulled the stainless coffee urn from its special cubby. Then it was over to the deepest sink, where she filled the urn with water before pursuing her kitchen stint in the "quick-cooking area."

In public, Pierre laughed at the kitchen labels. Privately, he adored them. They affirmed that his new kitchen was high end.

"I still can't believe the convenience," his gorgeous bride-to-be said as she drew the canister of coffee from the pull-out shelf under the counter. "I can't figure your mom and dad leaving this place."

"I promise, they're happy as clams now they've got just one house. And the cottage in Ocean Springs was always their number one. They like the beach. I, on the other hand, prefer the pool."

With more important things on his mind, though, he wasn't about to go into that now. "What do you think," he asked, "am I silly, having the crew and subcontractors over?"

"Depends on why you're doing it. A little camaraderie never hurts. Especially if you're looking to build morale." The cover clanged lightly as she set it on the coffee urn. "But do you trust them around your silver?" She gave him one of those cynical little smiles that she was so good at.

He played along. "No worry. I'll do a spoon check before they drive away."

"My favorite place," she said once everything was set up on the antique console in the parlor and they'd moved to the gallery. She'd settled in one of the wicker pieces that faced the alley of oaks and he sat in a matching one at her side.

"What's that?" she asked, sniffing.

"Confederate jasmine," he shot back, not missing a beat. It happened to be one of the plants he knew, mainly because it grew on the trellis over the walk at the corner of the house and as a kid he'd broken that latticed arbor and, with it, the thick old jasmine vine. It happened when he was trying to climb the trellis in order to drop a turtle on the brick walkway. Which seemed like a good way to see if a turtle's shell could withstand it. But Mama didn't care about his experiment. All she cared about was her "poor Confederate jasmine."

Her damn Confederate jasmine, he thought now, leaning back and giving out a sigh that covered not only the deal with the jasmine but other things that had been bothering him.

"Tired?" Louise asked.

He answered that he wasn't; that sitting here with her and the gurgling fountain amidst the live oaks and birds was just overwhelmingly wonderful. He might've added *overwhelmingly pricey*, because that was really the cloud that was hanging over him. How pretending that he had limitless resources was getting harder and harder, with bills piling up and payroll in two days and just about every subcontractor in Belmont Estates due major payments. Not to mention alimony and child support. That Mama and Pops had helped out with Louise's ring and the pool, patio, and kitchen renovation was great. Not so great was that they hadn't given him title to the property, title that could've acted as collateral on the loan he really needed.

"Pierre, for heaven's sake, what's going on with you. First you say things are wonderful, then you look like your best friend died. Is it your kids? Do you miss them terribly?" Eyes probing, she reached over and took his hand "When will they be back from Celeste's parents'?" She massaged his fingers. "Visitation must be hard."

He gave her a somber look. "It is, but what're you gonna do? I try to see them as often as I can. But you know how it is. One thing or another. Like last time the kids were on the calendar I had to beg off because Tim Cantor was passing through on his way to the Gulf. It was a spur of the moment thing, you know. I hadn't seen Tim in quite a while. And then . . . Oh yeah, the time before. Remember? The night Francois Plantation opened their new restaurant. Much as missing my date with the kids hurt like everything, we couldn't sit that out." He pulled his hand away and, signaling finality, slapped his knee. "Anyway, it's all so mundane. Not a pleasant subject."

"Well –" She smiled. "How about this – that amazing building crew of yours. I'd really like to hear more about them. You never did explain how it happened they all belong to the same church."

"They don't. Not all of them. Most of them. There are some outsiders. And it's not just crew that go to church there. Subcontractors do too."

"So how'd it happen?"

"Well, you know Benny."

"The only one I do know."

"A couple years ago he had the bright idea that I could save some dough by hiring from his church. They'd work for less than the crew I was using at the time, he said. Quite a bit less. So I set up a meeting at this 'Loving Kindness Church.'"

"Weird name."

"And the church was nearly as weird: an old block building with a bright blue Jesus sign on top. And inside? I mean, strange with a capital *S*. More like a salvage warehouse that had lucked into a gold mine of moldy-smelling green vinyl folding chairs than a place of worship. But heck, I thought, who am I to judge?"

"So how did all these guys learn the trade?"

"On the job."

"Totally green? That was all it took?"

He nodded.

"And you belong to this church too, right?" She obviously referred to the handout he'd asked her, as sales manager of Belmont Estates, to distribute. It was their first meeting, and he'd instantly been bowled over by her, thinking, *brains, poise, everything, and in one fabulous chassis.*

"No, I'm not a member," he answered.

"But your blurb says you employ *fellow* parishioners."

"A little hard to explain. It sort of slipped by without my notice."

"And you know what? I'm relieved. That building doesn't sound like the most romantic place for a wedding. Which brings up religion. We never talk about it."

"Unfortunately, now's not the time," he said as he noticed a moth-eaten brown Cutlass turn in at the end of the drive. "Looks like Diaz is early." A touch of sarcasm in his voice as he added, "This guy never disappoints."

"I don't know how to take that," she said as they both got up.

"Well, let me put it this way. He's a painter, and pretty good too, but a bit of a pain."

"Lazy?"

"Hardly. The opposite."

"Doesn't sound like a problem to me."

"Well, if that isn't, his looks might be. Forewarned is forearmed."

Louise was good. No sign of shock at the scars or eye, which were more evident than ever, being he wasn't wearing the bandana he wore while painting. She said she was pleased to meet him, repeated "Cedro Diaz" as though determined to remember the name, and even extended a hand. Which Diaz took while looking like it might bite.

"You're early," Pierre said.

"I wanted to talk to you in private," the Cuban answered, warily eyeing Louise.

"Don't worry about her," Pierre assured. "She'll soon be family."

"Well, then . . . . " Diaz still looked uneasy as he hit Pierre with his eye. "I noticed some things that are missing in the house we're working on and thought I should tell you."

"Like what?" Pierre snapped as the chirrs and trills of evening suddenly erupted, echoing the angry roar in his head.

Chapter Three

Losing Everything

At one time he'd probably looked a lot like Dakota, Cedro Diaz thought as he sat on the steps at the rear of Joseph Buford's construction van watching Dakota and Benny, who'd gotten their food from the lunch wagon and were heading back. He had never been that tall, but he'd had those good shoulders and curly black hair and skin dark and smooth as a bebe'. But that was years ago. Now, knobby shoulders, faded hair, rubbery lumps all over his face and, worst of all, the plastic shell in his left eye socket had turned him into a freak. A freak who now pulled to the side and tucked his legs in as Dakota barked "Comin' through" and, quick and athletic as any fellow called Dakota should be – at least judging from movies Cedro had seen on television – hopped up and found a seat under the rusty bolts way back in the corner. Benny, following, took more time, first setting the Styrofoam box that held his lunch on the bench running around the inside of the van, then bracing himself on the right doorjamb before heaving once, then once again as he boosted his flabby body in. The metal door rattled in its ceiling track and the big old vehicle creaked as, wheezing like someone with asthma, he picked up the box and settled himself on the bench not far from where Cedro sat.

"Wha'd you get?" Sharlene asked the two. She was sitting in the middle of the bench next to two small ladders.

"Roast beef po-boys, dressed," Dakota answered.

"You guys. Will you ever try somethin' new?" She did that scowl that was supposed to mean she was frustrated, and the long scar on her forehead stood out firm and pink. "You're stick-in-the-muds," she added before taking a bite of her cheese sandwich.

Benny, still rattling and puffing like a flooded engine, finally got up enough steam to croak, "The day Baldwin Johnson comes out here and eats lunch with us is the day I'll sample somethin' diff'rent." Opening his box and taking the tomatoes out of his po-boy, he went on. "You're his mom – " Facing Odile now. " – Gimme a clue. What's he doin' in there by himself all the time? Copyin' the Bible word for word?"

Odile wagged a bony finger in front of her lips, finishing her mouthful of banana.

Benny winked. "Is he sick in the head?"

"He's tryin' to learn the Bible," she finally got out, gooey teeth hanging over lower lip. "If he writes it down, he don't forget."

Benny sat back and grinned. The bench drooped even more and made a noise like it was hurting. "That's no excuse for bein' unfriendly."

"If he thought you was lonely or in need, he'd be out here." Poor Odile, still trying to explain.

Benny took a big bite and chewed, then studied his sandwich like he was planning the next attack. "I'll tell you what I'm worried about," he said, a crumb flying from the sticky, brown mass in his mouth and landing on the floor. "I'm worried the guy's goin' to turn into a preacher if he don't watch out."

A proud little smirk settled on Odile's black face as she ripped open a snack-sized bag, set it between her skinny thighs, and took out a potato chip.

"Hey, you guys," now came from the back of the van. A shrill voice, there was no mistaking it for anyone but Joseph. He'd been so quiet Cedro had forgotten he was there. But now, in the slant of light coming in from where he sat on the step, Cedro could just barely make him out. He seemed to be unscrewing the stopper from his thermos. "What did you think of the meeting at Pierre's last night?" he went on.

"He's doin' his best and I'll help all I can." It was Benny again, his tiny eyes on Joseph now. "All I know is I sure can't afford to lose my job."

"Me neither" Sharlene threw in. "I got kids to support."

"How about you, Diaz?" Joseph took a slurp of coffee and gave a satisfied sigh. "I've got this sneaky suspicion from what you said last night that you don't agree and that you're more worried about Pierre's customers than us."

Cedro's heart sped up. "I've just got a problem with a few things."

"Like Pierre making a profit?" Joseph's lips curled a little.

At least, low light and all, it looked to Cedro like they curled. It may just as well have been Cedro's sense of foreboding that made his lips look that way.

"Like Pierre making a profit at others' expense," Cedro replied, voice a little wobbly.

"He's not supposed to make money?"

"Not by fooling people."

"That's none of our business."

"I don't agree," Cedro said, aware that, having set his thermos cup on the floor, Joseph had gotten up and was slowly moving toward him. Again Cedro's sense of foreboding kicked in. The way the carpenter carried himself – that deliberate, slow pace – and the look on his face – that stony set to the jaw – were like the Cuban lieutenant's. And when he slammed his foot down on the metal stool right next to Cedro and jabbed his poker-hot eyes into Cedro's and passed the back of his long, black hand slowly across his mouth, Cedro felt himself flinch.

"Look," Joseph said, breath hot, "you think we're getting rich off some innocent babes? You think we're profiting like crazy?"

"Not – "

"If that's so, why'm I forced to drive this piece of junk? And why'm I stuck in the Myrtle Project, a trash bin you wouldn't put your smelliest garbage in. A snake pit. A hole of horror. I don't think I'm exactly – " he clenched his teeth. " – what you'd call rich."

"Not you." Cedro's words were little more than faint rattle. "Pierre is, though."

Joseph didn't seem to hear. "I'm lucky if my family has food on the table and shoes on their feet and if I can heat the place and if the water pipes don't bust and send down the ceiling and if the rats don't bite the baby and if the kids don't get shot in a gang war." He took a long, loud breath. "But you know what?" His eyes seemed to shine now. "I've got a job and I've got pride and I've got my faith too. And if you think I'm gonna start second-quessing the boss and take a chance on losing everything, you're off the mark."

Cedro's scalp tingled and he turned away, gazing out, seeing nothing while thinking *losing everything*. The words ringing in his head as he recognized that it really did come to that. Losing everything. Like last time. And all because of big ideas. Had he gone too far already? Was the ugly cycle starting again? If so, what would he lose this time? What was left to lose?

He slipped down from the steps.

"Where you goin'?" Sharlene called. "You feelin' sick?"

Chapter Four

Kindred Soul

When her fellow aspiring archeologists had finally driven off, Margaret walked to her car and opened the driver's side, settling herself sideways on the two cushions she used for a boost now that the driver's seat had given in to the sinking effects of age. Sun so warm, weathered shack in the distance so quaint, toll of "A Mighty Fortress" from St. Joan of Arc's bells so moving – it was a far cry from Spring Park, Minnesota, where it was likely snowy and cold, and where now – she checked her watch — yes now, the powerful voices of Good Shepherd Lutheran Church, led by the recessing choir, were booming out a similar strain. And where, but for Fred's job transfer, she would still be. Center stage, too, and loving it, anchoring the whole exhilarating spectacle, feverishly pulling stops, shifting manuals, and straining for organ pedals.

But she had to face it. She no longer sat at a newly built organ in the rear of a protestant sanctuary of contemporary design that was filled with people she'd known most of her sixty-two years. And, unless she abandoned Fred, she'd likely never sit there again. Rather, she was in a barren patch set between a swamp and sugar cane field. True, it had once been a racetrack. True also, it was located in the rear of a relatively new river road subdivision called "Belmont Estates" – in fact a subdivision where she wouldn't mind living, especially if she could find a low-priced, conscientious contractor to build the perfect little house for her (something she needed to get serious about). At the moment, though, all she could think about was how different what she was experiencing was from what the horse lovers and chance takers knew back then. Theirs was a world of linkage, of shared interests and histories, of fancy clothes and fine horses and mutual acquaintances. Hers was a world of detachment.

Yet, that feeling of otherness had eased a bit since earlier that morning. And what made the difference? It was Charlotte Bancroft, this lady who'd finagled her way into Margaret's life today. Who'd played the organ; who'd been taken from friends and family and plunked down in this godforsaken no-man's-land that in some ways was so appealing; whose husband had gambled; and who, for one reason or another, had abandoned that same husband as he lay dying. All of it occurring over a hundred years ago. Hearing about Charlotte had been like connecting with a sort of soul sister. Of course, Margaret recognized that she would never abandon Fred, especially if he were dying, and now that he'd scuttled the blackjack habit, she didn't have to think about that. Even so, the odds of two such kindred spirits as Charlotte and herself winding up in this unlikely place nearly took her breath away. And that no one in the historical society had mentioned either Charlotte or Albert Bancroft in all their earlier discussions of influential forerunners was equally surprising. The Bancrofts' was as tragic a story as any she'd heard.

The morning had begun quite normally, if *normal* meant a little problem with squealing hearing aids and a scare while making those perfect little half-circles with the metal detector. And these days, that's what *normal* meant. Of course, the problem with hearing aids was nothing new. Even these all-in-the ear ones that were supposed to be so great whistled when things like visors interfered with proper "nesting in the ear." The weird ache in the jaw that came on with metal detector exertion was more recent. At her last visit the doctor had even prescribed nitroglycerin. But because of her reaction to it – the intense headache – she didn't like the stuff and always left the pills in her car over by the stable. As far as jaw pain, she'd decided, it was less complicated and painful to just sit it out. Being careful, obviously, where she sat. This was water moccasin and timber rattler country.

Yet, why even think about that? In summer, when the old abandoned racetrack slithered with slimy creatures was the time to worry. This cool weather turned snakes sluggish, harmless. More than that, the historical society muck-a-mucks weren't a bunch of reckless fools. When it came to fieldwork, they covered everything. An example: right now over there near the brush pile, where that red first aid bag that Gilbert Kliebert and Leonce Batiste carried along everywhere rested on someone's spread-out sweatshirt. Their insistence that female volunteers, like the men, dress in long pants and boots, even when temperatures soared, was another example. Alma Delatte, working with them over there, was a case in point.

Of course, from the start, Alma wasn't the most feminine creature. She wore her hair in a man cut, avoided lipstick, and had a weird way of walking, legs a little wide-spread, as though struggling with jock itch. Skinny, sixty-four (she'd bragged on her last birthday), and, today, wearing a yellow t-shirt with

Acadi Frog Festival in bright green script, she looked much like a teen from a distance. Up close, though, she was fighting the same battle as Margaret. Apparently dark eyes and skin were no better at fending off wrinkles than blue eyes and freckles. Well, at least Margaret had one advantage. It was the extra pounds. True, a bigger *toosh*, as Fred liked to call it. But beyond that, fewer creases top front.

Margaret liked Alma. What she liked most was that Alma wasn't afraid of getting down on hands and knees and digging. She was supposedly Cajun, yet spoke like a U of M graduate, with an occasional slip into south Louisiana jargon. One of her favorite terms was *Cher* which, from what Fred told Margaret, meant *good friend*. Whenever Margaret was the target of the word she felt a ping of real friendship.

"Keep up the good work," Alma was calling now, having left her workmates for one of her infrequent calls on her *podna from the north*, another favorite label for Margaret. Stamping up in dusty boots, leaves and weeds crackling underfoot, she held out a lump resembling a chunk of dried putty. "This is what your detecting led me to earlier this morning. I found it in the old dump right near where your detector beeped."

Margaret used her arms to push up. First knees, then feet.

"Sore back?" Alma's lips curved in a knowing smile.

Margaret nodded, not about to let her in on the truth. Anyway, the pain was gone.

"Well, what do you think?" Alma asked, a touch of cool confidence in her voice as she handed the formless clump over.

Margaret studied it, then shrugged. "I don't know. Petrified wood?"

"Petrified wood!" Alma scraped grimy fingers through damp hair, leaving muddy spikes. "It's a kneeling woman." Eyes pained, she searched Margaret's. "You really can't tell?"

"Actually, Alma, I can't tell a thing close range without glasses."

"Well then, it's Saint Bernadette. Of course."

"And you say my detector helped find her? How's that? She's not metal."

"Easy. There was a button in the dirt right next to her. So tarnished I thought it was a rock at first. I've got it here . . . ." She fumbled in the huge pockets of the baggy pants that were obviously army surplus, then shrugged. "Oh well."

"So, this Saint Bernadette . . . I guess the reason I didn't recognize her is – "

"It's obvious. You haven't been inside St. Joan of Arc Church. Saint Bernadette is front and center up there." She wagged her head, squinted accusingly. "The most important landmark on the river road and you, so-called history buff, haven't even bothered to check it out."

"I'm really not a history buff," Margaret admitted. "Or at least wasn't till I got involved at the racetrack." A tugboat sounded its plaintive horn, and she looked toward the river.

Alma, meanwhile, took a deep drag from the cigarette she'd just lit and shot a tiny spurt from the corner of her mouth. "You really should check out the church." Wispy clouds floated out with words. "There's some great stuff there." She stared away, eyes fixed on her two workmates, who'd moved further out and were on their knees using trowels to scoop under a mossy cypress not far from the swamp. "What you might do is watch for one of those charters from New Orleans — I think they stop at the church on Thursday mornings — and drop in when the bus is out front. The tour guides are pretty good." Another drag, and a puff that faded into the crisp, blue sky. "You know, what I don't get, though, and only recently realized, is why the most important thing that happened at the church is totally passed over. The guides don't even give it a mention."

"And what – "

"A duel."

Margaret was relieved that this most important thing wasn't another one of those miraculous appearances of the Virgin to some tippling sugar cane farmer.

"But not just any duel," Alma continued. "It was one of the last in Louisiana. And hardly anyone, even locals, knows about it. Leastways, they sure don't let on. I never knew, and I've lived here a long time. Of course – " She dropped the cigarette, crushing it with her boot. " – I only recently got hooked on parish history." She nudged a ridge of dirt over the stub, then looked up. "It was just last week that I found out about it when I came across the duel in a book about Acadi in the public library. It's a weird story, this duel." Her eyes narrowed. "Turns out the organist playing Mass inside the church was no less than the wife of the guy lying shot outside. And get this – she finished Mass after they told her." Alma's eyes flickered with either the pride in owning such information or the pleasure of witnessing Margaret's interest.

"You're sure they told her?"

"No doubt. The book made a big deal of it. Said someone whispered the news in her ear during the Offertory and she didn't bat an eye. Just went on playing like nothing had happened." Alma's own eyes were slits, blacker than ever. "Brings up all sorts of issues, you think? Like, did she have any feelings for the guy? And if she didn't, how come? Had he been out tomcatting? Shoved her around maybe?"

"Could be she just didn't realize how bad off he was."

"He'd been shot, for God's sake!"

"It could've been a superficial wound."

"The impression I got was that she was told her hubby was dying." Alma fastened her eyes on Margaret's as though seeking some hint of comprehension. "Anyway, superficial or not, he was hurting and she didn't go to him."

"In a case like that, though, you never know if you've got all the facts. And to blame her . . . ." Margaret avoided Alma's incredulous eyes. "She may have simply misunderstood."

"If you ask me, it's pretty hard to misunderstand when you're told in plain English that your husband's breathing his last."

"Who were these people anyway?" Margaret was desperate to get off a subject that struck too close to home.

"Charlotte and Albert Bancroft. The book said he was a state legislator and doctor here in Acadi and she was, obviously, a musician. I guess Albert did a little gambling on the side too."

A musician who'd abandoned a dying loved one. And married to a man who gambled! Margaret could hardly believe her ears. It was as though Charlotte Bancroft had resurfaced, and in a transplanted Minnesotan with metal detector.

"In fact I guess it was his gambling that set off the duel. Gambling – devil's handmaiden," Alma hissed, wagging her head. "If I'd been in Charlotte's shoes I'd have been looking for a way out as soon as I realized." She glanced in the direction of a noisy commotion in the distance, where a hawk, having swooped and nabbed something, was flying off. "But when you get right down to it – " She faced Margaret again. " – she had no place to go. No brothers and sisters, dad passed, mom senile. Turned out, in fact, that with no one but Charlotte in the states, her old woman had moved in with her."

"No family?"

"They were in England. From what I understand, Charlotte's part of the Corbyn family – Corbyn being her maiden name – came here when her father's wanderings led him to New Orleans, where he took a job as first harpist — whatever that means – with the French Opera. I guess a few years later was when he came up here to teach at the convent."

Good God. Not just a trip north to Minnesota. In order to get back home, this woman had an ocean to cross. "The book, the one where you found all this. What's it called?"

"*Livre Riviere.*"

"Lasserre Parish Library?"

"Normally. But right now I've got it in my car."

"Do you remember if it said where the Bancrofts lived?" Margaret hoped it might be one of those old cottages on the river road that she drove by nearly every day. To see it, maybe even to get a look inside, would be pretty amazing.

"Not sure about that. I do know from a picture in the book that the house was a dogtrot."

"Dogtrot?" Wacky Louisiana lingo. It had been hard enough substituting *parish* for *county*.

"*Dogtrot* is a center hall with front and rear porches. Open the doors and you get a breeze through the house." She stamped out the cigarette she'd just lit. "Could be the caption tells where the house sat. Wait here. I'll get the book."

"And I'll get my glasses," Margaret said, following her toward where they'd parked.

On seeing the photo, Margaret's enthusiasm fizzled. Not that the little shuttered house wasn't charming. It had all the character of old New Orleans as pointed out in a tour they'd taken when she and Fred first arrived from Minnesota: Country French simplicity, with a chimney at one end and thin square columns supporting the roof and a balustrade around the front porch. There were trees and bushes, and an iron fence surrounding the whole thing. It was Margaret's kind of place. So that wasn't what bothered her. Her frustration was in not recognizing it. It definitely wasn't one of those halfway decent old cottages she drove by every day on the river road. It didn't even resemble one of the weary old falling-down shacks.

"In that little house – " Alma tapped the picture with the tip of a grimy finger. " – Charlotte Bancroft kept a valuable music library, a lot of it highbrow. First editions that ended up at the LSU School of Music. Papers, too, that are in the archives at the University. You know, there was even a Charlotte Bancroft Music Museum."

"At LSU?"

"Right."

"You're telling me that a culture maven lived in Acadi, Louisiana? Pretty hard to fathom."

Alma snapped the volume shut. "Acadi was a center of culture back then, I'll have you know. You need to read the book, Miss Skeptic." She picked up "St. Bernadette" and headed off toward her fellow workers, turning around midway and calling back, "I'll let you know when I'm done with it, Cher."

The idea that at one time there'd been a second – or in this case a first – self in Acadi, this one named Charlotte Bancroft, was going to take some getting used to, Margaret was thinking as she got back to work. And though she would've loved to just pack the detector away and sit there dreaming about Charlotte Bancroft and what it must've been like back then for this newly discovered kindred soul, Margaret wasn't about to sit down on the job. She was here to recover artifacts for the historical society and that's what she had to do. Reflection on her new-found alter ego, this duplicate, would have to wait.

So, upper lip stiff, she retrieved her electronic device and resumed little half-circles along the tamped down ruts horses had carved so long ago. Ruts that proved just as disappointing now as they had prior to her break. Now, though, she really couldn't trust herself. Half-circles were hit and miss; her attention to beeps sketchy. And even moving from one promising location to another – from those first ruts and then on to the area around the chunk of pocked concrete that marked the northwest corner of what at one time had been a roofed grandstand, and on to what had been the edge of the track, where pre-Civil War spectators had likely gathered behind a fence, mint juleps in hand, socializing while unwittingly parting with loose buttons, change, valuables, and who knows what – she had no luck. A good part of her problem may have been distraction.

But relief was on the way, and when at twelve o'clock the group gathered to appraise their finds, she could barely suppress a grateful sigh. Just as hard as restraining that sigh was feigning enthusiasm for the pile of trash they'd retrieved, starting with a horseshoe so eaten by rust it broke in two when Leonce tried to clean it, and moving on to something Gilbert said looked like a piece of a horse's bit (hogwash, for sure), and after that, tons of glass shards, all green, that could've come from a picnic within the past week and were as deadly as viper's fangs. And, of course, that precious "Saint Bernadette."

Chapter Five

A Gamble

After taking a right into the parking lot just past the sugar cane field, Fred Bohr drove straight to the rear, backing into the hindmost spot, near the chain-link fence. It wasn't that he wanted to avoid the sun; it was just as sunny back there as any place on the lot. No, the parking choice was a precaution, as was surveiling the entrance from behind the camellias across the road from the casino. (By then his shirt, under the supposedly lightweight navy sport coat, was clinging to him like a wet washcloth.) Equally precautionary was his stealthy crossing of the blistering river road after determining from behind those camellias that no one he recognized approached either on foot or in vehicle. And his final look back at the parking lot as he peeked from under the low-hanging fronds of the palm shading the front doors? That was to confirm that even Margaret, should she drive by, couldn't see his Volvo back there by the chain-link.

Feeling the need for further diligence as he stepped inside, he left on his sunglasses. Not much of a disguise, he supposed,

but better than nothing. From what he'd heard, the cheap –
and tasty – buffet attracted even non-gamblers, and that made
the corridor leading to the buffet the most precarious as far as
encountering acquaintances. He'd often thought that if he did
meet someone he knew he'd throw them off by getting in the
buffet line.

At long last reaching the men's room, he dropped the
sunglasses into a pocket of his sport coat and checked the
mirror. Strands over bald spot in place; lines around eyes just
as deep as the day before; paunch, despite the forty-five minute
jog and light breakfast, still revolting. Damn paunch. What
good the effort? Might as well indulge. Indulge in anything,
everything. Gratify the most egregious of urges, gaming
included. Why not? It was a heck of a lot better than spending
lunch hour in the office with a sandwich and newspaper, and
no worse for the aging body. Not to mention the deserved
diversion. That it wasn't guilt-free was unfortunate, of course.
This worry about rubbing eyeballs with someone he knew, such
as an employee, was what turned what should've been pure
pleasure into something less. He'd been lucky so far. Or was it
that his fear was overblown? After all, with salaried employees'
mere half hour lunch break there wasn't much chance they'd
drive ten minutes each way for a moment at the casino.

A little more relaxed now, he exited the men's room and
headed for the steps. Really, he was feeling more than a little
at ease. A kind of high was taking hold. A lot like when as a
kid he'd waited in line for the roller coaster. Back then it was
part anticipation, part worry he wouldn't find a seat. Actually,
same thing now. But scoping out the room, he saw there was
no need for concern. A stool at the middle table was right there
staring him in the face. And, after scanning nearby tables and
finding no familiar faces, he settled in, wingtips on chair rungs

and tie loosened, before appraising his cohorts. They were a veritable mixed bag: a young Dalai Lama, a blonde strumpet, and a Deadhead.

The dealer was the green-eyed one with round face. Scandinavian for sure. A cold fish who, when he shoved two twenties her way and asked for one-dollar chips, gave no sign she'd seen him before. And that was fine. All he wanted was action, which he soon got, but not to his satisfaction. From the beginning his hands were subpar. Worse, the hippie next to him latched onto a streak of luck so prolonged and unbelievable it was . . . taxing. Not that another's good fortune bothered Fred. He just would've liked sharing a bit of it, especially a hand like the one where the dealer had an ace up and the hippie got two nines and split them, resulting in mute reaction from tablemates: the Lama shaking his round head, the blonde unfurling her painted eyes, the dealer knitting invisible brows. Even the rubbernecking dealer at the empty table to the left got involved. "Not wise to split," he called.

But the hippie held out, first snagging a two and then a ten for twenty-one. "Far out!" he roared, gorilla arms skyward, barn odor westward toward Fred.

And the guy's second hand? Another two, another ten, another twenty-one. Beating the dealer's twenty. Luck at its most bizarre!

There was commotion at the table. No words. Scratching of ears, rubbing of chins, shaking of heads from the most reticent group Fred had ever played with. Except for the lucky SOB, who extended a hand and roared, "Gimme some skin, man." To which Fred responded with "Way to go" and the demanded extremity (which he silently vowed he'd wash on the way out).

The hand-washing vow came first. His second vow was that this would be his last game ever. A lunchtime sandwich and newspaper were looking better by the minute. At least at the grain elevator he had some control. Here, things were insane. Stressful. And worst of all was the clientele. Who were these people? Had they no better way to spend their time? Did they read books? Had they even graduated from high school? What would his long-departed mother think if she could see him now? His mother, who'd been so proud of her son's Ivy League scholarship. What was that son doing here in a casino?

No. Never again. No ifs, ands, or buts – this was his last hour at the casino.

That being so, and the uncompromising decision firmly settled in his mind, he celebrated with his last five chips. A sort of grand finale. Why not? Five paltry chips down the drain was no big deal. Especially when afterward he'd never again soil his fingers with the decadent (and likely bacteria-ridden) tokens.

But when his luck changed and the five paltry chips turned to twenty significant ones, there was no quitting. Who was it said "get 'em while the gettin's good"? Maybe Margaret, back in their fishing days. Anyway, his surge of pleasure was palpable. Pulling the chips in and piling them in neat columns was as good as . . . what? . . . watching grain silos go up? Actually, almost, and without the stress of construction worries. Chip columns just grew and grew into fat, stratified monuments, albeit small ones . . . until they slowly dwindled away. And when Fred's soon did, and the only recourse was an attempt to rebuild, all he found in his wallet was a mere four dollars. Four dollars, and he hadn't yet tipped the dealer or bought lunch. Truth was, though, that sullen Scandinavian didn't deserve a tip and as far as lunch, skipping it would be a step toward reducing the paunch.

A couple hands later, he was finding his way down the steps on the way to the exit. At the same time, pondering an excuse for being late. Another traffic tie-up at the levee, he knew, was getting old. As was slow service at Lambert's Restaurant or the post office or . . .

Yet, as chief in charge of the whole facility – probably because of that Ivy League degree – did he really need an excuse? Since he was doing his job in a responsible manner there was no need explain to anyone. Not even Margaret. What mattered was making sure Welbourne's grain business prospered while putting food on his own table, and in that respect he'd proved himself. At least, recently he had.

Waiting to exit the parking lot, air conditioner on high and windows open to expel hot air, he watched as one car after another streamed by. The cheerful yellow and white riverboat casino sat across from him now, and beyond that, the grim tanks, towers, and pipes of the oil refinery on the other bank. Two worlds. One oozing indolence and Southern charm. The other spewing industry and ugliness. The ugly part being where he spent a good part of those hours that gave rise to the need for escape. At least everything was a lot better than when, after personal financial losses and failure of his little compost business, he was in danger of losing his job with Welbourne Grain. At the time, Welbourne's offer of a job transfer and what sounded like a promotion – what else did it mean to be named Director of Engineering? – seemed heaven-sent. And it still seemed that way, except for the pressure.

What he really needed was to get out in the open, enjoy nature. It was why he'd loved the farm in Minnesota. And why he loved golf now. But there was no getting in a round of golf at lunchtime. So he was back to the few quick hands of blackjack that he'd promised Margaret when they left Minnesota he'd give up for –

A horn stopped him short. The offending car, past him now, was fancy. Most likely a Corvette. Bright yellow. Screaming money. The kind of car no one he knew drove. Of course, it might've just been someone warning him not to pull out. As far as anyone visiting from headquarters in Minneapolis? Not likely. Those guys drove economy rentals.

Even so, this wasn't good. If it ever got to Welbourne brass that he was spending the noon hour this way it could mean deep trouble. They didn't take to gaming. They didn't even call it gaming. They called it gambling. And when they said the word their faces twisted and they looked like they might lose their latest meal.

Chapter Six

Mr Lombard and the Museum

A year? No, more like two. And in those two years Louise had grown used to both the new nose and the name. It had taken longer for the name, and once in a while, especially when caught up in paperwork, she winced when she realized she'd been ignoring someone seeking her attention. Mary Jo had asked if she might be a little hard of hearing.

Other than the name, the only thing that never ceased to bring her up short, nearly to the point of a confirming pinch, was the three carat diamond mounted in a swirl of platinum ribbons and hearts on the third finger of her left hand and the gorgeous fiancé, Pierre Armant, who came with it.

Everything else had demanded adjustment, but the kind that one had to expect with any move as life-changing as hers. And some adjustments had been easier than others. The ins and outs of her position as sales manager of the up-and-coming Louisiana river road subdivision, Belmont Estates, was one of them. She'd mastered that by her second week.

On the whole, then, things were going pretty well. Granted, there'd been bumps in the road, getting her tubes tied being one of them. "Does it hurt terribly?" the snub-nosed nurse had asked when she was back in the recovery room dabbing at her eyes with a little lump of wet tissue.

"No," she'd answered, looking away.

But of course it did. Though not so much physically. What really hurt was that she knew there was no turning back, that those flesh and blood ties that had once seemed of no account were gone. First, her mother, whose heart she surely had broken and who even if generous enough to take her back would never trust her again. And then, even if only a possibility, a child of her own.

No mother, no kids, she had truly cut herself loose, she remembered thinking that day in the recovery room. A day she really would've liked to have had someone there. But there was no one, not even a friend calling to make sure the surgery had gone well. The only living being who seemed at all interested was the nurse, handing her tissues, asking if there was someone she could call to come and pick her up. "Oh, honey," she said when told Louise had said she'd call a cab. A moment later, she was moving a chair to the side of the bed so she could stroke Louise's forehead and murmur things like, "It's hard, I know."

And she was so right. It was harder than Louise had ever imagined when she first began planning. Back then, tubectomy hadn't seemed a barrier. She'd never wanted kids anyway. When she was little, she'd steered clear of dolls and as a teen, hated babysitting. Besides that, sterilization was such a big part of her scheme. There was no question it had to be done. To try to find another way of avoiding the risk of a throwback would be to put off the inevitable. And, she'd further rationalized back then, in the bizarre event she changed her mind, she could try reversal. From what she'd been told, fallopian tubes could be rejoined, unclamped. No promises as far as that. But did it matter? Hardly. Her mind was made up and for her to change it just wasn't in the cards.

So went her thinking before the operation. After, she was less philosophical.

Why the change? Maybe it was the trauma of surgery. Maybe the pain medication. Whatever, instead of optimism she felt sadness, sadness that surfaced whenever she had time to rethink what she'd done.

Happily, there wasn't much time for rethinking. The forethought involved in avoiding complications having to do with "passing," as some would have called what she was doing, made it easier. All that plotting and scheming allowed less time to second-guess or agonize over either the surgery or her mother. Practical matters, such as questions she was sure would come up regarding her background, held sway.

It was in a motel on her way south that she'd begun work on those questions. Following her mother's advice (there was no way she'd ever escape her influence) regarding benefit of practicing for oral presentations in front of a mirror, she did just that. Now, though, she practiced a slick spiel that wouldn't have gotten her an *A* in anything but a class on how to commit perjury. And though even in the best of times this mirror exercise made her uneasy, it was trickier at the moment. She'd not only had the tubal ligation; a few days later she'd had an "ethnic" nose job, narrowing and minimizing what had been her only trace of African lineage. So what she saw in the mirror as she practiced her oral performance was the broken face of a recovering patient. A face with swollen, bruised nose and blackened eyes.

Yet she controlled the urge to look away, and was soon earnestly explaining to her mimicking image that she'd been little more than a day old when she was found on a doorstep. "And from then on," she continued, "it was no bed of roses, believe me. I spent time in more homes than I care to think about. I don't even remember the names of foster parents. My whole childhood . . . really . . . better forgotten."

Practicing this way, she felt silly, ashamed. She imagined her sisters rolling on the floor, roaring hysterically when she brought up the doorstep. (Too clichéd?) And her mother, hurt and shocked.

Yet, she plodded on, explaining to her battered crony in the mirror that she was "likely of Southern European descent. Not totally confident about that, though."

Finally finished for the day, though she knew she'd need more run-throughs at some point, she felt such distaste for both the old Elizabeth and the new Louise that before she turned away she actually poked thumbs in ears, wagged her fingers, and crossed her eyes. A minute later, though, bolstered by what she knew to be the truth – that it wasn't her fault she'd been cheated and felt the need to pursue something resembling a decent life – she turned back to the unhappy face and blew a kiss. Bruised eyes blinked agreement: hard as it was, she'd done the right thing.

Even with all the planning, she kept fingers crossed long after settling on the river road. Truth was, she wasn't at ease. The Bancroft connection loomed in the background. At least she felt like it did. Like at any moment someone would come up from behind, poke her, and hiss, "I know who you really are and why you're here."

Still, she had no doubt she'd made the right decision in choosing Acadi. At least as a starting point. If it didn't work out she could always move on. But this drive to know her past was and had been for a long time something like a religious mission, and the only place she'd satisfy it was in this river road town. In the back of her mind, of course, was the question of where it would all lead. There was always the possibility of a fortune in unclaimed Bancroft memorabilia hidden away down here. Obviously, claiming it, she'd have to choose between old and new identities, so unless the hypothetical gold mine amounted to a major inheritance, she'd likely stay with the name change. Another scenario involved her great, great, great grandparents, who may have enjoyed such standing in the community that their race had been of no importance when they were alive and of just as little importance at the moment. Now that would be a turnaround. *Louise, Louise*, she had to warn at this point, *have you lost your mind? Remember what Grandpa said about the circumstances of Albert's death.*

Yet, from what Grandpa told her – when her mother, who banned anything to do with Albert Bancroft, wasn't around – it almost seemed plausible. Or was it that she wanted so much for it to be true that she'd convinced herself it was plausible? To be accepted on equal terms despite race had been her wildest fantasy ever since she'd realized what it meant not to have that footing. She literally dreamed of being free of the burden and, waking to the unhappy truth, would try to fall right back to sleep in order to regain the vision.

As to Albert and Charlotte and their standing in the community, there was no doubt they'd been influential. Fascinating too. But had they really been that important? And was there really a Bancroft museum at LSU or had her grandpa been making things up about Charlotte and her music and Albert and his career?

From the beginning, those were questions that bugged her. Yet even with the driving urge to figure it all out, it took a while to get around to the archives at LSU. She wanted, after all, to do it right, according to plan, no mistakes. (As if she'd ever feel totally confident that everything she'd done in the recent past wasn't a mistake.) And with finding a place to live in Acadi and furnishing it (after a fashion, because of scant savings), and studying for the real estate license and getting a job and then being doggedly pursued by Pierre — all the time keeping her lip zipped about her interest in the Bancrofts — she didn't get up to the archives in Baton Rouge until nearly a year after setting foot in Acadi.

It was on that visit that she got a look at some of the papers that verified her grandfather's claims about the Bancrofts' importance in the community. There were eight files, but only two were available to the public and, being she was supposedly part of that public, her access was limited. That fact grated on Louise. "You know, Mr. Lombard," she told the archivist, "when your card catalog says there are eight file boxes and six of those eight are off limits it's a real letdown. And when what's in those two available boxes turns out to be worthless, it's just plain – " She searched for the word. " – unjust."

She'd already introduced herself to Mr. Lombard, telling him that she'd gotten hooked on Lasserre Parish history through her fiancé, whose family had lived in the parish since the late seventeen hundreds. "Especially history that has to do with Albert and Charlotte Bancroft," she clarified. "From what I understand, Albert was killed in one of the last duels in Louisiana."

Mr. Lombard's cheeks flushed a bit and his dark eyes seemed to flash. Fortunate man. Not only good-looking, with curly silver hair and tanned skin, but obviously fired up by his job. By fifty-five, and he was surely that, a lot of people suffered burnout.

"I can count on one hand the inquiries I've had about that duel," he responded, "and I've worked here a long time. Most often, people want to know about the Long family, Avery Island, or our rare books collection." He studied Louise. "You're a rare bird."

"A rare and disappointed bird. That's why I asked for you. I need a real, live archivist. Someone who can help me figure out what's happened to all . . . . Am I right? There was actually a Charlotte Bancroft museum?" Feeling uncomfortable at the way he eyed her – a little too much fascination – she crossed her arms and shifted her eyes to the huge windows behind him, where drooping branches of a live oak loomed. "I suppose there are those who'd find Charlotte Bancroft's household ledgers and music programs fascinating." She turned back to him. "But not me. I don't give a darn how much liquor she bought and what she paid for it or what her choir sang on Christmas Eve, 1870. What I want is to see her stuff."

Mr. Lombard massaged his lips, and his brown crewneck slipped up, revealing a lightly frayed blue cuff. "Aren't there some letters and pictures?"

"One picture. Albert Bancroft in military uniform." Which, Louise silently recalled, she'd considered sneaking out of the archives. (He was *her* ancestor after all.) But having earlier studied the cursed rules that prevented such shenanigans – all baggage except pencil and pad restricted to downstairs lockers – she'd changed her mind. The photo, frame and all, was just too big.

Mr. Lombard, meanwhile, screwed up his eyes as though thinking. He was either really interested or pretending. "Weren't there some letters?"

"Three readable ones. And they were hopelessly boring. Depressing, in fact. About things like the death of a brother, a lonely girl in New York, sick kid. The rest were on onionskin, writing on both sides." She gave him a hot look. "Have you ever tried reading onionskin with writing on both sides?"

"I guess I haven't." He seemed to be suppressing a grin. What was it with this guy?

"Well anyway, you get the idea."

"I do." Serious again.

"Those onionskin letters were nothing, though, compared to finding that what I was looking for had been sealed away for a lifetime. A lifetime, mind you." A small sigh. Nothing too demonstrative. Avoiding suspicion was still crucial. "If I may ask," she said calmly, "what's the story with those six boxes I can't see?"

He shrugged. "Not sure. Could be there's a skeleton or two and the Bancrofts didn't want to risk embarrassing the rest of the family."

"But there is no family down here. At least that's my understanding," she quickly added.

His second shrug in less than a minute made her doubt earlier judgment about enthusiasm or interest. The man was jaded. He didn't have what it took to do his job. Add to that, he didn't take her seriously.

Yet, he was the only available archivist, and she'd better make the most of his expertise. So she changed course and in subdued, casual tone eased back into the Charlotte Bancroft Museum. "The girl at the desk said she'd never heard of it. Does it still happen to be around?"

"The museum was gone even before I took over as archivist. Long before."

"If that's the case, what were those inventories of museum artifacts and music doing in one of the boxes I was *privileged* – she pounced on the word – to look at? If the museum's gone, might as well toss the inventories as well. Or – " She gave him a sly look. " – have you got a roomful of that stuff sealed away too?"

A rosy cast similar to the early flush spread up his neck to his face. This time it looked more like unease than passion. "I wish I could help you," he whispered, and looked around warily. "But to be honest, that museum collection's been misplaced."

"Misplaced!"

He put finger to lips.

"You've lost the museum collection and you're acting like it's okay? If I felt like it, I could get you in deep trouble, you know. This is no small matter."

He took her arm and led her to the corridor, where he waited for the heavy wooden door to swing shut behind them. "It's like this. I haven't lost the collection, but – " He gazed over her head, apparently deliberating, before looking back. " – it'll take time for me to make arrangements."

"Arrangements?"

"For you to see it."

"Could you just give me some idea – "

"If you'll leave your address and phone number, I'll get back to you as soon as I can."

"But – " She stopped herself and unzipped her leather bag, taking a business card and pen from one of its pockets. After scratching out the address and phone number of the Belmont Estates Sales Office, she wrote in the phone number and address of the house she'd rented. "I'd prefer you get in touch with me at home," she said.

He took the card and reached for the door handle. "I'll do my best for you. You know," he added, "you're really quite beautiful."

The "Belmont Estates Five Percent Off Lot" promotion brought a flurry of customers to the subdivision during the next couple weeks, and Louise had hardly a moment to really think about Mr. Lombard's promise to do his best for her. Not that their conversation didn't pop into her head every so often. It was just that she had no time to press for further action. And, likely as not, it was for the best. It wouldn't be smart to spur suspicion by showing too much interest in the Bancrofts.

Then came the day his letter dated April 12 arrived.

Dear "Louise," she read, the thick black quotation marks around her name flashing like neon darts. What was this? How did he know?

She read on, hardly believing.

Here is the info you need. My storage unit is #15 at Best Value Storage. Address: 105 W. Magnolia Ave., Baton Rouge. That's where you'll find both the key (the owner will ask for identification) and the Charlotte Corbyn Bancroft Music Museum collection.

In the meantime I will have quit my job and left town. So I won't be around to look through the collection with you. And I'm sorry about that. I never really did get to sift through and figure out what went on back then.

I guess I'm a little dense, but it took a while for me to put my finger on who you were. You looked like someone, I thought, but who? Don't know if I showed it, but I was flabbergasted when I realized it was Aunt Alice. Not sure if you ever met her. She was old by the time you came along.

The bad thing about this whole affair is that once again I feel the need to pick up and leave. There are entanglements, as you well might understand, that rule out any kind of father/daughter relationship at this point. It's better for me to move on, change jobs, whatever. Maybe I'll even go back to teaching history.

Louise plunked herself down in a kitchen chair. As she braced her forearms on the trestle table the letter rattled in her hands and it was with some difficulty she read on.

There is one happy result of this decision of mine, and that is that I'm leaving the museum collection to you. But don't get your hopes up as far as those six sealed boxes in the Archives. There was no way I could get at them, so they're as sealed as ever. From what I understand, before she died Charlotte gave strict word to her daughter Lizzie regarding that hundred year provision. Who knows what awful secrets lie there!

Louise flipped the page.

Before I moved the collection into storage it had been moldering away in the attic of the old Music and Dramatic Arts Building at LSU for close to forty-five years. You may wonder how I moved it. Let me say, it was grueling. And I did it little by little. I suppose I really didn't have to be so careful. It had been stored since back in the late nineteen-forties and no one had looked in the card catalog for it in the past five years.

I doubt anyone will ever show interest again. For all practical purposes, it's lost. And now it's yours. I've taken care of everything with the storage owner and security should be no problem. All the information you'll need is enclosed. It could be you'll want to move everything to storage nearer where you live.

First edition sheet music and old scores are fairly valuable, and who can say as far as the artifacts. I suppose if you were to think about selling things, though, you'd want to consider ramifications as far as anonymity.

Amazing, Louise thought. First time he'd been in touch in twenty-six and a half years, and this man who she should by rights call "Dad" was lecturing on nuts and bolts. *Callous creep*, she was thinking when the phone began ringing. Probably Pierre. As it jangled on and on, she shivered.

When it finally stopped, she read on.

What a twist that you and I should meet down here in Bancroft country. Breaking away from Albert's legacy, we both ended up chasing it. But now I'm free and you've got the burden.

May you find whatever it is you're after.
B.A.B.

Louise set the letter on the table, glanced at the sheet of information he'd enclosed, and took the breath she'd nearly forgotten, clearing her head enough to start sorting through this crazy tangle she'd begun snarling the day she turned up at the archives. A sad tangle in its way, but wonderful too. Charlotte's collection had been dumped in her lap, and without any strategy on her part.

The sad thing was that her father was lost to her again. That he hadn't been interested enough to set up one – just one

– meeting in order to catch up on her life showed the depth of his detachment. And she hated him for it. She would've liked to return the favor by not giving his sudden appearance and disappearance another thought. But she couldn't make herself do it. Instead, as soon as she had time she stopped at the local library and looked for his name in phone directories of Baton Rouge and nearby towns. Her plan was to find the address and drive by the house. But "John Lombard" either had an unlisted number or no phone at all.

At least there was the archives. Certainly she'd get some information there.

But that, too, was a dead end; a cool "Sorry" to her request for his former address. "Well, then, forwarding address?" she'd said, all the while aware that if they wouldn't give out the old it was unlikely, even if they had it, they'd hand over the new. The answer from the woman on the other end was another "Sorry," still frigid but with impatient overtone now.

And since Louise didn't want to raise questions about her own motives, she gave up her search even while thinking someone at the archives knew where her father had lived and probably where he'd moved as well, and could likely even expand on his "entanglements." A wife? Children?

Maybe a wife, she decided, not kids. Kids were too risky. Like her, he would've wanted an untainted identity.

But that didn't mean that those already born to him, especially this attractive newcomer from Brackenville, New York, who shared his dream, could be easily dismissed. And as days wore on, Louise began thinking that he might reconsider. That he might decide to get in touch again. Not by showing up at the Sales Center. He'd be more careful than that. But what if he wrote another letter or phoned, or even drove down to where she lived?

Hope brightened her days. She rushed home at lunchtime to check the mail. Each time her home phone rang she ran to it, later hoping disappointment when she recognized that the voice wasn't her dad's wasn't too obvious. After work and before she either went out to dinner with Pierre or to Valeria Plantation to relax with him, she listened for the knock on the door, heart thumping even as she imagined opening it and finding her handsome, blushing dad. And despite bitterness that hung on, she even pictured a long, warm embrace.

Meanwhile, she took to rereading that one letter, analyzing it, looking for hints as to what he was like and where he'd gone. But it offered little satisfaction. Her only consolation was that one of these days she'd get the chance to sneak away to his storage unit in Baton Rouge. Maybe there she'd find information that would unmask this man who was so much like herself.

Qualify that. So much like herself as far as challenging the hand life dealt. Otherwise the two were very different. And she wasn't sure just how to explain it. Perhaps it was the wisdom of years. Maybe intuition. Or it might have just been her dad's long experience with duplicity. Whatever, while she hadn't had a clue as to his identity and had tagged him as a run-of-the-mill middle-aged archivist on the make, he had known early on who she was. And that was more than a little baffling. Yes, he said she looked like his Aunt Alice. But after all these years and in a town hundreds of miles from where he and that aunt had last met? It was amazing. Troubling too. Why hadn't she sensed something – if only that she'd seen him before – and put two and two together.

Yet, maybe that was being too hard on herself. How could she have known? He'd abandoned the family shortly after her birth. Her mother had done a meticulous job of getting rid of everything, including photos, that had to do with him. Her grandfather had lost everything related to all Bancrofts in the fire that left him with nothing but the clothes on his back. And the last thing she'd ever dreamed was that her father would turn up on the campus of Louisiana State University. An incredible bunch of events had conspired against her even suspecting.

Chapter Seven

Storage Unit

Perfect. With her fiancé at the Home and Garden Show in New Orleans, Louise finally had time to get up to Baton Rouge to really look into that mixed lineage that that same fiancé knew nothing about. She'd gotten a quick look at the Charlotte Bancroft collection when she'd moved it from her father's distant, messy, poorly lit and much too small unit to the one she'd rented at Silvain Self Storage. Now she was going to start a fine-comb look-through that would likely take some time.

She set her coffee, hazelnut fumes pluming from Styrofoam cup, on the concrete apron of the unit, then unlocked and pushed up the door. As it rattled in its track, sunlight rolled in, casting its harsh glare on the dusty old things she'd hauled in four weeks ago. Four weeks today. And what a day it had been. In more ways than one.

First, she'd had to get to her father's unit at break of dawn to remove the museum cards so that when Clyde got there he'd have no reason to doubt her song and dance about the collection being just a bunch of things left her by a very dear friend who'd died.

And then Clyde, who the storage company's owner recommended to help with the move, had turned out to be slow and careless, in need of constant supervision to ensure nothing got broken, torn, or placed where she couldn't easily get to it. To guard against having to come back on her own to rearrange things, some of them heavy, she'd directed his every move, from setting up the card table and brick and board shelves to making sure the magazines from the boxes were kept in order. All of it taking time.

Then once Clyde had left, she'd had to search out the big yellow envelope in which she'd hidden the cards, finally finding it at the bottom of a stack of sheet music. And after that there was the placing of those cards on or near their referenced items.

When sometime after nine she turned off the light and rolled down the door, she had doubts she'd make it home without drifting off. When she did, and dragged herself to bed, she was exhausted but gratified. She'd made it through a day as long and hard as any and, because she'd stayed the course, the going would be easier from here on in.

Here on in, next phase, or whatever to call this most special of days, Louise was "sunny side up" (her mother's words) when she arrived at her self storage. Grateful, too, she'd taken care preparing for this day. Even taking into account the hours spent, it had been worth it. More than that, she was grateful for the fluky way she'd met her father and the even more fluky way he'd up and informed her that these treasures were hers. The whole affair was beyond belief, yet here she was, sun warm, coffee waiting, heritage about to be enjoyed. She was feeling a lot like when as a kid on Christmas morning she'd gotten past the frantic opening of gifts and was ready to settle in and play.

And the gifts on this day? Among them, a wicker-covered wine bottle saved from Charlotte and Alberts' engagement party, a lacy black shawl Albert gave Charlotte as a wedding present (the color struck Louise as ominous considering the turn their lives would take), and a music case. That the card accompanying the music case indicated Charlotte had used slave labor to get it built surprised Louise. From what her grandfather had told her, Albert had squared with Charlotte regarding his race early on. As well, Charlotte certainly knew he'd fought on the Union side. That being so, Louise could only assume the music case had been built before Charlotte met Albert. Which didn't change the news of Charlotte's apparent lack of conviction.

Yet, though surprising, that lack of conviction was something Louise could understand. She, too, had compromised: she was well on the road to marrying a man with an elitist attitude, an attitude she didn't much care for. And her reason for choosing him? Mostly because he was a member of that very elite. A real contradiction, but one that proved that old adage about people wanting things they can't have until they get them and realize they've made a mistake. Which was definitely the way it was with her. But then, with her twenty-seventh birthday around the corner and the need to get on with life, she wasn't about to back out of this less than ideal spot she found herself in. And though being in Pierre's company at times grated, he was the best this isolated river road community had to offer, and the only plausible choice among those in pursuit of her. Lawrence Hymel, futureless bank teller with atrocious breath who claimed she was the most beautiful woman he'd ever seen, was simply not in the running. Nor was Emile Lambert, sugar cane farmer twenty years her senior who still lived with a mother who showed no signs of departing this world.

So went Louise's unchecked thoughts until, out of the blue, a bee buzzed her head and she froze, pupils straining corner to corner, lid to lid. When the threat finally faded, humming into the blinding light outside, she took the lawn chair from against the wall and pulled it over to the stacks of old music on the brick and board shelves, where she sat down. Even then, though, she couldn't make herself begin the organizing that was to be a big part of this day's mission; she was hard put to block thoughts that had been popping up all morning. Thoughts that centered around both the choices she'd made and her options now that she'd realized those choices weren't as great as expected.

There were two options. One was to move on, setting up shop in some other state or, maybe, in New Orleans. That would be tricky at best. First, there were her plans regarding Charlotte and Albert and what happened back then and the dream of figuring it all out. At this point she'd only begun looking into it. Was she willing to abandon this goal that gave her life real purpose? And if not and she moved on, how would she manage the Bancroft memorabilia? Would she move it again? Where would she find the funds to take that on? Money was always an issue. Savings gone and credit card maxed, she was living hand to mouth, every cent going for living expenses or payments on the Cadillac. Even a pre-owned luxury car cost megabucks.

No doubt about it, she was stuck. Acadi was and would have to remain home. Aspirations regarding ancestors and qualms about the drop-dead looker with influence and assets who, good or bad, she'd promised to marry – these were her destiny. Her fate, to put it simply. Yes, it was compromise. But, really, life was compromise. Take Charlotte and Albert. Their compromise involved deceit in public and honesty in private.

Considering the repercussions of the truth of his race getting out, theirs must've been anxious lives.

With that final bit of reflection, Louise committed to buckling down. First, off with the bulky knit that had felt so good earlier in the morning, hanging it on the strapped chair frame before tucking sweaty shirt into jeans. Next, neglected coffee on the self storage apron outside, lukewarm now but still giving off the suggestion of hazelnut, dumped in the grass. Finally, back to the chair in front of the shelves and getting down to work.

She'd already done some homework. Granted, not a lot, but enough to have some idea as to current prices of collectible paper goods. Which weren't half bad. In some cases, forty dollars for first edition sheet music. Add scores and the rest, and prospects looked good. What she needed now was an inventory, at least of the paper goods, to give some idea of the collection's value. And that was what she'd start this morning. Later, when she had time, she'd get a professional out for appraisal.

One thing was sure. It would be a while before she found time to look through the battered boxes in the corner. But they could wait. There was likely nothing of real value in cartons as bent and broken as those.

Chapter Eight

What Can I Say?

No metal detector today. Instead, carrying a screen box with a trowel in it, Margaret was on her way to the old racetrack dump, where she and Alma would spend this Sunday morning sifting through soil, looking for artifacts perhaps not as unusual (or suspect) as the St. Bernadette statue that had already turned up in the dump, but more befitting a racetrack.

After parking not far from the stable where Belmont Estates residents boarded their horses, she crossed one side of the oval track and headed for the other. She was still out of range of the stringed-in area of newly turned soil marking the location of the dump, but she could see the pile of brush that sat at its side. And that's where she was headed.

About halfway there, though, that familiar tightness gripped her chest and she decided she'd better sit down until the spasm eased. Luckily, the path was trampled from frequent visits by her digging sidekicks so, feeling no worry about what might be hiding in the grass, she stayed there, legs stretched out and arms as a brace. It was best to take it slow at a time like this. Besides, Alma was nowhere in sight and the view was . . . well . . . interesting: that moss-draped cypress that never failed to bring to mind horror movies she'd watched when she was six or seven. Movies with eerie, spectral trees steeped in steaming swamps, branches twisting toward threatening skies. Movies that brought on nightmares that had gotten her a slot in bed between her mom and dad.

As she rested there, the throb of a helicopter broke in, chuffing away, making it hard to think about anything but . . . chuffing. It was probably the parish spraying for mosquitoes. Although it could mean the powers that be were searching for an escapee from the new courthouse. Or on a happier note, a helicopter delivering a CEO to one of the plants. Whatever, twentieth century activity in the sky over a crazy neighborhood that prided itself on ties to the past. It was a contradiction, this melding of old and new, past with present, ancient plantation homes with oil refineries.

But she was getting used to it. And, actually, for all her earlier doubts about these new surroundings, she was content. It was a feeling that at one time she'd thought she'd never have again, at least not in these parts. *God-forsaken* was what she'd called Acadi back then. It was when everything about Louisiana bothered her. Humidity that fogged her windshield. Monsoons every summer afternoon. Caterpillars that fell from live oaks and stung like jellyfish and fire ants that attacked in droves and left stiff white blisters. Not to mention rotting communities where old people in slippers, flanked by rusted appliances, sat on crumbling porches.

Back then, nothing was right. She worried about toxic air and high tension wires and tank farms and cooling towers and gas flares and mid-stream loaders. Everything was unhealthy, she thought, and, one way or another would kill her. Which, she also thought, might be for the best anyway. Better to end it all early, fish out of water, than to founder indefinitely in an alien pond where there were none of one's species. She was an outsider and that was that. She could learn to suck crawfish heads, play a washboard, dance to zydeco, she could even convert to Catholicism, but it would make no difference. The natives would still think of her as a stranger, a trespassing northerner, and keep her in check. Those whose families went back generations – centuries in some cases – had little time for newcomers without ancestors in France, Germany, or Nova Scotia.

From the beginning Fred had seemed okay with the move, what with the prospect of year-round golf and all. (She hoped, with a casino in the neighborhood, he'd be able to keep his promise about gambling.) But as far as her? Without kids to ease the way, to get her involved in church and school, she'd balked. What would a sixty-two year-old who loved good music, and played it pretty well, do in an all but deserted town in south Louisiana where the inhabitants preferred washboard/ accordion dance tunes? she'd asked both herself and Fred over and over.

Then, with that business with her mom in February, she'd lost even the strength to ask.

"Margaret Bohr?" the female had asked when, still in flannel pajamas with lacy collar, she'd picked up the phone in the apartment on that gray midwinter morning.

Noting gravity in the voice, Margaret sensed a quickening in her chest. "Yes," she answered.

"One moment for Dr. Mitchell, please."

Her heart began bumping.

"Yes, Margaret," he said. "We've missed you in church."

His curt pleasantry increased her unease.

"Sorry to alarm you," he went on, "but I've admitted your mother to Ridgeview Hospital in Waconia. Her cleaning lady brought her to my office this morning. Said she'd found her in a confused state. Sick to her stomach as well. She was all alone there on the couch in the back room, unable even to clean up the vomit."

"Oh, my," Margaret had groaned. "What – "

"With her history of heart problems, I thought it best to admit her and find out what's going on, even though she didn't seem to be in great pain. Her biggest concern seemed to be if this was it, as she put it."

"She means – "

"I know what she means, and I think she needs someone with her, whether this is it or not."

His words stung. Yet Margaret understood. Dr. Mitchell was concerned. To him, it looked like neglect. A feeble octogenarian with soft doughy face and widow's hump who'd been his patient ever since he'd opened his office in the town of Mound had gotten the shaft from her own family, which at this point amounted to one selfish daughter and a couple preoccupied sons.

After Margaret had gotten off the phone and made flight arrangements, she packed her bags, all the while mulling over the difference between the way it looked to Dr. Mitchell and the way it really was. Dr. Mitchell didn't know the half of it: what a good daughter she'd always been; how since the day she'd left Long Lake she'd called her mom every evening; how she'd begged her to come South and live with Fred and herself; and how from the beginning she'd planned what she'd do in a situation like this. How she'd drop everything, even if it meant putting off finding a place to live, in order to fly home and stay at her widowed kin's bedside. As long as her mother lived, she'd be there for her. It was her duty.

A duty that when she lived in Minnesota she could have at times done without. Especially since with each passing year the hours involved in honoring her vow had multiplied. Though her mom had still insisted on the right to drive back then – right foot on gas, left one on brake of the yellow Valiant Lawrence had bought her – Margaret found that more and more she was the one behind the wheel, the one bringing the aging matriarch shopping, to doctor appointments, to lunch. Sometimes, after a long period with her mom's saggy, freckled arm twined in hers she'd felt like a congenitally joined twin. Other times, especially on hot days, a sticky crutch would have been a more apt analogy.

Even so, it was okay. She might've preferred spending time with her best friend or even reading a book, but this was okay. She was discharging a debt that had begun piling up the moment she came into this world and had continued to the moment she left home to move into a rooming house at the University of Minnesota. Daughters Regina and Nancy would one day do the same for her. Kurt was questionable. On second thought, no, not even Regina and Nancy. This mother wasn't going to burden her kids.

Her recollection of those hours spent chauffeuring her mom around always brought up one particular day. It was shortly before she and Fred had moved to Louisiana. They were sitting across from each other in a booth at Betty's Buffet in Minneapolis, her mom delicately dipping into a small bowl of mashed potatoes and gravy and Margaret attacking the Swedish meatball special, a most appealing and generous deal at four dollars and ninety-five cents, with two sides, cloverleaf roll, and dessert. Between bites they reminisced about family. Such things as Margaret's grandmother's Seventh Day Adventist faith and the panic her predictions of impending apocalypse stirred in Lawrence, Arnold, and herself; and her mom's brother, Buddy, always getting drunk at family Christmas parties; and Margaret's mom's favorite subject – her husband's inability to provide for the family of five, Margaret being the youngest.

During a pause in their exchange, her mom studied the spoon in her withered hand. "Well," she said, lifting her eyes, "at least it wasn't all bad. We had our blessings too. Lawrence was such a bright, talented little tyke and Arnold was so cute and you – " A hushed break. " – what can I say?" She looked back at the spoon, turning it, studying it as though in the shiny finish now reflecting the red, blue, and brown of the Tiffany-style lamp above the table she'd discover Margaret's defining attribute.

Margaret gave her time. Her mom wasn't as quick as she'd once been. Sometimes it took a while to bring up the right word.

But if there were a right word, it never came, and with a sigh, her mom resumed her delicate intake of mashed potatoes and gravy.

Margaret, meanwhile, lifted the heavy green café curtain and looked out. There, parked diagonally, a burst of orange in the otherwise ordinary bunch of cars parked in rows at the side of the building, sat her car. If she chose, she could jump up, stalk out, be on her way. Let the ungrateful biddy find her own way home.

Instead, she dropped the curtain and turned back to the pleasant face, agreeable blue eyes, barely moving mouth from which the gooey spoon had just been withdrawn. As she started to speak she thought better of it.

On the fifth day of her stay in Minnesota, the sixth after Dr. Mitchell's call, her mom suffered a stroke. A severe one that garbled her speech, crippled one side, and got her transferred first to the rehab wing of the hospital and then the long-term care facility. With Fred in Brazil monitoring progress on the construction of the soybean extraction plant that, as director of Welbourne engineering, he was in charge of and Margaret's prolonged absence from Louisiana of no real concern, she made plans to settle in. She'd have all the time in the world to think about finding a permanent home in Louisiana when she got back. For now, she'd return to the caring, unappreciated mode. The mode of daughter who had always been there but simply didn't compare to her *bright, talented, cute* brothers.

Then Kurt called from Denver saying Noreen had given birth. Margaret had expected the call but had given no thought to what she'd do once the blessed event was reality. But when Kurt said, "You really should come and see the baby, Mom," adding, "She's beautiful, the image of you," the reality of her bond to this newborn hit home. Not that Margaret took his words as gospel and expected to find a tiny clone in Denver. Her thinking tended more to the significance of the event in the life of her family. The fun she'd miss if she didn't go was a consideration too. It hardly seemed fair that she be stuck guiding a wheelchair up and down the foul-smelling, over-heated hall of a nursing home or sitting in a hard, armless chair listening to her mom respond "ata imcabory" or "bimmu" to the speech therapist's "How are you?" while Noreen's mother on a comfy couch in a room filled with flowers cuddled the toasty, sweet-smelling bundle that was the progeny of not just Noreen's family, but her own.

Besides, a trip to Denver didn't mean lengthy separation from her mom. If she went – and that was a big *if* – she'd stay only a day or two. Just long enough to get some relief from her grueling vigil. Long enough, as well, to lay claim to the title *devoted grandmother*. True, the way her mom's health had been lately, a day or two was chancy. But only in the sense of missing something she didn't want to witness anyway. And if she really worried? How about asking Arnold to take over while she was gone? It seemed he (with his wife) spent as much time traveling the world in search of the perfect vacation spot as in the office peddling insurance. With all that free time on his hands maybe he'd be willing to take a turn at his mom's side. Especially since he'd been so *cute* when he was a kid.

But Margaret knew she'd never ask either of her brothers for help. It would be like asking Ronald Reagan to come home and weed the garden. Or Michael DeBakey to take a break from heart surgery in order to clean the attic. It would be beneath either of them. They had more important things. They'd always had more important things. The most she'd ever been able to expect when her mom was ailing and hospitalized, which in recent years had been more than she cared to re-member, was a fly-in and grand entrance. Then, after parading beautiful, well-dressed wives and displaying undying love (an extravagant peace offering always scored) and impressing with talk of success and travel, they'd be on their way "back to the salt mines." Just enough time with Mom to maintain the ap-pearance of caring offspring.

The good thing about those visits was that they always made her mom's pale, timeworn face glow with pride. Like an ember rekindled by the wind.

Not so this time, though. Not after the disastrous clot that had killed so many brain cells. There wasn't a sign of fire in her now, and Margaret's brothers left not in a flurry of regret about the necessity of returning to work, but in a low-keyed, somber mood marked by comments about how much they appreciated this sister's sacrifice.

A sister who, hearing those comments all over again, suddenly saw everything come together as far as flying out to see her new grandchild. And in a moment of audacity – or was it rage at mistreatment from all sides? – made up her mind to cease self-sacrifice, if only for a time.

When Margaret first heard the news she felt like either that Denver kitchen was short of oxygen or her lungs had shrunk. No amount of gasping satisfied the need for air. Kurt and Noreen wanted to drive her to the emergency room, but she said no. And she was glad she did. By the time she boarded her flight for Minneapolis she was pretty much back to normal. Except for a dull pain she suspected was as much, maybe more, due to emotional strain as to problems with the heart. A lot of the time it wasn't even a pain. It was more an emptiness, as though something essential was gone. The feeling was some-what in her chest, but in her throat too. And in her head. And as she might have expected, it was really intense when later she began disposing of her mom's belongings after the will had been read.

That day of the reading was one she'd never forget. It could've been yesterday. The odor in the lawyer's office, where someone had recently smoked a cigar. The red and white peppermints in the crystal candy dish on the desk. The wooden blinds slanted up to hold back glare from the sun. The framed diplomas beside the file cabinet. And most of all, the feeling after the lawyer read, "To my beloved daughter, Margaret, who has always taken care of me, I leave all my personal effects."

Having finally taken care of the seemingly never-ending tasks involved in wrapping up her mom's affairs, she came back to the apartment in Louisiana. At first she slept a lot, her soft wool blanket gathered around her like a cocoon. Her dreams, quite naturally, centered on her mom. On the old homestead as well.

In one of those dreams, she was in a boat on the channel watching her mom who, perched on a rickety ladder while painting blue-green trim around the second-floor windows, was about to topple. Sitting there, hands gripping fishing pole, Margaret knew she should row over and save her. But she couldn't seem to take her hands from the pole.

Another dream placed her mom behind the display counter in the front room of the house, where her dad's bake shop had been in early years. While she bagged a dozen donuts for Dr. Mitchell, a snaky column of jagged-toothed rats ascended the basement steps on their way to the very room where the two went about their business. But when Margaret tried to scream a warning she found she had no voice.

Other dreams were just as disturbing and Fred, wakened by her shrieks, would shake her and ask if she was alright. To which she'd murmur that she was fine. A reply that never seemed to satisfy. He'd pose the same question each night when he came home from work. And there was little wonder why. That she was suffering from something that kept her immobile from dawn to dusk was more than apparent. If it was grief, it had gotten out of hand. Even she knew that. She'd never in all her life felt this bad. And it was all due to her mom who, along with her optimism and lifelong dreams of making a fortune – the bake shop, cafe, boat rental, rental apartment

– was now part of the past. The cruelest twist – she'd died without so much as a friend at her side.

One evening as Margaret sat humped over the kitchen table staring through the sliding doors at the haloed lights in the foggy parking lot below, Fred let her know how he felt. "This can't go on," he erupted, slapping his palm on the table so that his coffee cup rattled in its saucer. It may have been passion but seemed more like anger. "You've got to get out of this place. You can't sit here and grieve forever."

Margaret kept her eyes on the lot below. "There's nothing I want to do," she said, voice grainy.

When she finally looked up, he was chewing on a knuckle, squinting. "Well . . . " It took a while before he sat back and folded his arms. "How about gardening? You've always loved that. And being outside might make you feel better."

She shook her head. "We've got no yard."

"You really think the apartment manager would object to you sprucing up the grounds with a few flowers, or some herbs. Heck, everyone loves flowers and herbs."

She turned back to the misty lot below. "Anyway, I don't feel like it."

"That's my point. You've got to make yourself do it. You've got to start somewhere."

"What if I don't feel like starting?" she said, getting up and slumping to the sofa in the living room, where she sat down in an imprint that perfectly matched her posterior.

When he came home the next night, Fred told her he'd seen an article about the Lasserre Parish Historical Society in the local paper. It seemed they were looking for volunteers for a dig at the old racetrack in the rear of Belmont Estates

Subdivision. "You've always loved history and old stuff," he said. "At least you did back home. Remember the Indian mounds?" A pause, and a look of expectation.

Margaret lifted and dropped a shoulder, not about to argue even though he had it all wrong. It was her mom who'd really liked the Indian mounds that had given the town of Mound its name. It was her mom who liked history.

"And an old racetrack in Louisiana, Margaret. Who would've thought?" Fred's eyes were wide now and he was nodding like a pigeon out for a walk. "Why not give it a try, Margaret." (Second time he'd used her name in less than a minute, and she was finding it annoying.) "It might get your mind off your mother. And – " He smiled. A gentle smile. " – it'll get you out of those pajamas."

What he didn't seem to realize was that she didn't want to get out of those pajamas. Nor did she want to dig at an old racetrack. For that matter, she really didn't want to forget about her mom.

But Fred didn't give up. "Did you call the historical society?" he'd ask on coming in the door after work each day.

"No, and I'm not going to," she finally shot back, flinging herself off the couch and heading for the steps to the upstairs bedroom.

"You're going to go bonkers if you go on sitting around this place," he called after her. "If you want to know the truth, I think you're going bonkers already." Under his breath, but loud enough to hear, he added, "You might recall, you've got a history of bonkers."

That was what stopped her.

Bonkers. Crazy. He was actually calling her crazy. And the sad part was that he was speaking from experience. Back in college there'd been that period after the ear surgeries failed when she'd gotten so depressed she'd hinted at self-destruction. It was unlike Fred to refer to something so personal and devastating – and in such a mean way – and it brought her up short. Was he trying to shock her out of a sure path to disaster? Did he see something she didn't see? What if he had it right and she was on the verge of mental collapse? And all because she couldn't come to terms with a bad choice. Lots of people made bad choices, and those same people were out there going on with their lives. What was wrong with her?

What was wrong, she finally decided, was that she'd given up, just like after the ear surgeries. Back then it had taken an inspiring little girl to pull her out of the doldrums. Since she didn't have anyone like that now, what did she have? Nothing, really, but this fear she might be losing her marbles. Was it enough? Considering the ramifications, quite possibly yes. And all she had to do was make the effort. Get out of the pajamas, take a bath, comb her hair, and . . . maybe even give Fred's advice a try. Volunteer at the racetrack.

The very next day, shoving grim thoughts into a closet in her brain and slamming the door (if Fred knew this was how she'd decided to deal with her misery he may have had her committed then and there), she got cleaned up, went about chores just as she'd done prior to that midwinter call from Dr. Mitchell, and called the historical society. As well, while out shopping she stopped at the hardware and, as the society representative suggested, bought a trowel.

And the next Sunday and every Sunday after that, she followed the gravelly road and three-rail fence back to the Belmont Estates stable. Once out of the car, she'd scurry past the whooshing tails and smelly stalls, hoping to avoid the jodhpurred horsey crowd, that superior Belmont Estates Subdivision group who were impatiently awaiting completion of the racetrack dig so that show ring construction could begin. If she happened to run into one of them, she lowered her eyes and pretended deep thought. But at this point the truth was that she avoided thinking deeply. No more of that painful soul-searching. Each time the closet door opened a crack, she nudged it shut. She'd learned her lesson.

At the racetrack, she scooped with her trowel, dug with one of the society's shovels, or hunted with one of their metal detectors. And it wasn't long before her efforts paid off. It was on her second Sunday.

"There's something down here," Alma, her Cajun partner, had said, the metal detector in her hand beeping as she motioned Margaret to move closer.

A moment later Margaret was on her knees following Alma's instruction: using a knife to cut out a square of soil and slicing it down the middle before passing half to her partner. Then, following that new friend's lead, she pulled her portion apart. And found? Gold. Literally. It was a dollar. A tiny one, smaller than a penny and in rougher shape than any of the coins in Fred's collection. But still . . . .

After setting it in the grass next to her trowel, she unbuttoned her shirt pocket and took out her glasses. "Holy Moses," she said. "Eighteen-forty-nine. Can you believe? And I bet mine are the first hands to make contact with it in nearly a century and a half." Goosebumps climbed her back. "What do you think? A mustached fellow in top hat and long coat, jangling coins in his pants pocket, reaches out to pat his horse and, unawares, drops this little gem."

"Or –" Alma, not to be outdone. " – mustached man in top hat and long coat, buying mint julep for gorgeous lady in hoop skirt, fumbles, losing coin under her skirt."

"You think they sold mint juleps at the track?"

"Doubtful. Good story, though."

Truth was, neither were very good stories. But that didn't matter. What mattered was that Margaret was standing right there in the middle of history, at the same time thinking something she'd only briefly considered before – that Belmont Estates Subdivision might be a good choice as far as a place to live. In Minnesota, tract communities tended to be sterile, without character. But Belmont Estates, with antiquity underfoot, wasn't like that. Yes, there were the security fence and guard gate and manicured lawns, but beneath it all was straight-out history, stuff that gave value to a subdivision that at first glance looked perfectly ordinary.

And this house that Margaret would build there (she was already making plans) would be true to location. Yes, spanking new, but looking old. That was something she'd have to make sure of: that it looked like one of those vintage places she'd been searching for nearly since they'd arrived. Back then, driving up and down the river road, she'd been hell-bent on finding a syrupy century-old Creole cottage nearly hidden behind bananas and live oaks and camellias. Those she found, though, were dark and dingy with rotten moldings, sagging floors, and antique plumbing. Beyond that, burglar bars on windows and doors hinted at problems with crime, and industrial plants – often much too close – promised noise and pollution. With a new house in Belmont Estates she wouldn't have any of that. What she'd have was the best of both worlds: a quaint reproduction with modern amenities on a lot planted with all manner of native plants and in a community brimming with a past.

Snooty neighbors aside, she'd be quite happy.

Shortly after the decision to build in the subdivision – which Fred, having preferred new construction from the beginning, wholeheartedly approved – they went out, bought a half-acre lot that visiting grandchildren would love, and started planning their home with Vernon Breedlove, the disabled architect recommended by the subdivision's sales manager. That same sales manager, Louise Dennis, also introduced them to Pierre Armant, whom she described as "a contractor who really knows what he's about and who, incidentally, is my fiancé." Red flag? The sales manager's promotion of her fiance' sounded like it. But when architect Breedlove added his enthusiastic recommendation, Mr. Armant began looking like a pretty safe bet.

Margaret's thinking went something like this: Belmont Estates was a fine community populated by intelligent professionals who'd no doubt demand the best, and when the sales manager of such a place made a big deal about someone's competence, there could be little question – sales manager's personal involvement or not – of that contractor's capabilities. Much the same could be said for the architect's support, but without the "personal" caveat.

Even so, having by then studied every home-building book she could get her hands on at the library, Margaret knew the proper sequence of events, and she wasn't about to skimp on anything. Since her search for that antique Creole cottage had proved disappointing and she'd had to settle for second best (though second best was looking pretty darn good at the moment), she'd at least get her money's worth. The next step, she knew, was to get bids from at least three contractors. Bids that she and Fred picked up at a meeting in Louise Dennis's office a week or so later, when they learned that Pierre Armant's was lowest.

The meeting was pleasant. Louise – she insisted they call her by her Christian name – once again bragging up the benefits of living thirty miles upriver from New Orleans: French Quarter and great food and antique shops and jazz and, if they chose, Mardi Gras parades. Addressing Fred, who on this day in bright green pants and yellow sweater looked the part of golfer, she also boasted about the town of Acadi being within twenty miles of no less than five golf courses.

Finally, pleasantries dispensed with, Louise slid some glossy flyers across the table, explaining that they were a little more info on each of the three builders they were considering. Being the contractors themselves had written the brochures, she said, they were "straight from the horses' mouths."

In the car, flyers in lap, Margaret took her glasses from the plastic attaché she'd inherited from her daughter. "Since both the architect and sales manager seem to like Pierre Armant so much, you want to hear more about him?"

"Sure." Fred, sharp nose and chin in profile, was looking over his shoulder, backing out of the parking space.

Margaret began. "Over the past five years, Pierre Armant, President of Choice Construction and personification of excellence in the building industry, has been committed to the creation of superb custom homes as well as to using the fine skills of his fellow parishioners at Loving Kindness Church in Kenner, Louisiana. The homes he builds not only benefit you, his customers, but needy members of this close-knit Christian community. Mr. Armant's promise is that the quality of your new home will be the highest and your experience with his company totally agreeable."

"The business about quality sounds good and I guess an agreeable experience is important. But – " Eyeing the road, chewing the side of a finger. " – that spiel about church really is a bit much. As you well know, I've never trusted people who use religion." His eyes met hers. "So what do you think?"

She took off her glasses and slipped them into the attaché. "I think he's low bid."

Chapter Nine

Low Bid

On a cool, pleasant evening a few weeks after giving the nod to Pierre Armant, Fred parked his car a short ways from the fire hydrant in front of their building site. Margaret was at his side, her dog in the rear.

"Look at that," he said, pointing toward the new concrete slab twenty-five or so yards from the street. In the waning sun it glowed like a golden dance floor. "Pretty darn exciting, don't you think? We've now got something to show for our effort. And from the way it looks, Pierre's relocating the slab a little to the rear of what the plans indicated makes not one iota of difference."

"A little to the rear?" Margaret's eyebrows arched and her pale eyes widened. "Without telling us, he turns the back yard, where we plan to play croquet and have parties, into a postage stamp and the front, with little purpose but to look pretty, into a . . . a . . . ."

"Block of stamps?"

She frowned, apparently unimpressed with the metaphor, and unfastened her seatbelt before reaching to the floor for Wolfgang's leash.

Her mood may have been less than sunny, but Fred wasn't going to let it get to him. "Well, look at it this way, he did save some trees."

"So he claims. But they're scrub trees. Not worth a dime." She adjusted her seat toward the rear, then climbed on her knees, facing Wolfgang in the back. Not the easiest maneuver for one with generous hips, and her heavy breathing attested to it. "Our fine contractor also saved himself the work and expense of cutting and hauling the trees away."

"Lot, trees – anything else eating you on this gorgeous evening?"

"Actually, I'll never feel okay about the fill." She was stretching over the center console, struggling to get the leash over the Airedale's long head. Each time she had the loop perfectly centered, ready to slip up and over, he dipped in ill-timed anticipation.

It was kind of funny to watch. Even so, Fred didn't let on. "Dwelling on things like how much sand was dumped on our lot is pointless, Margaret. The architect assured you there was enough and that means there *is* enough."

"Even so – " Never one to surrender the last word. " – the lot looks low."

And with that definitive, if breathless, observation, she got her timing right, slipped the leash on the dog and, sliding it over her headrest, opened her door before doing some kind of complicated maneuver through the rear window that ended with her outside, leash in hand, opening the rear door to let the dog out. "Poor sweetheart. Look at you," she said, addressing Wolfgang as he warily stepped down from the car. "Penned up in the apartment so long you hardly know what to do. Look, Fred, how pathetic – "

The dog yanked the leash from her hand and, ignoring her strident commands, began single-footing it around the lot before, pitching up and down like a rocking horse, he returned and – front low, rear high – bounced around in front of her. If dogs could tease, this one was expert. Even when Margaret finally trapped the leash under her foot, he kept at it, breaking loose, nabbing the leather strap in his teeth, and snapping it back and forth before prancing off again.

"Let him be," Fred told her. "He won't go far."

"Good riddance if he does," she snarled, swinging around and setting off toward the slab.

Pausing there near the old oak that made this lot nearly as appealing as their former place in Minnesota, Fred took a deep breath. He was a lucky fellow. And no matter what Margaret said about the house, things were coming along nicely. Plans done to perfection, construction financing secure, and now with the foundation finally in, they were truly on their way.

Breaking into a trot, he caught up with Margaret, grabbing her hand as she approached the clean, angular plain of concrete that signaled another beginning.

But his exuberance evaporated when, jerking her hand free and moaning "My God," she broke for the slab and reaching it, dropped to her knees. "Just what I feared," she wailed. "Lumps, bumps, ridges. It just won't do."

And, being that she'd planned to simply stain and score the concrete, making it look like those polished stone floors in *Architectural Digest*, he silently acknowledged that she was probably right.

At least on the way back to the car they found the earlier problem, namely the recalcitrant and forgotten Wolfgang, resolved. He was now comfortably sacked out – fast food bag pillowing his shaggy, bearded muzzle – on the mound of trash not far from the oak tree.

Chapter Ten

You See What I Mean?

It was Fred's first day back after a three-week trip to Sao Paulo to make sure the elevator he'd designed for Melbourne down there was progressing according to plan, and he was glad to be home. There was nothing like routine to keep one on the straight and narrow. Travel, with unhealthy food and little time for exercise, was hardly conducive to staying in condition. Just getting out there, jogging around the town of Oakview that morning, had felt fantastic.

Too bad the magic couldn't last. But there was no magic in being driven around by Margaret. With the volume of fatty food consumed behind that steering wheel and the associated crumb drop, putrefaction was a fact of life. The stench today was nothing short of ghastly. It was like rotting road kill. Worse, the longer they sat in the car waiting to get out of the apartment building parking lot, the stronger it seemed to get.

"You and your finicky nose," she said, when he opened the window. "That smell is nothing but the air conditioner. It's been leaking on the carpet under the dashboard for a few days."

"I wish you'd told me before we left. I could've driven." He was holding his nose.

"Waste of time. I've got everything we need back there." She flicked her thumb toward the rear seat. "And you'll get used to the smell." She glanced over. "Patience. My byword these days. Perseverance too. I'm patient about the odor because I've got to persevere in making sure we get the house we're paying for. This is no time to be foolish with money. You remember what happened a couple years ago." Another glance. "When I get time I'll get the cooling system fixed."

"You have that much to do?"

He soon regretted asking. Hearing her response was like listening to a recitation of *The Odyssey*, only without the fascinating plot. She went on about the seven-mile drive between the apartment in Oakview and Belmont Estates that she made two – sometimes three – times a day, explaining that the way things were going with Pierre, with all the necessary oversight, she had no choice. There were other things she'd like to do, like visit Baton Rouge to look into Charlotte and Albert Bancroft or spend an hour or two at St. Joan of Arc's organ (the priest had given permission), but regular site inspections were more important.

"I don't understand why, when we're paying both a contractor and architect, you, as well, need to supervise," he told her.

"When you're building a house this expensive you can't be too careful."

"Is it possible you're a little paranoid?"

"I was the one who would've been happy with an old Creole cottage. Remember?"

He stayed silent, thinking he really didn't see what the "old cottage" had to do with her paranoia. What he could've said was that she'd gotten just as excited as him about building in Belmont Estates. What he did say was, "Seems like you're implying materialism."

She gave him a quick, wise look. *You said it, not me.*

He bristled. "A little contradiction, don't you think?"

"How so?"

"You're the fanatic about the house."

"I'm just not fond of wasting money."

"I doubt you're wasting money. I do think you're wasting time."

By now she'd pulled out of the apartment lot and was parking in front of Roussel's bakery, just a block away. "Want a donut?" she asked, getting out.

It was at this point that he nearly gave in to silent despair. Nothing about her made sense. Why ask if he wanted a donut when she knew he never ate donuts and disapproved of her — of anyone – eating donuts.

She began her first deep-fried, powdered sugared artery clogger while they waited for Oakview's only light to turn green. The treat was little more than a sticky crescent by the time they passed Emile's Grocery, *Home of Boudin, Famous Cajun Sausage.* (Thank God she didn't stop there.) The remainder of the donut went in as they rolled by the newspaper office, that ancient building with *General Merchandise* bleeding through new paint.

And all this time she licked fingers and sucked teeth while itemizing the infractions her construction oversight had uncovered. Among them, French doors with muntins that were too thin and a shiny brass fireplace, now sitting in the garage, that didn't fit with French Country decor. Neither doors nor fireplace were those specified in the contract.

"And what, may I ask, are muntins?" he asked when he got a word in.

"Divisions between window panes."

"Window pane divisions too thin. I see. And –" he tried to mask exasperation. " – is there any possibility you might just live with the doors and fireplace despite the fact they're not in the contract?"

"Are you kidding?" she responded, meanwhile rustling in the bag in quest of another debilitating treat.

It was then that he turned away, searching out escape among the sun-bleached sheds and grassy fields on his side of the car. And, blessedly, she went to work on that second donut.

Finally, Belmont Estates sign in sight, he heard the click of the signal light. Reaching the guardhouse, Margaret turned in, stopping, waving, waiting for the uniformed guard to lift the gate and let them go on past the massive houses – many under construction, some completed, a good number sporting horse vans in their drives. It was a decent neighborhood, and if he had the time he'd grab a lawn chair, set it out front of their place and, while learning the art of home building, get to know the neighbors. Neighbors whose names would one day be familiar, he was thinking when his fair wife broke into his thoughts with "You haven't mentioned my eyebrows."

"Right," he said. He wasn't inclined to go into how he'd puzzled over why at this stage in life she'd taken to painting her face.

But she was inclined to explain. "The reason they're so dark is that I'm on stronger blood pressure pills that turn my brows black. Too much stress, the doctor says."

Maybe too much stress, he thought as she pulled up in front of their house and turned off the car. Likely too many donuts as well.

He opened his door and viewed the so-called source of his wife's affliction. Progress was amazing. The frame was now sheathed in blue Styrofoam and there was a tar-paper roof. True, it wasn't a huge structure, but when it was finished – with treed courtyard in front and cool blue pool in u-shaped rear – charm would make up for size. It was a classic.

"Forgot to mention," she said as she got out of the car. "There's a diagram of the island on the kitchen slab, and I feel like it points to another problem. Being you design elevators and are up to snuff on this kind of stuff, I'd like if you'd take a look."

She had it right. He was quite good at this kind of thing. So, following her suggestion, he made his way into the kitchen area.

The moment he saw the Sharpie-drawn diagram on the concrete floor his already unstable mood plummeted. It was obvious someone had measured wrong. A matter of at least a foot. And from what Fred could tell, that foot was going to make for a very congested kitchen. With the refrigerator open, there would be no room for passage around the island.

"You see what I mean about problems?" she said, snapping the long strip of measuring tape into its shiny case after using it to drive home her point. The satisfaction in her voice set him off, and he wrestled out of his sticky tee shirt, flung it to the floor, and stormed out the door to the rear deck.

Chapter Eleven

Finger to Lips

Pierre parked near Mrs. Bohr's obnoxious BMW and got out, tucking his crisp linen shirt into his tailored Italian slacks. The old biddy was around, but where? Ah yes, there, bustling toward him from her "house in progress." Obviously in busybody mode: camera dangling from Shar Pei neck and monster tape measure in stumpy paws. Decked out as usual too. Was that a cat on her tee shirt? And that flowered visor with the enormous bow – how many times would she turn up in that before someone, maybe good old Fred, clued her that it was just plain gauch? And those overdone brows. What was the story there? Had she, in her sunset years, suddenly stumbled into a cosmetics clearance?

In spite of his annoyance, he put on the sincere face – a little gnawing at the lip, some concern in the eyes – as she closed in. Her expression, of course, was sulky. Nothing new, that sullen look. She'd been that way for a while now.

"Got your blueprints?" she snapped point-blank, no greeting, no change on grump-face as she opened the driver's side of her car, pushed the seat up, and leaned into the rear of her clunker, tossing her spy gear on the floor and exposing her jumbo tush before emerging with that grotesque plastic attaché that was a mainstay of her trappings. Then she slammed the door. *Thwock* went the driver's side window as it slipped from sight. Shocking was the blasphemy Mrs. Bohr uttered before dropping the case and sticking her fingers into the slit where the window lay entombed.

"Problem?" Pierre asked, barely able to stifle a snicker.

No reply, of course. She was busy. It seemed that she now had the barest of grips on the glass and was tugging. And slowly, very slowly, the glass was coming up. A quarter, a half inch, one inch, and . . . .

Thwock.

A few seconds of silence followed before she turned to Pierre, an even sharper edge to her voice now. "Got your blueprints along? I left mine inside and I've got some questions."

"Sure 'nuff." A little folksiness to turn down the heat. "They're in my car." He nodded toward his new yellow Corvette and, with Mrs. Bohr in tow, walked over.

It wasn't long, though, before he got to thinking that he should've said *hoped the plans were in his car* because after making his way through the ski brochures and golf shoes and big red road atlas, and setting them aside, he began wondering if he'd left the plans in the Mercedes. Even so, he plugged away, that ugly glare in Mrs. Bohr's eyes serving as motivation as he shifted a few more things, including the boxes of nails and a level. (He was down to the nitty-gritty now.) Meanwhile, even though he'd always raved about the scent of new leather, he was wising up to the truth in that saying about too much of a good thing. More than anything, though, he was wondering why she needed the blueprints anyway.

"You need a truck," she said, hands on hips now. "Have you ever thought of getting one?"

"I need an administrator," he shot back playfully, sweat rolling down his face and dripping onto his freshly-pressed shirt. "Well, maybe not," he corrected as, at the very bottom, he turned over a sample board of shingles and came upon the roll of drawings. Which were now quite flat, but at least still blue.

"So, here we go," he said, slamming the door and carrying the blueprints to the front of the car before unrolling and smoothing them against the long, streamlined hood. Lord, how he loved the sleek, low –

"What's that?" Mrs. Bohr spat.

"That?" She'd caught him off guard.

"That." Her pudgy finger jabbed at the drawings. "And that."

Dear God, what was at this moment causing her to even more foully crimp her crumpled brow?

"I see now why the refrigerator water line connects with the food processor and the plumbing stub is four feet from the utility sink," she ranted. "You're working from outdated plans that should've been thrown out weeks ago. Where are the revised ones?"

"Revised?" It was news to him.

"Breedlove changed the drawings at least two months back. He moved the refrigerator from that spot – " She jabbed at the drawings again. " – and put the food processor there instead. And the utility sink changes are on the new plans too."

"I don't think I got them," he said. (If he did, he sure didn't have them now.)

He could've known his response wasn't going to sit well with her. That it would lead to major haggling. But this was more than that. This was a first-rate blowup. First, Mrs. Bohr snapping that Breedlove had sent the plans to him. Next, him saying that maybe because he'd recently moved his office he hadn't gotten them. Finally, Mrs. Bohr thinking long and hard, eyes pinched, jumbo visor in hand, fat fingers scratching at wild, white cowlick before finally nearly shouting "Ah, yes" while slapping her hat back on and roaring, "Breedlove said you picked them up at his office." And all this followed by her leaning on the hood, drumming her fingers, and dissecting him with those small steely eyes before again shooting them toward the plans.

What else did she think she'd find there? This was crazy. She was crazy.

"Hey," he said as agreeably as mood allowed, "not to worry. We're on a roll. Fireplace tomorrow, rough-in after that, and then windows and doors. And I just ordered your roofing. You'll be in before you know it."

"Get the amended plans," she snapped, not even looking up. "And while you're at it, tend to the kitchen. You're a foot short in there."

Oh, wow. She was onto the square footage discrepancy,

"Those infernal framers must've measured wrong," he said, snatching the blueprints from under her nose.

"So what are you going to do about it?" Her eyes were hot steel, straight from the furnace.

"I'll have to talk to Breedlove when he gets back. I guess one alternative is to chuck the island."

"Are you kidding? I want to look out on the pool while I cook."

"A new fridge then? That one from your other house juts out too far. And much as I understand your economy, a slim new built-in might just do the trick." He shifted the blueprints to the other hand and opened his car door just as Fred Bohr, slipping into a gray tee shirt coated with what looked to be sawdust, sprang from the house and trotted toward them.

Mrs. Bohr must not have heard him coming, because she raged on. "But that refrigerator would've been fine if you hadn't shorted – "

Her husband broke in. "We'd better be on our way. I need to be to work by eleven and I've got to shower and change."

Mrs. Bohr turned back to Pierre. "Give me a ring this afternoon," she ordered, shooting a last hot look his way before taking off for the house and calling over her shoulder, "Be right back, Fred."

Which was when Pierre hit old Fred with, "Any luck at the casino the other day?"

Old Fred's answer was a finger to lips.

As they drove off, Pierre imagined their exchange. Mrs. Bohr raging about the problems, perhaps even suggesting – she was that mad – that it was time to sue. And Fred, explaining that with forty percent of the house paid for and only twenty percent of the work done, it wouldn't be wise; there could be no filing a lawsuit, sitting back, and watching things play out. That wasn't the way it would work. All they'd accomplish by taking him to court was stopping things cold while still paying interest on their loan.

No, Fred Bohr was smart. He knew he was in no position to bug his contractor. He might even try convincing the grody hag that it would be best to just live with some of the headaches. Which wouldn't be easy. The hag was anal about following the contract word for word, about "getting the most house for the money." And beyond that, she didn't seem to be a quitter.

Chapter Twelve

So Many Questions

Thank God she wasn't in charge of maintenance of Belmont Estates, Louise was thinking as she sat at her desk looking out on the street in front, where two workmen had just finished leveling fresh concrete around a manhole cover. It was hard enough being a sales manager whose job included connecting builders with clients.

Yet, not really. In most cases it wasn't that hard. Pierre and Mrs. Bohr were the exception. What was going on between them was no ordinary matter and may have largely been due to personalities. Mrs. Bohr's was up front, confrontational. Pierre's was indirect, ambiguous. Ambiguous to the point of arousing doubt even in Louise. And though Mrs. Bohr's behavior was irritating, Pierre's was concerning. This was the man she planned to spend her life with. And if what Mrs. Bohr charged was true, he was not only self-serving, but devious. True, the same charge might be leveled at Louise, but in her case the behavior was justified. It was the only way to wangle a level playing field.

As to the fray between her fiancé and his client, it had been hard to keep a distance. But she'd done her best. Whenever Mrs. Bohr came around with complaints about Pierre, Louise claimed conflict of interest and told her to talk to Vernon Breedlove.

"But he's always out of town," Mrs. Bohr had said last time.

"I guess you'll just have to catch him when he's around," she'd replied, silently noting how much easier it was to dismiss Mrs. Bohr's complaints about Mr. Breedlove than those about Pierre. She'd hated when the fusspot told her Pierre was not only ignoring terms of the contract but working from outdated plans. And when Mrs. Bohr said that his framers made an error in square footage, Louise actually felt the need to talk to him, to warn that his reputation was at stake.

His response? "Don't worry your pretty head about it."

Which, instead of relieving concern, was troubling. Yet that was the way he liked thinking of her, and with tiny skirts and platform heels, she was quite aware that she didn't exactly discourage it.

All of this, though, was beside the point. What concerned her right now was his way of doing business. Had he recently changed or had he always handled things this way? And if he'd always been this way, why had no one complained? Was Mrs. Bohr right when she said clients hadn't bothered to inspect his work, that they were either too busy or hadn't taken the time, and that he'd been heading a slipshod operation all along? It did make some sense. As did Mrs. Bohr's complaints about work on her own house.

Louise supposed she could talk to the architect about the allegations. Maybe he'd set her mind at ease. Yet what would Vernon Breedlove think of her doubts about her own fiancé? Besides that, what if, Vernon and Pierre being close, Vernon told Pierre?

So many questions. It was at a time like this she really missed her mother. She'd always been a good listener. More than that, a clear thinker. And that's what Louise needed now. Someone to help sort things through. Someone she could really have confidence in. Yet, that meant trust from the other side as well, and there was no likelihood her mother would ever have faith in her again. Especially if she knew of all her compromises. But just as Louise didn't miss a day without thinking of her mother (wondering how she was doing and if she was pretty much back to her normal regimen of reading and teaching and bird-feeding and shoveling snow and baking deep-dish apple pies and watching the news in the evening and even still wearing those faded red pants and the wedged slip-ons with worn-down heels), she didn't fool herself into thinking she could ever go back.

Chapter Thirteen

No One Will Ever Know

Having sat there for a few minutes now, Cedro's arms were still a little numb, but his fingers weren't cramping any more. And in the shade of a tree at the side of the lot, he felt almost cool. The electrical transformer wasn't the most comfortable place to sit, but Joseph's van, just a couple feet over, was in the sun and, having been in the sun painting eaves on Stimson's garage for the past couple hours, he didn't want any more of it.

He'd been watching the *garcetas* (the rest of the crew called them *egrets*) on the marshy shore of the canal running alongside the mansion. White and graceful, they flapped their wings each time a car came toward the tiny bridge over the canal. A few minutes back, a flatbed loaded with foundation pilings had thumped past, drowning out the saw buzz, hammer crack, and gospel music from the house, and the birds flew away. Now they were back.

"Time for morning break" in a voice that could only be Sharlene's put a quick end to his thoughts. Even though she was the friendliest of the crew and often took her breaks with him, her turning up – and on his blind side – was a surprise, and he quickly fixed his sweat-soaked bandana so it covered the worst scars on his face.

Sharlene meanwhile had stepped up and into the van, and there'd been the click of cooler latch and pop of can tab and sigh like she'd taken that first swallow and felt better already before she'd come back out, hair wet like his own and sticking to her forehead.

"This is the kind of day you gotta be careful about heat-stroke," she said. "Sweepin' up that sawdust in there – " She pointed toward Stimson's mansion. " – I felt like I was gonna pass out."

She sat down on the step at the back of the van, stretching out her long, straight legs and crossing them at the ankles. While she took a drawn-out look in the direction of the house, Cedro shoved over to the other side of the transformer so he could see her better. His pants were wet with sweat, and he left a streak that he hoped she wouldn't notice.

"You know," he said, "I've been thinking."

She gave him a silly smile. "Oh no, not that." She took a swig of her Pepsi, swishing it around in her mouth before swallowing.

He went on. "There still are no anchor bolts or roof clips or reinforcement plywood in this house, and the drywall subcontractors will be here any day. You know what that means?"

"That no one will ever know there are no bolts or clips or plywood, because drywall will hide it. So?" Her soda can clanked as she set it on the step next to her. "Really, Cedro, give it up. You gonna risk your job just because Pierre doesn't care if this house is perfect? Like I said, no one will ever know. Not even the Stimsons. And I don't think they'd care if they did. I've never even seen them out here." She ran her fingers through her long brown hair, front to back, separating it into wet parts that showed every inch of her face, including the long scar on her forehead. "God, it's hot," she moaned.

"But the Stimsons don't live around here," he told her. "They don't know what's going on as far as hurricane protection on their house."

"Okay. Right. But what are the odds of a hurricane anyway?" She took another sip of Pepsi.

"This is hurricane country."

She rolled her eyes. "Look. If there are problems with the house it's the architect's job to find them, not yours. And if Mr. Breedlove says Pierre can go ahead with drywall, who are you to question it?"

But who else would? he wondered. There was Dakota, of course, who right now, hands on hips and toothpick in teeth, was standing near the end of the drive over near the dumpster. But would he care? As supervisor, he should. If he was serious about his job, he should have already noticed. Yet, maybe he hadn't. If so, it seemed only right to tell him. Yes, Dakota was the one.

Cedro got up and started toward him, taking quick steps so that he'd get there before a lady who'd gotten out of an orange car and was heading in the same direction.

"Sir," he said, a nervous flutter in his voice as he aimed his good eye at him, "did you notice there are no anchor bolts – "

The supervisor fired a mean look his way, stopping him before turning to the short, white-haired lady who'd gotten out of the car and was now a few feet away. "Good morning," he said, tossing the toothpick and sticking his hands in the back pockets of his jeans. "What brings you over here?" He looked pleasant.

She looked unhappy. "Where's Pierre? We need to talk and I can't get him on the phone."

"He'll be here any minute," Dakota answered, no smile now.

Her stony look softened and she turned to Cedro. "Sorry. I don't think we've met."

"This is Diaz," Dakota cut in, grabbing Cedro's shoulder and squeezing too hard. "Painter. He's from . . . ." He pinched his eyes.

"Cuba," Cedro said.

"Diaz. Nice to meet you." Her eyes were a very pale blue. "And your last name?"

"My full name is Cedro Diaz."

"Cedro." She extended her hand. "And mine's Margaret Bohr. I guess we'll get better acquainted once painting starts at my house. You'll be there I presume."

Dakota grinned. "If he shapes up."

The comment seemed innocent until Mrs. Bohr, saying she'd wait for Pierre inside the house, walked away and Dakota swung around, hissing under his breath, "And I meant that about shaping up. You'll be out of a job if you go on stickin' your nose where it don't belong."

Chapter Fourteen

Bound by a Sad Truth

It had been a hairy morning, with Margaret thinking she might be having a heart attack, even giving thought to heading for the hospital. But she soon changed her mind. Getting admitted only to be released a day later with new blood pressure meds and even more hard-nosed rules regarding exercise and diet just wasn't worth it. Nor was an angiogram, the next likely gimmick in her cardiologist's bag of tricks. Fat chance of her having one of those "procedures" after having watched her mom's reaction to the dye. She could've died.

Anyway, morning scare over, she was fine now. So fine that, on her knees on a blue rubber mat in the "courtyard" – that ho- hum space between two of the buildings in the apartment complex – she was going ahead with her plan to plant marigolds around the bushes. Digging those little holes, sprinkling in the plant food, and placing the plants to their best advantage – best side out, poor side hidden – was just plain engrossing. So engrossing that it wasn't till her laughing racetrack buddy barked "Hey, you" that she was aware of that narrow, olive face looking down on her. Blame it on her visor or her hearing or her complete absorption in the task, whatever explained the fog, she was a little embarrassed. "What are you doing here?" she said by way of greeting, patting the soil around her latest planting before slipping off the garden gloves. "I didn't think you knew where I lived."

"Well, you mentioned an apartment compound, and this is the only one in town."

Margaret set her gloves next to the watering can and trowel and got up in a manner that wouldn't either send her head spinning or clue Alma as to her withering limbs.

"Just wanted to show you what I found at the racetrack this morning." Looking like a kid with a great report card, Alma held out a big silver coin. "Too bad you weren't there. Talk about high spirits." She shifted the coin to her left hand before fishing around in the breast pocket of her coveralls, coming up with a crushed cigarette pack. "Damn," she said, crumpling and putting it back.

Margaret responded with a butterscotch from the pocket of her clam diggers, and took one herself, peeling off the wrap and stuffing it in her shirt pocket before getting out her glasses and taking the coin from Alma. "Half dollar, huh. Where'd you find it?"

"Behind where the grandstand stood."

"Goosebumps?"

"Goose bumps and – " Alma put her hand beside her lips. " – nearly embarrassed myself." She didn't explain. Whatever it was induced a butterscotch-scented giggle before a return to sobriety. "A while back," she said, "you mentioned that your husband collects coins."

"In fact he's pretty serious about it."

"Well, we – Gilbert Kliebert and I – thought maybe you could ask him what he thinks this one's worth. Not that it really matters. Just curiosity's sake."

"He's out of town right now. But . . . let's see." Margaret studied the coin, burning it into memory. "Eighteen fifty-three – "

"No need for that. I'll just leave it. And, obviously, no hurry."

"Well, I'm as excited to know as you. Just wish I'd been there. But I wasn't quite up to it this morning."

"Nothing serious I hope." Alma checked her watch and looked toward the parking lot.

"No. Just needed a little rest, I guess. I stayed in bed till I felt better. Pretty darn boring without a decent book to read. I cursed whoever checked *Livre Riviere* out of the library and didn't bring it back."

"Hmm. Could be Kliebert. He's gotten all interested in Fernando de Soto. Maybe he forgot he had the book."

"If I could, I'd buy it. But it's out of print."

"When I see him, I'll remind him."

"Tell him it's kind of important."

"Kind of important, huh." A wry smile exposed Alma's tobacco-stained teeth, teeth that soon were working on the final bit of butterscotch.

Margaret let Alma's comment go at that. Her preoccupation with the Bancrofts – how she'd even been thinking maybe she'd one day get back to writing and, if she did, this intriguing couple were just the kind of subject she needed – was private, and would be for quite a while.

Meanwhile, Alma was wagging her head, seemingly amazed. "I'm still trying to figure how it happened Charlotte Bancroft finished that Mass. What she was thinking. And then her guilt afterwards. The torture of knowing she'd deserted her husband at death's door."

After Margaret had walked Alma to her pickup and watched her drive away, she lingered there next to the parking lot, musing on the torture Alma spoke of, that burden Charlotte and she shared. Finishing Mass was no more immoral than cuddling a new grandchild, but when either took the place of presence at the side of a dying loved one, self-blame was inescapable and never-ending. And Charlotte and she would always be bound by that truth. For now, though, Margaret would try to give it the blind eye and again slam shut that imaginary door in her head.

Chapter Fifteen

She Could Be Reasonable

Fred was standing in front of the range, and swung around when Margaret, in nightgown, walked in. "Hey, just in time," he said.

She sniffed, wrinkled her nose. "What's going on? What's that smell?"

"I'm making seafood crepes." It was Fred at his best: sweet, kind, beautiful.

"Oh, nice." Quick adjustment to her face and tone. "Need help?"

"Nope. We're ready. Plates and orange juice on the table, piece de resistance coming up. I was about to call you."

Having finished at the stove and with sandals slapping flecked old linoleum, he carried the serving plate over and set it in the middle of the table. The presentation was really quite pretty. Around the tiny pancakes he'd arranged rounds of sliced zucchini and strips of carrots.

"Low-fat. Better for you than bakery goods," he said, pulling his terry robe tight around his waist before sitting down across from her and picking up his fork. Ready to dig in, he paused, eyes meeting hers. "You really think they smell bad?"

"Only in the context of rotting crawfish."

He tilted his head, apparently confused. And since she really wanted to tell him about the nightmare that woke her in a sweaty panic – a nightmare that included stapled papers titled *Ongoing Building Concerns* and *Concessions* screaming at her and a smelly dumpster filled with rotting crawfish and maggots – she didn't hesitate. At the same time, she didn't hold back on the food. Nor did he. Amid the clank of silverware and crunch of vegetables and whatever other noise went with attacking a good meal, she went full speed into her dream as he listened intently, at times studying her, at times peering out the sliding doors and past their balcony to the building across the parking lot.

When she wrapped up, he shook his head and cleared his throat. "This thing you've got about Pierre and his work, and these lists! *Ongoing Building Concerns. Concessions.* What next? *Evidence of Indictable Crimes?*" He didn't wait for her answer. "It's just not healthy to get so wound up, Margaret."

"Well, I sure don't want to forget things like the refrigerator I was forced to buy, and that's where *Concessions* comes in. *Ongoing Building Concerns*, on the other hand – "

"I know. Self-explanatory. But really, don't you think you're getting a bit obsessive? Does Pierre know of your lists?"

"Not the concessions one."

While Fred got up to refill their coffees, Margaret considered his words. Unfortunately but quite possibly, he did have a point. Especially about her single-mindedness. She'd always known she had tendencies that some would call perfectionist. There was no doubt that sometimes she got obsessive about things. And when that happened she prided herself on being able to slow down, ease off, follow one of Fred's favorite by-words – "get back to nature." Which, if she did, didn't mean she'd change anything about her dealings with Pierre. She'd just take a break.

So, while Fred picked up dishes and loaded the dishwasher, she slipped upstairs and into one of Kurt's old jerseys from his soccer days (she hoped it wasn't too heavy for the weather) and the trusty clam diggers she could no longer find in stores and her sturdy Dr. Martens lace-ups and the picture hat (to protect her freckled skin) she'd worn to Regina's law school graduation.

"Great idea," Fred said when – finding him downstairs on the nubby gray sofa across from Wolfgang, in his usual place on the matching easy chair – she told him of her plan to do some gardening. "When you put in those flowers between the apartment buildings it was a lift for everyone. The lady next door – "

"But this time it won't be flowers. This time I'm trying herbs."

A big nod and another, "Great idea."

"And this time I'm planting out at the site, where I can water every time I come. There's no available water here at the apartment buildings."

He rubbed the back of his neck, obviously not taken with her idea. "Seems a bit early to plant out there, don't you think? What if they grade over it?"

She swatted away his words. "I'll take the risk." Having acted on his earlier advice regarding obsession, she wasn't about to give more ground.

He began saying something, then paused, a flash of uncertainty in his eyes.

"What?"

"You understand what I was getting at earlier, don't you?" A weak smile. "It isn't that I think you're wrong. But you've got to be careful. Like I said, you can get obsessive. And then . . . well, you know, sometimes you turn people off."

That he insisted on going back to his breakfast lecture was irritating and even more irritating was his fixation on an inborn trait of hers that had generally served both of them quite well. She felt a surge of hostility. "Turn people off! Certainly I don't want to – " She mocked, voice high, wobbly, affected. " – turn people off. Especially Pierre."

"C'mon, Margaret. I didn't mean – "

"I'm in a hurry," she said, wheeling toward the coat closet, it's door ajar and the sound of scratching from inside.

"And you're angry."

She pulled the closet door open and, as the cat shot out, reached up to grab her garden gloves from the shelf. "Well who wouldn't be? After trying hard to be reasonable, you tell me I'm not."

"You're not unreasonable. It's just that you're a little different sometimes."

"Different from what?"

"From your old easy-going self."

"For your information, I've never been easy-going." She grabbed the doorknob. "I've gotta go."

"Fine. Run off. Angry, headstrong – "

"Headstrong now. Well, maybe I'd rather be headstrong than – " She searched. " – pleasure-seeking."

"Hedonistic is the word, if you want to know."

"Oh. Shall we play word games? Or golf? Talk about hedonistic."

"With all the high pressure travel I've been doing I think I deserve some time off."

"While I'm struggling to keep my head above mounting problems with the house? You think that's fair?"

It was a perfect opportunity for dramatic exit, and she swept out the door, slamming it, rattling windows that sounded like applause.

Building site deserted, she ignored holes in the blue fiberboard on the side of the house (they were already noted in *Ongoing Concerns* anyway) as she marched straight to the stick that marked the right corner of what would one day be their back yard. She could be reasonable. She'd proved it when a while back she'd planted the apartment garden instead of stewing over building concerns and she was proving it right now. "Obsessive," she snorted, setting her new shovel and the tray of little pots of herbs from Lagasse's Nursery in the middle of a patch of dry weeds not far from a sickly-looking tree that all-knowing Yale graduate Fred had said was a water oak. Tarragon overpowered everything, even the oregano, and brought back memories: third row, Mound theater, around eight years old, Sunday afternoons chomping licorice while reading Roy Rogers's lips.

Now, she stared out at the field beyond. Gold, tan, and charcoal, like a Van Gogh. Or was it Seurat? But for the squawking gulls she might've remembered those artists she'd learned while playing *Masterpiece* with the kids back in the early seventies. For now, she'd just open the doors of her hearing aids and let sweet silence relieve her of all care. Silence that lasted until, midway through her work, six pots down and six to go, she bore down on the shovel with one of her wide brown shoes, but without the usual crunch of sandy soil.

Actually, at first there was a small crunch, but more the feel of it than the sound. After that, however, came the unmistakable clank of metal. Metal shovel meeting metal object. So distinct that even without hearing aids she knew what she was dealing with. If she'd been working at the old racetrack, that clank would've meant some kind of success. Another artifact. Maybe something of historic interest. But since she was sowing rather than reaping, it meant setback. At the same time, she wasn't of a mind to just pass it over and dig someplace else. The neighborhood was too rich in history to make light of buried things, pesky or not. She had to stop, interrupt her planting, and check it out.

So, using the point of her shiny new shovel first as a pick and then a lever, she zeroed in. But under the topsoil she found the ground to be hard as rock, and neither method worked well. Having probably sat there for years, the piece was really stuck. Even if it hadn't sat for years and was just something that had gotten packed in tight by heavy machines when surrounding homes were razed to make way for Belmont Estates, there was a good chance it could turn out to be quite interesting. Maybe even valuable. Which meant, she suddenly realized, it wasn't such a good idea to be banging at with a big metal tool.

With that in mind, she put the shovel down and, finding a nearby twig, got on her knees, using the twig and her gloved hands to scrape and brush, and with each move, reveal just a tiny bit more of something that was beginning to look like rusty cutwork. But, oh the numbing tedium. And when she finally took off the sweat-drenched gloves and tried to curl her fingers around the rim, she still found it impossible to budge. There was no place to get a grip. And with the twig about to fall apart, it was of little use in making that notch her fingers needed to get a decent hold.

What to do? She needed more than a twig. She needed something sturdy. Something like . . . how about that ice scraper she'd used on the windshield in Minnesota?

It turned out the few minutes it took to locate and bring back the scraper from the car were worth it. Now able to dig around the edge, she began breaking through a bond that in places was so solid it seemed like metal and soil were one. A fact she hoped meant the piece had been there a good long while.

When she finally curved her fingers around and got a good hold on the thing, she knew it was now or never. Aside from twisting it out of shape by prying with her shovel – or worse, breaking it – she'd never get it out.

What a relief, then, to feel the release, the crack. Relief, but also alarm as she pitched back, slamming into the ground, wind knocked out, terrible twinge near the rib cage. Twinge that lingered.

Lying there, she wondered if she'd pulled a muscle or if it was her heart. And, if her heart, whether this might be the big one. If so, who'd find her body? Fred, she decided. But not till much later, after he'd arrived home hungry.

When the pain did go away, she sat up cautiously, testing to be sure. Fairly confident she was okay now, she plumped her hat and set it back on her head before picking up the prize from where it had fallen. Studying it, she found (as she'd suspected) that it was fretwork. A curling snake of reddish-brown metal. Nice find. Interesting. But she'd have to come back to it later. First, the herbs.

Rubber-legged and a little dizzy, but other than that okay – at least for the moment – she dragged herself to her feet and got back to work sprinkling plant food in holes, unpotting plants that smelled heavenly, and sticking them in. She worked fast, racing toward that moment when she stuck her gloves in the pockets of her clamdiggers, left the shovel and pots near the water oak and, with the newly-found treasure in hand, trudged around the house to the front. Now would come the fun, and she was ready to indulge. She even found a dip to settle herself in the massive roots of the live oak. The craggy bark didn't make for the most comfy nest but after taking off her hat and putting on her glasses, she made do.

At first, while poking and scraping at her prize, she suspected it was a trivet. But looking more closely and noting jagged edges where it must've broken from something, she began to think it might be ironwork from a sewing machine. If that's what it was, though, why the monogram *CD*? It seemed like it would be more fitting with an *S,* as in the old standby Singer Sewing Machines. What's more, and important too, was that she'd recently seen a similar combination of initials and ironwork somewhere. Now if she could only remember . . .

Ah, yes. Fences in the French Quarter in New Orleans. A monogram from a fence, that's what it was. Initials CD. Or were they . . .

She took off her glasses, folded one stem, and used the other to poke out more of the stuck soil. Then she put the glasses on again. That was a *B*, not a *D*, she decided, sitting forward so she could pull a tissue from her back pocket to wipe stinging sweat from her eyes. All the while thinking how perfect this was. Just the sort of thing that made her glad they'd bought property in Belmont Estates. The sense that people had been here before, years and years ago. And this time it was even more special. This time it looked like these folks hadn't just passed by. These had likely settled here. Maybe even on her lot.

More fascinating, though, in fact so much so that it made her scalp creep, were those initials. Married couples had been joining surname initials in monograms for as long as she could remember, and that *CB* could just as easily stand for *Corbyn-Bancroft* as anything. Unless she was losing it, she was quite sure Alma had said *Corbyn* was Charlotte's maiden name. If she was right, might Charlotte and Albert have lived here, planted this old oak, looked out (maybe from a porch) on the same view? Might Charlotte herself have hand-picked this monogram?

Incredible. But stranger things had happened.

When she got to her car she put the monogram in the plastic bag that the plant food had come in and set it on the passenger side. Then, tossing picture hat in back and snapping hearing aid doors shut, she roared off toward the Lasserre Parish Historical Society Museum. She'd think about the pots, shovel, and badly needed shower later.

Chapter Sixteen

C and B

It was already too late to inform the receptionist that she wasn't in, Louise decided as she stood at the front desk watching Margaret Bohr, plastic bag in hand, bustle into the sales office. "Wish I could talk, but I'm snowed under," she told the cheeky nuisance who not only looked ridiculous but smelled like she'd just finished work at a licorice factory. And who replied, "This won't take but a minute" as, smudged face beaming, she pulled something grimy from the bag. "I was on my way to the historical museum when it occurred to me that you could probably help me out."

Louise conspicuously checked the clock.

"This," the oblivious Mrs. Bohr said, proudly thrusting the nasty thing toward her, "might be right up your alley."

Louise extended an unwilling hand toward what seemed to be a filthy metal ornament. "What is it?" she asked, holding it arm's length from her new raw silk blazer.

"I'm not sure. I think it's a monogram. Maybe part of an old fence. I dug it up near the back of our lot."

Louise drew it closer. *CB.*

The realization that *C* and *B* might, and quite possibly did, denote two names of great significance — like Charlotte Corbyn and Albert Bancroft — didn't occur all at once. What it did was seep in. And by the time that seepage had grown to a threatening, black pool, Louise had taken a long breath and scrutinized each twist of the metal. Was that really a *B*, or was her overactive imagination playing tricks? It could be a *D* with a bit of dirt stuck in the center.

Yet, she knew better, and she also knew at this moment that it would be her first real test, not so much of facility in lying but of skill in winging it. For, it seemed, Mrs. Bohr knew something. What it was Louise wasn't sure. Nor how Mrs. Bohr had found out.

"You'll burn a hole, the way you're ogling," the white-haired pest said. "Something wrong?"

"Oh no. Nothing, really." She gave the monogram back, then clasped trembling hands behind her back. "What gives you the idea this is up my alley?" She was resolved to stay in control.

"From that tour you gave." The bag rattled as Mrs. Bohr's grimy fingers battled to get the monogram back in.

"Tour?" It took a moment. "Oh." She almost sighed aloud. "You mean the drive through old Acadi."

Louise had never thought of that little expedition as a tour. When she'd show prospective home buyers the old historic area, it was more an effort toward selling a style of pastoral life than a sightseeing excursion.

"The drive, the tour, whatever you call it, you *do* know a lot about old Acadi." Mrs. Bohr seemed to be reassuring herself.

"To be honest, I'm limited on that score." Louise felt more confident now. "What I told you that day we drove around was pretty much the extent of it. And even that wasn't my own.

The office staff did all the research and put it together. I just memorized it."

Mrs. Bohr frowned. "And here I thought you knew this place like the back of your hand."

"Hardly. I'm new here, you know."

"New?"

"I grew up in the northeast."

"I can't believe. The northeast? How can that be? You even look like you belong. Although your accent – "

"I'm sorry, but since I really can't be of help – " Again Louise glanced at the clock above the receptionist's desk. " – I hope you'll excuse me."

"But . . . but . . ." The impertinent matron caught Louise's arm as she turned toward her office. ". . . just one more question." Mrs. Bohr's eyes pleaded. "Remember when we drove by those old live oaks and you said that meant someone once had a house on the property?" Leaving no time for an answer, she went on. "Well, I don't know if you've noticed, but we've got a huge live oak on the corner of our lot." Her pale eyes shone as she waited for a response.

Which was as bland a look as Louise could muster.

No less excited by the poker-face, Mrs. Bohr continued. "It makes me wonder if someone once lived there. Then when I add this monogram to the picture . . . ." The pale eyes now probed Louise's. "What do you think?"

"In the first place, I was referring to plantations with a number of old oaks, like an avenue of them."

The phone on the front desk jangled, and Mary Jo picked up. A moment later, "Hey, how you doin', Pierre?"

"I can't talk right now," Louise said under her breath.

"Pierre! That's who I should talk to." For all her enthusiasm, Mrs. Bohr might have just recalled a very dear and long-lost friend.

But since Mary Jo had already relayed Louise's message and hung up, this wasn't the moment for a tete-a-tete with the fellow who'd up till now been the woman's nemesis. And that reality was an oddity Louise couldn't ignore. She pointed to the plastic bag. "You want to talk to Pierre about this thing?"

"Well, he may know who lived on our lot. Wasn't his family one of the first in the parish?"

"Where'd you hear that?"

"Alma Delatte. She and I dig at the old racetrack."

Dig at the racetrack. Now what did that mean? As if Louise really cared. Besides, Mrs. Bohr was now going on non-stop in her fervent, nutty voice about this woman, Alma: "And if what she said is true, Pierre's got to be out-and-out tops for questions like who lived where, and when. He might even tell me if I'm right." A pause. "If I can ever get hold of him, that is."

"Right about what? If I may be so bold."

"About whether or not these people, the Bancrofts, had a house on our lot."

A terrific flutter shook Louise's insides and she swallowed hard before making a valiant effort to control the tremor in her voice. "To be frank, I think you're barking up the wrong tree. This monogram likely has nothing to do with your property or – " She played it well. " – these people called . . . you say the name was Bancroft?" The way she said it made clear *Bancroft* was as unfamiliar as one of those crazy Cajun words that made no sense. "Anyhow, the way I see it is that this monogram probably washed in from someplace. Maybe when the levee broke years ago. "And now," she said, turning toward her office, "I've got to get back to work."

Chapter Seventeen

Lord, Do I Trust My Eyes?

By the time she got to the Lasserre Parish Historical Museum, it had closed for lunch, so Margaret headed for the local library, where she aimed her inquiry at the most venerable face behind the circulation desk.

"Anyone here know much history of Lasserre Parish?" she whispered.

Blurry eyes came alive behind metal-rimmed half-glasses in a parchment face. After covering her mouth with a skimpy paper napkin, the ancient finished chewing what definitely included onion. "Forgive me," she said in a wobbly soprano before using shaky hands to spread the same napkin over a soggy burger and catsup-soaked fries and then pushing the mound aside. Facing Margaret again, she offered a smile that revealed sticky goo on very pink gums. "History of Lasserre Parish, huh. Well, you might think I'm crowing, but you sure came to the right person. I've lived here all my life. Name's Elmira Keller."

Margaret introduced herself and explained about the monogram before pulling it from the bag and handing it to the librarian. "Do you have any idea whose initials those are?"

Ms. Keller's knobby fingers followed the metal swirls as though defining the monogram by touch. "*C* and *B*?"

"That's what they look like to me."

"Well . . . ." She set the monogram on the desk and gave it the eagle eye. Finally, she turned to Margaret. "I seem to be drawing a blank."

"How about this, then. Do you know where I might find out who *C* and *B* were?"

The librarian sucked her teeth and narrowed her eyes, staring somewhere behind Margaret. After what seemed an eternity, she came back to life. "There is one place we might look." And without a word, she got up and set out across the room, body sloping right, left arm out.

Margaret followed.

When she got to a wall of metal files, Ms. Keller began pulling out drawers and examining contents, eventually finding what she was after. "I have no idea how old the monogram is, but there's a chance you'll find what you're looking for on this map. If you don't find the answer here, you might try the historical society."

Margaret put on her glasses and unfolded what amounted to an oversized reproduction on which, under the title *Lasserre Parish 1894*, the Mississippi River twisted like a thick slice of snake, starting top left, drooping to the treacherous bend known as Hardscrabble Turn, and then gently curling back up and out of the map. Along both banks, in tiny black lettering and interspersed with dots and dashes and numbers and lines, were the names of plantations and homeowners. She could tell it wouldn't be an easy read, but knew she had to give it a try. So, with Ms. Keller tagging along, she headed for the nearest table, where she spread the map out and leaned in.

It took a few minutes to find St. Joan of Arc and even longer to locate the Riverbend House of Retreats because, as

Ms. Keller explained, it had been called Washington College for Young Men back then. And after Margaret found those, it took a while to figure out where her lot sat. The way she did it was by placing her left index finger on the church and her right one on the school, then estimating the distance between her property and each of those landmarks. Because her land was much closer to St. Joan of Arc than Washington College, she moved her right finger from the school to near where she thought her property lay. Then, left finger advancing eastward, began a halting journey down the road going east. "Post office . . . Fernando de Soto . . . J. D. Melancon . . . Arceneaux Plantation . . . racetrack a bit to the rear — " A pause and then a gasping, "Lord, do I trust my eyes?"

"What is it?" Ms. Keller's hot onion breath grazed Margaret's cheek.

"Albert Bancroft. I think Charlotte and Albert lived on our property." She threw her fists in the air, knocking Ms. Keller's glasses askew.

"The Bancrofts?" Ms. Keller's timeworn eyes went blank as she adjusted her glasses. Then, and with a glimmer of recognition, "The Bancrofts. Of course. English couple. *C* in *CB* would be Charlotte . . . what was it again . . . *Carlin?*"

"Corbyn."

"Oh yes, Charlotte Corbyn and Albert Bancroft. I haven't given a thought to those two in years."

A goateed fellow at the next table cleared his throat, and Ms. Keller lowered her voice. "Now that was some team. Have you read *Livre Riviere?*"

"No, I've seen it, though. Is it in?"

"I'll check." And with that, Ms Keller sailed off, returning a few minutes later with the book. "There's a part about the Bancrofts – " She was paging through now. " – Ah, here it is."

After handing it to Margaret, she sat down across from her, pushing the map aside. "You read, I'll listen."

Margaret sat down too, and was soon either summarizing or reading, all the while keeping in mind the "library voice" she'd learned in elementary school.

First was the description of Charlotte. "Woman of superior character and beauty, music teacher at Sacred Heart Convent as well as organist and choir director at St. Joan of Arc Catholic Church. Statuesque, cultivated, genial, with intelligent eyes and flowing hair. A true intellect and faithful Catholic. The clatter of her carriage as she and daughter Lizzie rode to the convent each morning was a signal to the neighbors that it was time to get up."

Margaret sat back. "You know, that sounds so familiar. When we lived in Minnesota my kids came along to church on a pretty regular basis and, believe it or not, at one time I had a rattling car."

"Oh?" A vacant look on Ms. Keller's face.

But instead of explaining the alter ego business, Margaret went on, at this point scanning text that was wordy and awkward. "It was during the Civil War in 1863 that Albert and Charlotte met. Albert was stationed with Union troops at a place called Upper White Hall, and he and a friend took a carriage ride to Acadi, where they had an accident near the Corbyn home. Not a major one. But they had to wait for repairs. And that was when the Corbyns invited them into their home. Albert and Mr. Corbyn, both being from England, made friends right away. And when Albert saw Charlotte and heard her play the piano he fell head over heels. They got married in 1865.'"

Holding her place, Margaret leaned back. "So amazing."

"Right-O. An Englishman serving with the Union — "

"That too. But what's really amazing is that I met my husband at someone's house and it was shortly after that we started dating."

"So you . . . ." The librarian's eyes narrowed. "So you met your husband . . . . And the correlation?"

"Shhhh," from the goateed fellow at the next table.

"Charlotte and I both – " Margaret stopped mid-whisper. "Too much to explain. I'll tell you about it some other time."

Returning to the book, she read on in a voice so low it was a mere hum in her hearing aids. First there was the account of Albert as an unwilling but honor-bound participant in the duel (Which happened on Sunday, August 23, 1874). Following that were a few lines about Francois Dupuis, the plantation owner who killed Albert. After that were details – the fifteen paces and Smith and Wesson revolvers and how when first shots turned out to be either wide or high, Dr. Bancroft's second, David Nicholas, insisted (contrary to everyone's wishes) on another firing. The sad result being, of course, Dr. Bancroft with a bullet through the heart and Dupuis with a nasty wound to the stomach.

"Talk about stomach, that just turns mine. A second insisting – "

"And they were supposedly friends."

"Best friends, in fact. I mean, the guy was Bancroft's second." Her eyes met the librarian's. "Does it make sense that the man Bancroft chose to watch out for him got him killed?"

The goateed fellow's chair screeched on the wood floor as he pushed away from the adjacent table. After slapping his papers together, he stormed to a chair in the far corner of the room.

Margaret gave Ms. Keller a guilty look and resumed library voice as she finished up with a paragraph about Dr.

Bancroft's popularity in the Acadi community and how the people of the community had missed Charlotte, too, when she died nearly fifty years later. And – leave it to Alma to get things right - an account of a music museum in her honor at LSU.

As to the essential photo, the one Alma had shown her that day at the old racetrack, it didn't take long to find it and the proof Margaret was seeking – *CB* monograms on each side of the front gates. "Yes!" she breathed, flipping to the title page to check the book's publication date. Nineteen fifty-seven. Nearly forty years ago. Would LSU still have the stuff? Was there still a music museum? Wouldn't it be fun to just go there and poke around.

"You're a dear," Margaret told Mrs. Keller as together they copied what they could of old newspaper clippings about both the duel and the music museum. Then, with those copies and *Livre Riviere* in hand, she said thank-you and promised she'd be back.

"You been cleaning chimneys?" Fred said when she came in the door. "Scratch that." He did a double sniff. "You fell in a licorice patch."

"That's tarragon," she said, reaching into the plastic bag and taking out the monogram. "Look at this." She handed it to him.

"From the fire in your eyes, I'd say this filthy trivet is priceless treasure that was buried with either de Soto or – "

"No smart remarks," she said, launching into a recount of her day and ending with, "So what do you think? A second insists a duel go on, a state legislator is mortally wounded, his wife finishes Mass when she hears the news, and there's no explanation for the whole ugly episode."

Fred set the bag, monogram on top, between them on the sofa and she reached over and brushed it with a loving hand. "Seems impossible, doesn't it? Me, amateur archaeologist so to speak, choosing as my building site the very spot where two significant figures spent a good part of their lives, and then finding a spectacular artifact there. Just makes me shiver."

"I'm glad you feel better than when you left this morning."

"You think we'll find the other monogram in the backyard?"

"All of a sudden I is we."

"You mean you'll help me dig?"

A dim glow from the parking lot seeped in on both sides of the bedroom blinds as Fred, in pajamas and with freshly brushed teeth, turned off the bathroom light.

As he got into bed Margaret raised up on an elbow. "You know, at the library today I found nothing about gambling in the stuff about Bancroft's duel. You think Alma made it up?"

"She said he gambled?"

"She said the duel had to do with gambling."

"Interesting."

Margaret sighed and turned to the other side. "All I can say is, thank God for Gamblers Anonymous."

Delicate whistling preceded the soft scrape and clack of the nightstand drawer as she put her hearing aids away. "Good night," she whispered contentedly, throwing her arm above her head and banging the wobbly rental headboard into the wall.

"You know, Margaret . . . . Margaret?"

But she was either so worn out from her eventful day she'd already fallen asleep or didn't hear him. Besides, there was always tomorrow. And he'd do it first thing. He had to. Both admit and quit. But how? Gamblers Anonymous again?

Or on his own? Easing off, like he'd done with smoking. Or cold turkey?

What a relief it would be when he was free of the habit. No more worry about either Margaret or Welbourne. Or Pierre, in a fit of pique, informing.

Chapter Eighteen

Not an Ordinary Joe in ihe Bunch

Fred was back from Brazil. A two-week trip this time. And because Margaret, as usual, had the blueprints, tape measure, camera – everything – in her car, he reluctantly agreed to let her drive to the site. She'd stopped using the air conditioner, she assured him, and with the carpet dry now, the odor was gone.

"I love this car," she said while waiting for an opening in morning traffic snaking past the apartment building parking lot on its way to the river road. "I've loved it since the day I saw it in the Vintage Classics lot in Minneapolis. I'd never seen an orange BMW before. White, black, silver, even red, but never orange. It reminded me of Indian summer."

"Well, if you love it so much, why don't you get the air conditioning, driver's window, and vacuum hose fixed?" Restraint, he reminded himself, aware that his voice was getting high and his toes curling. "It's either that or get a new car. And I don't mean new to you. I mean really new this time."

"You've changed, Fred. Remember when you had no qualms about driving that broken-down Ford?"

"The truth is, Margaret, we've both changed. It used to be you wouldn't have been caught dead in some of the things you wear these – " He stopped himself. "I didn't mean – "

"Forget it." She offered a weak smile and switched on the radio, switching it off a moment later. "I've never told you about the day I visited the house over on Hialeah Street, have I."

"Nope."

"Well, while I waited for Pierre – he was supposedly on his way – I went inside to look around."

"Nice place?" He was still kicking himself for his earlier words and was grateful for the break from nit-picking.

"It was big. Impressive. But not as impressive as the finishing crew. It's an interesting bunch our contractor has working for him."

"How so?"

"They're gospel freaks."

"Really, not very surprising. Remember the PR about Pierre and his employees belonging to a church with a funny name."

"Well, the crew's funny too. Not an ordinary joe in the bunch."

"Special, huh."

"In a questionable way. One guy, a painter, is fat enough to headline a sideshow. Another, a Cuban, is scarred like you wouldn't believe and seems to have trouble with one eye. Then there's a standoffish carpenter who goes on about sickness and broken hearts and ultimate victory as though he's Elmer Gantry."

"If they do decent work – "

"That's my point. I don't know about the unfortunate Cuban. He was outside with the supervisor. But this carpenter – I think his name is Joseph – didn't know beans about installing molding. There were gaps everywhere, some as wide as my little finger. And the fat painter was friendly enough – he may have even done decent work – but he didn't seem to realize that this woman madly sweeping up sawdust in the same room was messing with his enamel finish."

"So what did you do?"

"Dragged myself outside, demoralized, dreading the day they start work inside our house."

"And Pierre? Did you talk to him about it?"

"He never got there." She pulled up in front of their house and got out, leading the way into the garage, where she emitted a gasp so loud Fred's heart did cartwheels. "What is it?" he, too, gasped.

"The latest deliveries." She flung a hand in the direction of two louvered wooden things that resembled small windows without glass.

"What are they?" Whatever they were, he was thinking, they looked quite ordinary. In fact, quite fine.

"Gable vents, and they're the wimpiest gable vents I've ever seen." Stooping, then slapping her plastic attaché on the concrete floor, she grabbed pen and paper from inside. "Aside from making it look stupid," she said, finished writing and breathlessly pushing up, "I don't see how these vents are going to add anything to the house. They sure won't make the attic any cooler."

"I may not be a designer, " he said, hoping a little humor might help, "but I think they're kind of cute. "

"Kind of cute, huh." She studied him. "What is it with you, Fred? You can get so worked up about my car, but when it comes to the house you fizzle. Why is that? Don't you see? Even if Pierre doesn't read plans, wouldn't you expect, just from what he wears, that he'd have some sense of taste? I doubt his home is brutalized."

She probably meant *bastardized,* but Fred kept it to himself because by now she was brandishing the page and working herself into another tizzy. "At least half of *Ongoing Building Concerns* are Pierre's shabby trade-offs, and I just don't understand. Why's he bringing in all this junk? Is he getting deals on discards and overage? Does he think we're too dumb to notice?"

"What does he say? Have you asked him?"

"Like I told you, he's never around. Besides that, he ignores my phone messages."

"Hmm. I wonder where he is."

"More than that, when he's going to send this stuff back. All of it has to be changed out."

"All?"

"Of course."

"At the risk of him walking off the job?"

She nodded.

"Well, one thing's encouraging, and that is that he hasn't installed any of it. Makes me think he might be waiting for the right things to come in. At least we can hope. At this point it's all we can do. Give him the benefit of the doubt. It's a better idea than – "

"Being obsessive and paranoid?" She gave him a calm, knowing look.

Chapter Nineteen

Vernon, You Just Don't Know

Margaret's calm, knowing look was long gone when three days later she got to the site and found gable vents and French doors installed and windows going in fast.

A quick drive home, a scramble through her metal file box for the contract, and she was soon on the phone, hearing aid whistling shrill support as she jammed the receiver to her left ear and blurted her message to Pierre. "That stuff in the garage didn't belong on the house, and you damn well know it. And there's not a chance it's staying there. Article 9 of the contract reads – " Document rattling in her hand, she found her place. "' – Work not conforming to contract documents, including substitutions not properly approved and authorized, may be considered defective.'"

After she'd hung up and calmed down a bit, she began to wonder if she'd made any impression at all. What she'd quoted didn't seem tough enough to change the mind of a stubborn fool who couldn't grasp that plans and specs were part of the contract. A fool who had no idea – or didn't seem to care – how much time she'd spent driving here, there, and everywhere in search of the perfect stuff for her house. More than that, taking care that those items were stated explicitly in the drawings and specs before they went out for bid.

What had it all been worth? How could Pierre be so casual about it? Had none of his customers ever done the same? Certainly, if they had and, after all that effort, found him sneaking in cheap substitutes, they must have complained. By now he should have learned his lesson. But he hadn't.

So, what to expect? Would he go on ignoring her? Might she have to take him to court to get the junk torn out? Or, in the end, would she just give up and accept a shoddy house?

As long as she had some control over the purse strings, she knew the latter wouldn't happen. Somewhere along the line, maybe when he was expecting the next draw, she'd put a stop to the finagling.

Meanwhile, Vernon Breedlove was just a phone call away. And with the number drilled into her brain from frequent use, she dialed it, getting through in an instant. But connecting with the office and Fiona, was as far as she got. Which wasn't that unusual. Such things did happen. There was a casual attitude about the office. More than once Margaret had been ushered in only to wait while Breedlove, in trademark string tie and button-down, sipped chocolate chestnut coffee while finishing up with his travel agent, going on about who knows what as though to hang up was to end all contact with humanity. Finally, with a jolly "have a good one," the architect would battle to his feet, reach for his cane, call to Fiona to find the blueprints, and direct Margaret to the conference room.

That's the way it usually was and now, as Margaret waited for him to pick up the phone, she suspected the hangup was similar. Because of that and not expecting his response any time soon, she was a little surprised when his voice boomed "How are you, Margaret?" from the other end. But it wasn't the end of the holdup. He was on the other line, he said, and would call her back.

"If you don't mind," she replied, recalling similar unkept promises, "I'd rather hold." She said this despite the friendly lilt to his voice, that little flip that meant he was open to hearing her out. There'd been a time when she felt like he might've grown tired of her. That was when he often forgot to call back. She'd noticed the behavior in that period around some of their get-togethers aimed at fine-tuning drawings for the house. Meeting after meeting he'd say, "Time to wrap up. Blueprints and specs are ready for bids." And meeting after meeting she'd respond, "But . . . . " and go on to tick off amenities that, as long as she was building, might as well be in her new home.

"Margaret." She was roused from her musings by his voice on the line again. "Hey, it's been awhile. Sorry for the wait, but you know how it is." A breathing space. "What's on your mind?"

"I hate to turn your day bad, but I've got problems with Pierre."

"You mean the kitchen measurements?"

"No, that's taken care of." She explained about Pierre moving walls and the built-in fridge she'd had to buy. She didn't mention that both were now in her Concessions list and would be taken into account in final payment.

"It's other problems that are bothering me," she said, "and there are lots of them. So many that I think I'm going to have to pay you for extra inspections."

"Will you hold a minute, Margaret? Fiona's got a question for me."

While she waited Margaret pondered what his response to her hint would be, for that's what her suggestion about inspections was. She was letting him know, without coming out and saying it, that he was doing a half-assed job of overseeing her jobsite. He, after all, was the one charged with making sure the contractor's work met certain standards. *Administration of the contract* was what it was called.

Would her hint tweak his conscience? Would it remind him that he was being paid for contract administration that wasn't happening? Hopefully, yes, and without provoking him. She needed him too much to risk a breach.

"Now, you were saying – " He was back on the phone.

"I was saying that I need someone with clout to stand up for me. Pierre's been sneaking his crew in and doing mischief when I'm not there. Then when I leave messages for him he doesn't call back."

"I'm sorry to hear that, Margaret. I was under the impression the house was coming along nicely, other than those little slips we have to expect. It looked wonderful the last time I was out."

"Oh Vernon, you just don't know. I've got a list of problems a mile long."

And she started in.

Chapter Twenty

Not Your Typical Easy-Going Broad

The phone rang and rang, and the answering machine finally kicked in. "Pierre. Vernon Breedlove here. Will you give me a call? I – "

Pierre lifted the receiver. "Yes, Vernon."

"How you doin', man? Where ya been?"

"Oh, around. I moved my office into the house, you know, and am loving it."

"Great place to live and work, Pierre. If I were up there I'd be eating every meal at Brignac's. Ever tried their stuffed shrimp? Recipe's out of this world. Crabmeat stuffing, you know. Not too much Worcestershire. And their bread pudding . . . . "

Yammer, yammer. If the guy ever stopped babbling and gadding about he might get some work done.

"Hey." Breedlove was serious now. Finally down to business. "These issues with Mrs. Bohr. What do you think?"

"I think she should get a life."

"I know." A polite snicker. "But the situation with the structural engineer?"

"Oh that. Slip-up. Those things happen, you know."

"We've got to be careful."

Pierre held the receiver away from his ear and glared at it. Breedlove telling him to be careful? The guy who drew two sets of plans now advising prudence?

Phone back in place, he listened, silently mocking, head bobbing back and forth with each wacky remark from the other end.

"Seems like Mrs. Bohr isn't your typical easy-going broad," Breedlove was saying now, "and if she starts spreading the word – "

"To who? To you? Louise? And where's it going from there? Or is Mrs. Bohr going to call the incompetents at the Better Business Bureau?"

"There's always the Department of Inspections."

Pierre couldn't suppress a cackle. "I don't know anyone in that department who's averse to a little grease. Besides, if she starts spreading the word, she's gonna be waiting till kingdom come for her house. I can walk, you know. And the Bohrs aren't in the most favorable position. Interest on loan, rent on apartment, furniture storage – all go on, construction or not. I doubt they've got funds for anything extra. Including legal advice." (Of course, Mr. Bohr's fear of him blabbing about the gambling likely didn't hurt either.)

"You're pretty confident." Breedlove sounded doubtful.

"Totally confident. Partly because, except for that first draw and their little delay concerning insurance and termite questions, the Bohrs are good about paying. With the last advance, I'm set. For the moment, you understand."

Breedlove cleared his throat. "Now, to the other reason for my call. Which is, Mrs. Bohr asking me to do extra inspections."

"You turned her down, right?"

"And allow some other architect in? We'd really be in trouble."

"So what's your plan?"

"I'm not sure. Play it by ear, I guess. You know, Pierre, I think the time has come when we've got to accept that some of our substitutions will have to go. You'll make a little less, but that's life."

"I'm not making that much right now. My bid was too low in the first place. You know that. If we can't cut costs with a few trade-offs I'll barely break even, especially taking into account the extra work on the damn concrete floors and the walls I had to move for the island. That idea you had about two sets of plans, one for the Bohrs and one for my workers, did me in."

"Sorry about that. I guess I didn't take into account how a few less square feet would change kitchen dimensions. Anyway, I promise – " Upbeat again. " – we'll make it up on the next house."

Chapter Twenty-One

Tacit Blackmail

Good news for a change. Conconco, the company Pierre had hired to fix the slab, had done top-flight work. Even Margaret agreed that the floors looked great. Smooth, slate blue, flowing from one end of the u-shaped house to the other, they resembled a pristine pool. It was too bad it would be a month before the colored concrete could be stained with the green that would make it look like old copper. More than that, it was too bad that during that period, even with plastic and cardboard overlay, there could be no foot traffic. So whether or not he planned to, Pierre couldn't change out the windows, doors, and gable vents that were by now weathering.

Meanwhile, out of the blue, Margaret answered an ad for an organ/carillon player at The Holy Church of River Road and got the job. Which wasn't a development as surprising as the concrete floor. She'd always been a good musician. Her mother had seen to that, shelling out one dear dollar each week from the time Margaret was six until graduation from high school.

On the phone Fred told Regina, "Part of the reason your mother took the organ job is that she's worried about finances. With nothing happening at the site I'm not that upbeat either."

"Nothing new with Pierre?" his daughter asked.

"Not really. We're still waiting for the concrete to cure." He peered out his office window, trying to recall if there was anything else. Regina being the lawyer in the family, it was always good to pass things by her. "I guess I should take that back," he said a moment later. "The brass fireplace Pierre left sitting in the garage is rusting and he's gotten what your mother calls shoddy furnaces and water heaters delivered."

"Oh boy. I bet that plays havoc with her blood pressure."

"She doesn't mention it, but I suspect you're right. It's probably off the charts."

"And all because of Pierre."

"In large part."

"What can be done? You got any ideas on how to handle him?"

"Not at the moment. It's complicated."

Especially complicated, Fred was thinking, when one was dealing with tacit blackmail.

Chapter Twenty-Two

Memories

Driving up to the Saratoga Springs site and finding Pierre there was a surprise to Cedro. Pierre wasn't one of those contractors who hung around his construction sites. He wasn't even one who had meetings with his crew, except for that gathering at his house months before when, after Cedro told him of his concerns, Pierre ignored him for the rest of the evening – and beyond. Today, though, Pierre could no longer ignore him. At the same time, Cedro wasn't feeling that urge to look after an innocent client as strongly as he had back then. He was still feeling the urge, but in a more private way.

So, when Pierre snapped, "What are you doing here? There's no call for a painter, nor will there be for a while," Cedro avoided Pierre's eyes. And when a burning desire to flee closed in, he quietly replied, "Just looking."

"Just looking, huh. And may I ask for what you are looking?"

The image of Duardo in the prison yard under the flood-lights flashed into Cedro's mind and in an instant of bravery like he seldom felt these days, he corrected his chicken-hearted reply. "I'm checking for anchor bolts."

"Anchor bolts. My my." Pierre was like a mad dog about to attack. "And may I ask what business that is of yours?"

"I've read that every house down here should have them."

"Well, not every house does. So what?"

"The fellow I worked for in Florida, he always put them in. And he was on the Florida Building Commission."

"La-di-da." Pierre said, raising a limp wrist and fluttering his lashes.

Voice a little shaky now, Cedro went on. "He said he'd never known a contract that didn't call for them."

"What the . . . . If you want to practice law, join a firm. If you're going to paint, stick to that."

"But what if someone gets killed when one of your houses blows down?"

"Blows down? Phooey. Nonsense. Even my clients don't worry about it."

"They don't know."

"Have you never heard the old saw, 'What you don't know won't hurt you'?" He folded his arms and gave Cedro a long, cold look. "Now, if I'm not mistaken, aren't you're due over at Stimson's?"

After that it was a long day, with Cedro trying more than ever to figure out what he should do. It was a little like when back in the sixties he'd had to make up his mind about fleeing Cuba. If he did, there was risk. If he didn't, there was risk too. Now, though, it wasn't so much a matter of life or death. Now it was a matter of conscience. And now, having survived and known what it meant to live in a country where he could – and should – speak up, he was torn. Afraid. In America they'd call it "lily-livered." His brother Duardo would have called him a *cobarde.* Coming in and painting sheetrock that he knew had been installed over missing bolts that would have connected the bones of the structure to the concrete foundation – making the home much safer – made him an accomplice, an ally. Yet, what could he do about it? He was caught. It seemed he had no influence on anyone who mattered. And if he quit his job, who'd hire him? For that matter, who'd give him a decent recommendation? For sure, there was no asking Pierre for one. And after the past two years, did he even want to go on in construction? But what else could he do? It was much too late to try to go back to the practice of law.

The question was still on his mind that evening as he sat on the steps of his trailer watching Sharlene, shoving her kids ahead, make her way toward him while telling them to "Show Cedro what you have for him."

Bradley – younger of the two and blue-eyed, skinny, wearing a Superman sweatshirt – held back more than Gina, who finally handed over the prize Sharlene seemed so proud of. It was a picture, the one Sharlene had taken the day they'd come to pick up the stray kitten, and in it the children sat in the grass, each with a hand on the tiny, orange shape in front of them. They were wide-eyed, likely wondering how something so soft and cute could come from someone so scary.

"Thank you," he said, staring at the photo and then putting it in his shirt pocket. "How is the kitten doing? Is he happy at your house?"

When they shyly nodded, he took the picture out again, forcing a smile as he pretended to study it.

After they left, he lay on his bed thinking about the children, especially Sharlene's Gina and his own Adria. They really weren't very different. When he was first released from prison in Cuba, Adria too had been wary, running away and hiding. Only after seeing him a lot, and realizing that under it all he was quite normal, did she loosen up.

Adria. Such sadness. Better not to remember. Better to leave those memories and dream himself back to happy days on the plantation. Those days before Adria, when he and Duardo were young and didn't have a worry in the world.

He closed his eyes. It soon was all there. The hills in the distance. He and his brother heading home on their horses. Duardo leading the way, of course. The pound of hooves on the hard, dry road as they got to the entrance and made their way through the huge iron gates. The shade of the sabal palms along the drive, and Duardo pushing his straw hat off, letting it hang on his back. The scent from the spit – hoping it was pork with peppers and onions – as they left their horses to Elio to take to the stable. The maid and their mother in the kitchen, their mother in a brightly-colored dress that moved with her body when she swayed to the beat from the radio – Arsenio Rodriguez and his All Star Band. Her kissing their foreheads as they stopped to check the pots. Their dad reading the paper in his red leather chair in the library. Setting his glasses on the fancy little table at his side as he asked what they'd been up to. Their answer: watching the harvesters.

A perfect day. Without memories like that Cedro didn't know what he'd do.

Chapter Twenty-Three

Matching Monogram

With Fred at the wheel, Margaret was free to peek between the seats to where, on the rear floor crowding Carol's kennel and beneath Wolfgang's shaggy body on the seat above – where the dog scanned passing surroundings like a passenger on a tour bus – there were two cauliflowers, a cabbage, a paper bag of new potatoes, a couple bunches of carrots, and two huge mounds of turnip and mustard greens. "I hope we didn't get carried away with the vegetables," she said.

Fred smiled toward the road ahead, his one-over-par game earlier in the morning having bolstered an already upbeat mood. "With all the fantastic produce at that stand, there's always the possibility. But I doubt it. I've got plans for a lot of it already. As soon as I get home this afternoon I'm cooking up some mustard greens with low fat sausage. A pot of cauliflower soup too. A huge pot we can eat all week. There's a great recipe in Jane Brody's book."

Great and *cauliflower* – oxymorons, Margaret was thinking. Yet, as long as there were potato chips and Honey Buns hidden at the tippy top of her side of the bedroom closet she felt okay with whatever Fred chose to fix. It meant a week off from cooking, and that could open the door to some serious fun. Like going up to LSU to look into the Bancrofts. Which meant –

"Look at that, Wolfgang," Fred was saying now. They were at the guard shack and he was pointing at a calico cat on the window ledge. As the dog sprang around, looking every which way, his tail thumped against the seat.

"And look at that," Margaret said, nodding toward the red Cadillac in front of them.

"Well, well. Seems Louise Dennis works on Sunday too."

"And talk about working, look at her mouth go. That poor fellow with her."

"Well, she's gotta earn her board."

"You kidding? Pierre's loaded. Plantation on the river. Old money. It's why I don't understand the chintzy mindset."

The guard inside the shack finally got around to pushing the button that opened the barrier, and Fred waved at him as he followed Louise's car through. But where Louise took a right, he took a left, following the street bordering the river road. Margaret, meanwhile, leaned back and closed her eyes.

"Tired?" he asked.

"Tired of row on row of Georgian mansions. They're boring. Like the people in them."

"Sounds like a chip on the old shoulder."

She glanced over. "I have good reason."

"And may I ask what it is?"

"They're the ones who helped turn Pierre into a no-good. He got used to working for these Belmont Estates horse snobs whose idiotic social lives matter more than getting what they're paying for. They don't care what Pierre does so long as their houses are enormous and pass a superficial look-see."

"Yeah, well. I guess," Fred said as he pulled up at the site. And while Wolfgang furiously barked at the fluttering turkey vultures in the tupelos on the empty lot next door, he opened his door and got the shovel out of the trunk.

"There's no matching monogram in this yard," he spat an hour or so later, his mood having taken a dive.

Margaret swallowed her sip of Zinfandel. "That's the third time you said that. And in as many minutes."

"But this is ridiculous." He stopped shoveling and rubbed his back. "The only good thing about coming up here today is the cat got out of the apartment and the dog got some exercise."

"Don't forget the produce stand," she replied, pulling her knees up and resting her back against the water oak. Not that she'd shirked her duties. She too had searched, and though the day was mild, had worked up a sweat that soaked picture hat and tee shirt as well as waistband of bellbottoms. In fact, but for Fred's snippy comment about the missing iron monogram not likely having shrunk to minuscule proportions, she would have still been working away, sifting through his shovelfuls of soil, practicing those skills she'd learned at the old racetrack.

His snide comment, actually, had been a good excuse to pretend she was offended and drop out of their hectic – because Fred was in such a hurry get it over with – search. She would've preferred a more relaxed way of going about it, and that was why she'd brought Zinfandel along. Archeology and wine, she'd thought, were a perfect combination.

"To be honest, I don't understand what we're doing out here," he said now, voice bouncing with each blow as he chopped at the chunk of dirt he'd just turned. "I thought you were interested in the Bancrofts, not their goods." Sweat streamed down his face as he took a break, perching his foot on the shovel's metal scoop before taking off his Welbourne cap and mopping his forehead on his shirt sleeve.

"Well, wouldn't it be fun to have Charlotte Bancroft's matching monograms on the gates of our new house?" She reached over and patted Carol, and the cat, drunk with catnip from the flourishing herb garden, stretched her front legs ever so slightly. She'd been in the same dead curl on Fred's windbreaker for the past who knows how long. "Anyway," Margaret continued, right eye twitching like it always did when she indulged, "sit down for a minute and have a cup of Zinfandel. You'll feel better."

"I don't drink cheap white Zinfandel, especially not from paper cups. Nor do I drink when digging. Nor when I'm trying to make sense of – " He gave the sky a befuddled look and scratched his head with the hand that held the cap. "Am I understanding right? You're saying that if you found both monograms you'd keep them?"

"What's on my property's mine, isn't it?"

"I thought you planned to give them to the historical society."

"What's wrong with a little change of heart?"

"It's not like you."

"What's not?"

"Materialism."

She quieted her jerky eye with a finger. "This is much deeper than materialism. It's more like ESP. Or something like that. It's outside the senses." Her tongue felt lazy. "You know what I mean?"

"No, and I don't think you do either. My personal opinion is that you've got enough junk from our families without collecting monograms that belonged to some lady you never even knew."

"But this lady's a sort of friend."

"That's sad."

"What's sad?"

"That you've got a dead friend."

"Look at it this way. I don't need a live friend. I've got you." An enormous rush of gratitude enveloped her, and her eyes brimmed. "Which brings up how grateful I am to you for coming today. Have I said thank-you?"

"Over and over."

"Well, thank you again, you old sweetheart."

"You're going to have a wine headache tomorrow, Margaret," he said as he clapped his cap on his head and went back to shoveling. "I can guarantee it."

But he was wrong about the headache. It began early, even before the day was done, sending her to bed with brain matter beating against tight skull and body craving liquid replacement. However, with the help of pain relievers and except for the furry tongue, she was nearly back to normal when next morning she hurried down the hall of the blond brick music building at LSU, dodging two copper kettledrums while hearing the familiar scales of a vocalizing soprano and, in the interval between the opening and shutting of a practice room door, the ripple of arpeggios on the piano. It was much the same as the music school at the University of Minnesota in the fifties. Even the ponytailed fellow who directed her to the office looked like an old friend.

But when she entered that office and asked the green-eyed, pie-faced secretary about the Charlotte Corbyn Bancroft Museum and heard "Charles Bank what?" she felt a little less sure of herself. Even so, she dealt with it, explaining about Charlotte and the music her daughter Lizzie had sold to LSU in the early forties. All of it, clearly, was news to the secretary, who after consulting the dean came back with the news that he remembered a museum in the old Music and Dramatic Arts Building but had no idea when it had been dismantled.

"And the old Music and Dramatic Arts Building? Is that gone too?" Margaret was losing hope.

The answer was no, it was where it had always been, across the street. And (all this information from the dean via his secretary) that was where the museum collection would now be housed, in the Music and Dramatic Arts Building attic.

Well, then, might she take a look in that attic? Margaret asked.

The answer was yes, but not today. They'd have to locate the key. If Margaret would like, she could call later in the week to see how things were going on that score.

Great. One down, one to go, Margaret was thinking as she proceeded to the archives where twenty minutes later, having signed in and parked her attaché (minus the legal pad and pencil she was allowed to carry along) in a downstairs locker, she was standing at the main desk being informed that the new archivist, Miss Borovich, was the one she should talk to. "That's her over there," the girl said, pointing out a tall female with wild hair and big shoulders. "Just keep an eye out. When she finishes with the fellow, grab her."

So Margaret found a spot not far from Miss Borovich where she kept that eye out, meanwhile slowly scanning the wood-paneled room: book shelves, card catalogs, circulation desk, even plaster squares in the towering ceiling. After repeating the exercise, she gave out a sigh that would've alerted anyone with a sense of decency that a waiting library patron – in this case, a new Louisiana resident whose taxes paid for this institution – also deserved attention.

But to no avail.

Finally giving up on politely alerting the archivist to her lapse in judgment, Margaret grudgingly traipsed over to the card catalogs against the wall and, after studying labels, began casually flipping through a drawer covering *Balderson* through *Baptiste*. She knew it would be a fruitless effort. Nothing ever went that smoothly and, judging from her experience at the moment, certainly wouldn't now. A stroke of luck? Out of the question.

Out of the question until . . . right there, in that drawer and without help from anyone, she came across a card titled *Bancroft (Charlotte Corbyn) Papers 1860-1920, (8 boxes)*.

Of course, it took only a few minutes for her to fill out a special collections call slip and submit it to the assistant. And something more than a few minutes for that assistant to emerge from the door behind the central desk carrying two dusty, buff-colored boxes while giving Margaret an encouraging nod that didn't take into account what appeared to be a big-time shortfall in promised material. When the assistant placed those boxes in front of Ms. Borovich, now seated at the desk, Margaret couldn't hold back. "But where are– "

"It's all you can see," the frizzy-haired woman cut in, quick to squelch Margaret's objection. "The rest of the boxes are sealed under protective order. You can see them in the year two thousand thirty-seven or so."

Perturbed, but grateful for better luck than with the monogram the day before, Margaret took the boxes to a long table, where she opened the first one and inhaled an aroma from the past – boiled milk, Fels-Naphtha soap, whatever – that brought back those visits to Aunt Inga and Uncle Theos' farm in South Dakota back in the forties. The aroma was even stronger when she began paging through the endless ledgers of

Charlotte's household expenses. The scent and the awareness that Charlotte, like herself, had probably been a Pisces – proof being her extensive list-keeping – was strangely moving.

But the pleasant sensation took flight when, coming across onionskin letters with inky scratches on both sides – the back at right angles to the front – she had to give up on making out either what the letters said or who wrote them.

Yet, finding the framed photo of Albert Bancroft in his Union military uniform again lifted her spirits. There was no problem figuring anything out as far as this gem of a find. *Albert Bancroft* was right there, scrawled on the back of the picture. And he was handsome, robust, a casting director's dream. Judging superficially, it made even less sense that Charlotte had abandoned him at death's door.

But this was no time to dwell on looks and such. If Margaret didn't move on she'd likely get caught in afternoon traffic. So when, at the bottom of the box, she found an album with pages and pages of programs from music events – with pieces by Beethoven, Mendelssohn, and Chaminade featured– she was again torn. This was lovely, familiar music that took her back to when she'd been active in the music scene in Minnesota. She just couldn't make herself page through without reminiscing. Melodies, settings, friends – all of it like yesterday.

When nearing the final pages of the album, a photo slipped from beneath one of the many French Opera programs and caught on a loose corner mount, however, the memories came to an abrupt end. Pulling it free, she found it to be the heart-shaped face of a newborn. No doubt a relative of Albert, she decided, comparing it to his photo. Both were fair-complected, with dark curly hair, soft hint of widow's peak, wide-set eyes, and full lips. This picture, too, had an inscription on the back, and in perfect rounded script: *To My Love – 1863.*

That year, 1863, set Margaret thinking. What it told her was that this wasn't a picture of Lizzie Bancroft, because one of the things she recalled reading was that Albert and Charlotte hadn't tied the knot till after the war, in 1865. In fact, if she remembered right, eighteen sixty-three was the year they met. It would help if she knew the exact date, but unless their romance had moved with lightning speed and they'd behaved at an early stage in what society would have considered a most unbecoming way, this baby wasn't theirs. And even then it didn't make sense that this child belonged to them. They wouldn't have waited till she was two years old to marry. No one with any sense of propriety would have done that. Especially back then. And these were proper people.

No, the picture wasn't Lizzie. But, for sure, it was a relative of Albert.

All quite fascinating, yet was it likely to have any bearing on her search for answers about the duel? Well, she supposed, it could. And when she had time, she'd look into it. But not now. Now it was time for the other box.

In which – yes! – she found two inventories of the Charlotte Bancroft Museum collection. The first, a list of first editions, ran the gamut from Gottschalk's salon music to Dixie, and the list went on and on. The other inventory, listing musical artifacts and personal items "too numerous to detail" was just as impressive: daguerreotypes of Charlotte's family and medals Albert won for bravery in the armies of Queen Victoria in the 1850's and a cypress music case built for Charlotte by a slave and a music stand built for her by Albert and a black lace shawl he gave her on their wedding day.

But that wasn't everything. Three letters, legible this time and postmarked Brackenville, New York, lay at the bottom of the box. One, from his mother and addressed *The Honorable*

Albert Bancroft, House of Representatives, Baton Rouge, Louisiana, spoke of the death of Albert's younger brother, Henry:

. . . May 17, 1869 shall be remembered as one of the most heart-breaking days of my life. I miss your brother as much as I missed your father after that dreadful and unexpected event in London. (How blessed I was that Henry sent for me to come and take residence with him in New York when your dear father departed this world. May he rest in peace.)

You were near enough in age to know the joy Henry brought into the world. How, like your father, he was so infatuated with life. I trust you understand the tears that come when I recall that infatuation. My heart aches because of it, and because of the opportunities denied him. The dismaying truth that he hadn't yet found his life partner and had not felt the ecstasy of holding his own child throws an even more excruciating gloom over my existence.

Two paragraphs later, just as stilted, yet heart-breaking:

I can only pray that you never know the devastation of losing a child. The perfect agony. I find myself, having no appetite, compelled to refuse food. It is as though life is over. The long and dreary road ahead casts an overwhelming pall. I expect him to enter the room at any time and yet know he never will. Sometimes I ponder whether it would be less saddening had I had more than the two of you. Or if he had given me grandchildren to fill this agonizing void. But that would be saying that others could take his place, a dreadful thought.

Margaret sat back, hands in lap, thinking. Life was so unfair. Mrs. Bancroft had not only experienced the death of this son, Henry, but in five years her other son would die. And Albert's death would be violent. If this poor woman felt lost now, how would she feel then? Would she make it through? Might the next letter be one expressing worse grief?

Quickly retrieving the second envelope, dated September 17, 1890, Margaret found the letter inside to be not from Albert's mother but from a forlorn Lizzie to Charlotte. In it she said that after five months with her grandmother in Brackenville – apparently spent vegetable gardening and feeding chickens as well as canning most of it – she was homesick for Acadi and her mother.

No news there, Margaret decided as she reached for the third letter, dated 1895 and, like the first, from Albert's mother. But it wasn't about her grief. By now, twenty years after the duel, she'd likely adjusted. At least the duel wasn't on her mind at the moment. Instead, the newsy letter informed Charlotte that "little Byron" had been very sick. "However, I believe he's through the worst," she explained.

Maybe "little Byron" had made it through, Margaret was thinking after reading it, but it seemed like she, herself, was just beginning a test of endurance. Her search was getting more complicated by the minute. Now there was someone else to run down. Who, in heaven's name, was little Byron? Had Albert's mother, in her dotage, taken a waif under wing?

If she'd had access to those other six boxes – if *only* she'd had access - she might've found answers easily. But this was the way, it seemed, her search for the full story was going to go. Slow and exasperating.

And that meant she'd just have to work with what she had, taking down what seemed relevant and moving on from there.

So, pencil in hand, yellow legal pad at the ready, she began writing. *Bancroft family - Brackenville, New York. Baby – 1863. First edition of Dixie. Queen Victoria's armies. Little Byron?* As well, she added a few notes, one of them being that Albert's only sibling, a brother, died in 1869 at an early age. She had doubts about the significance of these jottings, but in one way or another they'd made an impression on her. Besides, to come home empty-handed just wouldn't have felt right.

With that in mind, she copied the photos too. And that took some doing. Obviously, taking Albert's picture out of its frame was off-limits. Yet, that was what she had to do. Secretly, of course, her eyes stealthily watching out for powers-that-be as her fingers worked the sepia image free. Thankfully, copying the baby picture and the inscriptions on the backs of the photos was much easier.

As far as looking into the three Lasserre Parish newspapers published right after the 1874 duel, Margaret got no satisfaction. All she found on microfiche was the article quoted in the book at the parish library. And that raised even more questions. Was there a reason the dueling death of a former legislator was ig-nored by two local newspapers and covered halfheartedly by a third, that latter one not even revealing what the argument was about or what charges were brought? Shouldn't it have been big news back then? Was there no criminal prosecution? Dupuis had, after all, committed murder, and Bancroft's second, David Nicholas, had been as responsible for that murder as Dupuis.

As to the cause, the gambling business Alma had suggested made no sense. Margaret could think of more believable explanations just by recalling what she'd learned in American History in college. For one, Dupuis being a plantation owner, would have hated Albert Bancroft simply because of his service in the Reconstruction legislature. Add to that Bancroft's service in the Union Army and you had one live shell waiting to explode.

But what of this apparent coverup by Charlotte's daughter Lizzie? Why did she seal the files? More than that, why had the family – Charlotte, in other words? – left instructions to seal the files?

So many questions.

Driving to The Holy Church to play her carillon gig, Margaret reflected on a day that had been neither total win nor utter loss, but that could turn into something very different if the old Music Building attic held all those items on the archives lists. If those things were up there, what else might be? Letters between Albert and Charlotte? Diaries? Or was that what was hidden in the other six boxes?

As far as the other monogram, it would be great if it were in the attic. But would she really, as she'd told Fred, keep it?

Well . . . . Finders keepers, after all. She did have a right to it. Yet, Fred had a point when he said that what she wanted was facts, not goods.

And with that in mind, how about Brackenville?

Back at the apartment, after going through two telephone operators to get the number of the Bancrofts in Brackenville (there was only one Bancroft listing in the town, she was informed by the final operator), Margaret dialed.

"Is this the Bancroft residence?" she asked when a dusky voice answered. A voice that, polite but cool, answered "Yes."

"My name is Margaret Bohr and I – "

"I'm not interested" was the curt response.

"But, please. You've got the wrong idea. I'm not selling anything. I'm looking for someone. You see, I live in Acadi,

Louisiana . . . or I mean I will live in Acadi. We're building there. A house, you know." She was a little flustered, and her heart was speeding up. This was important. "Do you know if you had a relative who lived in Acadi?"

"Who is this?" No longer polite or cool.

"My name's Margaret Bancroft . . . I mean Bohr. And my question is about a doctor who lived in Acadi back in the 1800's. His name was Albert Bancroft, and he served in the Union Army during the Civil War. Then he was killed in a duel."

"None of your business," Margaret heard before the dreaded click.

Chapter Twenty-Four

The Attic

As he stood behind the Music School secretary on the third floor of the old Music and Dramatic Arts Building, Fred tried to avoid staring at what was much too obvious – the jiggle of her hips in her clingy polka dot dress as she leaned over and unlocked the small door near the stairwell. It was almost a relief when she pulled it open, switched on her flashlight and, after squeezing in, clumped down an aisle of what looked to be boxes of all shapes and sizes. At least he could get his mind off jello.

"You're gonna die in here," she called back as, a ways in, she beamed her flashlight on the bulb in the ceiling. Grunting as her other hand went up, she grabbed the chain and pulled, lighting the space with a glow so bleak it seemed only befitting of what was likely to become a dreary afternoon.

"I'm sure not staying," she yelled, hands raised above the clutter as she carefully turned around and started back. "This record heat has turned the attic into a torture chamber. And – " She'd finally worked her way to the hallway where he and

Margaret waited, and lowered her voice. " – since it's Saturday, I won't be in the office long." Next to him now, green eyes wobbling behind strong tortoiseshell-stemmed glasses, she continued. "So if you're still around and alive after I've left – " She made a sound like a snort. " – just slip the key under the office door." She paused, apparently thinking. "Other than that I guess all I can say is 'Have a great day.'"

After the elevator door clacked shut, Fred flicked on his flashlight in preparation for what he knew would be as unpleasant as anything he'd done lately, including riding around in Margaret's car and digging for the monogram. Even so, he'd made up his mind to be patient, and did just that as he ducked his head and led the way in while calmly asking where she wanted to start.

"First, shine your light around so I can see if I recognize anything," she said before clearing her throat. "Could be that Charlotte's music rack or one of those other big pieces jumps out." She cleared her throat again. "A little musty in here."

More than a little, he was thinking as he beamed his flashlight beyond the dull glow of the ceiling bulb, where in all directions there were cartons and metal files. There were a few shelves and a trunk or two as well. No remarkable pieces that he could see.

"You know what I think?" he said.

"I'm not sure I want to know."

Her response hurt. Here he was, sacrificing for her, and here she was, cutting him down. Yet, he held back on what he'd planned to say. Maybe telling her that he thought no one in their right mind would store valuables in an attic as hot and humid and dusty as this would just egg her on, make her more determined to prove him wrong.

So all he said was, "That was uncalled for."

If she heard, she didn't show it. There was no apology. Not even an apologetic look. She just went on chewing her lip and bobbing every which way while appraising surroundings.

"I guess what we should do is start opening things," she said finally, nodding toward an area under the sloped roof. "You want to work back there?"

He focused his light. "That black hole? It'll swallow us live."

"If it swallows anyone, it'll be you. I'm working on this side, near the light bulb."

He nodded shrewdly. "I see."

"Well, would you rather sit under this hornet's nest?" She was pushing things aside, clearing a space on the floor under a rafter on which hung a papery gray ball that did appear to be a nest of some sort.

He backed away. "I'd rather — "

But he knew she wasn't listening. She already had her glasses out and was getting down on the floor next to a box, saying at the same time, "We'd better get started."

"Jesus," he sighed as he headed for his designated spot while pondering the crunch underfoot. Bat droppings? Petrified hornets? Rat turds? Better not to know.

At least there was one good thing, he decided on reaching the sloped roof and finding a trunk and two boxes: his workload wasn't overwhelming. On the other hand, hunching over in order to get into the space and then getting on his knees on wood as rough as cobblestone was about as agonizing as anything he'd done in years.

Still, he was here and whether or not his back and knees hurt, it was time to get down to work. So he took his half-glasses from the pocket of his running shorts, slipped them on, and opened the closest box. Which was filled with yellowed stationery imprinted *Louisiana State University School of Music*.

"One down, two to go," he called when he closed the box. It was then, as he straightened up, ready to go to his next assignment, that he slammed into a beam. No stars, but the pain was exquisite. Yet, worse than that, when he felt for blood, his fingers caught in something gauzy. A web?

He slapped his hand on his shorts, stamped his feet, jiggled all over.

"Something wrong?" Margaret calmly called as he approached his next project, the trunk. Which, it turned out, was just as disappointing as the box, being it was brimful of beards, long coats, and high boots. Costumery from some musical?

He slammed the trunk and made his way to the last box. Last and obstinate box. Big, and with stubborn cardboard flaps that took a foot and free hand to hold back as he shined the flashlight in, revealing plastic swords and pistols that for him, by now, held as much interest as watching a soccer game.

Finally – tank top, shorts, socks plastered to his dripping frame – he sagged over to his wife. "And what's going on here," he asked in a tolerant voice.

She picked up a typewritten page from the floor. "This is dated November 20, 1937. It's from Lizzie Bancroft to the Dean of the Music School." She set it back on the floor. "And this — " She picked up another page. " — is from the dean to Lizzie."

"Well I'll be. Anything interesting?"

She wagged her hand. "In hers, Lizzie says she can't come to a dedication concert for the Charlotte Bancroft Museum because she's sick. The dean's letter is in response."

"Mundane, huh."

"Maybe, but just that I found them is pretty exciting. It means we might find more." She mopped her forehead with her arm, then pointed. "I haven't looked there yet."

He walked over and called back. "Empty space."

She pushed herself up and, rubbing her back, slumped over.

"It is empty, isn't it. And why, I wonder." There was a flutter to her voice, as though she found emptiness positively captivating. "It really doesn't make sense. The attic's jam-packed, and here sits a void big as our living room." She leaned over and studied the floor. "You see what I see?"

"More amazing emptiness?"

Apparently unimpressed with his humor, she nosed her way down a side path to the little door where they'd come in. "More than emptiness. There are tracks. Look at that. Things have been dragged right through here, all the way to the hall."

She made her way back to him. "Just my luck if it was the museum collection."

"I don't think – "

"Look! In this corner." Now she was squatting. "See the pattern in the dust? Like a music rack sat here." Bracing herself with her hand, she pushed up. "Flashlight, please."

He handed it over and she trained its beam on metal shelving along the wall, then walked over.

He followed and, while she adjusted her glasses and studied one of the ledges, stood next to her, thinking how glad he was that no one was watching.

"Look, Fred," she said finally. "These shelves are not only empty, they're not as dusty as the rest of the place, as though not too long ago books or magazines or sheet music were stored here. You know what that means?"

"That they're clean and . . . . " Nothing clever came to mind.

And it didn't matter, because she was absorbed in her own crazy efforts. Stepping back. Scouring the shelving with the flashlight, top to bottom. Looking like a sweaty gumshoe on a hot case.

The whole thing was ridiculous, and, as before, his patience was wearing thin. "Don't tell me you think – "

She shushed him and, having moved closer to the shelves, crouched on her knees before reaching into the very bottom ledge and pulling out . . . magazines. Faded ones that at one time had very likely been bright with color.

After laboriously getting to her feet, she set them at eye level. There were three of them and, directing her flashlight at them for a better look, she made a sound like a cat in heat. "*Etude,*" she whooped. "My mom used to subscribe to it. And look, Fred. They're really old. Two from 1911 and one from 1912." She picked one up and studied it. "And, Mr. Doubtful – " As sweat dribbled down her face, she gave one of her big-toothed, superior smiles. " – see this?"

He put his glasses back on and read aloud from the upper right-hand corner. "Charlotte Corbyn Bancroft."

"And you know what that means?" She charged on, not waiting for an answer he wasn't prepared to give anyway. "It means these were overlooked by whoever moved Charlotte's stuff."

"Okay. I'm convinced." Even if he wasn't, he was about to collapse from heat, dust and too much exuberance.

"And," she went on, "it also means I've got to find that person."

He searched her eyes. "You really mean *I*?"

Chapter Twenty-Five

Looking at Things Rationally

As she sat on the front gallery of Pierre's mansion waiting for him to change to more comfortable clothes Louise couldn't help thinking about all the things she loved about this place. The scent of new-mown grass after a visit by the grounds crew. The sun blinking and sparkling and casting those long beams of misty yellow light through the rippling leaves of the live oaks. The red-centered flowers of what Pierre called *rose mallow* that bloomed beside the drive, big and white as the generous salad plates in her mother's kitchen. The sense that, except for the sugar refinery chimney and concrete levee, everything was much the same as when Pierre's ancestors looked out on it. Even the murky, roiling river still followed its winding course.

That she was to be mistress of the plantation didn't seem possible. Actually, nothing about life after leaving Brackenville seemed real – the trip from New York, staying at cut-rate motels; lonely days reading books and watching television and taking walks and eating solitary meals while waiting for her nose to heal; her first look at Acadi, with its jumble of unlikely buildings straggling the river (This is a town? she'd asked herself). And then there was the job, a job she suspected she got, in part, because of her looks. Finally, and most amazing, there was Pierre.

At first she couldn't believe he'd taken a liking to her. When it was clear he had, she was convinced it wouldn't last, that she was merely a diversion while he regrouped after divorce. But as time went on, and their relationship as well, she took it more seriously, daring to hope. She'd come home from evenings out with him and lie in bed savoring those special moments: the squeeze he gave her hand as they laughed at the same thing; the long, approving gaze when she came into a room; the intense interest in everything she said. She'd ask herself how it was she'd attracted someone so handsome, sensitive, perfect. Yet, she'd think, with her life up to now so miserable, maybe it was time things got better. (As if the improvement happened without her intervention.)

A few months after accepting the ring was when she came down to earth and started looking at things more rationally. It was then that she decided she'd been too optimistic. Pierre wasn't as perfect as she'd thought.

Be that as it may, here she was on the unbelievable gallery of his mansion and, judging from the click of latch and creak of floorboards, he was here too, coming up from behind and brushing her shoulder as he handed her a fresh glass of Chardonnay. Smelling of aftershave – a piney scent – he kissed her cheek, then came around and sat down in the wicker chair at her side.

"I'll be falling down drunk if you don't stop pumping me full of wine," she said, laughing. "And what's this with the fresh glass? You'll be washing stemware till morning."

"Not me. The maid. She comes tomorrow. Besides, it's quicker bringing a fresh glass than traipsing in and out to refill."

He slumped back and took a long breath before adding in a satisfied voice, "What a relief fall's finally arrived."

She took a sip of what she knew from his buildup during the earlier uncorking in the kitchen to be both expensive and quite fine, then smiled. "You and Mrs. Bohr. She said the same thing when she called today – 'What a relief fall's finally here.'"

"The last person I want to think about," he answered back, grimly staring out on the expanse of lawn between the oaks.

But whether he wanted to think about this client or not, Louise went on. "She asked when I thought you'd be back."

"I hope you told her I'll return when I'm good and ready." He looked intently into his glass before taking a long swallow and pulling himself up in his chair.

"Don't you think it's about time? She said it's been two months since she's seen either you or your crew and that curing concrete floors is no longer a believable excuse."

Pierre traced the *A* etched on his glass. Chestnut hair, patrician nose, bronzed skin (from a lot of time around the pool, she suspected), he was awfully good looking. And in white polo shirt and jeans and sandals, he was at his most attractive. "Don't – "

She stopped him. "I hope you're not going to say 'Don't worry my pretty head,' because that doesn't change the responsibility I feel."

He bolted his wine and, glass in hand, got up. "Want more?"

"I'm fine," she answered, confused by both the anger and the ease with which he dismissed this client who, though a pain in the backside, was after all paying for his services. This client who as well – and more importantly – was a threat to Louise. With Pierre's abandonment of the site, it seemed that the meddling biddy found so much time on her hands she was pursuing with fervor all things to do with Albert and Charlotte Bancroft. She'd even found that out-of-print book at the local library – a book Louise herself hadn't dared check out for fear of prying eyes – that had a chapter about the Bancrofts. What was most amazing was that she'd gone so far as to visit the attic. The attic! How Mrs. Bohr had figured that out she'd never know. Not that Louise didn't care, but the polite, indifferent response she was forced to pass off ruled out ever getting to the bottom of anything Mrs. Bohr said.

Louise did know one thing, though, and that was that whatever the busybody took an interest in was carried out with passionate determination. And that raised the question of just how far she'd get. She could ruin everything if she got to the point of connecting Louise with the Bancrofts. Which was why it was better for Louise to badger and push Pierre back to work on the house than to allow Mrs. Bohr in her free time, away from her own "supervision" of his work, to discover se-crets that could lay waste to one woman's future.

At the same time, Louise wondered, had she gone too far this evening with that so-called badgering? Sometimes, especially on an empty stomach, a little wine went a long way in loosening the lip.

Yet, thankfully, when Pierre came back he seemed okay with everything. "This Chardonnay is fine, you think?" he said, setting his glass on the table and slumping back in his chair.

She nodded.

The silence that followed, though, wasn't exactly com-fortable. And she was relieved when he started in about the wedding, asking if she was ready to set the date and location. "My parents are wondering. Especially Mama. I told her we'd get on it. She's worried about reserving the church, you know."

"And the church – ?"

"The Holy Church of River Road, of course. That's where Mama wants it. And actually, since Mama wants it there – " He smiled grimly. " – that's probably not where I'll choose to have it."

"All I know is I don't want to walk down an aisle between green vinyl chairs. On that score, did you ever get the handout about you and your crew changed?" It was a small thing, but it bothered her.

"You mean – "

"Where it implies you're a member of that weird church."

"Oh, that. I've still got to tend to it." He picked up his Chardonnay, sniffing, then swirling it, seemingly intent on enjoying it to the fullest.

"Hey, by the way," he said, sitting forward and facing her. "I've got some fantastic news." As though toasting, he held his glass high, then took a quick sip. "You remember me mentioning Franklin Couvillion?"

"The senator."

"Right." Pierre's glass clinked as he set it on the overlay of the wicker cocktail table. "Well, he called the other day. Says he's fallen in love with Ernest Strong's place over there on Pimlico."

"The one with the widow's walk?"

Pierre nodded.

"It's big."

"Biggest one I ever built. Anyway, Franklin asked if I'd be interested in looking at his plans and submitting a bid."

Louise suddenly wished she'd had a gallon of wine. She could've used fortification. A senator likely meant a lawyer and a lawyer meant a stickler for rules and regulations. Mrs. Bohr's complaints were a drop in the bucket compared to what might lie around the corner.

Chapter Twenty-Six

Greedy

Fred, in customary gray tee shirt and green shorts, was back from his morning run and, having poured himself a glass of orange juice, carried it to the table.

"That's all you're having?" Margaret said, pushing her generously frosted slab of carrot cake toward him. "Take this. It's good for you. Counts for veggies."

She waited. Wasn't he at least going to comment on the size of the helping?

Then she noticed his eyes. Always somewhat hooded, they were so much so this morning she wondered if he'd slept.

"What's wrong?" she asked before retrieving the cake and slicing into it.

He blew out, a long breath suggesting he'd been saving up. "Money," he said. "Welbourne stock is down another point today. Twenty-five. Ten points below when we signed the construction loan."

Her heart pattered. The forkful of cake on the way to her mouth clanked as she set it back on the plate. "I didn't realize. How did it happen?"

He explained about the company's earnings drop and the value of their stock following suit. Though they didn't risk losing the house, he said, they did risk losing retirement money they'd invested in Welbourne stock, money he'd hoped to grow into a tidy nest egg. The stock was collateral for the construction loan, he reminded her, and the bank wouldn't allow the stock's value to fall below the amount of the loan. Another few points on the downside and the bank, in order to maintain security, would demand he sell their stock – and at an all-time low. And this wasn't idle speculation. The banker had called yesterday reminding him of his commitment to sell at twenty-two.

"A nice house and no money to enjoy it? And in our old age? What's that worth?" Glaring, she sat back. "Bad as a great car and no funds for gas."

"Nothing we can do, Margaret, except hope for a turnaround. We're at the mercy of the market." He used his fists to rub his eyes. "What's so tragic is that we wouldn't be in this hole if Pierre had finished when he'd promised. The stock was fine in December. It was in January, when earnings came out, that it tumbled. And instead of picking up, it's dropped a few points since."

Outside, paper and dust began to swirl, and when rain started plopping through the screen door onto the linoleum, he got up and slid the balcony door shut. Then, sidelong on his chair, he stared out the window. "You know – " He turned back. " – I feel like we just got greedy."

"Greedy!"

"Too ambitious."

"You mean building a house?"

"In a trendy subdivision."

"If you recall, building in a trendy subdivision wasn't my first priority. Part of the reason I chose Belmont Estates was that I couldn't find a decent older home on the river road. You call that greedy?"

"I'm not accusing you, Margaret."

"It sure sounds like it."

He got up and carried his glass to the sink. "I've got to get ready for work."

As he headed for the steps, she turned back to the parking lot and rain and her cake. As far as the latter, it took a few minutes to feel up to scraping a healthy dollop of frosting from the top and licking it off her fork.

Chapter Twenty-Seven

Mama

Thinking that even if the afternoon had been sunny it wouldn't have felt like it, Pierre spun his Corvette to a halt in front of the Bohrs' jobsite. Like an omen, huge bald-headed vultures spread their wings, fluttered, and then settled back on the trees. And like a rotting jack-o'-lantern on an Indian summer afternoon, Mrs. Bohr's orange heap sat on the road near the drooping, mossy branches of the old live oak. The only thing missing was the witch herself.

Amend that. There she was now, being hauled out the front door by her mutt, plastic attaché swinging from shoulder, beloved and ever-present list in her free hand. The woman had a penchant for lists. For oversized shirts too. Her reasoning in wearing them, he suspected, was a lot like his reason for using duck blinds.

He zipped his leather jacket and got out, the wind slamming him like one more jinx as he struck out across the planks toward the entry courtyard, where his opponent and her canine, under cover from the wind, had taken position.

As he got closer he masked his hostility and called out in a pussycat voice "Finally back," realizing as soon as the greeting left his lips that *finally* wasn't a good word choice. In fact, there was no reason to even call attention to his return. All it would do was inflame Mrs. Bohr, whose metal-blue eyes were already shooting bullets.

"What's taken so long? Where've you been?" she asked in a voice so flat it brought to mind Celeste right before she freaked out that time he forgot to pick up the kids from school and they walked home on Highway 44.

"I've been with my mother," he replied, his best rendition of gloom clouding his face.

Mrs. Bohr cocked her head, studied him.

He, in turn, cocked his head, studying her while maintaining the gloomy facade. "You mean no one told you?"

"About what?"

"About Mama. She's been sick. Real sick. She's in Anderson Cancer Center."

Mrs. Bohr's eyes laid off the bullets, instead sending one long, gentle beam of truce. "Oh, Pierre."

"Yeah. She's been there for six weeks now, and I don't know when she'll get out." He tilted his head again. "You really didn't know?"

She gazed into the distance, eyes suddenly damp. "No," she said quietly, "I didn't."

"Well, it's been hectic, of course, shuttling between Houston and here, and her in such sad shape." He hung tough in maintaining the worried pose, even closing his eyes for a few seconds as though the pain of telling was nearly too much. "And then with partial custody of the kids and all that goes with that . . . . " He allowed time for Mrs. Bohr, now biting her lip while staring blankly at her list, to use her imagination.

"Sorry . . . I didn't . . . I mean . . . to bother you . . . ." Like a man exhausted, not thinking straight, he vaguely gestured.

"I understand," she said gently. "But what I don't understand is why you didn't let me know."

He shrugged, thinking it best not to get too elaborate with the story. "I don't know. I guess I didn't want to burden you with my troubles."

"Burden me? It would've been a lot better than me ranting about your absence to my poor husband day in day out." She reached up and patted his shoulder. "But I understand."

"That's a relief to hear," he said, hands behind his back now and encountering the damp roughness of what could only be a dog's nose. He shifted his hands to the front. "And I promise that, as much as possible, it's going to be full speed ahead from here on in. The crew will be here first thing in the morning and though I can't promise to be bright-eyed and bushy-tailed, I'll be here too. Let's see – " He counted on his fingers. " – does a May move-in sound okay?"

By now they'd stepped around a pile of waste concrete by the front doors, Mrs. Bohr on one side, himself on the other, and he let her pass first, giving him a chance to get a look at what she'd called "ski chalet dormers" a few months back. They were dormers that had cost peanuts to build and, from what he could see, still didn't look that bad. At least not bad enough to justify all the blather about not being the "West Indies design" she'd insisted was in the blueprints.

But the slow burn brought on by recall of the episode didn't affect his rosy spiel. He knew he had to get through this, and without rancor. So he steeled himself and went on with the planned walk-through of the skimpy house with the equally undersized crone and her mangy mongrel, who wouldn't stop snuffling his pants pocket. It was a sloppy inspection, the three of them dodging puddled sheets of plastic and soggy mounds of cardboard that had once overlaid the concrete floor. The wet mess, of course, didn't go unnoticed by him. Where had all the water come from? he silently wondered. It really was quite suspicious. Happily, not so suspicious that the now conscience-stricken matron ventured a critical word. Even when they opened one of the doors to the pool, where a dead turtle floated in murky rainwater and the smell was really bad, she held back. And when they were finally back in what would one day be the living room where, standing next to Mrs. Bohr and her dog, he stared out the front window with the most down in the mouth look he could muster, she was so caught up in his misfortune that she actually asked if *he* was all right.

"*All right* would be exaggerating," he said. "But what I can say is that I'm really glad we met here today so I could explain everything."

Her response was better than he'd dreamed: a grateful nod, "I'm glad too," and a dramatic folding of her list before shoving it into her attaché. What made the whole thing even more perfect was the secret flick he landed on her hound's nose.

After she left, he lingered there by the window contemplating not the untruths he'd laid on her but the sad truths that plagued the business he was in. And they truly were sad. There were two main ones. First, that you paid through the nose for topnotch people. Second, practicing economy with poorly trained workers was a gamble, and a very risky one. Especially when you had people like Senator Franklin Couvillion seeking you out.

"A week ago last Monday I had dinner at Ernest Strong's," Franklin said when he'd called Thursday night. "And when Ernie told me who his builder was, I said, 'I know Pierre

Armant. We went to school together.'" Now Franklin's resonant voice soared. "What a place you built there, Pierre. That widow's walk is absolutely choice. Marvelous. Well, the whole house is. And that's why – " He paused dramatically. " – I'd like you to look at my plans and give me a bid."

Ernest Strong's mansion. Why did it have to be that one that captured Franklin's heart? No question, it was a wowser. The biggest, most extravagant antebellum reproduction in Belmont Estates. And everyone did go on about it. As its builder he was awfully proud of the way it looked. So there was no problem with that. What was worrisome was that incident – it was before he and Breedlove had teamed up – when the architect noticed missing anchor bolts and insisted they be put in on the spot. At the time, it seemed like little more than an inconvenience that slightly diminished profit on an otherwise lucrative project.

But then Benny, who'd set aside his paint to do the job of connecting the mansion's wooden framework to the concrete slab with the huge bolts, said "Whoops" a few too many times. This particular day he was working right there on the west side under the library.

"What you got there?" Pierre had asked.

"Looks like honeycombed *ce*ment," Benny huffed, showing Pierre how each time he got an inch or so beyond the wooden sill plate with his drill, the bit slid like greased lightning into whatever was underneath. Which should have been concrete but seemed to be nothing. It brought to mind a fork penetrating Beef Wellington pastry only to slip into emptiness where the fillet should have been. Of course, there was nothing to be done at that point or at least nothing Pierre wanted to bother doing. He had three other houses in the works and any major step back would have thrown him off. Besides, he didn't like the thought of the way it would make him look. And anyway, there was little chance of dire consequences from a shortage of concrete in a few spots.

Or was there? The possibility of an eventual cave-in had been there in the back of his mind ever since, forcing its way to the forefront more and more often as time went on, sometimes surprising him by hurtling out of his subconscious like a cannon ball.

And now, it was that beautiful but questionable home that had turned out to be the one Franklin adored. Franklin, United States Senator, heir of the wealthy Couvillion family who owned Eventide Plantation.

Chapter Twenty-Eight

Friday Evening

Cedro took a right off the river road and headed toward the woods and his trailer. His landlady's little frame house was on the left and next to it, in the crooked shed at its side, was the battered Camaro he'd never seen her drive. Fat, slippered, and rocking, she sat – as usual – on the porch next to the washing machine. As he drove by, she waved, and he did the same while bumping on, his car rattling down the rutted road in a swirl of dust.

On pulling in beside the air conditioning unit there was the usual cat commotion. Today it was the black cat arching his back, hissing, and jumping down and the calico slipping out from between the bottled gas cylinders and shooting toward the pile of battered cabinets and tires at the side of the yard.

Inside, as always, the kitchen smelled of damp wood and gas. And the squeak of his soles on linoleum was like an ode to emptiness. No scent of cooking food, no sound of voices, no brush with human warmth.

It was Friday. The sun setting. A festival was going on in Oakview. Right now, cars would be jamming the intersection on their way to the parking lot near the high school and tiny white lights would be coming on in the trees on Main Street. Families would be standing around stalls talking and laughing and buying handmade white oak baskets and pecan pralines and ceramic magnolia paperweights. In the boat park across from the gas station a popcorn machine would be sending out its buttery aroma as kids begged to ride the ferris wheel and mothers bounced babies and fathers downed Cajun sausage and spicy rice dishes and beer.

And this solitary Cuban? Paint-spattered bandana in lap, he was now sitting on the bed in the rear of his trailer, eyes closed, trying to bring up another happy time. Not as public and social as the Oakview affair, but just as happy. And it was coming: he and Duardo, a rainy day, sliding on the floor planks of the gallery. Behind them, the long, green-shuttered windows. In front, the fountain with goldfish and coins. Lots of laughter.

He opened his eyes, lay back, shut them again. The inside of that home. That's what he wanted now. The kitchen, dinner time, Duardo and *madre* and *padre* and himself around the table smiling and talking.

But that part wouldn't come tonight. The glaring silence shut it out.

He got up, hung his bandana on one of the hooks in the knotty pine wall, and made his way back to the kitchen. Snap of light switch. Click of cabinet door. Crackle of bags. Each sound echoed like a rifle in a cave.

Outside, the rattle of pet food pellets in plastic bowls brought the bouncy gold kitten from his perch on the cast-off toilet tank and the Siamese from the roof. The rest of the cats came warily, slinking from under the trailer and creeping out from all over the junk-filled yard and surrounding woods.

What a bunch. The calico. The black one with bright gold eyes. A scrawny, swollen-nippled mother. A tabby with lame leg. A lanky black kitten, nearly full-grown. A gray longhair with matted fur. A white one with red, weepy eyes.

And then there was the limp-tailed brown and white puppy who, hearing dog food hit the pie tin, came out from his hiding place at the edge of the woods. "Come on," Cedro said gently, offering the pathetic creature the tin of food before setting it in the grass and backing toward the trailer, where he sat down on the step.

He and that puppy. Lonely partners. Damaged beings. Both fearful. Was it even worth it to feed and extend the life of a creature so miserable?

Chapter Twenty-Nine

FTD and Flowers

I just don't get it," Margaret moaned, collapsing on the other end of the sofa from where Fred sat watching television.

She waited for his response before going on. "That call a minute ago? It was FTD saying the flowers I sent couldn't be delivered because there was no Mrs. Letitia Armant at the Anderson Clinic."

Not only Fred, but Wolfgang, who was monopolizing the easy chair across from the door, and Carol, on Fred's lap, paid no heed.

Even so, she continued. "Why would Pierre lie about his mother having cancer?"

Fred put finger to lips. "Just a minute."

So she waited. Waited through the conservative blaming the liberal for illegal immigration from Haiti. Through the liberal shouting back that Haitians had been murdered because of conservative immigration policy. Through the Haitian guest's painstaking, incomprehensible (what language?) explanation of his government's problems. Through "We'll be back in a minute to wrap it up" and the endless commercials that followed. And, finally, through the wrap-up.

Which was when Fred came alive. "That program sure gets nasty," he said, shaking his head in satisfaction before tossing corn nuts mouth-ward, shoving the cat off his lap, stretching, slipping on his Weejuns, and standing up, all the while crunching away.

"Now, what were you saying?" he asked while turning off the television.

She jumped up, nearly upsetting the ginger jar lamp, a clatter that woke the dog – who patiently looked up and over – and sent the cat flying.

Margaret, too, was flying. Her destination the kitchen.

Fred trailed. "What's wrong, Margaret? What'd you say?"

Which was when, with thumb nails, she pulled the tiny battery doors of her hearing aids open. Turnabout was fair play. She could tune him out too.

Chapter Thirty

Looking Quite Fine

Pierre Armant was and always would be a liar. Margaret knew that. The deal with the Anderson Clinic proved it. And though it would have been gratifying to confront Pierre and watch him squirm, she didn't. She agreed with Fred: a fight over something as insignificant as get-well flowers could lead to another shutdown. Why risk it? Especially taking into account Fred's distaste for legal action.

So she went on as usual until, a few weeks after the incident, as things went from bad to worse at the site and her calls to Breedlove got more and more frequent (and his voice less and less bouncy), the architect took it upon himself to arrange a meeting for a serious walk-through. They might straighten things out that way, he said.

And, to her mind, straighten things out, they did. Whereas at the beginning of the walk-through Margaret felt like the whole exercise was hopeless, as the session wore on her thinking began to change. First off, Breedlove demonstrated what she'd later describe to Fred as "nothing less than strong architectural oversight." From the kitchen/dining room pass-through that had been framed too high to each crooked window that needed shimming, he missed nothing. He was so thorough, in fact, that he brought up things that weren't on her *Ongoing Building Concerns* list, problems she hadn't been aware of.

"You must have forgotten," he told Pierre. "Be that as it may, there seem to be no bolts connecting frame to slab." At that point he asked Louise to lift insulation so he could point at wooden floor beams. "And I checked the contract . . . ." Now he went on about size of anchor bolts and procedure for installing them, ending with, "Unfortunately, insulation that's already there complicates things. I guess you'll just have to lift it."

Lift it and cry, Margaret said to herself as Pierre, shaking his head as though he couldn't believe the slipup, jotted a reminder in his notes. "We'll fix it," he promised.

We'll fix it, we'll fix it, Margaret fumed to herself. If she could've had a dollar for each time Pierre repeated those words she could have eased Fred's worries about falling stock values. Add a dollar for the times Pierre looked shocked and sheepish, and she could've paid off the construction loan. As flawless as Breedlove's coverage of construction shortcomings, it didn't hold a candle to Pierre's award-winning performance.

But really, was it merely performance? Margaret began to wonder as the discussion of anchor bolts rumbled on in the background. Was it possible Pierre *had* changed? It seemed sudden, but stranger things had happened. It could've been he'd never really understood the problems and having Breedlove point them out was an eye-opener. Or that, though he obviously had strong connection to a church, he'd suddenly *really* gotten religion. But seriously, wasn't it worth it to give him the benefit of the doubt? What did she have to lose, other than more wrangling.

If asked at exactly what point her mind completed its turnaround, she couldn't have answered. But somewhere between the missing electrical outlets in the dining room and the badly bowed ridge support in the garage, Breedlove, Louise, and Pierre were looking pretty good. Breedlove had turned into a decent architect, Pierre an incompetent but concerned builder, and Louise a sympathetic ear. Watchful, attentive – they did care about her house. And that was what mattered.

"I heard your family's lived in Lasserre Parish forever," she told Pierre as they walked out after Breedlove, who was in a hurry to get to the airport. She stopped and turned to Louise, bringing up the rear. "Did you tell him about the monogram I found in our backyard?"

The sales manager, in three-inch heels, teetered on some waste concrete in front of the courtyard doors. "Not that I recall."

"Well," Margaret resumed pace at Pierre's side, "it turns out this iron monogram I dug up in my yard is from – "

He stopped, raised a hand. "Let me guess." And with a grin big as all outdoors amazed her with, "The Bancroft house."

"How'd you know?"

"This is where they lived."

"And you actually remember – "

"I don't remember the monograms. I was too young. But I do remember the Bancrofts. My history and theirs crossed in a most . . . how should I say? . . . devastating way. At least for the good doctor."

"Really." Because of his care with words and her reluctance to seem nosy, she held back on the obvious question. Instead, she asked if he knew when the Bancroft house was torn down.

"It wasn't torn down. It blew down in Hurricane Betsy back in 1965." His lips curved a little. "Does it bother you, building on a carpetbagger's spoils?"

"Not really." She didn't let on that this was news to her.

"How about the spoils of a black carpetbagger?"

"Black?"

"You didn't know?"

"He was from England."

"You think there were no blacks there?"

"Not at all. I think they'd be fools, though, coming here to be mistreated. Where'd you hear that anyway?"

"Family stories."

"Stories, huh?" She smiled skeptically.

"I read it in a book too. One that came out not too long ago. Written by Stuart Wilson, one of my profs at LSU. Ever heard of him?

"No."

"He's *the* authority on Reconstruction. Great mind. What he said was that, being black, Bancroft had strong feelings about the Civil War and wanted to fight for the cause. He was a military man, you know. I guess his brother was too."

Pierre squinted toward the steeple on the other side of the river. "Let me see . . . what was the book called? . . . Something about problems of peace in the South. Anyway – " His gorgeous brown eyes suddenly turned playful. " – you like bombshells?"

"Fire away."

"Well — " He slipped his hands into the pockets of his corduroys and picked up the pace again. There seemed to be something of a swagger to his step now. "My great, great, great – who knows how many – uncle was the second who forced the Bancroft duel to its deadly end and saw that the good doctor met his maker then and there."

"That is a bombshell." Despite disgust, she didn't miss a beat. "In other words, your 'great, great, great' was Mr. Nicholas."

"I'd say you've done your homework."

By now, they'd reached his car, and Louise, voice a little froggy, as though she'd swallowed wrong, piped up. "We'd better be on our way."

"You know what?" Margaret cut in. "You're the guy I've been looking for. Ever since I first heard about the Bancrofts I've wanted to know more." She hesitated, aware that what she was about to do was contrary to anything she'd considered up to now. "I'd sure like to . . . . Would you be interested in joining me for lunch?" She looked first at Pierre, then Louise. "Brignac's Seafood. And I'll buy."

Pierre turned to his fiancé, who didn't look all that happy at the prospect. "What do you think?" And without waiting, "Oh, why not. I was considering going there anyway."

"Wonderful, just wonderful," Margaret said, thinking this was becoming *her* day.

But after they'd driven away and she found her car in one of its obstinate moods, she pulled back on cloud nine enthusiasm. It was a good day, but not one without the usual snags. No day would ever be that perfect. Really, though, this one wasn't too bad. Once she'd done the trick under the hood and the magical roar and beautiful cloud of gray smoke erupted from the rear, she'd be on her way to what promised to be a fascinating hour or two. She'd be on her way, she soon realized, but in a very cold car. Flying high after success with the under-hood fix, she'd slammed the door with such gusto while getting back in that it sent the window into the impenetrable depths of the door frame.

Chapter Thirty-One

An Interesting Lunch

Margaret surveyed the room, searching out her friends (strange to include Pierre in that category), trying to recall what they were wearing. Ah yes, there, in the three-booth section hanging from a hook on the side of the booth was his plaid mohair blazer and in that same booth – glossy hair shimmering like a fine, black vase – sat Louise. Side by side, they faced the other way.

"I'd like to sit with that couple just beyond the bussing station," she told the waitress, who slipped behind the cash register and grabbed a menu before setting out across the swells and dips of the old wood floor. Following, Margaret felt less and less sure about how to behave. She didn't really know these people, and hadn't much liked them until about an hour ago. Even now she wasn't sure how she felt about them. Especially Pierre.

In the end, as far as a greeting, it was a simple nod that seemed to work. It felt just about right as she busied herself taking off and hanging her poncho on one of the booth's hooks. With Louise's shift from cordial to reserved, the low-key greeting was more in keeping with that change in mood, a change that could only mean Louise was annoyed at having to share with a pushy intruder what should've been a cozy lunch for two.

As with handling the poncho, sliding into the booth offered diversion. But not the kind that made Margaret comfortable. Her sweatshirt caught on table top butcher paper, toppling salt and pepper, Tabasco, and the rest, and after settling in, she had to smooth, right, and straighten the whole unfortunate mess. Meanwhile, the two across from her didn't offer help. And when she apologized, calling herself a clumsy oaf (something she knew she wasn't), they didn't even pretend to disagree.

By happy chance, that was when the waitress turned up.

"You go ahead," Margaret told the twosome, hoping to get some sense of what to order from what they chose.

Pierre didn't hesitate. "Louise and I will have the usual, Barb. Two house salads with balsamic vinegar on the side. No oil, of course. And water to drink. With lemon, please."

After a zip of pencil across pad, the waitress turned her heavily-lined eyes to Margaret, who silently asked, now what? She really hadn't planned on ordering light, but she'd look like a glutton if she didn't.

"Hmmmmm . . . . well . . . . " She frantically picked up the menu and searched for something that sounded like veggies but satisfied like steak, even while recognizing the futility of the effort. In this restaurant you ate big. The house salad – a few slices of crunchy, waxen tomato and a wedge of iceberg lettuce – was the last thing she felt like ordering. She'd made the mistake once, when she was trying to impress Fred, and had promised she'd never do it again.

"Hmmmmm . . . . well . . . ." she murmured a second time, now accompanied by the tap of the waitress's pencil. "I guess I'll get the – " There was no holding off. " – salad too. But with . . . do you have that mustard and sweet cream dressing today?"

"It's the house dressing." Impatience colored the waitress's words. "We have it each and every day." She looked toward three men waiting at the register.

"Now don't skimp." Margaret winked at the duo across the table who, she suspected, were already well into judging. Feeling a weird little surge of defiance, she let up a tiny bit more. "And how about a half cup of real bacon bits on the side too." No more winks. Just avoidance of eyes.

The waitress looked up from her pad. "So that's it for everyone?"

Margaret couldn't stop herself. "Not quite. I'd like turtle soup as well. And with a good squirt of sherry." She flashed a glance at Louise, then Pierre. "You sure you don't want soup? You'll need something more than salad to get you through the day."

Louise shook her head, Pierre said "No," and the waitress looked back at Margaret, pencil at the ready. "Cup or bowl?"

"Oh . . . . " Worry about judgment from across the table once again surfaced. "I guess a cup. A cup of coffee too." She held back, then added, "With cream."

Relieved when the waitress was gone, but once again aware of the strangeness of socializing with Pierre and Louise, who seemingly felt no need to break the silence with a little chitchat, Margaret finally nodded toward some primitive art, price tags attached, hanging on the wall. "It's nice, Brignac's giving artists an outlet. There was a restaurant where I lived in Minnesota that did the same thing. Unfortunately, the artwork was drab and depressing." She pulled her water over, squeezed the lemon wedge, dropped it in. "Everything's so different down here. Even Midwest history is bland in comparison. I don't ever remember hearing of a real live duel. You know, though, as far as the Bancrofts, it's not just the duel. It's the people themselves."

She took a sip of water. "As to the Bancrofts – " She was a little amazed at her smooth transition from art to soulmate. " – one of the things I really want to find out, Pierre, is where Charlotte's music and artifacts may have gone? Do you have any idea?"

He sat back, giving the waitress, who'd returned with their food, space to set it. "You're talking about the stuff from the dismantled LSU museum, right?"

Margaret nodded, feeling as she had earlier, that this was her day. The garlicky scent of turtle soup tickling her nose, the prospect of getting answers to Bancroft questions – things were looking good.

"Last I heard, it was stored somewhere at LSU. I know by the time I was in college, it'd long since been stashed away."

"In the old Music and Dramatic Arts attic, you mean."

"Wherever they store things like that."

"Which is that attic. And, to give you an update, the collection's not there anymore. I checked."

"Maybe someone from the family came in and loaded it up." He picked up his knife and fork and began slicing his lettuce.

"I think you're right That's what it looks like to me."

"As I recall, though, there's no family."

"There I think you're wrong. There are still Bancrofts in a small town in New York where Albert's mother lived. Which I guess is neither here nor there and certainly doesn't rule out someone outside the family taking it."

Gnawing on the side of his lower lip, he gazed at some point to her side; then, shaking his head, met her eyes again. "I don't think I can help on the museum stuff."

Margaret turned to Louise. "And I know you can't," she said expansively, feeling guilty about excluding her. But in that Louise knew nothing of the Bancrofts there was no way to include her in the conversation. Besides, she was behaving like a spoiled child.

Pierre, however, by now putting away with the delicacy of the well-born those perfect bite-sized bits of tomato and lettuce he'd so carefully carved, was most accommodating. "Other than where Charlotte's collection is, what else can I help with regarding the Bancrofts?"

"I'd just like to understand why what happened happened. As regards the duel I mean."

He patted his lips with his skimpy paper napkin and set it back in his lap. "All I know is what Mama told me."

"And that's what I want to hear."

"Well then, it all started . . . ."

And he proceeded to detail how his ancestor, Paul Corday, arrived in the late seventeen-hundreds, set up housekeeping in a shack on a few measly acres, and planted sugar cane that by the time David Nicholas – Corday's descendant and second in the Bancroft duel – came of age in the eighteen-hundreds had grown to a plantation of six thousand acres with the biggest mansion on the river road as its centerpiece.

"And that plantation is where you live now?"

"Right. With a lot less land. David Nicholas inherited it at a very young age when his mom and dad were killed in a carriage accident – I think it was at the beginning of the Civil War – and when David, who never married, eventually moved to France, he left it to his sister – my antecedent.

For a moment, staring down, he seemed deep in thought. "Have you seen the place?'

"I've driven by."

"Well, it really is quite marvelous, if I do say so myself." He seemed to have forgotten his food. "Anyway, back to David Nicholas. He apparently ran the place like a military unit. Very smooth. The story goes that when the bell rang at daybreak, slaves poured out of their shacks and lined up with their mules, carts, and plows while he made an inspection on a prancing white horse. Must have been quite a picture. Until emancipation, that is." Pierre's eyes dulled or narrowed or did something Margaret really couldn't put her finger on.

"Did he fight in the Civil War?"

"No, and I'm not sure why. There's no doubt he had strong feelings about it. Winning that war was his only chance of holding on to his inheritance."

Margaret ran her spoon across the top of her soup, nabbing a half-moon of egg garnish. "Well, at least he didn't lose everything."

"Not everything, but close. Growing sugar cane isn't cheap, you know. You've got dikes, ditches, and equipment in need of maintenance, and then comes harvesting. Without slaves, it was nearly impossible. The only way he could hold on was to mortgage crops and chain himself to a bank in New Orleans."

And that was the beginning of Pierre's tale. Only the beginning. It went on and on, through coffee and water refills and a rendition of "Happy Birthday" from a nearby table.

Eventually, with Louise by now fidgeting and her own mind wandering, Margaret began to wonder when the tedious account of David Nicholas's postwar problems would end.

And surprisingly, that was when, as though sensing impatience, Pierre changed course with, "David Nicholas would turn over in his grave if he saw the river road today. All those lazies sitting on their rundown porches waiting for the welfare system to drop checks in the mailbox. Shiftless, inferior . . . ." His face took on an eerie glow.

Margaret glanced at Louise, gauging her response. But the grudging ladylove was unreadable, seemingly fascinated by a fly dancing around her untouched food.

"And as to the reason for the Bancroft duel?" Margaret asked in an even tone. She wasn't about to start an argument with a racist when that racist might help her solve a most intriguing mystery.

"Simple," he said. "That carpetbagger got shot because a fellow named Francois Dupuis accused him of being black and, rather than admit, Bancroft chose to shoot it out. Strange, don't you think? A man who supposedly fought for blacks couldn't own up to being one himself."

"How did Dupuis find out Bancroft had Negro blood?"

"You got me. War records. Census. All I know is, he knew."

"How about David Nicholas's role in all this? He's the one who really doesn't make sense. He must've been one of Dr. Bancroft's best friends, yet got him killed. If the duel had ended when it should've, everything would've been fine."

"I see it this way, and I've thought about it a lot. My relative, Nicholas, pretended he liked Dr. Bancroft, and the doctor believed it. You know, Bancroft was a fairly influential guy and it didn't hurt to have him on your side. But when push came to shove, Nicholas did him in. The old tit for tat. Remember, Bancroft fought on the wrong side in the war and on top of that was one of the busybody legislators who passed those Reconstruction laws that nearly ruined Nicholas. And then when it was rumored Bancroft was black, well . . . . " He gave Margaret a compatible look and paused as though allowing time for her to consider.

"Funny, isn't it?" He finally continued. "Bancroft seemed to be top dog. He was even a good friend of Governor Pinchback, that stupid black who tried to force whites to observe the same curfew as blacks. But in the end, Nicholas was alpha canine."

"And Charlotte? How about her indifference when she found out her husband had been shot?"

"Put it this way – what would you do if you all of a sudden learned your spouse had lied about something as important as race?"

"But she couldn't have known for sure. It was only an accusation, and one her husband denied. I still have trouble believing it myself."

"I think at that point she added it all up and recognized the naked truth. There's no other explanation. Nor can I think of anything more disgusting."

"Than her indifference?"

"Than being married to a black who's a liar."

Margaret had already passed the courthouse on her way home from Brignac's when she decided that, being she was on some kind of roll, this might be as good a day as any to check census records. So she braked, turned around in a driveway, and within minutes was in a jam-packed room upstairs speaking with a secretary who directed her to huge, faded books lining a low shelf. It took only a moment to locate the book labeled *1870 Census – Lasserre Parish* and another few minutes of careful turning of brittle, brown pages to find *Bancroft, Albert*.

In the column after his name was his age — thirty-five. Charlotte and Elizabeth (who obviously was Lizzie) were next, and with no stated ages. (Which wasn't surprising, since a good portion of the entries didn't include age.) What was interesting, though, was the initial after all three. It was *W*, indicating white. Of course this may have been based on the census taker's personal judgment based on appearance. But if it were based on information Albert gave and if Margaret were to believe Pierre – his facts coming straight from that LSU authority on Reconstruction – Albert must have lied. Just like he'd lied to Charlotte.

Chapter Thirty-Two

What Do You Think She's up to Now

Having made it through the last couple hours, Louise was nothing if not relieved when she got into Pierre's car for the ride back to the sales center. And, she supposed, she was really none the worse although, while freshening up afterward in Brignac's ladies' room she'd still felt so traumatized by the revelations at lunch and the realization she was now part of the most bizarre narrative imaginable, she could hardly focus on her image in the mirror. Even taking into account her suspicions early on that passing in Acadi would be more difficult than passing somewhere else, she hadn't foreseen anything like the mind-numbing developments of today. Connecting with – becoming engaged to – someone who turned out to have an ancestor responsible for your own ancestor's murderous, cutthroat death was simply not a part of any credible story.

But truth be told, in Pierre she'd gotten what she wanted and a little more. Now she needed to integrate this "bombshell," a word he seemed to favor, with everything else and learn to live with it. Even more, she had to remember that, since she'd never known him, she'd never loved Albert Bancroft as one might love a living relative. If he were alive and she met him on the street, she wouldn't even recognize him. Further, for all she knew, he may have been a demon deserving of his fate. In other words, taking his death personally was silly.

As well, it had been silly to assume, as she had when she first began planning escape from Brackenville, that this wouldn't get extremely complicated. She'd been so wrong. Sorting it all out, covering all bases, was going to be an ongoing challenge. Pierre's revelation would always influence things. Yet, Mrs. Bohr's lightning bolt about the "small town in New York" was significant too. Did the prying busybody know the name of that town? And if she did, might she get in touch with Rebecca or Mary? If so, that would be a disaster in the making. Either of her sisters would delight in bringing down their wayward sibling. True, it would take some ingenuity on Mrs. Bohr's part, being that Rebecca and Mary now lived in the town of Penwill. But that was just down the road from Brackenville and that this Minnesota woman's previous success had demonstrated resourcefulness beyond expectation suggested that locating siblings would likely be little more than a pebble in the shoe.

"I wonder why Mrs. Bohr is so gung-ho on the Bancrofts," Pierre said now, putting an end to her musings. Traffic on the river road had finally slowed and he was pulling out of the parking space in front of Brignac's. "Did you see her face when I told her Albert was black? Total shock. I think she was pretty surprised when I brought up my connection to Nicholas too."

Louise stared out her window. *Mrs. Bohr* was surprised! Who could have imagined that David Nicholas, a man Louise's grandfather had mentioned in connection with Albert's death, would turn out to be part of Pierre's ancestry? Or that Pierre would know so much about him, as well as what went on back then.

So much, that is, except what went on with Charlotte. About her, Pierre was wrong. She hadn't found out right before the duel that her husband was of mixed race. From what Grandpa had said, she'd known all along. And Grandpa –

"Look at that." Pierre nodded toward the orange car in the courthouse parking lot. "What do you think she's up to now?"

Chapter Thirty-Three

A Solid House

There was a lot of gasping, slamming, even an expletive on the rainy day Margaret arrived to find Benny painting the front courtyard doors white. "My God. What are you doing? This is wrong, wrong, wrong. They're supposed to be stained, not painted."

Even as she ranted, she knew she was overdoing it, but considering the idiocy of the slipup, she couldn't help herself.

"Oh, jeez. You kidding? No one told me." Benny's porcine eyes searched hers. "You sure?"

She nodded, holding back the urge to shriek.

"Well, there's always turpentine," he said. "And the way we're movin' on your house, one little step to the rear means nothin'.

Without a word, he shambled to the far wall of the living room. "C'mere, Mrs. Bohr. Please." After lifting insulation batts, he pointed at metal heads in the studs meeting the concrete floor. "I just don't know how we coulda forgot anchor bolts. We never done it before," he said, grunting as he straightened. "Anyway, you got 'em in spades now. Even put 'em on inside walls, between rooms. It's not required, but makes for a solid house."

Chapter Thirty-Four

Better Get Your Camera

When Fred got to the site he parked in back of Margaret who, in Minnesota Vikings sweatshirt and grey sweat pants that bagged at the ankles, was getting out of her car. Meanwhile Cedro, paint stick in hand and patterned red bandana circling forehead and "Choice Construction" tee shirt splotched with paint, approached from the garage.

Fred greeted both and, dying to share details of one of the best games he'd ever played at Sugar Lake – and in late afternoon when he was wasn't even at his best – took out his scorecard.

Margaret, rolling her eyes irreverently, excused herself and headed for the house. But Cedro took the card and studied it, commenting on the best holes.

"You coming in?" Fred asked when Margaret interrupted saying it would soon be dark.

"No. I'd better get home. But – " Cedro was now madly slapping the paint stick on the palm of his left hand a ways down from a firm, rubbery scar running the length of his forearm. " – but you might take a good look at the anchor bolts."

"Unfortunate fellow," Fred said when he was inside with Margaret. "I wonder what happened. His face is a battleground. And he's so nervous. Worse than ever today." He shrugged. "So what's new here?"

"Just take a gander." The sweep of her hand took in new electric wires that snaked through studs as far as eye could see. "What do you think? Progress or not?" Her eyes shone like reflecting pools. "But here's the best part," she said, strolling over and again sweeping her hand dramatically, this time toward sill plates. "Benny showed me these when I was here this morning. He was so proud."

Fred leaned in for a better look. Then, without so much as a word, made for the front door. Returning a few minutes later, Volvo tool kit in hand, he got down on his knees, took out the screwdriver, and, biting his lip, used it to turn one of the metal heads. When it was out, he showed it to Margaret, whose eyes got wide.

"That's an anchor bolt?" she said. "How does it work?"

"It doesn't, and it's not an anchor bolt. It's a screw, and so small it doesn't even meet the concrete." He got up. "You know what we use in grain elevators? One and a half inch diameter bolts twelve inches long and they extend into the concrete eight inches." He slapped sawdust from the knees of his pants and picked up the tool case, shoving the screwdriver into its pocket. "There's a bit of fraud here, Margaret my dear. Better get your camera."

She winced, lowering herself to the floor. "I need a nitroglycerin. They're in my attaché in the car."

Back at the apartment Margaret sat, chin in hands, on the sofa. "My head," she groaned. "That nitroglycerin – "

"You should go to bed," Fred said, reaching over from where he sat on the arm of the sofa and massaging the back of her neck.

"If it were just anchor bolts . . . . " There was a slight frog in her throat. "But they're only a small part. Now I can't trust Pierre about anything. Period."

"I thought you knew that."

"But after the walk-through – "

"Margaret." He got up and moved to a more comfortable spot on her other side. "It's about time for a draw, right? You know, depending on his plan, Pierre either behaves better or worse when money's in the picture."

The statement made little sense, but she didn't object and he let it stand.

"What I don't understand is Benny bragging about the bolts. Seems like the whole crew's against us."

"Not Cedro. He told me to take a good look at the anchor bolts. He was warning us."

She grimaced, kneading her forehead with her fingers. "I don't know what to do anymore. Every time I turn around there's something. Maybe Breedlove was right when he said contractors get even with fussy clients." Her voice was deep, soft, as though thinking aloud. "At the time, I didn't take him seriously, thought he was just making it easy on himself; if I didn't dare complain, he could pretend there was nothing to complain about." She faced him. "If you hadn't taken out that screw, we'd never have known. It would've all been covered with sheetrock."

She sat back, squeezed her eyes, rubbed them with the heels of her hands. "We can't go on with this guy, you know. We've got to get rid of him."

"You putting out a contract?"

Not a trace of smile. "I guess I should see if I can hire one of the contractors who bid on the house in the first place."

"Why don't you let me give it another try with Pierre. I'll get on it in the morning. For now, might as well look on the bright side."

"There is none."

"How about Cedro and the way he's watching out for us?" Fred suddenly felt a surge of gratitude. "In fact, you know how he's so keen on golf? Well, you don't. But what would you think if I gave him one of my tournament passes? I don't suppose he's got much money."

She got up and slumped toward the stairs while he went on. "The only problem is club members. What would they say if they found out I gave a fellow I barely know – and a disfigured laborer at that – carte blanche to their fancy facilities?"

No reply from Margaret, whose baggy grey cuffs and ratty tennies were slowly dragging up the steps and out of sight. As far as Fred's thoughts about Cedro, they were soon gone too. In their place was his promise to give it a try with Pierre and what that would do to his unspoken moratorium with the contractor. Putting pressure on him just might – and very likely would – bring retaliation in the form of letting Margaret in on his gambling.

Chapter Thirty-Five

He Just Didn't Understand

Before they left for the meeting, Fred informed Margaret that he'd called Breedlove first thing that morning complaining about the fake anchor bolts; in turn getting a promise from Breedlove that he wouldn't sign off on any more draws until the problem was taken care of. As well, Breedlove said that before the meeting, he'd speak to Pierre about the issue.

Walking in, they found Benny over by the living room windows looking out at the turbulent, trash-filled hole they would one day swim in. Margaret held back, but Fred walked over.

"As long as you're here," he said in a controlled voice, "I'd like to ask something." By now, his hands were on his hips and he was rocking forth and back, heels to toes.

"Sure 'nough," Benny replied before folding a stick of Juicy Fruit into his mouth and offering one to Fred, who shook his head, stopped rocking, and began bouncing a finger in the direction of the screws in the sill plates. "What are those?" he asked. His voice was so even and innocent he might have been a three-year-old seeing acorns for the first time.

"You mean your wife didn't tell you?" Benny looked past him toward Margaret. A confused look. Then he faced Fred again. "They're anchor bolts."

"And you put them in?"

"Right."

Fred scratched behind his ear. "How far do they go?"

"Oh, I dunno. Way, way. Like twelve inches. And look here, somethin' else you'll like." He signaled to follow into the dining area. "I even put bolts on these inside walls. Pierre thought we should give you your due, so when he went out and bought 'em, he got extras."

Hearing the slam of the front door, they moved back to the living room, where Pierre was stuffing gloves into pockets of his double-breasted trench coat. "Brrrrr. Cold out there," he was saying. "Only crazies come out in weather like this. Not including you three, of course." He grinned and patted his thick, dark waves. "So, what's up?"

"I was just showin' Mr. Bohr some of the work I done," Benny said before picking up his paintbrush and pail of primer and heading toward the hall leading to the garage. "Anything else you need, I'll be out here."

Silently, they gazed after him.

"So, what can I do for you?" Pierre eventually asked. "You sounded a little grim over the phone."

Fred walked over and kicked at a screw. "I took out one of these anchor bolts yesterday." He gave Pierre a cunning look.

"Anchor bolts? You teasing? What do you mean?"

"Just what I said. I took out one of these anchor bolts." This time his voice was singsong.

"That's what you thought they were?"

"That's what Benny called them."

Pierre slipped his hands under his open coat, perched them on hips, and shook his head wearily. "I suppose he thought that. Bolts. Screws. All the same to him." He gave Fred a comradely grin. "He's a painter, you know."

"You're saying they're not anchor bolts?"

"Let's see. How's this gotten so mixed up?" He pulled at an ear and gazed away. "All I can tell you is – " He turned back. " – these were put in to mark the spot. We use them to open the wood. Then we come in later and put in the real thing."

"In other words, Benny lied?"

"He just didn't understand."

"Funny. He seemed to." Fred locked the contractor in a level gaze. "He said they were twelve inches long."

"Well, whenever it was. Tuesday I guess. I mean . . . . " His eyes scanned the room, searching. "Anyway, Benny couldn't find bolts. And he got these. What I'm saying is – "

"Just be straight, Pierre."

The contractor sighed. "I'm not sure I understand your question."

"It's quite simple." Fred's voice was trembling now. "Did Benny lie when he said these were anchor bolts and that *you* went out and bought them?"

"He's mixed up. Of course I suppose I could've forgotten. I buy so many things I lose track." Palms up, he lifted, then dropped his shoulders. "Whatever. What's important is that now we're ready for the real thing."

"But I want to understand better this business about screws. Isn't installing and then taking them out a waste of time and effort? Seems like Magic Marker would be a heck of a lot easier."

"Could be, but like I said, they hold the wood open as well."

"It shuts?"

"Not exactly. That is . . . . You want to do it right, is what I'm trying to say."

A muscle in Fred's cheek tightened as his eyes caught Pierre's. "If honest-to-goodness bolts aren't in here by tomorrow night," he said in that restrained voice he was so good at, "you'll be hearing from my lawyers. Is that clear?"

With that, he snapped around and headed for the door.

And Margaret, pleased with every last bit of what she'd just witnessed, followed.

Outside it was like a new day. Sun shining. Temperature climbing. And once they'd made it beyond the watery ruts and concrete chunks in the courtyard, they moved at a perky pace down the tottery planks toward the street. All that remained of the miserable morning was a brisk wind pelting wet bags and paper cups and bits of cardboard off the brimming dumpster.

"Good work," Margaret said to Fred when they were in the car.

"Right," he agreed, but without the confidence of a few minutes before, adding, "I've got something to tell you, Margaret."

Chapter Thirty-Six

Retribution

While she spent the rest of the morning in an oak swivel chair next to the greasy desk in the office of Red's Service Station waiting for repair to the car window that had caused much anguish during the wind and rain earlier in the day, Margaret considered her husband's "something." It was a disclosure that shocked her as mightily as if she'd suddenly been informed her father, who'd died what seemed a million years ago, was coming back and planned to move in with them. But she didn't know him anymore, she would have said.

And that was the way she felt about Fred. Father of her kids, mainstay of her life – yet she really didn't know him. As many times as they'd spoken of gambling, he'd never even suggested he was still doing it. As many times as she'd told him she was thankful he'd quit, he'd never said anything to the contrary. A steadfast, honorable man, she'd thought, who may have had a few shortcomings but at least didn't lie.

But this changed things. Essentially, what had happened was that he'd cheated on her. Not with a woman, but with another love.

So, what should she do? What could she do? From what she understood, gambling, like drugs, was hard to control, addictive. It wasn't as if he wanted to cheat on her. He was a good man. Kind. Generous. Smart. She could go on. That he had a fault, and that it was a major one, was unfortunate but didn't make him a criminal. He was simply human.

Or was she rationalizing? Making it easier on herself? Making it easier to forgive this lie that down deep she knew was too big to minimize.

Big or little, he had at least confessed. And without being forced. What accounted for his sudden need to divulge she didn't know. Maybe his handling of the situation with Pierre had spurred conscience, reminding him that there was the honest way and then there was the other, and that his own behavior was down there with Pierre's. Or he may have gotten such a lift from his success in dealing with the contractor that he felt the need to remind both himself and her that he was only human after all. On second thought, that didn't make sense.

Whatever his thinking, she hoped he realized that this ugly truth would be in the back of her mind from here on in.

Fortified with a burger and fries from the River Road Drive-In as well as the recognition that she was really none the worse for the morning's earful, she drove back to the site to see how things were going. And they *were* going. On stepping in the door her hearing aids picked up a noise so prolonged and high-pitched that if she hadn't turned them down she might've burst an eardrum. And who was behind that noise? It was Benny, who was on his knees facing the wall in the rear bedroom, cotton sticking out of his ears and forehead holding up a batt of insulation. Poor fellow was bent over the biggest drill she'd ever seen. And his "Choice Construction" tee shirt? Plastered to him from bulging neck to love handles.

"So that's how you install anchor bolts," she yelled, getting down close to his right ear. Drilling stopped and he snapped around. "What?"

Instead of repeating, she added a crack that satisfied to the core. "Those screws in the dining room, the complimentary ones. Will you be replacing – "

He lifted the insulation, positioned his head, and switched the drill back on.

Chapter Thirty-Seven

You Actually Could Live with Yourself?

One good thing – Pierre had gotten his favorite table at Brignac's, the one in the corner to the left of the plate glass window. It was a spot where he and Louise were a little isolated from the noisy goings-on between tables while at the same time out of view of the gas pump in front.

Beyond that, he was having trouble ridding himself of the hot, raging sensation he'd had ever since the meeting with Fred Bohr that morning. Thank God Louise hadn't witnessed the obnoxious business. If she had, to shift focus he might have confronted Bohr then and there. But this was going to be better. Less crass and just as – if not more – satisfying. "One of your trusted vice-presidents, Fred Bohr, has been observed at a casino not far from your southern Louisiana grain terminal during working hours, and I thought you'd like to know," he'd say once he had one of the major Welbourne players on the other end of the line.

And after that? He could just picture it. First Bohr's shock when confronted. Then his dodging and squirming as he found himself on the ropes. Just imagining the scenario, Pierre felt better. In fact, so good that when Louise pushed the menu away and brought up the anchor bolt situation — rumormonger Breedlove had called her about it earlier in the day – she added, "Why the smirk? Must have been a good day despite what little you've told me about this morning."

He shrugged. "If you mean the deal with the bolts, it was just a little problem with Benny."

"All taken care of, huh."

"Depends. As far as Benny, yeah. If he hasn't already, he'll finish up on them tomorrow. As far as Bohr, though, my response is in the works."

"Response?"

"A little something."

"'A little something.'" She wagged her head, mocking. "Like?"

"You'll see. Let's just say that truth will out in the end."

"An affair?"

He shook his head. "I think he's got a gambling problem. I saw him coming out of the casino."

"Lots of people go there, and not to gamble. I've heard they've got a good lunch buffet."

"This wasn't lunch. Not judging from the way he acted when I asked him about it. He obviously didn't want his wife to know. And I've got the feeling he doesn't want it to go public. What I suspect is that Welbourne Grain doesn't take kindly to their bosses gambling during business hours. I mean, who would? So when they hear about it . . . well . . . could be backlash."

"You'd get him fired? And all because he insisted on what he'd been promised in the contract?" She glared through narrowed eyes. "You actually could live with yourself afterward?"

She glanced around, lowered her voice. "The very thought that you'd jeopardize someone's career, and at this point in his life, is totally disgusting."

Face flushed and eyes burning with rage, his fiancé at this moment was the most beautiful woman he'd ever seen. Even so, her fury wasn't worth feeding.

"Let's forget it," he said. "You're right. Bad plan." He took a sip of wine. "Now, as to the wedding reception . . . .

Their exchange about the wedding reception had been stiff if not wooden. But on the drive home, Louise came out of it. At least mostly. It seemed her thoughts were still hovering around the morning's episode with Bohr.

"Vernon Breedlove mentioned that you continue to be plagued by substandard work," she said. "He seemed to think you might have better luck if you paid more."

"You and Breedlove sit around discussing my pay scale?" He'd tried to make it sound light, but it came out like an accusation.

"He was just wondering why some, quite a few actually, of the people working for you lack skills."

"If they lack skills, it's not underpay. It's that they're not the brightest in the world. And that's true of most common laborers. They're featherbrained. Lucky to have jobs. It's what I tell my people all the time – 'You're just lucky you're employed.' And they know it. They'd be on welfare if it weren't for me. Strange as it sounds, they're too proud for that. That's one thing you can say for them. They've got pride."

"It sure doesn't show in their work."

Maybe not, he thought, clenching both steering wheel and teeth while peering ahead. Regardless, those workers were what made him a success. Make that relative success. And with them bound to him by jobs, there was little worry they'd two-time. Except for the Cuban. And his days were numbered.

Chapter Thirty-Eight

A Fine Kettle of Fish

Louise made the letter short.

Dear Mother,

I think about you so much. I just have to know how you're doing. I'm writing because I'm not sure what you'd do if I called. I hope you'll find it in your heart to answer. My address is 6868 Hwy 44, Acadi, Louisiana, 70071. I go by Louise Dennis.

Just one more thing – please keep my whereabouts from Mary and Rebecca.

She addressed, sealed, and stamped the envelope before shoving it into the middle of a batch of outgoing mail where no one would see it. Then, sitting back, she fiddled with her engagement ring. Even in the garish light from above her desk it reflected amazing colors. If her mother could see it, what would she think? If she knew of Pierre and all that came with him, what would she say? "A fine kettle of fish" came to mind.

Yet the truth was that Pierre was exactly what Louise had been after and, for that matter – and despite the lack of principle that was getting on her nerves – still was. Sometimes he bothered her so much – his anchor bolt fraud came to mind – that she felt like ripping the three-carat, emerald-cut gem from her finger and pitching it in his face, but that was in less practical moments when she lost sight of why she'd chosen this path. Lost sight of the great clothes, fancy cars, unmatchable home that would've never been hers otherwise. Lost sight of other things too. One of them being escape from linkage of African-Americans with laziness. Another being escape from the automatic branding she'd seen so much of – that assumption that being colored spelled either a problem or a charitable cause. Living in a black community, she'd seen and hated all of it. And being she had the means to break away from the whole ugly cycle, that's what she'd done. Fulfillment was what she'd been after when she left Brackenville and, one way or another, she was going to get it. Elizabeth Bancroft, now Louise Dennis, was all that mattered. The sad history, the betterment of her race, the Martin Luther King model – none of those made any difference. There was nothing civil rights could do for her that she couldn't do for herself. There'd always be those, like Pierre, whose minds were made up. And the only way to beat them was to fool them. She'd been totally convinced of that ever since an experience years before in Freshman English.

It was a morning class and, as was her habit, she'd taken a seat next to the aisle. With her next class across campus, she always sat where she could make quick exit when the bell rang. On this day, the seat next to her was empty, and she'd set her books and purse there. But just as the instructor began his lecture, a rumpled coed in what looked to be pajamas shuffled in and targeted the space, standing in the aisle while Louise picked up her belongings and moved them to the floor. The commotion was distracting, with the scruffy girl squeezing through and tripping over Louise's books before settling in. But not as distracting as when, seated, she leaned over and whispered to Louise, "Thanks. The only other seat I saw was next to a black."

Up till then, Louise had never personally experienced such blatant discrimination. She, after all, was nearly as "white" as anyone in the lecture hall and it would take a real kook to detect anything suspicious about her nose. Her dark-skinned sisters, though, had often complained of what they called *microagression* (those insidious behaviors they'd experienced on a similar campus a couple years earlier) and Louise had never doubted Mary and Rebecca when they spoke of being forced off sidewalks when they passed or the surprise shown when they opened their mouths and the words that came out were like those of normal human beings. (As though all African-Americans used lower-class dialect.) Louise, too, had witnessed such treatment up close when she'd been in the company of neighborhood friends. But never, until that day in Freshman English, had anyone come right out with true feelings.

Strange, though, there was a good side to that bigoted coed's comment, in that it was proof of just how well Louise fit in with any group who, if they'd known the truth, might've shut her out. It was proof, too, of the possibilities open to her. More than that, it was justification for where she found herself now and why she'd never let go of what she'd won and why at this very moment it was more important than ever to tend to the business at hand.

Which was? Diverting Mrs. Bohr from her dogged pursuit of the Bancrofts. An effort that, if allowed to go on, could threaten Louise's future with her narrow-minded but successful fiancé. What was it he said the other day? Something about sending the whole bunch back to Africa. It was incredible that he even dared say such things. Incredible, too, that she'd stooped so low as to have agreed to spend the rest of her life with him. But this was where she was, and she wasn't about to backtrack now.

Thus convinced that what she was about to do would help safeguard her plan, she picked up the phone on her desk, dialed the Bohrs' number, and waited for the timeworn voice of the lady of the house to pick up. When she did, and after exchanging the usual pleasantries, Louise got right down to business.

"The president of the Auxiliary of Lasserre Parish Hospital called, asking if I knew of anyone who might be interested in volunteer work," she said in a jazzy voice that really wasn't in character. "It could involve any number of things, from manning the information booth to clerking in the gift shop." She paused, hoping for a show of interest from the normally gung ho Mrs. Bohr. But with nothing of the sort coming forth, added, "Your name came to mind right away."

"Oh, nice of you to think of me," was the eventual reply, "but I really don't have enough hours in the day as it is. You're lucky you caught me now. I was on my way out the door. Weekly stint at the racetrack, you know."

"I didn't realize you were that busy."

"Oh my, yes. As well as the racetrack, I do organ and bells at The Holy Church. I spend a whole lot of time practicing for that. Then I have to keep track of what's going on at the house, in itself a full-time job. And when I've got a spare minute, it's back to the Bancrofts."

"Still doing that, huh?"

"Oh sure. I'll never give that up." A spring to her voice now. "Did I ever tell you what my husband and I found in the attic at LSU?"

"I'm not sure." Best to pretend indifference, even when the heart was pattering.

"We found some magazines from Charlotte Bancroft's collection. Thinking about it just gives me chills. I couldn't believe my luck. "

"How do you know the magazines were hers?"

"Signature on the cover. Upper right-hand corner. *Charlotte Corbyn Bancroft.*" She emphasized each syllable. "It was so unbelievable. There I was, standing in front of these empty shelves when all of a sudden I notice some color down at the bottom and, like magic, the color turns into magazines. They were apparently overlooked by the thief." An ecstatic little moan. "And you know what else? There were tracks heading right out the door — "

"What a shame," Louise cut in, avoiding any more talk of apparent slipups.

"A shame? Hardly. I like detective work. And now that I know there's someone out there with the stuff, probably close by too, I'm rarin' to go."

"And when you find her? Or," Louise added seamlessly, "him?"

"Simple. I'll get all the facts and . . . . " Silence.

"And what, may I ask?"

"Time to let the cat out of the bag, I guess." A deep intake of breath. "You know, back in Minnesota years ago, after I got a degree in English and journalism, I did some writing. And what I'm leaning toward now is a book about the Bancrofts."

Chapter Thirty-Nine

You're Sure They're Lazy?

Margaret, black cape askew, came charging through the door gasping, "Worst ever with the cupboards today," sending Carol like a shot behind the sofa. But not before the cat's claws gained traction on Fred's thighs.

The weird thing was that, jolted and in pain, Fred actually felt a rush of relief. His wife was speaking to him. If nothing else, their marriage was salvageable. Now all it would take was some patience and restraint as he listened to the details of her latest grievance, a matter involving Joseph Buford ignoring blueprints and building base cabinets six inches too high.

For Fred, the matter was tiddlywinks. In his scheme of things at the moment a six inch difference in cabinet height wasn't that big a deal. Yet, it obviously was in Margaret's. To her mind, those cabinets that were supposed to look low and modern now resembled kitchen counters. Or worse, bathroom vanities. Besides, she'd have to handle this problem herself. She couldn't afford any more of Breedlove's extra inspections. His last bill had been three hundred seventy dollars. And as for her opinion of Pierre's crew? They were the biggest bunch of lazies she'd ever met up with. They couldn't even make the effort to read blueprints.

"You're think they're lazy?" Fred asked hesitantly. He wanted to be careful. At any moment she could turn on him. "I mean, whenever I'm around they're working their butts off."

"Working their butts off installing crooked moldings and gaping joints and leaning chimneys and – " A look like she was retrieving complaints from an ample list in her brain. " – bulging shingles and misplaced doorbells and – "

"I don't know, Margaret. It could mean laziness, I suppose. But couldn't it just as well be lack of skills?"

"Well, to me – " Voice muffled as she pulled her poncho over her head. " – it's laziness."

Chapter Forty

Making Friends

Margaret would've loved to confront Joseph about the cabinets the very next day. But she didn't get over to the site until toward evening, when the only person there was Cedro, who told her that most of the crew, including Joseph, were working in a nearby community at another of Pierre's jobs. She was about to leave when Cedro asked if things were going any better.

"If you're talking about construction, the answer is no," she said point blank before going on about the cabinet problem and how disappointed she was, yet how embarrassed to complain about a mere six inches. But the difference six inches would make to the way the interior looked, she explained, made her complaint crucial.

By the time she was nearly done – she was by now asking Cedro why he thought she was getting such shoddy work from Pierre's employees – her voice was coming in fuzzy and she asked him to watch Wolfgang while she ran out to the car for hearing aid batteries. She could've said good-bye and gone home at that point – she knew it was near suppertime – but truth was that if Fred had to wait, even if he worried, it might do him some good. It would offer more time for him to ponder the importance of trust. As well – and to justify what she knew wasn't exactly how one should treat a marriage partner – she rationalized (and she *did* recognize it as rationalization) that it was Fred who had felt so sorry for Cedro and who, if anything, should appreciate her time spent with him.

As far as Cedro, when she got back to the garage he was resting on a pallet, seemingly in no hurry to get home. "I've got coffee," he said, "and with chicory." He nodded toward his thermos. "Could I pour you a cup?"

"I love coffee with chicory, but this late in the day am limited to decaf."

"How about a bottle of water."

"No need. I'm fine. I'll just sit here on the ice chest." She suspected, lonely immigrant that he was, he wanted company.

"You know," he said, "if you hadn't brought them up I would have forgotten about your hearing aids."

"Thank you. Nice to hear," she replied. And though she'd hoped to go on about the shoddy work of his fellow employees and what he thought about it, she was instead soon baring her soul about her hearing, something she seldom talked about.

Cedro, on his part, seemed more than merely polite, listening intently, asking questions that made her think that on some level he identified with her. It wasn't till she'd finished the part about her grandma and how grateful she was to that sweet little lady for buying that first hearing aid when she was a kid – meanwhile tearing up and feeling so embarrassed that, to hide the show of emotion, she used the pretext of checking her watch – that Margaret had some sense of how late it had gotten. "Seven," she moaned. "It's really seven?"

"At least I'm none the worse for tonight," she told Cedro as they stood on the road next to her car. The evening was alive with chirrs, croaks, and honks, and the street light above glowed like a pearl in the misty gray sky. "But your poor bent ear. One of these days you'll have to tell me about Cuba. If you're willing, that is. When did you leave, by the way?"

"Nineteen sixty-eight."

"Hmm. Long time ago." She began to open her door, then paused. "In a boat?"

"No, we were on a raft," he said, meeting her eyes before looking away.

Driving home, Cedro felt good for the first time in a long while. Maybe, he was thinking, things had taken a turn. Maybe he was nearing the end of the lonely tunnel he'd been lost in. There seemed to be a light out there. A human light with hearing aids, wild white hair, devotion to a dog, and even signs of wanting to know him. Best of all, she was about his age. Sharlene was nice too, but too young. And then there were Sharlene's kids, especially the little girl.

Chapter Forty-One

Impatience

As they walked up the long drive to Valeria after an evening stroll on the levee, Pierre looked over at Louise. "It's about time we set the date, don't you think?"

"You keep saying that. What's the hurry?"

"Hurry! We've been engaged for more than a year. It's time you take on the role of mistress of Valeria Plantation."

"You mean quit my job?"

He glanced over again. She was dead serious. "But do you think you'd enjoy hanging around with nothing to do?"

She laughed. "I'd love it."

"With no one to talk to?"

"You'll be around. Or are you planning to move your office again?"

She had him there. And until he'd given it some thought, he'd avoid further reference to her employment. The truth remained – even without a little financial input he wanted her for his wife, and the sooner the better.

Chapter Forty-Two

Two Babies?

The crew was back. Though Pierre's car was nowhere in sight, Joseph's van was, and that was who Margaret wanted to talk to anyway. And if Dakota was there, it wouldn't hurt getting him in on it. Even if Fred was right and the whole group lacked skills, the supervisor might have the power to motivate toward more regard for those things that made a house a work of art as opposed to a piece of crap.

Inside, a sort of pedal point of activity hummed beneath a cheery voice from a radio on the floor that was claiming God commanded man to dwell with the wife in understanding and woman's complex need for love demanded that understanding.

"I need to talk to you about the cabinets," she said when she ran into the subject of her search, along with Dakota, in the rear bedroom.

"What about 'em?" Joseph never failed to give the impression of a chip on the shoulder.

"They're simply too high," she said, maintaining a level tone.

"Not my problem. I followed the plans."

Instead of arguing, she put on her glasses and sank carefully to the floor, where she unrolled her blueprints and sorted through till she found the interior elevations page. A page with a mind of its own, it seemed; when she pulled it out it rolled right back into a long spool. Not about to be thwarted, however, she used her left hand and right knee to help anchor it.

"So –" she said, finally ready to spell out the discrepancy between what Joseph had done and what he was supposed to have done.

But she was cut short by not only hot garlicky breath on her cheek but a strident voice in her right hearing aid. It was Joseph, crouching next to her now, poking at the drawings, braying, "Thirty-six inches. See?"

She responded in a voice less controlled than before and with a few pokes of her own, her index finger having a go at asterisks on the page. First the one right below the cabinet drawings and then the one at the bottom.

"Asterisk. Do *you* see?" She glanced over at him with what she hoped was a look of authority. "And – down here – matching asterisk. See?"

With a little frown settling on his forehead, he narrowed his eyes. "Asterik?"

That was when she truly grasped what Fred meant about skills and training. And, in this case, just plain reading.

"Asterisk. The star," she said, again pointing first to one and then the other. "See the stars?"

He said nothing, just stared.

"And behind the one on the bottom is the word *Note* with a colon (the two dots, by the way) and behind that colon it says, *All dimensions to be Verified On The Job.*" She nearly shouted it. "You see that?"

She checked his response again. At the moment, his eyes seemed to be squinting toward the asterisk at the bottom.

"And behind that the initials *V.O.J.* in parentheses?" She didn't bother to describe *parentheses*, suspecting it would either make things more confusing or be insulting. What she did do was translate *V.O.J.*: "In other words, no matter what the plans said, you should have asked me before putting the cabinets in. Thirty-six inches wasn't carved in stone."

Joseph looked up at Dakota and Dakota shrugged, as though in his role as supervisor the height of cabinets was low priority. "I don't know," he said. "I guess I can talk to Pierre about it."

And with that, Margaret's composure was swallowed in a fit of temper so violent she felt a twinge in her chest. Talk to Pierre about it! As though there were some question!

"Well, then, while you're at it – " Despite the twinge, she struggled for footing, releasing the interior elevation blueprint. It spooled back to its original roll while, giving little thought to whether it was Dakota's or Joseph's leg she used, she pulled herself up.

Finally on her feet, she stomped toward the front bedroom, her heart stomping right along as a quick glance to the rear assured her that her adversaries followed.

"While you're at it," she repeated when she reached her target, "talk to Pierre about this corner cupboard that's off center and – "

Now stomping all the way to the den on the other side of the kitchen. " – ask him what he'd like to do about this crooked chimney."

The twinge in her chest had by now turned to a burning tightness, so she left the two of them there, retrieving her plans from the rear bedroom before heading out the front door.

With the cabinet problem handled and the episode that forced its early wrap-up fresh in mind, she decided it was time to ease up. Further, she decided there was no better way than to get back to the Bancrofts. It had been a while. The last time she'd given Albert and Charlotte any real thought was that day she'd had lunch with Pierre and Louise at Brignac's. It wasn't long after that she'd combined courthouse information with what she'd collected from the library and archives, stuffed it in a folder, and shoved it into the metal file in the living room. Which was where she now found all of it, including notes about things that had seemed significant at the time.

One notation was about the 1890 letter from Lizzie in Brackenville to Charlotte in Acadi complaining about having to stay for months with her New York grandmother. Though that prolonged visit might not shed light on the duel – Dr. Bancroft at the time had already been six feet under for fifteen years or so – it was suspicious. Added to that was the grandmother's reference in a later letter to *Little Byron*. Talk about a baffling coincidence!

As to the two pictures she'd copied, the one of the infant with *To My Love – 1863* on the back and the one of Albert dressed for military combat, they were intriguing as ever. Being this infant who so resembled Albert wasn't his daughter, who could she be? There was no doubt, just from appearance, that she was Albert's blood and bone. A niece or nephew seemed a most likely answer. But judging from the letter Albert's mother had written after her other son – and Albert's only sibling – died, that other son had blessed the good doctor with neither niece nor nephew.

That Margaret was dealing with not one, but two, hush-hush situations – and all based in one illustrious family – seemed unbelievable. Yet, what else to think? Lizzie's stay in

Brackenville was as suspicious as the Archive photo and inscription. (Just as wonderfully salacious-sounding too.) Both were worth pursuing. Probably she'd have to go back to Lasserre Parish census records.

On the other hand, at least as far as the Lizzie affair, if Lizzie had gone to New York to have a baby, would she have brought that baby back to Acadi? To avoid scandal it would've made more sense to leave it with the energetic grandmother in Brackenville. And in that case? It was the 1900 census for Brackenville, New York, that would give the –

Wham! The significance of a baby suddenly slammed into her sluggish brain. With Lizzie an only child and spinster, and Albert's sole sibling childless, there was little chance that anything but a baby explained Bancroft descendants up there in that little town in New York.

Next morning, the Lasserre Parish Courthouse, as expected, proved to be a dud. So, following the advice of the clerk there, Margaret got on the horn to the Federal Information Center in Maryland, who directed her to Federal Archives and Records in New Jersey, who told her to get in touch with a local family history center of the Church of Jesus Christ of Latter-Day Saints in Louisiana. It was from them that she ordered the microfilm that would answer her question.

Chapter Forty-Three

Empty Space

This should read: A long day. Everyone had gone home and Cedro was wishing Margaret Bohr would walk in like she had the week before. It had been nice talking to her that evening. She was so different from his boss's other clients. Natural, honest, even telling him what it had been like as a hard-of-hearing kid who just wanted to be like everyone else. And that was what was interesting about her. As much as she must've tried, she still wasn't like everyone else, and at this point didn't seem to care. She was . . . how to say? . . . uncommon, with her wild white hair and crazy clothes and silly devotion to that dog of hers. If anyone made Cedro feel happy – almost happy, at least – it had been her, and every morning since that evening they'd happened to meet in the garage after work he'd even taken time to make the decaf coffee she drank, carrying it along to work in the extra thermos so that if she came she'd stay longer and they could talk more.

He was sitting on a pallet on the floor of the garage when it finally happened.

"So, what's new around here?" she said, walking in.

"Not much, except for Joseph working on the cabinet problem. So everything's going pretty good." His eye met hers. "At least right now."

"Right now, huh? I guess I should be grateful for even that. You know, there was a time, and not very long ago, when I thought the odds of this house ever getting finished, let alone surviving afterward, were very low. You wouldn't believe the trouble I had getting Pierre to take care of some things."

"I do believe." She was being honest about her problems with his boss and he was being honest too. It was like a confidence between friends. It *was* a confidence.

"Then all of a sudden," Mrs. Bohr went on, "the day before the guys started sheetrocking, everything came together – plywood corner bracing, flitch . . . . "

"Plates?" He'd been working construction for a while now and knew the words.

"Right. And those metal things above doors – "

"Lintels."

"Right again."

She finished with "diagonal wall studs," saying that for some reason they were easy to remember and adding, "Anyway, what I mean to say is, it pays to stand firm."

"When you're dealing with fraud there's no other way. It's too bad, but – "

A sound like snapping twigs or dry leaves just around the corner of the garage – a sound like someone was out there – stopped him.

Mrs. Bohr heard it too. "Am I imagining or . . .?

Cedro pushed himself up and wound his way past the sawhorse and through the clutter. Outside, he watched Benny trot across the yard in the direction of his red pickup.

Mrs. Bohr, beside him, whispered. "I feel like I'm in a thriller. You think my contractor's now stooped to spies?"

She meant it as a joke, he supposed, but he couldn't laugh. Watching his fellow painter slam the door of his truck and drive away was like watching a candle fizzle and die. Like this was the beginning of the end as far as his job.

Mrs. Bohr broke the silence. "You're quiet. Worried about Benny telling Pierre what we said?" She studied him. "Really, you shouldn't be. He may not have even heard."

"But if he did – "

"No worry. I promise." She was leading the way back in. "Someone like you can always find employment." She patted his shoulder. "Come on in and help me check my house-in-progress."

When they were back in the garage, Cedro reached for the extra thermos. "There's decaf tonight, and with that chicory you said you liked."

"You sweetheart, you remembered," she said, giving him a look like he was her dearest friend. "And does that mean the rafting story you promised?"

"If you'd like." He tried to sound like he was okay with it, but truth was, he'd hoped she'd forget what he'd promised in a moment of weakness. He wasn't even sure he'd promised it. Besides, he was pretty sure that what she expected was something like a tale about dodging boulders and swirling rapids in a rubber raft while enjoying beautiful scenery. And his story wasn't that. His story would make no one happier. Except, perhaps, himself. And that was something he wondered about: would it help if he got it off his chest? From what he'd read, people seemed to think that was the way to feel better. And if he could just feel better . . . .

He got up, taking a Styrofoam cup from the stack sitting with the paint on a newspaper on the floor, filled it with strong-smelling coffee from the extra thermos, and handed it to Mrs. Bohr. Then, after pouring some regular brew for himself, he sat down on the pallet, back against the wall, and, without prologue, softly began. "To get up the nerve – "

"Sorry, Cedro." She cupped an ear and smiled.

He started over, louder this time. "To get up the nerve, it took us two years. But once we got organized, it didn't take long to collect the boards, rope, and tires. The raft, it was big enough for the five of us and the stuff we brought along – powdered milk and crackers in black plastic bags, and water." He paused, thinking. "Oh yes, and the wood and bed sheet we planned to make into a mast once we were on our way. There were a few other things too. Not very many." Another pause. "It was about midnight when we shoved off."

"Hey, hold on." Mrs. Bohr laughed, took a quick sip of her coffee, and swallowed. "When was this and who were 'we'?"

"It was the summer of 1968. A cloudy night. There were five of us. My daughter Adria. She was six years old. Carlos, my law school professor, who was quite a bit older. Gerardo, a doctor and friend from childhood. And Gerardo's mother."

"How about – " Mrs. Bohr hesitated. " – your wife?"

"She didn't want to come. We were separated by then."

"And your daughter didn't mind leaving without her?"

"Adria had been living with me. I didn't think she'd care."

"Wasn't she nervous about it?"

"No. She was fine. I didn't tell her what we were doing until we were on our way to the raft, so she didn't have time to worry. Then I bragged to her about how wonderful Florida would be. So by the time we pushed off, she was going on about taking her puppy to Crandon Park Zoo in Miami. He would love the monkeys, she said." Remembering, Cedro couldn't help smiling. "I had to tell her to quiet down. Of course, I was already wishing I hadn't made so much of the zoo, and I was wondering whether we should have brought the dog along too. But he was a quiet little fellow. Never barked. And I'd wanted Adria to look forward to the trip, so I guess I'd been a little lax.

"That puppy." Cedro shook his head, remembering the ball of gold with black button nose. "He was even more lively than Adria. Jumping around on laps. Pulling shoelaces. A cute, little figurehead at the head of the raft. That was what he looked like when he finally quieted down. That is, until the seas got rough and he sneaked over to Adria.

Cedro paused, lifting his cup, savoring the bitterness of strong, black coffee. Then he studied Mrs. Bohr, swirling hers, staring back, waiting.

"By the time we'd rowed the thirteen or so miles to El Pino, the raft was already falling apart from the waves. So we found a place to hide in a swamp and did the best we could to repair it. The mast and sail, they were added there too. All the while mosquitoes eating us. We hadn't planned for them and by morning, when we left, we were covered in lumps."

He set his coffee on concrete next to the pallet, reflecting, ordering his thoughts.

"There was all kinds of traffic on the water that morning, I guess from a fishing cooperative, and we were worried about being seen. So as soon as we could, we stopped at another island. How long we stayed I don't remember. Might have been a day or two. Finally we just decided there was no way, on open water, we could be sure of being safe, so we took our chances and left.

"It was then, as I remember, that we started coming across boats with bullet holes in them. It was a shock, knowing that lying on those decks were people just like us, who had died trying to do the same thing. We didn't say it, but I'm sure it didn't escape any one of us. When Adria asked where the people were, I changed the subject."

"Oh, Cedro – "

"But we were lucky. For a time. Being shot wasn't our fate. As the days passed, the waves were more of a worry. At times they were like rolling mountains. And the raft was falling apart again. Surely a friendly boat or plane would find us soon, we said as we held onto each other in the scorching sun. At night, when it cooled, we huddled together under clothes we'd wrapped in rubber raincoats. To make things worse, we started worrying about food and water, and began rationing."

"Oh, Cedro," Mrs. Bohr said again. She was looking into her coffee, shaking her head, frowning. "I can't believe you made it."

He rubbed his chin, arranging his thoughts, aware that nothing could make the next part any less sickening.

"Not too long after that was when the raft broke apart and we all scrambled for inner tubes and boards. Gerardo helped his mother and I helped Adria. But the puppy slipped away. And even though we tried, we couldn't catch him." Cedro steadied his voice. "Strange how the picture of Adria and the puppy, her sobbing and him slapping the water, is so hard to forget. He was just an animal."

Mrs. Bohr looked horrified. "No need to go on, Cedro. I'm sorry I asked. I had no idea."

"I want to," he said. "I think I need to."

He picked up his coffee and slugged down the rest, girding himself for what was to come. How to say it? he wondered. Finally just blurting, "Carlos, he was the first to go."

Mrs. Bohr's damp eyes met his. "You mean – "

"He died first. We'd had no food for days, and with the sun and waves, Carlos was very weak." He battled for words. "Carlos . . . simply slipped through the center of his tire. Without a word. It was calm that night. Just a little breeze. I remember our silence, as though we were waiting for him to come back. So strange . . . . "

His words hung in the air.

"After that, things happened fast. Before the sun came up, a fog had gathered and as we floated in our circle, barely able to see each other, I felt a tug on my shirt. It was Gerardo. At first, because his voice was so soft, I couldn't understand what he was telling me. But his mother knew. He can't hang on any longer, she said.

"We fought, his mother and me, to help him stay up. But after an hour or so, with the sun out and the fog gone, we watched him slip away."

There was more to the story – Gerardo gasping "Save Mother"; his sinking into the water, then coming up and floating for an instant; his hand slightly swaying as he went down for good. But Cedro kept it to himself. And when Mrs. Bohr opened her purse and grabbed some tissues, keeping some to blot her eyes and handing the rest to him, he blew his nose and cleared his throat.

"I'm not sure how I did it, but somehow, even hanging on to inner tubes and boards, I put together another raft, a tiny one, and crawled onto it, pulling Adria and Gerardo's mother up after me. At the time, I thought the old woman might make it. But the sun, it was hot, and by then she'd given up. She didn't last more than a few hours." He stared at the crumpled tissues in his hand. "She was very religious, and as I eased her into the gulf, I made the sign of the cross. It sounds crude, but her loss wasn't as shocking as the others.

"From then on I lost all sense of time, all sense of everything. It was dark. It was light. The waves were bad. The waves weren't bad. We needed a colorful flag. Who cared about a flag.

"And then . . . my own daughter. She'd been sleeping, and when I tried to wake her, barely answered. 'Let me sleep,' she said. So I moved close and held her and told her not to give up. That it wouldn't be long.

"I think we were that way for quite a while, Adria whimpering and twitching in her sleep and me dozing. Next thing I knew – " he squeezed the lump of tissue till his nails bit his palm. " – she wasn't breathing."

He was weeping now, remembering the moment. His wailing "No, please, no." His holding her ravaged, feather light body while caressing her cheeks and hair.

His lips trembled as he avoided Mrs. Bohr's eyes. "When the wind came up again and the little raft broke apart, I let her go." Which wasn't all of it, but all he could say. What he kept inside was the part about the faded blouse and the way it billowed in the water and how, even now, he couldn't figure out how he could have been so foolish as to bring her on the trip. It was easier to just wrap it up and tell about how still it was and drifting between sleep and waking and how he cooled his head in the waves and drank from the ocean.

As far as rescue, there was little to be said. All he remembered was waking on a freighter in the Florida straits.

"So there you have it," he finished. "This was my raft trip."

He stared at Mrs. Bohr, who was mopping her eyes. And at that moment, something let go. He began to cry. And then to sob. Sobs that came from down in his stomach up through his chest and out through his throat. Sobs that, once they'd begun, went on and on, springing from that space that had emptied the day Adria died, yet never stopped leaking sorrow. The space that would never be full again.

Chapter Forty-Four

AK-47

The next time Mrs. Bohr stopped by in the evening she didn't stay long. "I don't mean to be unfriendly," she explained. "I'm just awfully busy right now."

But Cedro couldn't help wondering. Had he offended her with his raft story? Ever since that evening, he'd wished he hadn't told her. Burdening her with his pain, thinking it might make him feel better if he talked about it, had been selfish. She hadn't wanted to hear it. She'd even tried to stop him after she realized the horror. But he'd gone on, dragging her, unwilling, into his dismal dungeon. If now she thought of him as a self-seeking, whining coward who did little more than cause anguish to everyone he came in contact with, who could blame her?

That night, with the indignity of Mrs. Bohr's "awfully busy" echoing in his ears, Cedro hurried home, fed the animals and, without eating, went to bed early. Not that he could sleep. It seemed like his blanket had turned from soft wool to haircloth. And the throb and chirp of crickets and frogs outside was more like a brass band than soothing strings. The light on the pole outside his window was distracting too, casting icy grayness on everything from the knotty pine wall to the pint-sized dresser to the snapshot in the mirror frame above it. A snapshot not of the daughter he'd loved, with her long black braids and dark eyes, but of Sharlene Wilkes's kids and the stray cat he'd given them.

When he finally did sleep, the dreams were so scary he woke more than once in a state of horror, heart pounding like a pile driver. If it wasn't Adria and her billowing blouse, it was what had happened even before the raft trip: the lieutenant with his razor sharp bayonet and searing cigarettes and pointed boot. Or Duardo under the floodlights.

A big part of the problem was the little plastic calendar on the kitchen counter. He really should have turned it over long ago. Yet how would that help? He'd still know the anniversary was coming. Some chance force would drive him to remember. And come April 1, without his bidding, his mind, like an insect's antennae, would begin sensing and by the time the clock struck 4:13 on the morning of April 7, would have traveled to the prison yard in Cuba.

It wasn't April 7 yet, but already, with that date drawing near, he was reminded that the anniversary was around the corner and he'd better get ready.

And he could do it. He'd done it before. By forcing good memories, he could at least ease the pain. There had been so many sweet times. Ordinary days, but full of happiness. In the morning, Duardo and him sliding down that shiny mahogany bannister on the way to the kitchen for Café Con Leche and a tostada. The two racing to the stable for their horses. A lazy afternoon watching the harvesters in their huge straw hats and thick gloves and rubber boots, all the while both of them chewing sugar cane. On the way home, Duardo picking up a turtle and carrying it to the side of the road, setting it under a banyan. Before dinner, hands behind heads in chaise lounges under the palms by the pool, planning their lives. Afterward, legs slung over wicker chairs on the *galeria*, reading. Before bed, chasing lightning bugs.

Normally, Duardo led the way. He was three minutes older, after all. Then in law school he began changing, thinking new thoughts, spelling them out in a shrill voice, and, finally, quitting school. And estranging this twin, who was determined to follow the path they'd planned way back when. A path that involved graduating, marrying, and joining a law firm. A plan that was suddenly not enough for Duardo, whose views on takeover of farms and treatment of political *prisioneros* was, for sure, a quick path to trouble. And when he left to join the insurgents in the Escambray Mountains? Double trouble.

After he left, it took a while to understand what he'd meant. But when the plantation was taken away, Cedro finally did, and knew he could do no less than follow his twin brother's lead. He couldn't and he wouldn't.

After that? Loss of job, arrest, imprisonment, and torture. And finally, that night under the floodlights. Duardo's worn-down face, stubble of beard, hollow eyes. That moment before he was escorted to the post, and the hint of brotherly recognition. His brave waving away of the black kerchief. His shrug and long sigh.

And this brother? A realization that to continue to buck what was being forced on him would accomplish nothing more than leave Adria fatherless.

So instead of fighting, Cedro did as told, raised the AK-47 along with the rest of the firing squad, and aimed – a little to the right. And at that moment, lost all awareness.

Chapter Forty-Five

Spicy Facts

Hurray! The microfilm had arrived from Salt Lake City and Margaret was sitting at a projection machine in the family history center on the outskirts of New Orleans reading from the twelfth census of the United States, Seton County, New York. And the spicy facts were there. In 1900, the only Bancroft family in Brackenville was headed by Elizabeth Bancroft, obviously Lizzie's grandmother. She was eighty-seven years old. Her race? No fooling around in this census. She was black. More importantly, Byron, ten years old, lived with her.

Chapter Forty-Six

Elusive Worm

Louise suspected Mrs. Bohr was a bit tipsy that evening at Brignac's Seafood.

"Who would've thought I was so insightful?" the white-haired, black-browed braggart, sitting at a table near the front with her husband, said midway through her response to Louise's ostensibly polite inquiry as to progress on the Bancrofts. She'd already dropped the earth-shaking news that she'd found Grandpa Byron in the New York census.

"I mean, doesn't my locating little Byron Bancroft in Brackenville prove that business about a woman's intuition?" She winked at Louise as she took another sip of wine. "And the great part is that it's only the beginning. I'm gonna keep on with the Latter-Day Saints group. I'm going to trace that darn family till – " Her voice quivered. " – till I've uncovered the elusive worm who ran off with the goods. I think it's got to be someone connected to the family."

"Really." Louise pretended lukewarm interest, letting her eyes wander.

"Well, who else has a motive? Only family would value the collection. Or, for that matter, even remember it."

"It's not worth much, huh?"

"Not that much." Mrs. Bohr clamped a finger on her eye. "This damn eyelid. Whenever I drink wine it does a jig." She set the stemmed glass on the table and, after picking up her knife and fork, sliced into what could only be deep-fried catfish. "By the way, Louise," she said before depositing a generous chunk in her mouth, "will we see you at the meeting in the morning?"

Chapter Forty-Seven

Stone-Cold Dead

The same question Margaret had asked Fred a few minutes before, after washing the last bite of custard-filled Danish (she was taking a breather from carrot cake) down with some good strong chicory coffee, rolled around in her head as she brushed her teeth: was it fair of Breedlove to charge for his assistant's attendance at meetings when Breedlove was the one who'd recommended the builder whose incompetence made the sessions necessary? With one of those meetings scheduled in about an hour, the irony grated on her. Yet, she knew there was no way out. According to the contract, the architect was the one to interpret and decide matters concerning the builder's performance. Even if she thought it should go to arbitration, Breedlove or his assistant would be punching a time card while deciding if she had a leg to stand on. It seemed like any way she looked at it, she was the victim of highway robbery and Breedlove was the bandit.

The unfairness was still bothering her when she turned on the tap in the fiberglass shower and stood back, waiting for the water to heat up. It was her own fault, she was thinking, and rather than regret the day she'd hired Breedlove, she might as well just make sure she stayed on top of things for the rest of the term. Even doing that at this late date, though, couldn't replace gobs of money spent on a shoddy house. Well, at least the meeting this morning would help her stay on top of things. That is, if she was prepared. Which brought up the question of how well her papers were organized. She'd taken lots of notes. Some of them, like the pool man's claim that Pierre, not Mermaid Pools, was responsible for removing the mountain of dirt in the backyard, were on nothing more than scraps of paper. Was all that stuff in the metal file box, and in a sequence where she could quickly find each particular problem without a fuss?

She wrapped herself in a towel and, after fastening it at the side with a hair clip, made her way down the steps to the living room. A peek in the box assured her it was all there, the manila folder so full it bulged like a fanny pack. Though it wasn't as boiled down and orderly as she could have liked she promised herself that if she had time she'd tend to that later. For now, holding the sides so nothing slipped out, she'd just stuff the folder in her trusty attaché right next to *Ongoing Building Concerns,* that list she'd long since decided was like the hair on her chin: tweeze one and two grow back. The day after crossing off *cabinets,* water heater drainage and ceiling fan troubles emerged. Today, she hoped, she'd make some headway on all of it.

Upstairs again, bathroom steamy now, she slipped out of the towel, adjusted the water temperature, and stepped into the shower, drenching her head in the pelting stream before squeezing a pine-scented dollop of shampoo into her hand and massaging it into her hair.

When the splattering turned faint she mouthed a silent "Uh-oh," assuming she and Fred hadn't timed this well. Low water pressure meant he, too, was showering.

Yet . . . .

She raised her hand and met a force strong as a fire hose.

Strange, she thought. Faint patter, yet blasting water. It only made sense if there were suds in her ears or . . . .

She checked. "God!" she shrieked as her fingers met hard plastic ear molds.

Turning off the tap double-quick and with eyes squeezed against shampoo drizzling down her forehead, she pulled the hearing aids out and stepped from the shower. Then, with both molds in one hand, she groped for the towel hanging over the toilet tank.

Once she'd wiped her eyes and blotted the aids, she held them to her ears.

Stone-cold dead.

Not time to panic yet, however. She'd learned some tricks over the years. First, the hair dryer.

A banging on the door and the image in the foggy mirror of Fred in gray suit and striped red and blue tie peeking in behind her said it all; he was dressed and ready for the meeting. He also was ready to say something.

"I can't hear you," she hissed, switching off the hair dryer.

His mouth went elastic. "I didn't say anything."

"Well, don't," she shot back.

"What's going on? We're running late and you're standing here in the altogether shooting hot air at your hearing aids while foam creeps down your face."

Between his overstated articulation and her lipreading skill she understood it all. "Go without me."

"Without you!" A long look. "What's wrong?"

"Guess."

"We've got no time for games, Margaret, cute as you look this morning."

"Well then, I got the damn hearing aids wet and they're stone-cold dead."

"Oh boy." He glanced at his watch and mumbled something.

"What?" she snapped.

"What do you want to do?" he articulated so clearly that though his voice was a mere buzz in the ears she understood.

"You go. Maybe I'll come later."

"Maybe!" No longer mere buzz, now some fizz. "You're the one in charge. I don't even know what you want covered at this stupid meeting."

"Everything's in my case next to the file box downstairs."

"But – "

"Go," she said, shoving the door shut.

Chapter Forty-Eight

Daylilies and Hummingbirds

With his pressure on her to set a date, Pierre was on Louise's mind a lot lately. What bothered her most, of course, was his bigotry. But his recent treatment of Cedro Diaz and his handling of Margaret Bohr's legitimate complaints about the house were nearly as off-putting. There were half-measures and then there was sellout, the latter being the kind of thing – hurting other people to benefit himself – that Pierre was doing. Louise, on the other hand, was the half-measure type. Her deception had gone only so far, and she'd never meant to hurt anyone. That her mother suffered was and would always be a sort spot.

The difference between Pierre and herself was that she recognized the cruelty of what she'd done and agonized over it every day whereas Pierre seemed never to give his inhumanity a second thought. For him it was second nature. For her it was abnormal. Not so abnormal, though, that she was about to reverse course. She still wanted everything she'd wanted in the beginning, including the lavish lifestyle she'd enjoy with Pierre. With Margaret Bohr digging into the Bancrofts with the fervor of a passionate historian, however, there now was no guarantee as far as that. Louise could try to sidetrack the hearing-challenged snoop with stopgap measures, but it would take stronger steps than that to stop Mrs. Bohr. And what those steps should be Louise didn't yet know. What she did know was that nothing would change as far as her decision to pass. Growing up in a black community had convinced her of that. Even as a child she'd sensed that she was seen as second-rate. Less than second-rate by some. And when in college that truth really hit home, she knew it was something she could and would change. The only difference now as far as that choice was her reversal about the break with her mother. And that had made no difference anyway. Her mother hadn't even answered the letter.

Not that her mother's rejection was a surprise. But it was disheartening because, hard as she tried, Louise couldn't get this best friend who happened to have given her birth out of her mind. She'd been seriously mistaken when she thought she could just walk away from the one who'd been the base, the most important part, of who she was. No one, no matter how hardened, would have an easy time abandoning someone so significant. Lately, Louise had even been thinking about how, alone in that little blue house in Brackenville, her mother might fall or, worse, pass away without anyone finding her for days. Nearly as dismaying was the possibility of depression or ill health.

Maybe it was late for such considerations, but those were the sorts of things that came to mind. And it was no wonder; there was so much that reminded Louise of her mother. The daylilies in front of the courthouse. Hummingbirds in Pierre's rear garden. The faded jersey gown her mother had secretly sewn and surprised Louise with on her birthday. Despite a gaping hole under the left arm, Louise still slipped into it at bedtime, knowing that she'd do the same up till it fell apart and she reverently placed the remains in the top drawer of the bedroom chest next to the only picture she had of the loving seamstress.

Loving seamstress, such an apt label for this parent who'd shaped lives for her daughters just as thoughtfully as she'd put together those nightgowns. Was it any wonder that, though far away, she surfaced at unexpected moments. The other day it happened in the dentist's waiting room as, sitting across from another mother reading *Heidi* to her little girl, Louise had trouble with tears.

It wasn't just the memories that popped up all the time, though. It was the awareness, too, that though her mother may have loathed her youngest daughter's way of improving her life, she would have reveled in her success. What fun it would've been to show her the neat way she'd decorated her house, how smart she looked in designer clothes, how appreciated she was at work, how professionally she handled herself.

Chapter Forty-Nine

Botherin' the Boss

In an exuberant mood, Margaret parked her car behind the fire hydrant at the site. It had been one very good day. Not only was the early spring weather gorgeous, company stock, which had been climbing for a while now, had jumped two points today. Topping everything was the return from California of her hearing aids. The week before, hanging around the apartment, had been a long one. When she did escape, most often to take Wolfgang on his regular outings, she made sure she'd first peeked between the crack in the front window drapes to size things up as far as activity on the walkway outside her door. And once she stepped onto that walkway, and with that same goal of avoiding uncomfortable encounters, she'd eyeballed the courtyard below. Beyond that, to avoid acquaintances at the grocery store she'd checked out each aisle before turning her cart into it. And at Holy Church, where the organ now sounded like a distant calliope, she'd slipped in a side door and up the narrow steps to the balcony, where the instrument sat in safe isolation. In all cases, she knew she had no choice.

Meeting friends – as if she had many – would've been too embarrassing. Trying to explain that she wasn't her usual self, that she couldn't understand a word, that at the moment she was dumb as a stump had to be avoided at all cost.

Now, though, she was on top of her game, out of hibernation, relishing as she headed toward the garage the crackle of dry leaves underfoot and the squawk of swooping gulls overhead and the swish of traffic from the river road. Her world was right again. And if Cedro had been around, she would've stopped for a chat. Being that he wasn't, she got right to work checking progress since she'd last given the house a good going-over.

First, the Corian counters in kitchen and bathrooms. As expected, since she'd contracted separately for them, they were spectacular. On the other hand, the work and materials that Pierre was responsible for were of characteristic quality: scratched cupboard doors; cheap off-brand heater/ventilator lights in the bathrooms; garden-variety on/off switches where dimmers were specified; a powder room light fixture installed too high; a missing electric outlet behind the refrigerator; a whistling toilet; a crooked towel bar. And, most amazing, unpainted soffits above the pool deck already warping.

"Give this to Pierre," she said, handing Dakota an updated *Ongoing Building Concerns* list next morning. Halfway out the door, she remembered. "Where's Cedro these days?"

"He's out o' here. Fired." Having folded her list, he was stuffing it in a rear pants pocket.

"No. Really?" She stared at him. "Do you know why?"

"Musta been botherin' the boss."

"You mean the one decent . . . ." She looked away, recalling Cedro's reaction that night when Benny overheard their criticism of Pierre. "Do you know his phone number?"

"Uh-uh."

"Well, do you know where he lives?"

"Sharlene might," he said, pointing toward the door to the laundry room.

Before dark that evening Margaret followed Sharlene's directions to Cedro's trailer, turning right into a driveway not far from the ferry landing and heading into a wooded area. A small ways in, a battered Camaro sat in a crooked shed to the side of a little frame house where a fat lady, slippered and in a rocking chair, rested on the porch next to a washing machine. That lady, according to what a long-winded Sharlene had told her, was Cedro's landlady. As Margaret drove past, she sent a wave her way while bumping on, her car rattling down the rutted road in a swirl of dust.

Cedro's trailer was parked at the end, and when she pulled in front to park she was startled by a black cat on top of the window air conditioner arching its back and springing to the ground. And that wasn't the only cat. A second later a calico slipped out from between the bottled gas cylinders and shot toward a pile of old cabinets and tires in the front yard. If they were Cedro's cats, they sure weren't very friendly, she thought as she got out of her car and headed for the front door, where she mounted the steps and, without hesitation, rapped.

While waiting, she took in the setting. Over near a pink sink and nearly hidden by weeds sat a brown and white puppy, eyes sad and weary. Nearby, a gold kitten tight-roped the rim of another pink bathroom fixture, a toilet bowl. Across the gravel drive, brush was so thick it made her shiver. *Snakes.*

Finally she heard steps from within and turned to find Cedro behind the screen door. Not opening it, just standing there.

"Could we talk?" she said.

He didn't answer. A shadow in the gloom. Eerie.

"I'd like to talk to you, Cedro. Would you open the door and come out?"

He moved, and she heard the scratch of metal on metal. Hook and eye latch most likely.

When the door finally swung open it revealed a man transformed. Unshaven, matted hair, slept-in clothes, no shoes. Stepping out, his cuffs scraped the threshold.

"Are you . . . ? Is your . . . ? Are you alone?" she finally got out, recognizing the absurdity of the question even as she asked it. "Do you mind if I . . . ? She indicated the step and sat down. At a loss for words, she finally managed, "Looks like someone had a pink bathroom."

"The landlady." Not a hint of humor in his rusty voice.

"All these animals the landlady's too?"

"No."

"Tell me this." A weak smile. "Are you going to be civil or just stand there looking down your nose?"

He shuffled to the next step and dropped down across from her, meanwhile emitting an odor like stale bedclothes.

"You okay?" she asked.

He stared at his feet.

"Cedro?"

He looked at her, his real eye as lifeless as the prosthesis. This close, his scars were more grotesque than ever. Dark, firm, rubbery.

She rested her hand on his knee. "You know you can always find another job. In fact I bet my husband could get you one in a minute."

He was studying his feet again.

"How about it?" She patted the knee. "Should I tell him to go ahead?"

He shook his head just enough to say no.

"Well then, how about if I talk to Pierre? You were his best painter. I bet he's already got regrets about letting you go. You know how he is with that temper."

Another minimal shake of the head.

"You don't want to talk. I understand." She crossed her arms on her knees and rested her chin there, staring out toward the yard and the jungle across the road. "It looks to me like you could use some help. Is there anyone I can call? A relative? Friend?"

No response.

"How about money? Do you have enough to manage till you get a job? I'd be glad to chip in." She gave him time to consider. "Anything, any thing you want or need, Cedro, I'll get it."

"Food for the strays," he finally answered.

"Tell me what they eat and I'll have it here tomorrow," she said, relieved there was at least one thing she could do to help.

Chapter Fifty

Curling Fog

After Mrs. Bohr drove away, Cedro sat on the step, aware of animals ranging about, unsure how they'd gotten there, unsure how he'd gotten here. How he'd had the energy. It must've been some need that urged him on. That must have been why he'd taken on the strays. He needed to be needed. Yes. That was it. And now those strays needed food. It was getting dark and they needed food and he'd better drag his bag of bones inside to get it for them.

But he was so tired. So tired of it all.

He watched the animals. Grew tired of watching them. Looked for the moon. Couldn't find the moon. Felt sad without it. So sad he couldn't think. Had he been thinking? Maybe not. Yes, he had. Oh, what did it matter. He was sad and the strays needed food and there was nothing to do but watch them eat and he didn't want to do that anymore.

Next thing he knew, the sun was nearly up and he was still on the step. Had he been there all night? He didn't know. He supposed so. It was all a crazy blur.

Stiff and cold, he pushed himself up and went inside for pet food.

Outdoors, he filled the three plastic bowls for the cats and the pie tin for the puppy. Then he sat down on the step again, waiting, petting the cats who dared get close, talking to them about how this was the hardest part but he was sure they'd manage. That he was sorry.

When he got up, the Siamese rubbed against his legs and purred and the gold kitten bounced down the steps in the direction of a rotting cabinet in the front yard.

Back inside, he went about things in a calm, orderly way, pouring a tall glass of water, getting the sleeping pills the doctor had prescribed out of the medicine cabinet, and carrying both to the bedroom. He'd forgotten a pen, so he went back to the kitchen and took one from the catch-all drawer.

In the bedroom, sitting on the side of the bed, he picked up the book of Keats's poetry from where it sat on the bedside table next to the pills and water. He'd bought it second-hand, and its pages were thick with notes and underlining. He'd felt a bond with the first owner whenever it flipped to certain well-worn pages that he, too, liked best. Now, he let those flipping pages find the verse he wanted, the one about being half in love with easeful death. After circling it, he set the opened book back on the table. Then he pulled the pillow up against the wall, lifted his legs to the bed, and sat back.

Outside, the sun glinted through the leaves. Inside, the room was dim and same as ever – both red and green paint bandanas on a peg on one of the dark walls that crowded him on all sides, the picture of someone else's kids in the mirror frame, the slight smell of gas from the kitchen.

He pushed down and unscrewed the cap from the bottle of pills he'd been saving. There was nothing now but to do it. Yet . . . he had a half-quart of vodka in the cupboard. That would make it easier.

He set the pills next to the book and got up, carrying the water to the kitchen, where he drained the glass and poured in vodka. Then he returned to the bed, where he took a long biting drink, and another, waiting for courage. Was this really what he wanted?

"Yes," he said aloud, and with that, began swallowing tablets, one at a time, quickly, gulping vodka with each. He counted twelve before sliding down on the bed to wait, unsure how it would come, but relieved.

When a mist, floating like fog on the river, began to blur the room, he tried to remember what he was waiting for, and when his head got so heavy he could barely hold it up, he tried to think why. Then Duardo and Adria began calling. They were in pain, and he was in pain too, his heart ramming his insides. But he had to get up to help them. It was so hard, trying to walk in the curling fog, trying to keep from falling. The roaring in his ears . . . .

Chapter Fifty-One

I'm Coming In

The cat on the hood of Cedro's car – this one Siamese – turned out to be friendly, and while he purred and squirmed, Margaret scratched behind his ear. A response that, she soon realized, was a mistake; he energetically returned her affection by writhing in and out between her legs on her way to the door of the trailer. Between the animal's contortions and the uneven path and the bags of pet food in her arms it would be a real feat if she made it without tripping.

When she did and, relieved, set the bags in the grass, she mounted the steps and rapped on the screen door. Today, she noted, the inside door was shut as well. She noted, too, that the animals' empty dishes were right there next to the steps. Which brought up the question of whether to go ahead and feed them. With Cedro looking so worn-out the night before it seemed like the least she could do. And with this friendly Siamese obviously hoping for something more than a friendly pat . . . .

As she opened the cat food, her feline friend took note, and by the time Margaret was filling the bowls, the cat was nosing in, cracking away on pellets that smelled like the air around Fred's grain elevator when they were loading soybeans.

Finished with the cats, she went back for the dog's food. By now, he was peeking out from the underbrush near the edge of the yard. "Come on," she coaxed, holding out a handful of soft chunks and moving closer, pinching her lips and making those squinchy sounds most dogs love.

His anxious eyes considered her. Then, tail between legs, he sneaked back to where he'd come from.

Well, there was only so much one could do, she thought, filling the pie tin sitting nearby before heading back to the stoop to rap on the door again, a little louder this time. It could be that Cedro was a heavy sleeper. Poor fellow, she hated to wake him. But she really did need to see how he was doing. Just as important, to make clear she cared.

She sat down on the steps to wait.

A mockingbird, pale gray and long-tailed, sang his song from the roof, then repeated it, while a newly-arrived black cat, wide-eyed and nose quivering, forgot his food for the moment and, like a lame cricket, chirped at the feathered visitor. Margaret watched the cat and bird for a while, then caught sight of a green lizard hopping from a leafy vine to one of the concrete stepping stones leading to where she sat. He pumped and pumped until, under his chin, a red flap of skin like a flag popped out.

She could see why Cedro might like it back here in the woods. Despite rubbish, it was a nice place, a spot away from the clamor of everyday life. And, aside from a spat between two batting, hissing tabbies, one of whom withdrew in order to find a friendlier breakfast companion, everything was agreeable.

But where was Cedro? With his car out front, he had to be around. Was he taking that needed shower? Still in bed?

She checked her watch. Maybe she was a bit early. Or, just as likely, hadn't rapped loud enough.

She got up and did it again, actually banging this time.

If only she had something to read. Was there anything in the car? How about that music catalog? Better than nothing. While at it she might check in the rear. Could be, early though it was, Cedro was busy back there. Even if he weren't, it would interesting to see the rest of the landlady's junkyard. A pink bathtub maybe?

It was only ten steps or so, not far, before she was making the two jogs at the end of the trailer and finding – surprise! – neither a junkyard nor Cedro, but a pretty spot with wind chimes, a gardenia in full and fragrant bloom, some red petunias, and a plastic chair. A little paradise away from yard clutter. All it lacked was another place to sit. Unfortunate fellow. So alone and so damaged. With those scars and the fake eye there must be more to his story. What could have happened? She could only imagine. Really, did she want to know? She had plenty on her own plate. Yet . . . he was so alone, and he'd confided in her as though she were a friend. Now she must make time for him. What with the screwed-up hearing aids and all, she'd been remiss these past weeks. But now that things were back to normal and she could communicate, she'd make amends. If Cedro hadn't given up on her.

With a renewed sense of purpose, she walked around to the front and was about to open her car door when reality hit. What was she thinking? Obviously, something wasn't right here. He'd been terribly distraught the night before and now he was nowhere in sight and wasn't answering her knock.

She raced back, opened the screen door and, shading her eyes with her hand, peeked in the window of the inside door. It may have seemed nosy, but he was so alone, and if something had happened . . . .

Yet, there was no sign of anything amiss, at least as far as she could see.

Even so, she pounded on the door, this time using the heel of her fist. If he'd missed the earlier raps on the screen, he surely wouldn't miss this hammering.

She waited. And waited.

Still no response.

What to do? She hated to be a nuisance, but . . . .

She tried the knob on the inside door. Not locked! Weird. And convenient.

Poking her head in, she called, "Cedro, it's Margaret Bohr. I don't mean to bother you, but I want you to know that I brought food for the animals." She listened. "Are you alright?"

A fly buzzed around the light above the sink and the kitchen smelled like gas. Not strong enough to worry, though.

She called louder. "Would you just come out for a minute? I'd really like to talk to you. I promise, I won't stay long."

She glanced around the kitchen. It was dark, but with light from above the sink and opened door, she could make out pet food bags and a vodka bottle on the counter. Something like a calendar as well.

What to do? Standing there leaning in, trying to make sense of things, she thought she heard creaking from somewhere and backed out.

A few moments later, calling, "I'm coming in, Cedro. I need to know you're okay," she stepped inside.

With the shade on the window drawn, it took a moment for her eyes to adjust. As they did she saw that just about everything was dark wood. Cupboards, table and chairs, walls, even the hallway. Not a long hallway, but as dim as an underground tunnel. And as she made her way through it, purposely scuffing her shoes on the linoleum, she thought she detected the somewhat sweet smell of vodka. Was he drunk? Had he decided to drown his sorrows?

No. It was worse than merely drowning sorrows, she realized as she looked in the bedroom doorway, where a broken glass, pill bottle, and Cedro lay on the floor.

Chapter Fifty-Two

We Should Have Known

When an ashen, sobbing Margaret dragged in, Fred helped her to the sofa and got some tissues and a glass of water. After she'd gotten a confused story out, he bombarded her with questions.

"Was he alive?"

"He was warm. I think he was breathing."

"You say he has no phone?"

She nodded, sniffling.

"So where'd you call from?"

"Landlady's."

"How long did it take the rescue squad?"

"I don't know."

"You mean you didn't wait?"

"No."

"You waited, in other words." He shook his head up and down, prompting the nod he expected.

"I watched them take him away," she wailed, her face a grimacing mask.

"Oh, God," he moaned. "How awful. We should have known. We should have done something." He sucked in, pinched his eyes shut. "I knew. That night he and I talked about the golf and I thought about giving him one of my tournament passes. I knew then."

"Please, Fred, not now." She blew her nose. "I let him down even more than you. There he'd be, waiting in the garage. He had no one."

"How about the crew?"

"Uh-uh. Not that I saw. The only person who seemed to try at all was Sharlene." Her eyes filled again, and she got up from the sofa, heading for the kitchen.

A minute later, Fred heard the rip of a paper towel. Then a loud thump.

Chapter Fifty-Three

Margaret, I Love You

At City Hospital in Baton Rouge later that afternoon, Fred sat across the desk from Dr. Brandt who, ceiling light reflecting off his shiny head, was studying Margaret's chart. Looking up, he asked if there were any more questions.

"Not at the moment," Fred replied.

The doctor's eyes, round and gray behind equally round glasses, met Fred's. "As I said earlier, your wife's coronary was an incident waiting to happen. I've been telling her that for the past year. With her blood pressure history and lack of exercise and tendency toward overweight, she was a prime candidate." He closed the folder and stood up.

Fred got up too.

"As to the surgery," the cardiologist went on, "it'll take hours. If you're hungry, there's a cafeteria down the hall and to the right, and the food's not that bad. But don't wander too far from the waiting room. Someone will come out with updates periodically." He shook Fred's hand. "I think everything will be okay. Dr. DeNoux is a good surgeon."

Back in the waiting room, Regina, in jeans and sandals, and Kurt, in starched white button-down and charcoal pants, were waiting. Nancy hadn't gotten in yet.

"What's goin' on?" Typical Kurt, sounding as though he were meeting a college buddy for a drink instead of reuniting with a traumatized dad in the throes of a medical emergency. Typical, too, in that he had a can of Coke in hand. "Noreen said to tell you Mom's in her prayers," he said.

"How *is* Mom?" Regina broke in, giving Fred an extended back-patting hug. Her long red hair smelled of pineapple.

"The doctor seems to think she'll be okay. After surgery, of course." Having not brushed or flossed, he tried not to breathe on her. As far as the rest, the tee shirt and shorts that no doubt reeked of this morning's jog in the heat and humidity, he could only hope his fitness-obsessed daughter understood.

"And how about my favorite dad?" She took his hands in hers and stood back, studying him.

"I'm fine," he said, embarrassed by the catch in his voice.

Her eyes narrowed. "You sure?"

Seeking diversion, he turned to Kurt. "It's amazing you found flights that came in about the same time."

"Yeah, amazing." Kurt glanced at the clock on the wall. "When will Mom's surgery start?"

"Any minute. It may have already," he added.

"You know – " Kurt sounding a little too cheerful. " – if anyone's got the will, it's Mom."

Regina nodded vigorously. "She's tough."

"So . . . what else did the doc say?" Kurt shoved his attaché aside and sat down, knees spread.

Fred told them about his talk with Dr. Brandt.

"How about the surgeon? Did you get a word with him?" Kurt reached for his Coke.

"Briefly. He was in a hurry to get started."

"How was it you were home when it happened?" He snapped open the can, and took a swig while Regina broke in with, "Was she scared?"

"Hold on, you two." Fred tried to smile. "First, it just happened to be one of those days when I go in late. And as far as her being scared, I don't know. She came to right away and I got her a nitroglycerin. I helped her to the sofa and she just lay there while I went between her and the balcony watching for the ambulance. We really didn't talk. And when we got here, they brought her in on a stretcher while I parked the car." He looked over at a woman and youngster heading for the couch in the corner, then turned back. "Finally, a couple hours ago, I got to see her, and she didn't seem terribly worried then. Of course, she may have been sedated."

He ran his tongue around his fuzzy mouth. "And now, if you two don't mind, I'd like to go look for a toothbrush before things start happening."

It turned out the gift shop was closed for inventory and there were no dental supplies in vending machines, so he bought some lifesavers and stopped in a restroom to gargle before freshening his breath with wintergreen. Standing at the mirror, bloodshot eyes staring back, he thought about what might be going on with Margaret. It probably would've been better had he avoided that pamphlet in the waiting room that described the procedure – how the sternum was split and cranked apart, and all the rest – heart-lung machine to blood vessel graft.

The question of how much damage the doctor might at this very moment be finding sent him, post haste, back to the lounge, where Regina said that the first report from the operating room was in. Margaret's chest was open.

And so the late afternoon inched on. Next report was less terse, a little encouraging: "She's on the heart-lung machine. So far, so good."

Meanwhile, hands of the waiting room clock maintained their circular trek, dragging seconds into minutes and minutes into hours while the television, out of reach near the ceiling and tuned to rebroadcast of local news, was relentless. Over and over the mayor of New Orleans bit his lip before trying to explain the latest crime spree and the silly-sweet anchorwoman pouted preciously when the weatherman predicted rain and the sportscaster asked questions that evoked bleeped words from the Saints coach.

Lucky Regina. She'd fallen asleep, a cat mystery open on her lap and pages fluttering each time anyone passed. Hoping to follow suit, Fred slipped off his sneakers and stretched his hairy legs across the coffee table before pinching eyes shut and trying to picture a scene with cows, water, and trees. Instead, a situation in the operating room – shocked expressions, emergency beepers, doctors working frantically to restart an obstinate heart – wouldn't yield its unreasonable hold.

Why was this taking so long? he wondered, opening his eyes and looking over at Kurt, near the windows studying papers from his briefcase while twirling a tuft of wavy hair. That twirling, just one of his mother's mannerisms. The physical stuff – heavy eyebrows and dark eyes and hair – were from himself. If anything happened to Margaret, at least he'd have these kids to keep some part of their combined legacy alive. And to haunt him for the rest of his life.

What seemed like endless hours later, when Dr. DeNoux finally walked into the waiting room, Fred felt like his own heart was about to hammer its way out of his chest. "Quintuple bypass, and everything went pretty much as expected," the surgeon announced before sitting down and going on about the extent of damage.

"What I really want to know," Fred said when the doctor had finished and asked if they had questions, "is if she'll get back to her old self."

A frown clouded the taut, scrubbed face. "One can never say for sure. What I can say is that at this point I see no reason why she won't." He smiled a toothy smile that seemed artificial both in shiny whiteness and authenticity, then got up and extended his hand. It was cold, like the man himself. Fred hoped that meant he was one of those single-minded professionals who cared about nothing but his stock in trade.

A while later, hands clasped in front like mourners approaching a casket – having left luggage and the rest behind the receptionist's desk – the three sidled into the recovery room. Fred, first thing, stretched across the tubes and electronic gear to get a better look. What he witnessed twisted his insides into one huge knot. His rosy-cheeked, feisty soulmate was suddenly old and frail, eyelids grey and face ashen, body collapsed and flat. And her arm was like an icicle.

"Is this," he whispered to his kids, "what the nurse meant when she said your mother was waking up?"

Kurt shrugged. "Apparently so."

Fred silently sized things up. As bad as he'd expected, this was even worse. It was apparent that the life of the only woman he'd ever loved, his helpmate and kindred spirit, was hanging by a thread. It was also no wonder the surgeon had been eva-sive about prognosis. Margaret's survival was in the balance and the downside weighed a ton.

Eyes filling – and despite lifelong antagonism toward reli-gion – he said an awkward silent prayer, promising that if she lived – if *only* she lived – he'd make up for every hurtful thing he'd ever said or done.

When he moved aside, Kurt took his place, leaning in close, studying his mother. "The surgery's over, Mom, and you did just great," he said in a cheery voice.

She can't hear you," Fred croaked, tears starting.

Kurt wafted his hand across her face. "But her eyes are open and she's following."

Fred pushed in, waving his own fingers in front of eyes that moments before had been dead to the world.

Like crawling slugs, her pupils followed.

"Margaret," he whispered, voice ragged. "I love you."

Chapter Fifty-Four

I Been Feedin' 'Em

Cedro detected voices and opened his eyes, then let them flutter shut. "He's waking," he heard as he tried to twist from the blazing light.

Comprehension rolled in, and he forced his eyes open again. This bed with bars, this thing in his arm, these moving figures in blue meant only one thing: this was neither the hereafter nor sweet oblivion. This was a hospital, and he was in a drab, curtained cubicle. To his left, at the fringe of what he could see, sat a screen with wavy, colored lines and numbers. On that side, as well, a fluid-filled see-through bag hung from a pole. The tube that snaked from it seemed to be attached to a needle in his arm.

"What is your name?" he heard. "How old are you?"

He answered, his head pounding and his throat rough as sandpaper.

The hours following his unhappy waking were long and dreary, spent either deep in sleep or gazing down at his own furry legs sticking out from a hospital gown covered in maroon squares and circles and dots. When tea, toast, and crackers were delivered on a tray he tried to refuse, but the staff insisted. In between times he listened as the fellow on the other side of the curtain forced up sticky mucus with a harsh, gutteral blast while the nurse whooped, "Wonderful, Mr. Berthelot."

It was the same nurse who at this moment was pushing aside the curtain to let in a young man in a white coat who, fumbling with a stethoscope about to fall out of his pocket, was saying, "Cedro, I'm Dr. Shellstone. I don't know if you remember – I was in ICU yesterday."

Cedro grabbed the end of the sheet from the pile at the foot of the bed and pulled it up.

The doctor smiled, then leaned in, studying his forehead, gently passing his hand over the blue knob Cedro had earlier noticed in the bathroom mirror. "I see your goose egg is coming down. Good news. I bet that's hurting a bit." He mouthed each word as though speaking to a child. "You were lucky, you know. The lump is no big deal. Just a contusion. But if you'd gone a little longer before the stomach pump . . . ." He crossed his arms and gazed down at him, a softness in both voice and close-set eyes as he went on. "So you've got problems, huh man?" He reached down and patted Cedro's shoulder. "The unfortunate thing is – " He sighed. " – we can't do much for you here. But that doesn't mean we're abandoning you." He pulled a chair over and sat down. "What we plan to do is transfer you to a place that's geared to issues like yours. From what I understand, they'll start you on antidepressants right away." Crossing one knee over the other he sat back, as though planning to stay a while. "There's just one thing you'll have to do. Nothing big. It's just that you'll need some clothes. Toiletries and money too. So what we want from you is the name of someone we can call to bring that stuff to the facility where you'll be staying."

By next morning he was settled into what felt to him like a home for the *criminalmente loco.* He'd never been in one, but it was what, if he'd ever thought about it, he'd imagine dangerous, unstable people wandering around in. It was the window in his room that really convinced him. Such an innocent-looking window until he raised the green curtain and saw the bars. Yet, beyond those bars was a basketball court. Well, being an athlete didn't protect against being mean and crazy.

As far as the accommodations? The twin bed looked comfortable, shelves and closet were more than he'd ever need, oak furniture was nicer than anything in his trailer. If this was the place he'd get help, it was as good as any. Now if all the helpers could just take those silly grins off their faces.

But no, in walked another. Some kind of aide. Sappy smirk, voice fluttering, "I've got a surprise for you." Next thing, he thought, she'd offer him three guesses.

But she didn't. She did, however, make a grand gesture, arm swinging and hand swooping, toward Sharlene, behind her. Green dress, brown shoes, all arms and legs, and loaded down with a cardboard box topped by a bouquet of wilting marigolds, Sharlene's round face puckered and her thin lips quivered as she whimpered, "I'm so glad to see you. I missed you. Your animals miss you too."

"You've seen them?" The cats and dog hadn't entered his mind since he'd asked Mrs. Bohr to bring food for them.

"I been feedin' 'em. Sure. Every day." She seemed to be in control now and smiled a little. "An' if you don't get home pretty soon, I'm gonna steal every one of 'em."

Chapter Fifty-Five

Holy Joes

Pierre stood in front of Bohrs' house watching two workmen unload a roll of rusty reinforcement mesh from the bed of a dusty black Ram pickup. It was miserably hot, and the sweaty odor from one or both was powerful. But far be it from Pierre to complain. He was just thankful they were here. How Ernie Douga, the concrete subcontractor, had missed the uproar over Cedro Diaz was hard to figure. It seemed like word had gotten to all the other cursed creeps working for Pierre. Crew, subconstractors – all had stopped work in protest of his treatment of Diaz. Diaz, of all people! A half-blind Cuban Pierre never should have hired was to blame for this catastrophic mess. Scaffolding in place, but no painter. Shutters and window screens and hardware and thresholds and pet doors and air conditioners in the garage, but no one to install them. Or to install the mirrors, shower doors, and light fixtures waiting in the house. Not to mention the inside painting yet to be done and the finish work on the fireplace. Where would it all end?

Not likely here and now, Pierre suspected, as a junker rattling like a coaster wagon on clam shells, spun to a halt next to the fire hydrant. It was, of course, Sharlene Wilkes' Volkswagen Beetle, and she was soon rolling out of the nasty red bug, ski pole legs in cut-offs leading the way.

"Morning," he called, and glanced at his watch. "You sure are punctual. Ten a.m. on the nose."

Gawky, self-conscious, she approached.

"Now, what's this business about a – " He suddenly remembered Douga, there within hearing. " – time off?"

She didn't argue terminology. On the phone the day before she'd used the word *strike*. Face to face she sounded less confident.

"Well – " She studied her ratty black sandals and, though it was steamy in the sun and her face was red and damp with sweat, hugged herself. " – you remember I told you I had a brain aneurysm?" Her voice was husky.

"I didn't remember exactly what it was, but I knew you had something wrong." To put it mildly. Case in point: her bringing it up now.

"I think the Lord was watching that day the doctor went in and fixed it. He coulda let me die, but instead He guided the surgeon's hand and I came out okay." She looked at him long and hard, as though what she'd said meant something, then flicked her small, deep-set eyes in the direction of the river road and levee. "Lately I been wonderin' what it was God saved me for." She passed the back of her hand across the nasty scar on her forehead, brushing aside wisps of stray, mousy hair while giving off a spicy scent. "It sure wasn't to go around lying and cheating. It had to be for somethin' better than that."

The scrape of metal on metal as the two concrete men removed a roll of mesh from the truck bed distracted her for a moment. Then she went on. "That's why I'm not gonna do it anymore, no matter if my kids do go without. And the rest of 'em aren't either. That's what they asked me to tell you."

"The rest? Lying and cheating? Slow down," he said under his breath before motioning her over to his Corvette, parked far enough away that Douga and his men were out of range.

"Now," he said, stopping next to the car, "what's – "

"The rest of the crew and the subcontractors," she broke in, words now coming at breakneck speed, like she'd memorized the spiel and was antsy to get through it, "we got to talkin' about it after Cedro's recent – " She apparently couldn't call it for what it was, and shrugged. " – and decided it was time we stood up for somethin' instead of just pretending that we didn't know what was goin' on."

"Give me a clue as to what you're trying to tell me, okay?" As if he didn't already know from her phone call that it was Cedro's firing that was freaking everyone out.

"You've been profiting at your customers' expense and we've been making like we didn't know. Cedro was the only one who admitted it. He told us he didn't think it was right."

"That I profit off building a house? What do you think I'm in business for?"

"Profits are one thing. What you're doin' is something else." She gave him a drawn-out, accusing look. "You know what I'm talkin' about."

"I'm totally clueless. But what's this got to do with walking off the job anyway? You're getting paid what we agreed and – "

"Now that Cedro – "

"Oh, I get it. I've done the same myself. When bad things happen to friends, I feel sorry and make them out to be saints."

"We're not turnin' Cedro into a saint, even though what he said did have a lot of truth. It's just that up until now he was the only one who stood up for anything. Now we decided to stand up for something."

She stared down at her sandals, right foot working the sandy soil into a little mound. Finally, after a deep and apparently fortifying breath, she met his eyes. "You know, we think you fired Cedro because he questioned your tricks."

"I'll have you know I fired him because he was gabbing about me – bad stuff and with a client – behind my back. Benny even heard it. No boss has to put up with that."

"Benny feels real bad about tellin' you, too. Now he's blamin' himself for what happened to Cedro, including . . . well . . . everything."

"He shouldn't. The Cuban was making trouble. Not that I like that he tried to kill himself, but it just proves he's even wackier than I thought."

The concrete workmen were pounding stakes into the ground now and Pierre looked over. "Anyway, no point in rehashing that," he said, turning back. "What's important is to get things back on line."

"We're not getting things back on line till you stop the tricks."

"Tricks!" He laughed, but gently. "You make me out to be some kind of monster when all I'm trying to do is make a living. And in the deal, you're getting jobs. Do you want to go on welfare?"

"Welfare's better than selling our souls."

"Dear me. You do think I'm the devil. How can I convince you otherwise?" Brain on overdrive, he deliberated. This group was by far the cheapest labor he'd ever find. He couldn't afford to lose them. What he needed was something to get their minds off Cedro.

And he knew what it was. A raise. Some of them had been beating around the bush for just that for a while now, and when he hired them he'd hinted at one sooner or later. This would be sooner than he'd like, but what else was there to distract them? Besides, it didn't have to be megabucks. Just a morale-booster. Something to sweeten the pot.

"This is what I'll do," he said. "If you're all here ready to work at eight tomorrow morning, I'll have paychecks in my pocket that include raises for each and every one of you."

"If you think that'll change our minds, you're whistlin' Dixie."

"Well then. What if I try to do better?"

She eyed him suspiciously. "What does that mean?"

"Let's put it this way – from now on, any time you see something that bothers you, let me know and I'll take care of it."

He wasn't exactly sure what he'd just promised and he was quite sure she wasn't.

"I suppose we can give it a try," she said.

Which brought up the question of whether he could have gotten by without raises. Too late to think about that, though. At least she hadn't approached nor had he made any promises about rehiring the Cuban.

"Trust me," he said, raising his right hand as though swearing an oath. "I'll try to do better. We'll get this thing straightened out yet. I guess I just wasn't thinking."

Or at least not thinking his workers would suddenly turn into a bunch of Holy Joes who were going to make profit even harder to come by.

Chapter Fifty-Six

Another Try

Weeks after she'd walked in with the box and wilting marigolds and the same number of weeks since he'd started the anti-depressants and "behavioral and stress management training," Cedro was sitting on his bed dressed in plaid shirt and khaki pants waiting for Sharlene. Everything was packed for the ride home. He'd been told he was well on the road to recovery. Which didn't mean, the therapists explained, they were going to release him and let him flounder on his own. Their plan was for him to go on taking the pills at home while coming back to the clinic for group sessions. With PTSD – which was what they said he had – this was accepted treatment.

As far as feeling better, he supposed that was true. He'd talked a lot about his horrible past – all of it this time – and maybe he didn't feel as anxious when he thought about it. But the memories were still there, no doubt about that. And even as he packed his things and said his thank-yous and good-byes, he wasn't sure that all the therapy and medication had helped that much.

Yet, on this day, walking out of the facility with Sharlene and feeling the sun and hearing the birds, he thought he'd give it another try. "You call this car a beetle?" he asked, trying to sound interested and positive.

"Some people do," she answered. "I call it a roach. My red roach." She laughed. "And since it's gotten hot sittin' here in the sun, let's open the windows and cool the dirty bug off."

She was right about the heat, but he wasn't sure if it was the temperature or a smell like sweaty tennis shoes that made her hurry with the windows. Anyway, that smell soon blew away – or he got used to it – and the wind tossing his hair every which way felt good. Before he knew it, the one-story brick building with window bars and basketball court was out of sight and he and Sharlene were on their way out of the business park in the direction of the expressway, leaving further and further behind those nice people who'd tried so hard to help him. They'd become friends. Better friends than anyone on Pierre's crew.

Except, of course, Sharlene who, as she drove, updated him on what had happened while he'd been gone. Most shocking was Mrs. Bohr's heart attack. He hoped he hadn't been the cause but suspected from what Sharlene said that he'd been a big factor. It must have been a shock, her finding him that way. But he hadn't meant it to happen. Still, what had he meant to happen? He'd asked her to bring pet food and she wouldn't have wanted, rain and all, to leave it outside the trailer. She would have knocked and wondered why, with his car out front, he didn't answer.

"I didn't know she had heart trouble," he said. "Has she recovered?"

"No word on how she is, so I suppose she's doin' all right. What is it they say? No news, good news." Sharlene slouched

back in her seat. "Sure has been different without her poppin'
in at the site."

They were on the twelve-mile bridge crossing Lake
Pontchartrain now, and gulls swooped and squawked overhead.
Sharlene silently pointed as one dove into the water and brought
up a small fish. "You know, Cedro," she said, briefly facing him,
"that was a close call you had. You really scared us. We felt so
bad about you and so mad at Pierre that we even stopped work."

"What do you mean?"

"The crew walked out. Left Pierre high and dry. And
you'll never guess what I did." She sent a crafty glance his way.
"I negotiated a deal with Pierre, just like one of those union
bigwigs. Told him we wouldn't come back till he stopped his
hanky-pank. You know, the stuff that drove you mad." Brown
hair flying, elbow out the window, she glanced at him again.
"And you'll be glad to hear that he vowed to do better."

"You think he will?"

"I think . . . I don't know. It hasn't been that long. Hard
to tell." She shifted in her seat. "But how about you? What will
you . . . Oh heck, we'll talk about that later."

She was quiet as they headed west, turning off at the
exit to the town of Oakview where, in the cypress swamp to
the right, an alligator and egret shared a log. A few minutes
later, having turned onto the river road, the route he knew so
well, he was feeling like he'd been gone for months. The crape
myrtles at the entrance to the courthouse were covered in red
and pink flowers and the snowball stand not far from the ferry
landing had opened for summer and had a line in front.

"I've come up with the most fantastic idea," she finally
said, breaking the silence. "Want to hear?"

"Sure," he said. He was beginning to think she, too, had
taken a happy pill. The difference was, hers had worked.

"I've got to expand on it, but I've got this plan that just might turn us guys into super home builders." She checked his reaction, then went on, outlining the most far-fetched scheme he'd ever heard and finishing right before she shifted into second and made the turn into the drive where, as usual, Mrs. Willis was on her porch next to the washing machine. After asking if he'd like to stop and say hello and his firm "no," she told him it didn't matter anyway; she'd informed the landlady he'd be back today so she wouldn't wonder what was going on.

"The place looks pretty good, don't you think?" she said, pulling in in front of the trailer.

He nodded. "Who cut the grass?"

"One of us from the crew," she said, getting out. "We been takin' turns."

After flipping the driver's seat forward and getting the box out of the back, she handed it to him, and he followed to the steps where, holding the screen door open with her hip as she unlocked the main door, she explained how when she'd first come to pick up clothes for his stay in the facility she'd found the key on the kitchen counter.

Inside, he set the box on the table and she flicked on the light before whirling around, arms wide, like a kid showing off a clean room. "What do you think?" she said, smile so big a missing tooth showed in back.

"Looks like new paint." He tried to sound really pleased.

"Right. We brightened it up a bit."

"You shouldn't have."

"We wanted to."

"We?"

"Benny and me. And lookee here." She opened the refrigerator. Same old refrigerator, but clean. The burned-out bulb had been replaced too. What she seemed to really want to show off, though, was the food. "Milk, cantaloupe, lettuce, tomatoes, margarine, lunchmeat, coffee. And – " She slammed the door and stepped over to the counter. " – Ta da!" With a dramatic swoop of the arm she pointed out a narrow loaf in cellophane. "Special sour dough from the bakery. You like sour dough?"

"How much do I owe you?"

"No worry. The whole crew pitched in. Not a big drain on anybody. If you don't like the groceries, though, you'll have to blame me. I picked 'em out this morning."

He felt tears coming.

"You okay?" She touched his arm. "How 'bout a sandwich and coffee. I'll fix it."

"Thanks," he said. "I'm not hungry."

"In that case, why don't we just turn around and head over to my place. The kids would love to see you. My mom's there too."

He shook his head. "I'm tired. I need a nap."

"You could sleep at my house." Eyes wide, eager nod.

He shook his head again.

"Well then, I'm off." She turned toward the door. "But don't get used to me bein' gone. I'll be back in an hour or so."

"Please, Sharlene, it's not – "

"I know, I know."

She pushed the screen door open and, lifting her skirt, hopped down the steps.

Chapter Fifty-Seven

The Battle

When Margaret's endotracheal tube, the big one in her mouth, had been removed, Fred asked nurse Huguet why his wife could do nothing but whisper. He wondered if the tube or the surgery could have damaged her vocal cords.

"No worry" was the reply. "Her cords are fine. She'll be talking like normal before you know it."

But Nurse Huguet had been wrong. When Margaret's voice came back a day later it still wasn't normal. It reminded Fred of one of those weak and whiny stops on the organ she played at Holy Church. Poor thing. He could only imagine what she felt like. Throat scraped, sternum cracked, arteries stitched. Yet, though he felt sorry for her, especially when the nurse slammed her on the back to make her cough up the mess in her lungs and she moaned "I'll split apart," he also was grateful for her complaints. She was back to her spunky self.

Then progress slowed. Really slowed. "What's wrong with her?" he'd asked the RN the day she was scheduled for release from the hospital. He was standing at the nurses' station down the hall from her room. "She's not coming out of it. She's depressed. I can hear it in her voice. Are you sure she's ready to come home?"

"In fact that's where she'll shake the doldrums more quickly," was the response. "And, frankly, if you want my opinion, she's a little self-indulgent. I'd treat her with less patience if I were you. She tends to feel sorry for herself." At this point the nurse actually winked. "But then, that's just my opinion."

It was easy for a young, healthy individual to criticize an older, sickly one, he thought at the time. Nurse Huguet was really overstepping bounds. She had no right judging his wife, and even if Margaret did seem a little self-pitying, he wasn't going to treat her with less patience. He'd made a promise in the recovery room.

But now, three weeks (that seemed like an eternity) since dear mate had been released from the hospital, that selfsame mate was really starting to get on his nerves. It was Tuesday. He'd just gotten home from work and, having changed from sport coat and tie to khakis and polo shirt, was getting supper. Cheerless queen bee, still in her pink piqué nightgown, was again glued to the spot at the kitchen table that had been her throne since the day he'd begun acting as both cook and bottle-washer. "So you're not feeling any better today," he muttered once she'd answered "no" to his daily query about physical wellness. (Even this never-ending inquiry about her health was getting old by then.)

Her follow-up response on that Tuesday was equally consistent with her recent demeanor: the forlorn wag of the head, the slouch, the cupping of chin in one hand while using the other to separate a greasy clump from her mat of white cowlicks and twist it around her finger. That twisting being a habit that though once endearing – back when her hair was shiny and clean and she was thinking deeply about something other than herself – was, like everything else, getting very old.

When she finally whimpered, "I just don't have any energy" was when he let loose. Not in outright violence, but with enough vigor to demonstrate frustration and, as well, release it. What he did was fling the utensil drawer open, seize the vegetable brush, and then slam the drawer shut before going on to attack the biggest of the baking potatoes – her favorite Yukon Golds, of course – that he'd gone a mile out of his way to pick up on the way home. After first pelting the potato with a blast from the tap, he scoured and scrubbed till the skin was a mere patch of yellowish-brown. Meanwhile, in a voice seething with sarcasm, he told her that maybe she should follow the doctor's advice and force herself.

"Force myself to what?" she asked mid hair twirl.

"You know. Get some exercise." He shoved the cruddy, clabbered breakfast dishes aside, making room next to the sink for the potatoes. The clattering perfectly fit his mood.

"I'm just not up to that yet," she said, adding a sigh as though even the thought exhausted her.

"When do you think you'll be – " His voice took on a mocking tone. " – up to it?"

She was still slouching and twirling, but – something new – looking mildly amused. "Bad day?" she said.

"Why do you ask?" By now he'd finished with the potatoes, having set them in the microwave and set the time.

"You're cranky."

"I wasn't cranky till I left work," he said, switching on the right front burner and banging the frying pan down on it before shooting the pan with cooking spray. "Then after checking on progress at that fabulous house we're building (which you haven't shown interest in for weeks) and driving all the way over to Rouse's grocery to get the damn potatoes you love, I come home to breakfast dishes and unmade bed and laundry and cat litter – "

"And me, right?"

"You're the one who said it."

Now that he was pretty sure she sensed his frustration, he let up on histrionics and calmly opened the refrigerator, taking out the chicken breasts and slipping them into the pan. When the oil sputtered he turned down the heat.

"You just don't understand," she said in that feeble voice that evoked in him not sympathy but annoyance.

"That's for sure – " He was struggling to maintain calm. " – and with each passing day I'm more confused. Judging from what the doctor says, you should be doing more than lying in bed."

"He doesn't understand either. Besides, I don't lie in bed all the time."

Which was true. The kitchen chair was another favorite, especially while, as now, he was slaving over her food. Slaving and at this very moment again feeling intense frustration as he beat the bushes for a space to set the cutting board so he could finish up with the broccoli. "Why in hell . . . . what do you do all day?"

Swearing had always been verboten in their home, and the reaction was immediate. First a dumbstruck look. Then the screech of her chair as she pushed it back before bracing herself and getting up. Following that, and with a few brittle and cautious steps, she was on her way.

"Where are you going?" he called as the scuff of her slippers trailed off.

Twenty minutes later, when he sat down to eat, he didn't bother to call her. She'd be back. She never missed a meal. In fact, right now, what was that? Shuffling on the steps? He cupped an ear rearward. Like he'd expected, on her way already. So like her – never mad for long. Especially with baked spuds involved. When she limped back in she'd likely whine about being starved. Likely expect an apology, too. Which she wouldn't get. He'd meant what he said. It was high time she faced truth and showed some pluck.

The scuffing stopped. Maybe it hadn't been slippers. Could've been Wolfgang scratching fleas.

He got up and walked over, again cupping his ears, this time toward the upstairs bedroom. A swishing sound. Or was it sloshing? Perhaps she was cleaning up. At any rate, still avoiding him.

So what? Big deal. He sat down at the table and sliced into his sauteed chicken.

When he was done with supper he checked the clock on the microwave. Nearly seven. Unusual for her to stay mad so long. Of course, she might've fallen asleep staring at the ceiling.

Should he take a look?

He began sneaking up the steps, then considered the impact of her catching sight of him, how she'd know he was concerned about her and how that would diminish the impact of his words. Concern was what had gotten them to this point. Too much concern on his part. There could be no backtracking, no sugar-coating now. Better that she deal with the truth, that she know that he'd expected better from her. She was, after all, of hardy Scandinavian stock. Take her dad. He, too, had suffered a heart attack. But did he give up? Not on your life. As soon as he was able, he headed right back to his bakery, where he worked long hours – and gratefully – till he finally succumbed to a stroke. (On his way to work, no less.)

Fred took a few steps back, then retreated totally.

It was after he'd finished loading the dishwasher and was beginning to scrub the frying pan that it occurred to him that something had happened. True, she may have just fallen asleep. But without eating supper? Very unlike her. Best he check.

He set the pan on the drain board, dropped the chore boy into the dishwater, grabbed a kitchen towel, and headed for the steps. Upstairs, approaching the bedroom, he heard that same swish, scratch, rasp . . . . whatever to call it. One moment quite distinct, the next fuzzy.

The bedroom door squeaked just a little as he pushed in. But she didn't notice. She was sitting there on the floor, back to him, shoe box alongside, pink piqué nightgown in a ball near the foot of the bed. In its place on her drooping body, the shiny salmon and blue running suit he'd picked out for her last birthday. It swished and whooshed as – perspiring, panting, ashen cheeks sagging – she intently worked on the shoelace of one of the cross-trainers that had been part of his gift.

He stepped into the room and around to the side just as she finished, sat back, and . . . clutched her chest? The pained expression on her face said it all.

What in God's name had he been thinking? That scarred heart of hers wasn't even ready for the simple exertion of get-ting dressed.

"Margaret," he said gently.

She still didn't hear him. Probably had taken her hearing aids out.

"Margaret," he said again, this time louder. "I'm sorry. I was wrong. Come on back to the kitchen and I'll warm supper."

She wiped her damp face on her sleeve, tugged a sock on, and picked up the other shoe. With each move a small, pained grunt.

He stepped closer. Touched her shoulder. Small, defenseless shoulder.

"What are you doing?" she gasped, surprised.

"First tell me what you're doing."

"I'm gonna get some exercise," she panted. By now she'd loosened the lace on the other cross-trainer and was battling to work her foot into it.

He gestured toward the window. "But it's dark out."

"There are . . . plenty of lights . . . around the apartment buildings." Her breathing was labored.

"But I don't think you're ready for exercise."

He thought he detected a slight roll of the eyes, but went on even so. "Here. At least let me help you." He came around front and dropped to his knees, setting the dishtowel on the rug before reaching for the shoe.

Glaring, she held on.

He got up, chastened, and stood there watching every excruciating move till she was done and heading for the steps. Then he followed, close, hands reaching out ready to save her, as she pumped and wheezed her way down.

After the front door latched behind her he ran to the balcony and stood there waiting for her to come around the corner of the building and cross the parking lot below. When she did, it was like watching a seasick sailor fighting a gale. A gale he now felt like he was part of.

Chapter Fifty-Eight

Dinner

"This dinner will show Cedro how much I care," Margaret told Fred, "and I want to do it all myself. No help, understand? You did your part by getting him a job. Now it's my turn."

Her "turn" was undertaken with incredible enthusiasm, that was sure. But whether Cedro appreciated the effort was debatable. From the moment he and Sharlene walked in, his response was puzzling. Perhaps medication was to blame. Or Cedro may have still just been depressed. Whatever the case, it was hard for Fred to even imagine him caring enough to dress for the occasion. But in navy pants and neat striped shirt, he'd somehow managed.

It took some orchestrating on Margaret's part, once they were in the living room, to get everyone where they belonged. Wolfgang needed to be shooed out of his spot in the easy chair to the bedroom upstairs, to which the cat and her litter had already been moved. That accomplished, it was Sharlene who sat in the dog's chair while Cedro and Fred took the sofa. For herself Margaret brought in a kitchen chair. A little uncomfortable, Fred suspected, but it made for easy access to the kitchen.

She already had the appetizers on the coffee table and, now in their designated locations, Fred, Sharlene, and Margaret snacked on pita wedges dipped in hummus, potato skins made with nonfat "butter" granules, and melon balls rolled in lean ham. As well, the three sipped Chardonnay. Cedro, because of antidepressants, nursed a glass of water and, as far as Fred could tell, ate nothing.

It soon was apparent that Sharlene was a talker. Her kids – the girl was about to celebrate her eleventh birthday and the boy was eight – kept her busy. Especially the girl, who played softball in summer and soccer in cooler months. Tonight their "maw-maw," who spoiled them with homemade chocolate malts and nonstop card games, was staying with them.

When Sharlene took a breath to dip a couple pita wedges in hummus and place them on her plate, Margaret broke in for a word with Cedro about his strays. And it truly was little more than a word from Cedro. "How are they?" "Fine." "Is the puppy getting friendlier?" "No." The latter response evoking a comment from Margaret as to what sort of abuse had made the pup so afraid as well as if anyone could ever earn the animal's trust. Then Sharlene told a story about a dog she'd had as a kid that turned out to be so clingy and needy that her mother dubbed him "Underdog."

After that, Fred sneaked in with a compliment about Cedro's work at Welbourne as well as a couple questions geared to luring him from his silence, one about mileage from elevator to mobile home and the other, whether the grain smell bothered him. "That odor," he said, narrowing his eyes as though addressing a most profound issue, "how would you describe it? Malodorous? Cloying?"

Cedro shrugged, and Sharlene offered "Stinky."

As far as mileage from home to work, Cedro didn't know (and wasn't much interested) in what it was.

By the time they'd moved to the table for dinner, Fred was convinced that trying to include Cedro in any sort of conversation was futile. At the same time he hoped the unfortunate Cuban's behavior wasn't too disappointing to Margaret. She'd really put her heart into the evening, from ambience to edibles, having draped the chrome-legged table in white linen, drawn the vertical blinds against parking lot lights and activity, and switched off the shiny brass ceiling fixture, using candles instead. She'd even made sure the kitchen table wouldn't wobble by taping a matchbook under its shortest leg. Beyond that, she'd contrived a sort of buffet, placing a bouquet of yellow roses on a big linen napkin on the kitchen counter as near as possible to where they would eat. On it were placed all the delectables.

And those delectables! Truly befitting of the word. Shrimp broiled to a turn, moist inside but with a bit of crunch. Green onion/caraway brown rice, both attractive and tasty. A spinach salad with lots of cherry tomatoes and red onion tossed in a light honey/mustard dressing she'd concocted herself. And yeasty wheat rolls she'd picked up hot from Roussel's bakery and now kept warm in the oven.

As she flitted from stove to counter, serving plates piled high, Fred marveled at her transformation. Had it really been mere weeks since he'd confronted her and she'd staggered off across the parking lot in a swishy running suit and spotless cross-trainers? She already looked better. Beneath that overblouse and full madras skirt was a body in transition.

When she finally sat down, Margaret said how happy she'd be when they were in their house, even if that house was less than perfect, a statement that was a perfect launching pad for Sharlene to defend what she admitted was a questionably proficient crew and subcontractors who, she interjected vehemently, were redeemed by "good hearts." Those hearts being another launchpad for Sharlene, this time into a play-by-play of the job shutdown she'd implemented.

"I had no idea you had shut our place down" Fred said when she'd finished, which wasn't precisely true and he knew it. At one point he'd wondered where everyone was, then decided they must have been called to another site.

Margaret, at the counter uncorking another Chardonnay, broke in with "I *have* noticed a change in attitude. Even Joseph's behaving," and that inspired Sharlene, holding out her glass in anticipation of a refill, to add more to her shutdown account. "I was really hopeful at first," she explained. "Everyone was doing their best and things were lookin' up. But before you know it, there goes Pierre pullin' his old tricks. And the raise he promised? A couple bucks a week. What's that worth?" Her glass clinked as it met Margaret's bottle. "We're fed up. All of us. But what can we do? No decent employer will hire us unless we have decent training and we'll get no decent training with Pierre."

"Difficult," Margaret agreed, refilling Fred's glass before turning to Cedro and asking if he'd like more water. When he shook his head, she topped off her own Chardonnay.

"But I got a plan," Sharlene went on, her small, deep-set eyes taking on a bit of a glint as she impaled a shrimp with her fork and took her time finishing it off. "I need help to follow through with it, but if I can get that help I'm pretty sure I can make things better for the whole bunch. Actually, less for me than for the rest. Bein' a cleaner, I don't need that much trainin'."

"Enough prologue." Fred chuckled. "Let's hear your plan."

"Okay. This is the way it goes." She studied the ceiling as though for inspiration. "What I want to do is – " Facing Fred. " – get a fund goin'."

"A fund," he repeated.

"Right. I want to get local businesses to contribute to a fund that would get job trainin' for the guys I work with. You know, I saw a story in the magazine my church puts out that described somethin' like that. Really, it was more than a fund, though. It was . . . like . . . a program. They called it 'Learning House'?" She glanced around as though expecting a response from someone else who'd heard of it. Seemingly satisfied no one had, she continued. "The money they collected – I mean, it was a lot – was used part to pay for land, part for supplies, and part for teachers from a vocational school who were hired to train the students, who were guys like Pierre has workin' for him. The way it worked, money was collected from local businesses. Donations too, like from manufacturers and suppliers. You know, goods. And then the students, gettin' paid from the fund and bein' supervised by the teachers, built a house on the land. When it was done, they auctioned it off and the profits from that house paid for the same thing all over again – land, teachers, workers, supplies. It just keeps going, new workers gettin' good skills and good jobs, and people who buy the houses makin' out 'cause the houses are well-built and don't cost a fortune." She leaned back in her chair, folding her hands on the skirt of her washed-out green dress, and beamed. "So. What do you think?"

What naivete, what unabashed ignorance, was Fred's silent response. Sharlene had no idea how hard it would be to raise money and encourage donations and then get teachers from the nearest vocational school twenty miles away to come up to Acadi. The whole thing was impossible.

"Have you figured how long it would take to get this organized?" he said carefully, tossing a secret glance Margaret's way, thinking he'd find mutual skepticism there. But she was waiting for Sharlene's answer.

"A while, I s'pose." She speared the last shrimp on her plate and did away with it. "God, these shrimp are great."

"I'd help," Margaret erupted.

"After the way Pierre's workers tried to hoodwink you?" Fred suspected Chardonnay had softened his normally judgmental partner. For the moment.

"They've reformed, don't you see?" Margaret's eye twitched like it always did when she imbibed, more proof of Chardonnay involvement. "Besides, I don't believe in retaliation."

"Me neither," Sharlene said going on to support her claim with another of her stories, this one about her dad getting back at her mother. Her mother didn't appreciate him, he'd claimed, so he left her. But it backfired. While he pined away, her mother found a gem of a second husband. It had been twenty years now, and Sharlene, having never forgiven him for breaking up the family, hadn't spoken to him since.

And with that bit of convoluted reasoning, they retired to the living room where, over coffee and meringue shells filled with raspberry sherbet, Sharlene continued on about her "plan."

Chapter Fifty-Nine

Bradley

After dinner at the Bohrs', as Cedro walked with Sharlene to her car, she asked if he'd mind driving. She'd had too much to drink, she said, and with kids depending on her, didn't want to take chances. They'd be in a bind if she were gone. Besides, she'd learned her lesson, having lost her husband two years before in an accident involving alcohol. Which driver had been under the influence wasn't clear and Cedro was so tired he didn't much care. The long evening had now gotten longer. That nap he'd planned for the ride home was out of the question.

"You can drop me at the end of my street. I'll be fine," Sharlene said as she stumbled in on the passenger side. "Tomorrow I'll get Maw-maw to drive me up to your place to pick up the car. She's stayin' till Sunday, so no problem." She slammed the door and rolled down her window. "Gorgeous night, you think?"

He nodded and opened his too. Maybe fresh air would revive him. There was nothing else that would do it. The town was asleep, its arched street lamps casting sickly light on plate glass windows. The closed Shell station, the blinking red light at the crossing, the chain-linked yard of the old brick school – there was nothing to make him sit up and notice. Nothing, that is, until Sharlene pointed and said, "There it is. First road past the sugar factory parking lot. See that skinny white sign? I'll get out there."

The sign, tapered like an arrow and lit up by one of the street lights, read *House for Rent.* Nearing it, he slowed. "Where now?" he asked.

"I'll walk from here." She reached for the door.

"You can't. It's dangerous."

"Well, then – " No argument. She obviously knew he was right. "Take a right a block down. It's the third house on the left. Watch the potholes."

Two of the ruts were so deep he had to drive on the wrong side. The third nearly blocked her driveway. "What should I – ?"

"Just plow through," she told him.

The scrape on the bottom of the car was like fingernails on a blackboard.

Sharlene, meanwhile fiddling in her purse, mumbled, "I know the key's here someplace."

As he waited, Cedro studied the house. Inside, a dim lamp peeked through a gap in drapes on the picture window and outside a gutter hung crooked and a lightbulb glared where a frosted panel was missing in the small black lantern above the front door.

And there was something else, something that Sharlene suddenly noticed too: on the concrete step half in half out of the light from the lantern sat a little boy in glasses staring out.

"Bradley," Sharlene moaned, key in hand now, flinging the car door open and stumbling out. Shadow long, black purse flapping, she ran – suddenly fleet as a deer – in front of the headlights and across the lawn, catching the boy in her arms, mussing his hair, laughing, kissing him.

Then she turned toward the car and waved. "Thanks, Cedro. See you tomorrow," she called as he reached over to shut her door.

She got there about ten next morning, a white paper bag in one hand and skinny, bespectacled Bradley holding the other. Her mother followed, and as soon as the group was inside, introduced herself. Daughter Gina was at a friend's house.

Most surprising to Cedro was that Sharlene showed no sign of misery from wine the night before. Once they were crowded around the corner table with donuts on a chipped yellow plate and coffee and milk in cups that were seeing the light of day for the first time, she began happily sharing her views on everything from the best kinds of donuts to the benefits of girls' soccer.

"You want to go out and play with the animals?" she asked Bradley when he began fidgeting. She used her thumb to wipe powdered sugar from around his lips. "It might be better than sittin' here with us old people."

He leaned into her, glasses slipping up as he hid his face in her shoulder.

"Remember that dog I told you about last night at the Bohrs'? The clingy one? The one mom named — "

"Underdog," her mom broke in.

"Well, this guy — " Sharlene indicated Bradley with a nod, Bradley none the wiser as he nestled in her arms. " – is likewise."

As if to prove the opposite, Bradley wriggled from her grasp, stepped to the screen door, and slipped outside.

"Hope he didn't scare you last night," Sharlene said under her breath. "But that's the way he is. So needy. Ever since the accident he just hates when I leave."

"He didn't scare me," Cedro said, getting up and looking out the door, where Bradley, sitting on the top step, was petting the Siamese cat.

But when Cedro stepped out and sat down next to him, the boy got up and headed for the end of the trailer. The black cat, warming himself on one of the concrete stepping stones, saw him coming and, tail big, ran toward the woods. A moment later, the boy was gone too. And Cedro, hearing the clatter of cleaning up from inside and suddenly feeling exhausted, decided to go in.

"I'll do that later. Please don't bother," he said. "If you don't mind, I'm going to lie down."

Next thing he knew, he was looking up at Sharlene. "We're goin' home now," she said. "Can you help find Bradley?"

It took a moment to understand. When he did, he got up and led the way out the door and past the cars to the side yard, the direction Bradley had been heading when he'd last seen him. Sharlene, sounding worried, kept calling his name. In between and near tears, she went on about how he should have been in the yard and why he wasn't. She worried about poisonous snakes. Child molesters too.

But no snakes or bad people were in sight when they found Bradley in the underbrush. That didn't mean he was alone, though. On his lap sat the brown and white pup who'd always been scared. Not much of a pup now. He was getting big.

"Why didn't you answer?" Sharlene scolded.

"I didn't want to scare the puppy," he said. And a moment later, quietly, "I didn't want to go home."

As the boy aimed pleading eyes toward his mother, Cedro felt a rush like he hadn't felt since Adria, after the divorce, had said he was the one she wanted to live with.

"If it's alright," Cedro said, "I'll bring him home later."

Afterward, sitting on the plastic chair in his "patio" on the other side of the trailer, Cedro listened to the small voice of a child coming from beyond the elderberry bushes. Talking? Singing? In any case, a happy voice. And when the bushes parted and the boy, sneakers flopping and cat trailing, pushed through to tell him he thought the animals were hungry, Cedro felt something he hadn't felt for so long he wouldn't have known how to describe it. It just felt right. And as that child followed him first to the kitchen for the pet food and then to the yard, where he made ready to dump pellets into the plastic bowls by the step, Cedro was still trying to figure out why he felt different.

His thoughts, though, were cut short by a whisper. "What?" he said.

"Yuck" was the response.

"'Yuck?' What does that mean?"

"The cats will get sick if they eat from those bowls. They're filthy."

He might have told Bradley that they weren't as filthy as they looked; that, in fact, what seemed to be dirt was simply stain from sitting outside in the weather and that Bradley's own mother had been feeding the cats from those very bowls for weeks. Instead, he set the bag in the grass and went around gathering the rest of them as well as the dog's pie tin, then carrying them to the side of the trailer where a hose and rags hung from the outside faucet. "You wash, I'll dry," he said.

"With these dirty rags?" Beneath his glasses, Bradley wrinkled his nose. "Yuck."

"And yuck on you," Cedro said, unable to restrain a smile as he headed for his car and clean paint rags.

Soon, bowls and tin as clean as they'd ever been and Bradley finished feeding both cats and dog, the boy was making plans. "By the time I come next time," he said, "I'm going to have names for every one of these guys."

Chapter Sixty

If You Want To Talk

Louise had finally gotten an answer from her mother. She'd stopped at home to check the mailbox after lunch at Brignac's with Pierre, and there, sandwiched between the phone bill and a Bloomingdale's catalog, was the off-white, square envelope with *Arvilla Bancroft* in fine, familiar hand in the upper left corner. Strange as it seemed, connecting with her mother had become such an obsession that each day, even before she reached for the mailbox tab, she felt her body tense. It had been the same today, except that when she saw the letter the hair on her arms flicked straight up and a shiver shot down her spine.

Once she'd opened it, she read not once, but three times: *Dear Elizabeth, If you want to talk, you may call.*

In the car again, she slipped the note back into the envelope and set it on top of the rest of the mail on the seat next to her before backing out of her drive and heading downriver toward the office.

She'd call her mother tonight.

This fast walk in her soon-to-be neighborhood was Margaret's after-lunch routine now, and with Wolfgang on the leash hauling her along, she pushed on at breakneck speed past Georgian architecture, luxury cars, horse trailers, and ornate iron mailboxes. Pushed on until her fleet-footed pacesetter decided to take a break at the hydrant next to the sales office parking lot.

As he turned and sniffed and sniffed and turned Louise Dennis's red Cadillac, soft rock coming from open windows, pulled into the lot. Perfect, Margaret thought. If she'd planned this it couldn't have been better. She'd been wanting to talk to Louise about Sharlene's fund and now she wouldn't have to make that phone call she'd been dreading. She'd get it over with here and now. Louise always made her uncomfortable. Sometimes she felt like under that serious facade Louise was smirking. If not smirking, rolling her eyes.

Still, Margaret knew that getting Louise behind Sharlene's plan could make the difference between success and failure. The people Louise dealt with in Belmont Estates had money. Influence too. Now the question was – did they have conscience as well? As far as conscience, Margaret's mission would answer the same question about Louise.

So with Wolfgang finished at the hydrant, Margaret made tracks to Louise's car where, as she set her arms on the frame of the opened passenger side window, her watch banged, alerting a seemingly preoccupied Louise. "Mrs. Bohr! What are you doing here?" she said, looking over, apparently surprised.

"To be perfectly honest," Margaret began, "you're my first hit." Despite the sudden realization that *hit* wasn't the best word choice, she went on, launching full tilt into an explanation of the Learning House Project and its benefits. In order to avoid casting aspersions on either Pierre's workers or the man himself she emphasized that Learning House would benefit *all* construction workers, parish-wide, in need of training.

It must've been a pretty good pitch, because when Margaret finished, Louise took a pen and small pad from the shoulder bag perched on the center console and propped it against the steering wheel. "Let me take a minute to jot a few notes so I remember some of the details," she said. "When the homeowners' group meets next week I'll pass the info on to the president."

"Take all the time you want," Margaret replied before standing back, rolling her shoulders, and taking a quick look at her dog who, nose on paws, had fallen asleep at her feet.

When she leaned in again, Louise stopped writing to look over. "I'm a little poky," she explained, "but you know how it is sometimes. Write it down or forget. And I just remembered something else I want covered when the homeowners meet."

"Oh, trust me, I understand. I'm a fanatic about note-taking." Never, at least in recent months, had Margaret seen Louise so downright happy and, whatever had brought about the change, she wasn't about to take a chance on jeopardizing this bit of luck.

So she stayed pat, arms on window frame, breathing as quietly as she could, eyes wandering past the mail on the seat – it would've looked nosy to focus on it – to the soft leather shoulder bag and gleaming wood console to Louise's black hair glistening in the sun and her skimpy black skirt and tight little jacket and pointy-toed heels. The way women dressed these days!

When Wolfgang nudged her leg, she pulled out and checked, finding him fine, simply restless in his sleep. It felt good to straighten her neck and shoulders, and she took a few seconds to do a good head roll. Whatever Louise was writing definitely wasn't short and sweet.

"Just about done," Louise remarked as Margaret resumed the awkward position and began another round of the car, this time stopping at the mail on the seat not far from her chin. (With Louise preoccupied, she wouldn't notice.) The small stack was just far enough away that her farsighted eyes, with help from a bit of squint, could make out beautiful script on an envelope sitting on top of a Bloomingdale's catalog. First-rate penmanship, she thought, the kind she'd give an eye and tooth for. The *A* on *Arvilla* exquisite and the *B* on *Bancroft* fine as calligraphy. Best of all, the *B* on . . . . *Brackenville*? "My God!" she blurted, scalp bristling, "how do you know the Bancrofts?"

Louise's pen stopped.

Maybe it was the whining of the distant chainsaw or the glacial silence that followed. It could have been a combination. Or it might have been the eternity it took for Louise's small tablet to drop from steering wheel to lap. Whatever, Margaret felt like she was part of an authentic thriller.

"How do you know the Bancrofts?" she demanded, more forceful this time.

And while Louise vacantly studied her pen, slowly running her thumb over it, back and forth, back and forth, Margaret added a breathless "Why didn't you tell me?"

When Louise finally twisted toward her – eyes glazed, a helpless look – Margaret thought the crucial explanation was in the works and backed off. But when Louise again turned to her pen, Margaret lost hope and hurtled on. "How can it be you've got a letter from a Bancroft in Brackenville? The *only* Bancroft in Brackenville. I thought you said you'd never heard of the Bancrofts." She glared at Louise, narrowed her eyes. "What are you hiding?"

But the sales manager who earlier had been surprisingly easygoing had reverted to stony, close-mouthed demeanor. Dropping her tablet and pen into the shoulder bag, she rasped, "I'm in a hurry . . . I'll give you a call," before picking up the mail and opening her door.

"But . . . just a quick answer. Please. Tomorrow is moving day. You may not be able to get hold of me for a while. I'll be – "

The slam of the door put an end to her pleading, and she was left with a rear view of Louise, steps a little wobbly, heading toward the entrance to the sales center.

Chapter Sixty-One

Not Funny, Louise

Virtually paralyzed, Louise sat behind the closed door of her office for the next hour. The misstep she'd worried about and worked so hard to avoid had finally happened. She'd messed up, and so badly that any hope of holding on to her assumed identity, any hope of marrying Pierre, was out the window.

The longer she thought about it, the more hopeless it seemed. There was no way to keep the truth from Mrs. Bohr now, no lie that would explain away the letter. That she had all along pretended ignorance of the Bancrofts ruled out a new story. All she could do now was square with her nemesis. And before squaring with her, square with Pierre. Better to bear up to a confrontation now than spend torturous weeks or months waiting for him to get the news through the grapevine.

But how to tell him? In a note, with the engagement ring enclosed? Or in person? It would be so much easier to send a note. Easier in the short term. But in the longer view, doing it that way did little more than postpone the inescapable. No matter how she let him know, there was a showdown in the making. And then . . . .

Yet . . . what if it turned out he loved her so much he'd stay the course no matter what the complication. Now that *would* be a shocker. Yet, such things did happen and unless she gathered her wits and summoned courage now she might never give him the chance to show that under that bigoted exterior hid a true heart.

She was still arguing with herself as she stood on the rear gallery of Pierre's Greek Revival waiting for him to answer the doorbell. She could change her mind, she was thinking, and pretend she'd just dropped in for a quick visit. Yet, what would that help? One way or another, he was going to find out, and this was as good a moment as any. Judging from puddled footprints leading from the pool to the French doors, he was inside. Likely getting dressed after a swim. Likely in a good mood too. Which in this case wouldn't much matter. Knowing his mindset regarding race, she wasn't expecting goodwill.

While waiting, she looked around, already nostalgic. She loved this place. Being honest, it was Valeria Plantation more than Pierre that had enthralled her. And now it was likely it would be off-limits. The crumbling shack way back in the field; the alley of oaks in front; the patio; even that hummingbird – there seemed to be only one – that was now flitting around the potted cigar plant. All of it –

The latch in the doorknob clacked and she wheeled around, heart cranking up.

"What's with ringing the bell?" he said, first peeking out, then swinging the door wide. His hair was dripping and he was in swim trunks. A towel draped his shoulder.

"I . . . just felt like it," she stammered. "I – "

"Well, come on in . . . stranger. If memory serves, I saw you a couple hours ago." He leaned in for a kiss. A kiss she avoided by twisting away.

"Hey. Why the cold shoulder? What's going on? Something with the Bohrs again? Another so-called problem?" He closed the door after her. "Must be some kind of emergency, you driving all the way over here in the middle of the day." Studying her as though the answer lay in her eyes, he began drying his hair with the towel, then stopped, letting it drop to his shoulders again. "There *is* something wrong, isn't there. What is it, Louise?" Stroking his chin, he looked away, then turned back, a cynical smile on his face. "I know. You've made up your mind to call it quits. I've suspected it was coming for a while now. You're here to tell me it's over."

She stared at him, thinking how close he was to the truth. The only difference being he'd be the one to cut the cord.

"Well?" Crossing his arms, leaning against the kitchen island. "Let's have it."

She felt a little woozy, waved a hand helplessly, sighed. Finally opening her mouth, she wheezed, "I'm African-American."

He stared at her, eyes searching, then chuckled. "And I'm part gorilla." Quick as that, his tone changed. "Actually, not funny, Louise."

"I didn't mean to be funny." Her heart was thundering. "And I'm not Louise either. My name is Elizabeth Bancroft."

"What's gotten into you?" His voice was strained. "Get off it. Not funny I told you."

"Not meant to be funny," she said again. "I came down here from Brackenville to – "

"Brackenville! And your name is Elizabeth Bancroft?" His jaw tightened. He'd gotten the drift.

"All I wanted was a fair shake," she said, a tremble in her voice that warned of a dive toward tears. Self-pity, shame

– whatever brought it on – she somehow held back. What helped was seeing in his eyes the hatred that she'd dreaded and knowing that he didn't, and would never, understand or sympathize.

She'd dreamed about just this sort of confrontation often. Most of the time the nightmare included a court convicting her and a judge coming down hard. The strange thing was that now that she was facing judgment, she felt numb, distant. It was as though she were watching it play out but wasn't part of it.

Pierre, though, was all involved. Swallowing hard, clenching fists, eyes like fire. When he stepped toward her she shrank back and reached for the door. And in a quick move before pulling it open, tossed the engagement ring on the floor in front of him.

Outside, it seemed like everything echoed. The kitchen door when it slammed, her heels on the gallery floor, her keys when she dropped them getting in the car.

Chapter Sixty-Two

Mother

The air inside Louise's gloomy bungalow was stale and after setting her purse and papers on the kitchen table she pulled up shades and opened windows. On the levee side the sun was setting, the sky red beyond the ragged pines in front. She leaned on the sill, gazing out, wondering what to do with the rest of an evening that was looking unbearable. Should she try to eat? Turn on the television? There was also that call she'd intended to make to her mother, the one she planned before everything fell apart. But really, the only thing she wanted was to go back to Valeria and resume life as Louise Dennis.

An hour later, having changed to her old jersey nightgown, she lay on her bed wrapped in the comforter waiting for sleep that wouldn't come. Instead, the terrible moment Mrs. Bohr noticed *Brackenville* on the envelope and the pounding in her chest as Mrs. Bohr kept demanding to know how it was she knew the Bancrofts and Pierre's fury when he heard the truth rolled over and over in her brain. What had happened, she knew, was irreversible, yet it seemed there should be some way to go back, find the letter in the mailbox, and start over. At the same time, was that really what she wanted? For a while now she hadn't been comfortable with the prospect of marriage to Pierre. In fact, she'd been thinking that what he was, what he'd become to her, was simply a barrier against loneliness. If she'd still been living in Brackenville her mother would've filled the space, though in a much more lovable way. Now that Pierre was out of the picture . . .

She wriggled out of the comforter and threaded her way through the shadowy, cluttered living room to the kitchen, where she turned on the overhead light, lifted the handset from the wall phone, and dialed the Brackenville number she'd earlier planned to call. "Mother," she said, the word like a foghorn in the night, when the familiar voice answered.

"Yes, Elizabeth," she heard from the other end.

The image of her mother, likely in the brown terry robe that never wore out, resting her elbow on the arm of the blue and white striped sofa, was as real as if she were there, and a rush of longing drifted over Louise. "You can't imagine how good it is to hear your voice." She sat down at the table. "How are you?"

The silence that followed was so prolonged she feared the line had gone dead or, worse, her mother had changed her mind about talking and quietly replaced the phone in its cradle. When the words "The same" (in a hardened tone) assured her that at least her mother was on the line, Louise held back on affectionate wordiness. "How are things?"

She hadn't planned what to say and risked repetition.

Her mother's response – "The same" – was just as worn-out.

"And your health?"

"Nothing new there either. And you?"

Though there was a coolness in her mother's voice, Louise felt relieved that she'd at least shown interest.

"Well . . . I'm down here in Louisiana – I'm sure you realize that from my letter – doing pretty well." She waited for a response, then went on, hoping that if she kept talking her mother would keep listening. She needed so much to know she was there on the other end.

She didn't tell everything, of course. It was a matter of picking and choosing and then letting her mother, if so inclined, silently fill the gaps. Mostly, it was run-of-the-mill – her job, the house she'd rented in Acadi, the car she'd bought – and ignored the topic most on her mind, her rejection at the hands of her fiancé. Knowing her mother's feelings, she didn't even bring up meeting her dad in the LSU Archives or all the Bancroft stuff she now had in storage. To approach either would be to trade already cool indifference for icy bitterness.

"Tell me what's going on up there," she finally said.

"Oh, you know, pretty much the same. One day following another."

"Are the daylilies blooming?"

"They're at their prime, in fact."

"Anything new in the neighborhood?"

"Well – " She was warming. " – you remember Pete Robinson?"

"Sure do."

"He got married. Someone from a block or so over. His mother had some of the neighbors in for a barbeque after the wedding. I baked a couple pies and brought them. Poor dear. She works so hard." She paused. "Oh, and Belle's Grocery burned."

Louise was relieved to have missed both. More than that, relieved that her mother was loosening up. "Sounds like . . . well . . . sounds like . . . good old Brackenville. I often think about the place. Not exactly the place – " It seemed as good a moment as any. " – I think of you. I think, too, of how awful I was to – "

"I don't want to hear it."

"You don't know what I'm going to say."

"I think I do. And what I want you to know is that, though I may not have shown it, I always knew how unhappy you were. No one knew better what you went through growing up." Voice, subdued, she sounded tired. "It nearly killed me, knowing that nothing I did made things better."

"You did make things better. You – "

"But I never thought you'd just leave like that. I thought, unlike your father, you'd one day come to your senses. I guess I didn't realize how much you two were alike." She breathed out. A heavy breath. "Well, it doesn't matter now."

"But it does, and I'm sorry."

"You think saying you're sorry takes care of my grief after you left?"

"Well, I – " A choking sensation.

"I still can't believe it. No warning. Things seem okay. And then you're gone."

"I'm – " She stopped before *sorry*. "I was just overwhelmed. Had been for a long time." Even to Louise the words sounded lame. "But I didn't mean to hurt you. I hated doing it. I hope you know that."

"That you didn't mean to hurt me? To be that cruel and then think it wouldn't – "

"That's not what I mean. I knew it would hurt. It hurt me too. Why do you think I finally wrote? I've missed you."

"And now you think you can dance back into my life as if nothing happened."

"No!" Her response was too intense, and she toned down. "I don't think that. Some things did happen and, because of them, nothing will ever be the same." She was about to go on. But to explain motivations would be to provoke. Besides, her mother knew. "Let's just forget it. At least we're back in touch." She swallowed. "And I still love you."

A sigh. "*Love.* Easy to say. I wish I could, but can't. Whenever I think of what you did, how you let me think things were okay – at least stable – and then left, I can't even pretend."

"If you thought things were okay, it was only because you wanted to. What was it you used to say? Something about nothing happening to anyone that they're not fitted by nature to bear." Louise had often wondered if that reasoning made it easier for her mother to accept that she'd brought a child into a world where she just didn't fit. "Anyway, no reason to argue."

Fearful their exchange was about to wrap up, Louise asked about Rebecca and Mary.

"Are they still – "

"Still active in the rights movement, if that's what you were going to say. They're not like you. You know that. But at least they mean well."

Louise chose to ignore the innuendo. "No one brought up by you could possibly turn out really bad. Lately I've been thinking about how you used to read to us. A chapter or two each day. You know, I've got that copy you gave me of *Meditations* by Marcus Aurelius beside my bed right now. I still use the last nightgown you made too. It's got a big hole, but I just can't make myself toss it out."

"I could – " Her mother paused "Oh, never mind."

"I'd love it if you'd make another, if that's – "

"Actually, it was."

With little more to be said on nightgowns Louise, in the silence that followed, again feared an imminent break. "Still plagued by high jinks at school?"

"Oh, that. Whoever said teaching eighth grade English was easy sure had it wrong. Even so, it's got its good points. I've got some really special kids this year. Most could definitely do college work. What's sad is that their parents can't afford it."

"We were poor and you made it happen."

"Don't forget that I had a decent job and a house to borrow on." Her mother cleared her throat. "And with that . . . my decent job is calling. It's late and I've got tests to grade."

"But – " Louise hesitated, then let it out. " – would you ever think of coming down to Acadi to visit?"

Her mother hesitated too. "I'd have to think long and hard about it," she finally said. "It's a place I've never really had a hankering for."

Chapter Sixty-Three

The Straight Story

Though Louise had promised to call Mrs. Bohr regarding the Brackenville letter, she didn't. In that regard, she owed the woman nothing. Of course that didn't stop the cheeky, white-haired zealot from phoning her at home in the evening as soon as she'd finished her move.

"Before I tell you anything, I want a promise you'll keep it under wraps," she told Mrs. Bohr.

"That's asking a lot. You know, I was thinking of writing a book."

"No deal then."

"No deal! Do you realize you're spoiling one woman's dream?"

"Better than destroying another woman's life."

"It means that much?" A breathing space. "But why?"

"Just because." It was her mother's favorite response when she was little. The truth was, she didn't know why any more.

"Oh, let's get on with it," Mrs. Bohr said after a cautious pause. "I promise."

"Well, then . . . the story's simple enough. I'm the one you've been looking for." Cool and reserved, knowing she no longer had anything to lose, she went on to explain how she'd been *passing* (Mrs. Bohr didn't know the term, and she defined it for her) and how she, indeed, was a descendant of Albert and Charlotte and had at one time been known as Elizabeth Bancroft.

"Elizabeth! Another Lizzie?" Mrs. Bohr squealed. "As in Charlotte and Alberts' daughter?"

"Yes," she answered before going on about how the whole business had been painful and she really didn't feel up to rehashing it at the moment.

Of course, Mrs. Bohr didn't let it drop there, going on about how the Bancrofts of Acadi meant so much to her and how the day she'd found out about Charlotte was the day Acadi had transformed from boring backwater to fascinating frontier. (To be fair, Louise thought on hearing this, Mrs. Bohr *did* have a way with words.)

Further argument from the wordsmith included the claim of a special bond between her and Charlotte and the words *kindred spirits* in describing their relationship. "You see," the babbling windbag went on, "Charlotte and I were both outsiders. Both musicians too. And we had the same experiences, or at least similar. I could go on. But the point is – Charlotte saved me."

"Saved you? Really, now." Louise smiled to herself. "You may be alike, but – "

"Got a minute?" Mrs. Bohr broke in. "I'll tell you a deep, dark secret."

And Louise, whether or not she had a minute, listened – first impatiently, then with resignation, finally somewhat sympathetically.

"So you see – " Mrs. Bohr wrapped up, voice shaky, as though about to break. " – Charlotte and I are linked by grievous mistakes: Charlotte abandoning Albert and me abandoning my mom. And doing it when they needed us so desperately. I know why I did what I did. I wish I knew Charlotte's reason. I guess that's what drives me."

It was a crazy explanation, yet one that hit home. Louise knew abandonment, and from all angles. She'd suffered its piercing blows at her father's hands, then turned around and lashed her mother with it.

A little more receptive now, she pulled a chair out from the kitchen table, sat down, and asked what her troubled colleague wanted to know.

"Oh, there's so much." Mrs. Bohr hesitated. "First off, where the museum stuff is."

"I've got it in storage in Baton Rouge," Louise told her, half expecting a request to see it on the spot.

Instead, like a distracted kid with too many new toys, Mrs. Bohr fixed her sights on the fellow who got Dr. Bancroft killed, the second who insisted the duel continue after first shots. "Did you know when you got engaged that David Nicholas and Pierre were related?"

"No. The first and only time I heard of it was that day at Brignac's."

"You know – " Mrs. Bohr was slow to get it out, as though she were analyzing as she spoke. " – when you add it up, Nicholas knew he had Albert Bancroft both ways. If Albert had survived the duel, he would've likely been tried for attempted murder before a jury of white plantation owners. And can you imagine a group like that deciding the fate of a black Unionist turned Reconstruction legislator? One who'd maimed, perhaps killed one of their own in a duel?" A few seconds of silence. "I still can't figure why no charges were brought against the other guy . . . what was his name? . . . for killing Albert."

"His name was Francois Dupuis, and what I think is that race had something to do with it."

"I suppose." Mrs. Bohr's voice, sounding resigned, drifted off.

Louise got up, ready to set the phone back in its wall mount. "Well, if that's it, I guess I'd better get back to supper dishes."

But Mrs. Bohr wasn't to be put off, and now she turned to something even more personal, bringing up Louise's relationship with Pierre and how it seemed to be a replay of the "Albert and Charlotte drama," as she called it.

"It might look that way" Louise replied, feeling almost relieved at the prospect of getting off her chest something that no one but Pierre and Mrs. Bohr were even aware of, or at least cared about. "It's not true, though. Not at all. The only thing similar was the attraction between two people who normally wouldn't connect. And in case you haven't heard, the engagement's off."

"All for the best, if you ask me," her new confidante judged. "To connect with someone like that for a lifetime would have been disastrous. That aside, you have to admit, you and Pierre were following in Albert and Charlottes' footsteps."

"To the contrary. Albert and Charlotte's relationship was nothing like ours. From what my grandfather said, Albert was up front with Charlotte even before they married."

"But remember the day at lunch when Pierre said Albert lied to Charlotte about his race?"

"All wrong. Albert had told her."

"Do you know if he told anyone else?" She probably had Dupuis, the accuser and assassin, in mind.

"Grandpa said he didn't. That it was just too risky. If the Acadi community had found out, they would've run him – Charlotte too – out of town. Back then mixed couples even risked arrest."

"So Albert was forced to deny Dupuis' accusation." A pause and "hmmm, hmmm, hmmm" as Mrs. Bohr seemed to digest it all before posing another question, this one as to how Dupuis found out Albert was African-American if Charlotte was the only one who knew.

"Something to do with Civil War records," Louise answered. "I never got the straight story."

"And Charlotte. What about Charlotte after Albert died? Do you know if she ever got over it?"

"Grandpa said she hardly spoke of Albert."

"Strange, huh? But how did your grandpa know?"

"I guess the story just passed down. I suppose Lizzie told her grandmother about it when she spent all that time in Brackenville."

"Years after the duel, you mean."

"Right. Something like sixteen years. That grandmother must have been one of the few Lizzie could confide in. Probably the only one. And maybe she needed to talk."

"You know, I finally figured out why Lizzie was up there for all those months." Mrs. Bohr was silent for a few moments, as though waiting for a response. "Did Charlotte ever see Lizzie's baby?"

"I don't think so."

"Did Lizzie ever see her baby again?"

"Yes. She went back to Brackenville several times."

"Was the baby by any chance a throwback?"

"You're asking if my grandpa was black as shoeshine?" She swallowed. "That I can answer from first-hand experience. And the answer is no. No one but my sister Mary is really dark."

"Who was the father?"

"Not a clue."

"And you don't care?"

"Right."

Which actually wasn't true. Of course she wondered about Lizzie's lover. Grandpa had wondered too, and wondered with a passion. But that spry old grandmother who'd taken him in and raised him never let on that she knew.

Chapter Sixty-Four

Tending to Business

"Good grief," Margaret gasped when she finished the punch list. She'd never dreamed this document listing work not conforming to contract specifications (that the general contractor must complete prior to final payment of five percent) would add up to thirty-five items. Or had she? Anyway, with construction on their house supposedly complete, it was time for Pierre to finish up on this list that she'd previously called *Ongoing Building Concerns.*

Surprisingly, except for two deficiencies the architect insisted Pierre wasn't responsible for, Breedlove agreed, copying the list on office letterhead and sending it off to the contractor. Whether Breedlove really believed that once Pierre had done the work on the list the case would be closed was a matter of speculation. Yet, since she'd never shown the architect her concessions list or her photographs, Margaret assumed he did. In that case, Vernon Breedlove was going to be very surprised when at the end of the thirty days Pierre had in which to finish the work on the punch list she brought out pages of contract deviations (titled *Concessions*, of course) that added up to more than the five percent she and Fred were withholding for punch list items and asked for satisfaction in the form of cash payment.

When Pierre sent Benny and Joseph back to do the work on the punch list, she thought maybe the contractor was going to finish up on the house after all. Which only made sense, since (Pierre would think) there were thousands of dollars to be lost if he didn't. Then, when Benny and Joseph abandoned ship, she tried to figure it out. Did Pierre have some intuitive sense that she and Fred wouldn't be good for the last five percent? Did he realize that continuing work would get him nowhere as far as collecting? If so, he was smarter than she gave him credit for.

Pierre's fencing contractor was among the most substantial individuals, girth-wise, that Margaret had ever seen and when, swarthy and sweaty, he arrived one morning at her side door demanding payment for the iron fence, she gave him her undivided attention before explaining her side of the story. "Your agreement was with Pierre, not us. And I paid Pierre for the fence already. It was part of the May draw. He even gave me a lien waiver he said you signed."

"Lien waiver? I signed no fuckin' waiver," he bellowed, spit shooting from his cavern of a mouth.

She stepped back. "Well I'm sorry, but this is really between Pierre and you."

"Pierre and me! I can't even find him."

"I know how it is. But, in my experience, he eventually turns up somewhere in Belmont Estates."

"Not this time. I can tell you that for sure."

"Why do you say that?"

"You haven't heard?"

"I guess not."

"He was kicked out. It was about a week ago. That Senator who's building up the street? He found Pierre cheating him. Got on the horn with Belmont Estates management and before you know it, Pierre Armant is out. Replaced."

"Really."

"Yeah."

"I guess I'm shocked."

"Yeah. Well. So what you gonna do about my dough?"

"There's nothing I can do. Like I said, I'm not responsible."

"You got a fence and I'm out thirty-five hundred dollars?" His eyes narrowed and he positioned gorilla hands on hips that were nearly level with the yoke of her flowered housecoat. "You won't get by with this. If I don't get that money, I'm putting a lien on your property."

And with that, he swung around and stomped to his dirty white pickup, bumbling in and slamming the door. As he roared off, hot rubber stung her nose.

When she told Fred about it that evening, his face paled, as though blood had been sucked dry. "I wonder how many waivers we have that Pierre signed in other people's names," he said. "We could be forced to pay a lot of subcontractors twice."

She disagreed, arguing that she was positive forged documents wouldn't stand up in court. She added that this waiting around they were doing was really getting on her nerves. "The time for patience is past," she said. "It's time we take the bull by the horns and get going on the punch list. More than thirty days have passed. It's obvious Pierre has no intention of finishing the work. I think we should hire the people we need and then follow up with letters asking Pierre for payment for their work. It wouldn't hurt to send the list of contract deviations and damages to Breedlove now either. It'll clue him as to what's coming his way as far as arbitration."

Fred didn't argue.

Margaret felt pure, unmixed fulfillment next morning when she mailed the deviation and damage figures off to the architect. All her meticulous record-keeping was finally being put to use.

Gratifying as that fulfillment, though, it didn't compare to what she felt a couple weeks later when she typed up the first of a series of letters to Pierre. The letters were like a catharsis, and once she'd started, it was hard to stop. Each began, "To keep you apprised of activity on the punch list," the redundancy meant to grate on him much as his constant malfeasance had grated on her. She was taunting him, reminding him that she was still around and tending to business.

After the repetitive intro, she'd get down to details of the corrective work she'd had done by independent handymen: shiny door knobs replaced with the brushed bronze ones she'd asked for; all the ceiling fan problems corrected; dining room doors finally installed; sagging dishwasher re-attached to the kitchen cabinet; crooked doors shimmed; rusty screws replaced with galvanized ones; crooked electrical outlets straightened; wrought iron tie backs to keep shutters secure during high winds finally installed; decent (nice and deep) holes drilled for pegs so that screens didn't fall off; inadequate weatherstripping around doors as well as ugly thresholds replaced; door stops finally put in; furnace vents, replacing those violating code, installed; and so on.

With the letters she enclosed bills for the work. And each letter closed with "Hoping to receive payment soon, I remain," or "Making slow progress toward completion of the punch list, I remain," or "Thanking you for early payment, I remain." Yes, Pierre, she'd think, I'm still around and tending to business.

She didn't expect or receive a response to any of the correspondence. (Was it correspondence when there was no exchange?) Until, that is, the mailman brought the certified letter that was addressed to Vernon Breedlove, Fred, and herself. It read:

> The undersigned represents Pierre R. Armant, d/b/a Choice Construction Company, with regard to monies owed to him for services rendered in connection with the construction of the home located at 87 Santa Anita Road, Acadi, Louisiana. Pursuant to Article 1 – Administration of the Contract . . . Mr. Armant requests that this claim be submitted to Arbitration with the initial presentation to be held at Mr. Vernon Breedlove's office on February 29. . . . It is further requested that Mr. Breedlove make the necessary arrangements for the arbitration hearing.

Chapter Sixty-Five

So Nice of You

Though Mrs. Bohr looked more slender, she was still frumpy, Louise was thinking as, waiting in front of the new West Indies style house, she watched the silver-haired matron approach. She was wearing that ghastly black-fringed poncho. Where in God's name did one find anything so ugly? Second-hand store? The poor woman seemed to have an innate leaning toward the common. She likely shopped at outlets and ate at cafeterias and loved Neil Diamond and flea-bitten cats too. It was strange that her home was really quite attractive. Credit Vernon Breedlove for that.

"This is so nice of you," she said now, getting into the car.

Louise checked the side view mirror and pulled out. "Better not get your hopes up. I can't promise anything. There are papers and things in some boxes, but whether they'll be of interest to you, I don't know. I haven't had time to really look them over."

"I'm just grateful you asked me along."

Asked her along? After months of hints regarding a visit to the storage unit, what was Louise to do?

"Oh my," Margaret swooned as the door to the storage rolled up and she caught a glimpse of black lace. No one had to tell her it was the shawl Dr. Bancroft gave Charlotte on their wedding day. And the music stand it hung on? Slipping on her glasses and reading the museum card, she assured herself it was the very stand mentioned in the archives inventory, the one Dr. Bancroft had made for his new wife.

From there, things only got better, or at least stayed as good, as she scurried between demijohns from Albert and Charlotte' engagement party to an eight-shelved, square-nailed cypress music case built by a slave, and then on to the magazines on the card table. *Etude Magazines* like the ones she'd found in the attic were there, as well as *Musician, Musical Leader*, and – she counted – seven other periodical collections. When had Charlotte found time to read them all?

And the first edition sheet music! She suspected that the ones Charlotte's father brought when he came over from London were the most valuable. But *Dixie*, published by Philip Werlein's of New Orleans, was definitely in the running. And what was so wonderful was that all these items – from what she could see, every single one – had either Charlotte or her fathers' signature in the upper right-hand corner.

"You take this," Louise said, bringing the lawn chair over. "I'm perfectly comfortable on the floor." She took off her little red jacket, setting it on top of the magazines on the card table and, looking streamlined in black knit top and what Margaret took to be designer jeans, went back for one of the battered cartons from near the rear of the sun-drenched storage unit, setting it beside the chair. Margaret moved the other box. Then, having worked up a sweat, she followed Louise's example, taking off her poncho and setting it on the table. After rolling up the sleeves of her old grey batwing and pulling up the legs of her sweats, she sat down and, letting Louise lead the way, started work.

If she could call it work. These cartons were what could be termed a gift from God, likely holding all of Albert and Charlottes' personal papers, plus some. In the first box, wrapped in tissue and at the very top, was the satiny wood baton, well-worn where Charlotte's fingers had gripped it, that she'd used to direct St. Joan of Arc's choir. Likely thick with Charlotte's prints. Now a few of Margaret's as well. A palpable link. Thrilling.

In the same box were Albert's documents for bravery in the service of Queen Victoria (Crimea in 1855, Sebastopol in 1854-55, and Lucknow during the Sepoy Mutiny, 1857). Underneath, again neatly wrapped in tissue, sat two medals, one for Sebastopol and one for Lucknow. If there'd been a medal for Crimea, it wasn't there now.

After that came parched and yellowed certificates certifying Albert's 1861 enlistment as a surgeon with the New York State Volunteers.

"The thing I can't figure out is how a New York Volunteer ended up in White Hall, Louisiana," she said, handing the documents back to Louise.

"If I remember right, Grandpa said that toward the end of the war Albert was with . . . I think he called it an 'army of occupation'. I suppose that army was stationed at White Hall." She carefully set the papers next to the tissue-wrapped medals on the floor and reached back into the box, coming up with letters Albert signed while serving as a Louisiana state legislator as well as ones from when he was in charge of the New Orleans Sanitary Commission.

"Influential fellow," Margaret said. "You come from good stock."

Louise smiled slightly before putting everything back, pulling the other box over, and getting on her knees. First things first, she retrieved an envelope from the top, opened it, and read "October 25, 1874, London, England." After pausing to clear her throat, she continued: "Dearest Charlotte, I was astounded to read in your letter dated September 15 that no one is aware of the reason for the duel. It certainly seems plausible, as you suggested, that it had to do with the chance or careless remark of one involved in politics. I agree that it was against Albert's principles to duel and that he must have been goaded into it." Louise took a break, this time bouncing her head as she apparently skimmed irrelevant material. "Signed, Aunt Caroline."

She handed the letter to Margaret. "Sounds to me like Charlotte wasn't completely candid with Albert's aunt. I distinctly remember Grandpa saying that Charlotte knew full well the reason for the duel."

"Maybe she didn't want his relatives to find out he'd been pretending – " The suggestion that black and white were mutually exclusive suddenly struck her as preposterous. Louise was no different today than six months ago, other than being a lot nicer. Yet she was now "black." And if Louise was "black," who else? Breedlove? Pierre? Fred? Herself?

So much for speculation. Margaret was ready to get on with it. Especially now that she'd gotten a glimpse of what was next in line in the box, which looked to be a leather-bound journal. Her glamorous pal, dark hair shimmering and bouncing as she took it from the box, looked like she, too, was fascinated.

But fascinated or not, after checking her watch, Louise put the journal back. She was worried, she explained, about being late for an appointment with a client. "Why don't you just take the box home," she said, getting up. "I'll come by later to get it." Hands on hips, she deliberated. "Better yet, call when you're ready to go through it. If it's tonight, all the better."

Chapter Sixty-Six

An Adoption

Louise had a feeling that Mrs. Bohr would, no matter what got in the way, find a path making it possible on that same evening to get a gander at what lay in the second box. And she was right. By the time she arrived at the Bohr home the enthusiastic lady of the house had even put the dog out, leaving him to stand, wet nose smudgy, at one of the French doors gazing in pitifully. Where her husband had been sent wasn't clear, but from what Louise sensed, he wasn't within hearing. It wouldn't have mattered anyway; Mrs. Bohr would surely give him the scoop as soon as they were alone.

Having decided that it would be easier to go through the box while sitting on the floor, the efficient hostess had spread huge, cushy pillows (that she'd picked up half-price at Dillard's, she bragged) on the gorgeous concrete flooring that had caused such consternation during construction. As well, so there was plenty of room to spread out, she'd pushed the dining room table against the wall. The setup – a view of the pool and, between them, a tray with wine and stemmed glasses – was deluxe compared to their morning venue.

But Louise wasn't tempted by the wine, white Zinfandel being much too sweet for her taste, and was soon on her knees shuffling through the contents of the musty-smelling container. First in line was the journal that had nearly waylaid her that morning. With *Albert Bancroft* embossed in gold on its cracked leather cover, it had a substantial look. "Do you want me to read?" she said on opening it and finding the script to be faint and splotched with brown spots.

"By all means," was the reply.

"Well then, it begins on November – " She squinted at the blurred date. " – anyway, sometime in November of 1862. The heading is *Fredericksburg,* and this is what Dr. Bancroft writes: 'Campfires in the streets and sharpshooters in rifle pits and I'm self-prescribing for debilitating dysentery. Also trying to set up a hospital for the wounded while lying in half a foot of mud and water inside this tent. Some of my recent surgical patients are being transferred to Washington and I've been telling the bigwigs that by so doing they're sacrificing many of their lives. Care of the wounded, Union's efforts at Vicksburg, the war in general – disgusting.'"

On a lighter note, in 1863 and still in the military, he described an incident while stationed with a garrison of federal troops known as Scott's Cavalry at White Hall, Louisiana. As the story went — a story Mrs. Bohr quietly suggested she'd heard before -- one afternoon he and a Captain Beatty were out riding in the town of Acadi in a horse-drawn buggy when the harness broke. In the course of getting it fixed Beatty discovered that an acquaintance, Charles Corbyn, lived next door to the repairman. Soon, Beatty and Albert, on the doorstep of the Corbyns, were being "implored" by the family to stay for dinner. They did, and afterwards enjoyed the piano and vocal skills of Corbyn's daughter Charlotte.

From that day on, according to his journal, Albert did his best to stay in touch, through letters, with the beautiful woman. And despite his claim that the Union's conduct of the war was disgusting, re-enlisted as soon as his commission expired.

Harsh comments regarding conduct of the war did come back to haunt him, though, and he was arrested and held in Baton Rouge. "My court martial has now been going on two days and up to this time everything is favorable for me," he wrote at one point.

It was right after Louise finished the words *favorable for me* that Mrs. Bohr, seemingly having forgotten her new-found decorum – behavior Louise had taken note of and appreciated both in the morning and since she'd joined her on the dining room floor – whooped, "Court martial! You mean this prominent doctor – head of the sanitary commission, legislator and all that – now has a court martial to taint his fantastic reputation?"

Louise was meanwhile paging through, searching out the next entry. It seemed Dr. Bancroft had gotten lax in posting updates. One month, two months, three months – still no entries. Finally, four months later, a penciled item showed up that spurred a sort of rebuttal to Mrs. Bohr's court martial blowup. "Tainted reputation or not," Louise said, "Charlotte seems to have had no qualms. This says they were married in early1865."

She flipped through the journal seeking out more. When she felt sure she'd covered everything, she set it aside, grabbed a batch of documents from the box, and lay them near the pillows.

"That's all for Bancroft's diary?"

Louise took a paper from the pile and began unfolding it on the floor. "I'm afraid he wasn't much of a journal-keeper."

"I thought there'd be more about his court martial." It seemed Mrs. Bohr neither forgot nor gave up easily. "You know, it's possible Francois Dupuis found out about it and started spreading the word, embarrassing Albert, forcing him to defend his honor."

"Could be, I suppose." Louise was trying to make sense of what she was at the moment trying to read.

"But there are so many possibilities. Like Pierre said, Albert may have been defending his honor against an accusation about his race. Or, like my friend Alma said, a gambling debt may have come back to haunt him."

"Or how about this?" Louise held up what she'd been studying. "Albert's membership in a group called the Union League. It required that the inductee promise to – " She found her place and read aloud, finger leading the way — "'do all in one's power to elect true and reliable Union men and supporters of the government to all offices of profit or trust from the lowest to the highest, in ward, town, county, state, and general government.'" She locked eyes with Mrs. Bohr. "What do you think?"

"Amazing. I guess I sensed Albert was a carpetbagger, but . . . . " She shook her head, picked up her wine, stared into it. "There were major problems, you know, among Republican lawmakers back then. They were divided. There were those who belonged to this Union League and there were those Southerners who'd fought for the Confederacy." She was sounding a lot like a professor. "If I remember right, that last group called themselves the White League. I read about it recently. An article in *The Times-Picayune* that told about a fight between the two sides that got really bloody. People died, in fact. It was called something like 'Battle of Freedom Plaza.' And it was right around the time of the Bancroft duel. Reading about it I got to wondering if the two may have been connected."

"Interesting," Louise said, half meaning it. Her mind was by now crammed with possible connections to Dr. Bancroft's untimely death. Setting the Union League document aside and reaching back into the box, she came up with a loose page, apparently from Albert's journal. "Court martial's out," she announced after reading it. "He got an honorable discharge on July 21, 1865."

The next batch she set on the floor were newspaper clippings, the first, an account of how the duel came about. What she read – and what her obviously enthralled friend heard – was how on Saturday Dr. Bancroft refused to fight but on Sunday morning, after Dupuis – who turned out to be a deputy sheriff – had nailed up placards throughout the parish claiming Bancroft was a "villainous liar, infamous scoundrel, and contemptible coward," changed his mind.

Having finished that – and acknowledged with a nod Mrs. Bohr's wholehearted sympathy for Bancroft's hurt feelings – Louise moved on to an item that described the scene. "'The distance agreed on was fifteen paces. The weapons chosen were pistols (Smith & Wesson's No. 2). First and second shots proved harmless, but on the third and at the word 'two,' both principals fired simultaneously and both went down – one a bleeding corpse and the other thought to be mortally wounded. Dr. Bancroft was shot immediately under the right arm, the ball passing through and completely severing the main artery of the heart, when death ensued without a struggle. Mr. Dupuis, upon examination, was found to be shot about one inch and a half or two inches to the right of the navel, the ball passing between the stomach and the intestines, striking the inner side of a rib on the left side. It glanced upward and remained in his body. He was brought to his home and is now undergoing treatment . . . with but little if any hope of recovery.'"

Another newpaper item quoted Francois Dupuis after the duel: "If I live I will kill the man that says Dr. Bancroft was a coward."

Still another alleged that the duel's seconds deemed it prudent at the moment to travel for their health, a bit of humor from a reporter who explained that the code of honor required seconds stop a duel after first shots and that the parish community was up in arms over losing the popular doctor.

Finally, having read contradictory accounts of much to do with the shootout, including where it took place and who called for second shots, Louise shook her head. "One story says it happened in front of St. Joan of Arc, another that it took place in some judge's back yard. Then there's the matter of second shots. In one, Albert's second makes the call; in another, Albert himself." She met Mrs. Bohr's bespectacled blue-eyes. "What are we supposed to think?"

"Whether Albert asked for more shots or not, the seconds were the responsible ones. That's the way I see it. And the guy who demanded another round, Pierre's relative, was the unquestioned scoundrel. If he did insist on it, I mean. And since I've gotten used to the idea of Charlotte inside St. Joan of Arc playing Mass and Albert outside dying, I'm going to stick with the church as the crime scene."

"And I'll stick with Pierre's relative being the detestable second who made the call." Louise allowed herself a little smile before picking up a single-columned clipping. "This is from a paper called *River Republican,* dated August 25, 1874. It says,

'Dr. Bancroft was buried at ten o'clock this morning in the cemetery of St. Joan of Arc Church.'"

Her eyes met Mrs. Bohr's. "I wonder if we could find his grave."

"No luck with that. I've looked. At some point the river changed course. The oldest part of the graveyard is now under the Mississippi. It's eerie. If you stand on the levee in front of the church and look down, there's one gravestone still sitting there, sticking up in the water."

"Well, then," Louise found her place and resumed reading. "'Dr. Bancroft leaves here in America his bereaved wife, a mother-in-law, and eleven-year-old Lizzie, his adopted daughter – '" Her heart skipped. "What in God's name? Adopted? Why would they say that? It's not true. I'm Albert and Charlottes' blood relative. Grandpa never said anything about adoption, and he knew everything."

Mrs. Bohr gazed across the room and out toward the deck, where her dog, head flopped over the side, lay at the edge of the pool. "You know, it's funny" she said, "I feel like I knew that. Like I read it somewhere."

Louise's heart, still acting up, banged away as she tried to make sense of this most shocking news. What did it mean for her? If it was true, there was no reason to be here on the floor of this house in Acadi, Louisiana, looking through papers that had very little to do with her. She wasn't really a part of this family and to have come all this way, gone through so much only to find that the bloodline that was now her only source of pride didn't include her was like falling off a cliff.

"I don't know what to say," Mrs. Bohr said quietly.

"No need to say anything," she replied, getting up and grabbing her jacket from a dining room chair. "I need air. I need time to think. I'm going home."

Chapter Sixty-Seven

On to Something

Alone now, sorry her companion was so bothered by the latest discovery (also a little hurt that their friendship was based on nothing more than mutual interest in the Bancrofts), but not sorry or hurt enough to give up on the box and what it might hold as far as insight into her soulmate Charlotte, Margaret picked up the clipping Louise had, in her unglued state, dropped and set it with the other clippings. What she really wanted to see now was Charlotte's input. Hopefully, a diary.

Yet, what she found in the little that remained in the cardboard carton included nothing as substantial-looking as Dr. Bancroft's journal. What she found were some daguerreotypes of Charlotte's family in England, a few poems and stories Charlotte had written in her small, straight-up script and even a list of her favorite "maxims," but nothing as personal as a chronicle of daily life.

Among her "maxims," however, was a curious piece dated February, 1870, and titled "Words That Make Sense." Whether it was something Charlotte had concocted in her own mind or something she'd read in a magazine, liked, and later copied in pen and ink was unclear. It went like this:

Many a home-god grows heartily sick of the reverence with which his family devotees pursue him, and sighs for freedom and for his life, and to be off of the pedestal on which his dependents would have him sit forever while they adore him and ply him with flowers and hymns and incense and flattery. Supposing a lady to have a fine genius, a brilliant wit of her own, and the magic spell and infatuation removed from her which had led her to worship as a god a very ordinary mortal, and what follows? They live together, they dine together, and they say "my dear" and "my love" as heretofore, but the man is himself and the woman herself. That dream of love is over, as everything else is over in life, as flowers and fury and griefs and pleasures are over.

Finally, Margaret thought after reading it through twice, she had some insight into what Charlotte may have been feeling on that fateful day Albert died. If after reading this she was still thinking Albert and Charlotte didn't have marital problems she was, for sure, short on brain matter. This was the sort of thing she'd been looking for. Unlike what Albert wrote in his journal – skimming over things as though facts were all that mattered – Charlotte's words had depth.

If only there were more of them. Instead, what was now left in the bottom of the carton was more input from Albert, this time in the form of a bunch of letters bundled in a rubber band that split like cooked spaghetti when Margaret pulled it off. Postmarked in late 1865 when Albert was apparently traveling to New York to muster out of the army, they didn't offer much promise of anything interesting. Being they were written less than a year after their wedding and a long time before the duel, they were likely to be pretty dull.

On closer inspection, though, Margaret found them surprisingly revealing. One in particular, written while stopping over at Bayou Sara to wait for a steamboat, was a jaw-dropper. In it Albert told Charlotte to "meditate over the little squabbles we have had and try to form a new plan for our future guidance despite the unfortunate matter regarding Lizzie."

On seeing the words, *unfortunate matter regarding Lizzie,* Margaret blinked in disbelief. After months following a distinguished family and noteworthy careers, most all of it the stuff of remarkable people — granted, with a misstep or two – was she about to unearth some buried trash? And about Albert, of all people?

Of course, this *matter* could have been anything. Disagreements between Charlotte and Lizzie, say, or just the fact they didn't like each other. But what did such shallow concerns have to do with Albert and Charlottes' "future guidance"? More than that, how old was Lizzie at the time? Wasn't she a baby? Had she even been adopted yet? If she was eleven in 1874 when Albert died in the duel, she was two when he wrote this letter.

It was those words *unfortunate matter* that bothered Margaret. Not bothered so much as intrigued. *Matter* implied some kind of situation. One that required a euphemism to mask its squalid truth. Which, if as sensational as she suspected, would probably bring Louise back to the fold. And in that case . . . .

Margaret stuffed the letter back in the envelope and carefully set it aside. It was a treasure she didn't want to misplace. Even if she found nothing more, this was the clue that, as far as Charlotte's behavior, cracked the case. Hopefully, she'd find even more.

So she slogged on; opening, reading, and returning endearing but humdrum letters to their envelopes. It wasn't till the second to the last one that she came upon another statement that gave pause. Penned by Albert while staying at the Astor House in New York, it claimed: "I can read every flitting thought of your mind. All sorts of imaginations have you, I can fancy, in your bed alone, wondering what your Albert is doing, whether he loves you as a husband ought to love a wife, the temptations he is subject to, the chances that may turn up during his travels which may be the means of his being led astray."

Setting the letter down, Margaret took a deep, satisfied breath before gazing out at the pool where Wolfgang, awake now, was clambering to his feet about to take off after a squirrel. She tapped her lips, fine-tuning her thoughts. Which were pretty simple: unless Albert had already been led astray and proved himself less than honorable there was no reason for Charlotte to have the concerns he referred to.

"Yes!" Margaret said under her breath, more positive than ever that she was on to something. First the Lizzie *matter*, now this. Both pointing to Albert as a far cry from the exemplary husband he'd seemed. In plain uncomplicated terms, he was a philanderer; the daughter he'd generously adopted was likely his very own, a result of errant ways. What's more, his wife knew. The big question now was, had she known about Lizzie before the wedding and, even so, gone through with it or had Albert told her later, when either conscience or Charlotte's suspicion turned the screw? More than that, did he divulge the name of the mother as well? Albert may have been honest up to a point.

Poor Charlotte. It had to be a strain living with proof of her husband's shenanigans following her around, calling her "mother" while at the same time playing second fiddle as the community worshipped that husband for his accomplishments. Carrying on in a situation like that would've demanded much in the way of tolerance. And that, judging from what little she'd written, eventually failed Charlotte.

As far as Albert, was it that abundance of worship that finally got to him? Was the guilt just too much? Was that why he told Charlotte when he did? From what she'd written, that's what it sounded like. On the other hand, if one day she'd unexpectedly come across the picture inscribed "To My Love," the confession may have been forced on him. Maybe that was the day Charlotte really decided she'd had enough. The day, too, when groundwork was laid for finishing Mass.

Next morning right after her regular yogurt and blueberries, she looked up Louise's address and got out the old iron *CB* monogram she'd found in the back yard that day she'd planted the herb garden. As she pulled it from the plastic bag, loose soil tumbled to the floor, and she made sure before putting it back that she'd shaken every bit of that dirt out. What made it so important was that the two letters that proved Lizzie's blood relationship to Albert were going in next and she didn't want to soil them.

Feeling a little, she supposed, like that guy from Publishers Clearing House when he walked up to a front door and got ready to personally notify a winner, she knocked, and when Louise, in bedclothes and with mussed hair and puffy eyes, peeked out, began her spiel. "I have something here . . . after you left last night . . . " she stammered. Finally, holding the bag for Louise to take, she blew out, "Since you're a Bancroft, this is yours."

"I'm sorry?" Louise gave her a look like she'd sprouted horns.

"It's yours. The monogram from the Bancrofts' fence. And . . ." Margaret hesitated, unsure how to handle the next incredible part.

"But – " Louise took the bag, peeking in as though afraid of what, besides horns, was in store.

"Shh, shh," Margaret broke in, finger to lips before taking the bag back and retrieving the two critical envelopes. "After you left last night I found these," she said, pretending not to notice the beginnings of an eye roll. "What I've got here is proof positive that your grandfather was right about the Bancrofts. That all of you up there in Brackenville didn't descend from anyone other than Albert." A warm, satisfying rush swept over her.

Louise, meanwhile having taken the envelopes out of the bag before setting it on the steps, took her time slipping the letters out and, eyes sliding like slugs across each page, taking in what should have but didn't draw the response Margaret expected. Instead, finally finished and working at getting the crackly notes back into their envelopes, she muttered, "Nice try, but these prove nothing."

"But those words *unfortunate matter*?"

"What about them?"

"They sound awfully suspicious."

"Not to me. I think they sound like an ordinary family with ordinary issues."

"You don't find it strange – Albert talking about some serious matter involving Lizzie when Lizzie was little more than a baby? She was two years old when he wrote that letter."

"Could have been terrible twos . . . or colic."

"Colic!" Margaret swatted away the word. "Infants get that, not two-year-olds. And a stubborn kid? Not exactly the stuff of – " She stopped herself. Actually, a really stubborn kid could've been pretty difficult. Regina had given her firsthand experience. "Well anyway, the other letter, the words about Charlotte's suspicions. That sure supports the idea of indiscretion on the part of Albert. And then in combination with the talk of Lizzie and the unfortunate matter . . . Don't you see?"

But Louise merely shrugged and, after picking up the bag, dropped the envelopes back in.

It wasn't but a few minutes later that Margaret, with the bag sitting on the seat beside her, slammed the car door and headed home.

Chapter Sixty-Eight

Bang-Up Job

Margaret and Regina were a team today. A faction that, pretentious as it sounded, were on the side of justice. And on the other side, sitting right there at the conference room table looking sleep-deprived and rumpled and crabby sat Pierre Armant. His lawyer was there too, in a green plaid sport coat of the wrinkle-free fabric popular in the mid-seventies. And who was this newcomer who was about to represent Pierre? Alvin Fisher was his name. And he wasn't merely Pierre's lawyer. Mr. Fisher was his client as well; Pierre was building a home for him in Barrelleaux Parish. All of which was explained by Vernon Breedlove after he'd limped in beaming and asking how everyone was and apologizing for being late. He was, of course, attired in bolo tie and button-down. New to his look were cowboy boots and a cane that sported the silver head of a horse.

When a few moments later Breedlove directed Mr. Fisher to go first, "since he represents the complainant," the lawyer's ears took on a pinkish glow. "I'm a little out of my comfort zone," he admitted, opening a brown accordion-style folder and taking out a number of typewritten pages. "My normal field is animal law," he said, fumbling in his breast pocket and pulling out a pair of thick-rimmed glasses. "But I'll give it a try." He cleared his throat. "My client, Mr. Armant, asked me to call this meeting because he believes the Bohrs still owe him – " He picked up the top page, studying it, rubbing the back of his neck with the fingers of his other hand. " – eleven-thousand seven-hundred and fifty dollars. That amount is the – " He adjusted his glasses; then, like a first-grader finally grasping what he's trying to read, finished in a burst of confidence. " – the five percent due at the end of the lien period."

"Both the amount and who owes who are in error," Regina cut in. "I've found after careful review that it's not the Bohrs who owe Mr. Armant, but Mr. Armant who owes the Bohrs. However, we can get to that later." She sat back in her chair. "Since you called the meeting, Mr. Fisher, go on."

And he did, his extended statement – the gist of which was that during construction the more Pierre tried to please, the more these clients demanded – being interrupted intermittently by well-placed shots from Pierre that Fred recognized as blatant lies. Even after Fisher finished up by accusing Margaret and Fred of holding back five percent as a ruse to get out of paying up, Pierre went on. "A ruse that's backfiring," he barked, addressing Fred. "I put a lien on your house, you know." The statement elicited a sharp intake of breath from Margaret and a stony-eyed glare from Regina. As to Fred, he remained calm, quite sure that if there were really a lien on the property the bank wouldn't have agreed to the new mortgage.

"If there's a lien on the house," Regina said dismissively, "I'm sure we'll know soon enough. Now – " She turned to Breedlove. " – May I begin?"

He nodded.

"What I want to do is go back to the beginning, way back to the contractor's first little bit of deception, when he had delivered to my parents' low-lying lot inadequate fill and began building on it. I want to explain something you may have been wondering: why the Bohrs didn't get suspicious then." She paused as though expecting the architect to admit the very puzzlement to which she referred. "The reason for their naivete was that at that point they presumed Mr. Armant meant to do his best by them. If he put that much fill down, they thought, it was the right amount."

"And it was," Pierre muttered through his fingers.

"It wasn't until later," Regina continued, "that the Bohrs awoke to Mr. Armant's deception. Of course it was too late then to do anything about major problems already affecting their house. All they could manage from that point was to keep track and let Pierre know each time another shortcoming surfaced. And even that didn't remedy the situation."

Pierre sat forward in his chair. "You remember what it was like, don't you Vernon? You simply couldn't please them."

"May I continue, Mr. Armant?" Regina gave him a long, cold look. "Recently the Bohrs sat down and figured up what all this mischief cost them. And that's what we've brought along today. You've seen the figures, Mr. Breedlove?"

He nodded.

"But before that," she said, "I want Mrs. Bohr to show you a few photos that illustrate the contractor's flagrant disregard for the word of the contract."

So far so good, Fred thought, turning his attention to Margaret who, face flushed, had slipped on her half-glasses and was disgorging the contents of her attaché onto the table. From the pile, she took one of the many gold and blue photo envelopes, opened it, and began passing pictures – describing each in turn – across the table to Fisher. The way her voice fluttered, she could have been flashing snapshots of grandkids. "Here are the furnaces that were the wrong brand. And the water heaters that were the wrong size. Oh yes, a shot of water in the garage. It floods every time it rains, you know." With Fisher's hands full now, she slapped prints on the table. "This – the property line and where the fence should have been." Another slap. "Here – an idea of the elephantine chunks of concrete we found in the garden." Slap. "Here – pools of standing water in the yard because of Pierre's stinginess with fill and poor grading. Here – "

"Thanks, Mom," Regina broke in. "I simply wanted to make clear that if there were any questions about the validity of complaints, we've got plenty of proof."

"Just a couple more, dear," Margaret replied, now emptying a second gold and blue envelope and furiously sorting. Fred meanwhile was watching Fisher and wondering what, with that vein pulsating in his temple, was going through his mind. Was he second-guessing his deal with Pierre? Regretting the barter of legal advice for cut-rate house?

"Here," Margaret said, finally locating the photos she was after. She snapped both of them down on the table, tapping first on the one she'd taken of the textured and dappled gray shingles on the house up the street. "That was the roof I wanted," she said, eyes lingering fondly. Now she tapped on the photo of her own roof, black and plain as a coal stove. "That," she spit, pale eyes glinting like steel, "is what I got."

Breedlove reached for the pictures. He may not have seen them before, but he certainly knew of Margaret's disappointment with the roof. She'd kept nothing a secret. So it wasn't Breedlove's reaction that Fred was waiting for. It was Fisher's. Strange as it seemed – and even recognizing that it was the architect who needed to be convinced of malfeasance – it was the lawyer's reaction that Fred was focused on.

Margaret obviously felt the same. She waited till Fisher had both pictures in hand before going into a long-winded explanation about Pierre's responsibility for the discrepancy between what she wanted on the top of her house and what she got. Midway through, she locked shimmering eyes on Breedlove. "I called you. Remember? And you told me that for the time being we might as well try to live with some of these deviations. That we'd settle differences later."

The architect ran his tongue over his upper lip while Regina poked her mother's shoulder. "All right, now – "

"One last thing," Margaret said, picking up the two huge plastic cups of "evidentiary rocks" sitting next to her on the floor and setting them on the table. "This – " She reached into one and pushed a fistful of lustrous, chocolate-colored aggregate toward the center of the shiny mahogany surface. " – is what I specified for the driveway. This – " She shoved some pale, chalky pebbles from the second cup to an adjacent spot. " – is what I got. I could just as well have ordered riprap."

Fisher picked up a few from each pile. When he set them back, Breedlove got up, gently gathered the rocks one by one, and handed them back to Margaret. Then, with a tissue, he carefully wiped grit off the shiny surface and into his hand, depositing it in a nearby wastebasket.

"Time to move on," Regina announced when he was seated again. Fingers to chin, massaging thoughtfully, she studied her notes before looking up and, with narrowed eyes, addressing Breedlove. "A few months ago, Tony Bacino, Mr. Bertrand's fence contractor, turned up at the Bohrs' asking for money, and when Mrs. Bohr told him the facts – that she didn't owe him anything and that she had a lien waiver proving it – he claimed he'd never signed the waiver." She swung around now, fixing keen, accusing eyes on Pierre. "What I want to do right now is establish if you, Mr. Armant, might be in the habit of – excuse my language – forging."

"I'm sick of this," Pierre exploded, cords in his neck tight as bridge cables. "The only place I'll get justice is a court of law. That's where this case should be decided."

"Okay." Regina slammed her briefcase shut, sending papers flying. Backing her chair out, the screech on the wood floor was like a cat in heat.

"One minute," Fisher said before frantically covering his mouth with his hand and whispering in Pierre's ear.

And while Breedlove went after the papers, Regina waited for the other lawyer to finish his confidential monologue. Which ended with a halfhearted nod from Pierre, now slumped in his chair staring at his fingers, and Fisher saying, "Mr. Armant didn't mean that."

"Well what did he mean?" Blatantly confrontational now, Regina's hands were on her hips. "I thought he made himself perfectly clear."

"He wants to rescind his last statement," Fisher said wearily.

Regina let out a prolonged, exasperated sigh and sat back down. "Alright then," she muttered, straightening her papers before turning to Breedlove. "Okay if we give Mr. Fisher the figures now?" she asked in a voice even more weary than Fisher's.

When Breedlove nodded, she patted Margaret's arm. "All yours now, Mom."

Without hesitation, Margaret thumbed through, picking out one of the documents Fred remembered her struggling over. Formatting of numbers and columns and tabs had been a challenge on the word processor, and when she'd completed her painstaking work she'd broken into a few lines of "Ode to Joy."

No silliness emanated from her dissonant soprano today, however. "First, a little background on what it was like working with Pierre," she began, again directing her explanation to Fisher. "There was hardly a day we weren't worried that he'd walk off the job. He threatened all the time and followed through twice. The second time, he was gone for weeks, months." She paused, studying the document, probably making sure she had the right one. "So these numbers I'm giving you show what we paid because of that delay: extra rent for the apartment and furniture storage, refinancing charges, interest."

Fisher took the list. And while he studied it, Margaret licked her thumb and nabbed another. "This," she said, "is our accounting of what we paid Vernon Breedlove for extra architectural supervision which, of course, was necessary because of the way the work was going.

"Now – " Blue eyes flashing above glasses, she pushed two more pages across the table. " – these are substitutions and deviations that were never authorized. You know," she said, shaking her head, sounding a little giddy, "it seems like I've been writing notes and taking pictures forever. But I knew if it ever came to a lawsuit I'd need some kind of record. And, like our daughter said, it wasn't as if we didn't complain. The problem was that in most cases Pierre just wouldn't listen. Yet – " She paused, thinking. " – I've got to be perfectly honest. Sometimes we were just too late in catching things, especially at the beginning when we trusted him to a fault. Like with – "

"Thanks, Mom. We've got to move on. What's important is that you followed Mr. Breedlove's advice when he said to live with things and settle cost differences later. Which is why we're here today. The time to settle up has finally arrived. And that's why we're asking you, Mr. Breedlove – " She gazed down at what looked to be a copy of the contract. " – as per Article 10, Section 10.5 of the agreement between owner and contractor that says the architect is to make the initial decision on any disputes – we're asking you to decide for the Bohrs in demanding Mr. Armant pay the nine-thousand, two-hundred and fifty dollars he owes them, which is the amount left after holding back the final five percent from the twenty-one thousand he owes for everything on Mrs. Bohr's lists, including substitutions and deviations."

Fisher punched away at his pocket calculator. Trying to determine if figures added up? Or calculating what he might lose on his own house?

"I'll declare Choice Construction bankrupt," Pierre threatened, voice high, face feverish.

"Your threats don't scare me," Margaret replied, grinning. "From what I've heard, your plantation is worth more than that stupid company anyway."

"Right." Pierre managed a smile too, a shifty little one. "It's worth more, but it belongs to my parents. You can't touch it."

At this point Breedlove got up. "Unless there's something else," he said, "I think we should call it day. There's nothing to be gained by shouting. When I've made my decision, I'll get in touch with all of you. And Mr, Fisher, it was nice meeting – "

But Mr. Fisher was already out the door.

"You did a bang-up job," Fred told Margaret when he got into the car. She was setting her attaché and the cups of rocks on the floor next to her feet, and looked over at him. "You don't think I went on too long?" she asked, beaming.

"I think you did a bang-up job. You, too, Regina." He met his daughter's eyes in the rearview mirror before turning the key. Then, back to the mirror, he caught her eye again. "Just one question."

"Okay, shoot."

He began backing out, forgoing the mirror in order to look over his shoulder and check the rear. "Do you think Breedlove will decide we should go on to binding arbitration."

"Not much chance of that. He'd look bad. After all, he was largely responsible for your problems. Mark my word, he'll put this whole affair behind him as fast as he can."

"So today we both won and lost."

"Right. You'll never collect what Pierre owes you. On the other hand, you'll never have to pay him another cent." She sat forward, resting her arms on the back of her mother's seat, the scent of her cologne wafting his way. "I've been looking into AIA standards and am convinced Breedlove's got his own problems. In fact, I think he'll be my next project."

"AIA . . . architect group, right?"

"American Institute of Architects."

"You want to elucidate?"

"You and your big words." She laughed. "If what you mean is do I want to spell it out, this is what I mean: If what you've said about your suspicion there were two sets of plans – one for you and another for Pierre's employees – is true, I think Breedlove's in big trouble."

Chapter Sixty-Nine

Trees and Birds

Ouch! Traffic beating at his ears and all shades of gray smoke stinging his nose, Pierre stood in a parched field a half-block from Airline Highway waiting for his chance to make a few bucks. Since this wave of bad luck with Belmont Estates Homeowners Association, he really needed the dough. To be banned from building there had been a major downer.

Low-cost was the word today. And what struggling young family could resist the package: their choice of any lot on the three-acre parcel and a new house to boot. Having paid next to nothing for the land, he'd make out too.

"Chuck and Barb Morgan," the short-faced, sturdy fellow in gray and blue-striped shirt, blue shorts, and heavy knee-length socks, said when he and his family were out of the ancient Isuzu Trooper. He shifted his kid, the little darling's mouth dribbling a curdled mess, from one arm to the other and extended his hand. "Excuse the twinsy look. Saturday morning soccer, you know."

"You both play?" A nod and smile to disguise his stupefaction.

"It's a couple's league. Teachers." Chuck twisted his head away from the kid, who was now trying to snag one of his old man's gargantuan ears.

"Teachers! Love it. Salt o' the earth. My aunt's an English teacher. Smartest woman I know." A genial look that gave no hint that Auntie Harriet wasn't Pierre's favorite. She was stuffy to the nth degree. Cheap too.

"Yessir," Chuck went on. "Barb's kindergarten. I'm history and coaching. And I guess you know what that means." The kid began whimpering, and Chuck bounced him. "That's why your deal in the classifieds sounded interesting." He looked around. "But – "

"I guess this is reality, huh?" Barb whined, looking around as well, hands on oversized hips stuffed in shorts identical to Chuck's.

"I was lucky to get this parcel," Pierre said before any real flak could fly. "Right after I nabbed it, the prices around here skyrocketed."

"But is this residential?" Barb was staring at the rail cars on the other side of the highway.

"Right here it is, and you've got your choice of lots." He paused long enough for a groaning semi to exit the warehouse area. "I own the whole three acres."

Barb shaded her eyes with her hand and, like the proverbial Indian, rotated slowly, taking it all in this time. "To be honest, this isn't what I expected."

"No?" At his asking price it had seemed like a deal to Pierre.

"Well, I thought it was country. Trees and birds. That's what your ad said."

He rubbed his chin, leaned against their car. "That's where landscaping comes in. Trees, then birds. Finally you don't even know you're anywhere near a highway."

"Yeah but landscaping costs so much, and we've – "

"What are those?" Chuck broke in. He'd noticed the metal bus barns next to Pierre's parcel.

"Not sure," Pierre answered. "I'll check into it though. You know, what's really special about this area is that it's not in the floodplain."

"Mmhmm." Chuck gazed away.

In the silence that followed Pierre considered a new approach. "Ever heard of Belmont Estates?"

"Who hasn't?" they both said at once.

"Well, I built some of their fanciest homes."

"Impressive," Chuck said before bouncing and shushing the fussing kid and then giving Pierre a sidelong glance. "This might seem nosy, but I have to ask – what are you doing out here when you could be in Belmont Estates putting up mansions?"

Pierre met his eyes with the true-blue gaze of a bleeding heart. "It was a matter of principle. I decided I'd rather provide lodging for good, simple people who deserve better."

"Interesting." Chuck narrowed his eyes and went back to bouncing the kid. Who all at once gave out a whopper of a yowl. When he handed the brat to his wife, she growled, "He's hungry and we've got to go." With that, she snapped around and headed for the door on the passenger side. "Thanks," she called back in the rock-hard voice of a female soccer player.

"Yeah, thanks," Chuck said, reaching for the door.

Pierre thought fast, reached for Chuck's arm, took one last shot. "If you'll wait a minute I'd like to show you something. Got a sec?"

He didn't wait for an answer, instead hustling to his car, where he picked up some flyers from the pile on the seat.

"These were done up by Belmont Estates," he said, handing a few to Chuck when he got back. "They might give you some idea of my background."

Chuck opened the door of the Trooper and got in.

"You know, you won't find a cheaper deal. And – "

"Thanks," Chuck said again. He slammed the door, started the car, and burned away, leaving Pierre in a cloud of acrid smoke.

When he got into his own vehicle Pierre sat for a minute, staring out, thinking this might not be as easy as he'd hoped. He'd need to revise his plan, draw attention away from drawbacks and toward strengths. Maybe start with the handout?

The handout. He picked one up and put on the reading glasses sitting on the console. *Over the past five years, Pierre Armant, President of Choice Construction and personification of excellence in the building industry, has been committed to the creation of superb custom homes as well as to using the fine skills of his fellow parishioners at Loving Kindness Church in Kenner, Louisiana. The homes he builds not only benefit you, his customers, but needy members of this close-knit Christian community. Mr. Armant's promise is that the quality of your new home . . .*

He stopped reading. He had it. Start with the church part next time.

Chapter Seventy

A Medal

It was just past eleven on a bright Thursday morning, and the fried onion smell from the River Road Drive-In next door was tempting as Margaret, visor low on her forehead and eyes on the buckled sidewalk, carried an armful of Fred's soiled button-downs toward the dry cleaner. She was taking small, careful steps and giving little thought to anything but keeping from stumbling when she heard her name and looked up to find her racetrack buddy.

"Where were you last Sunday?" Alma asked, already digging in the bib of her overalls and pulling out a pack of cigarettes and a shiny red lighter. "Things aren't the same at the racetrack when you're not there."

"Too much going on."

"Still on the Albert and Charlotte kick?"

"Oh yeah."

"That reminds me – " Alma inhaled and blew out, then crammed the lighter and cigarette pack back into her bib. " – the other day we got something in at the historical museum that had Albert Bancroft's name on it."

"Really."

"It was a medal – " A bus whipped by, flipping Alma's short dark hair straight up and flapping her dangly Mardi Gras mask earrings. She turned her back to the lashing dust. " – a medal with Bancroft's name on the rim. For service in . . . . " She gazed away, concentrating.

"Crimea?"

She turned back. "How'd you know?"

"Well, it's one of the things that's missing."

"From where?" But Alma didn't wait for an answer. "You'd never guess who had it." A cagey look, a long drag from her cigarette, and a whoosh of smoke from deep in her lungs. "It was in a box your contractor brought in. Pierre Armant said he was cleaning his attic and found the box in a trunk that belonged to some long-deceased relative. He said she was the younger sister of David Nicholas, that guy who played a big part in Bancroft's duel. Her name was Olivia?" A pause as though expecting a sign of recognition. "Anyway, Mr. Armant said this 'Olivia' was his forebear, and because of her relationship to David Nicholas and the duel – and the fact this bit of Nicholas history was moldering away in his own attic – he felt like the historical museum should have it." About to take another drag, she added, "You know, the way Mr. Armant bragged up Nicholas you'd think the guy who got Bancroft killed was a god or something."

A car with a faulty muffler roared out of the drive-in lot, and Alma's eyes followed. When the racket faded, she turned back. "You should take a look. Actually, what Mr. Armant brought in was more like two boxes. A box within a box. A little one and a big one. I found the medal in the little one.

Ten minutes later – if that – Margaret found herself in the "Lasserre Parish Culture and Heritage Center," looking through the smaller of two boxes. It was what she'd call a keepsake box, and had definitely seen better days. Inside, along with a hodge-podge of dried flowers and tarnished jewelry she, of course, found the medal. Along with it was a locket with initials ONM on its case. The medal not only had *Crimea 1855* on the front but in tall, thin capitals on the rim *Dr. Albert Bancroft, Medical Staff.* And the locket? Inside was a snippet of the same photo that had slipped from beneath the French Opera program in Charlotte's album. No mistaking the newborn's heart-shaped face; widow's peak; round, wide-set eyes; full lips.

Proof of a serious liaison with Albert? Margaret now had it. Now if she just . . .

She got down on her knees, sorting through papers in the big box, searching for the clincher. At the bottom was a Bible, and she opened it to the first page where, above the dedication to King James, she found it.

"You want me to photocopy this *one* page?" the secretary asked when she brought the Bible to her. "It isn't even scripture."

At home, comparing the inscription she'd copied in the archives months ago – the one from the back of the newborn's photo – to the signature on that dedication page in Olivia's Bible, Margaret confirmed her suspicion. *To My Love – 1863* was in the same script. The slight backward slant, the round letters, the extra curls on T, M, and L – everything identical. If she'd been convinced she had incontestable proof when she found the baby picture in the locket, she had a superabundance of incontestable proof now. The baby in the picture had to be Lizzie, and Lizzie was Albert Bancroft's daughter. The mother – Olivia Nicholas.

"Whoa!" she whooped, dropping her steamed up body into a kitchen chair as her wired brain pondered how it was back then and how David Nicholas must have felt. How angry at the source of his sister's infamy.

She glanced at her watch. The courthouse would still be open for more than an hour. Plenty of time for a gander at one of her favorite old tomes to answer her final question.

When she got to the second floor, she headed straight for the big room and the faded red books on the bottom shelf. After pulling out *1860 Census – Lasserre Parish*, she took it to a table and carefully turned the crisp, yellowed leaves until she found the surname *Nicholas*. Under given names there was a Joseph and a Pierre. Pierre seemed not to have married, so it was Joseph and his family that she honed in on. In 1860 he was forty-five. His wife, Mary, forty-two. Their children, David Robert and Olivia Marie, were nineteen and fourteen respectively. That would have made Olivia seventeen at Lizzie's birth in 1863. Seventeen!

And Albert? If Margaret remembered right, he was thirty-five in 1870 census records. So he would have been twenty-eight when his teenage lover gave birth. Eleven years her senior. Sex with a mere child.

How could this have happened? No family would have encouraged a relationship like this, much less condoned it. Did that mean Albert and Olivia met on the sly? That her family wasn't aware? If that were so, did her brother know?

Margaret leaned back in her chair and began twirling a convenient cowlick, trying to sort the whole thing out. If, to hide the truth, Olivia was sent away and then talked into surrendering Lizzie to an orphanage right after birth, and Lizzie wasn't adopted by Albert and Charlotte until a few years later, maybe her brother hadn't put two and two together until he'd seen Lizzie, taken note of her age and resemblance to Albert, and done some investigation on his own.

But if that's what happened, why didn't David Nicholas himself come right out and challenge Albert? Yet, there was this – to publicly confront Albert about Lizzie would have tarnished the whole Nicholas clan.

If he'd planned it, Nicholas couldn't have experienced a more fortuitous conclusion to the disgrace that secretly plagued him. It was in the heat of off-and-on-again duel challenges between a man named Dupuis and Albert, with Dupuis apparently accusing Albert of something pretty bad – at least pretty bad back in those post-abolition Reconstruction days when hatred of blacks was at a peak – that Nicholas got his payback. The accusation was that Albert was Negro.

Margaret couldn't swear by her suspicion. The only thing she knew for sure was that, in defending his honor, Albert had chosen David Nicholas as a second. David Nicholas who, of course, had no idea how the duel might end. He could only hope. And hope even harder if Dupuis, piling indignity on indignity, truly did charge that Albert lied about his lineage. The bitterness, the humiliation Nicholas must have felt at hearing that the father of his sister's child most likely had mixed blood! That is, assuming Nicholas was as bigoted as his relative, Pierre Armant.

And that was what was hardest for Margaret to grasp: how that bigoted relative had remained in the dark, with not an inkling that Albert Bancroft had fathered a child with his very own antecedent. It was ironic, this puffed-up fellow bragging that one of his forebears was responsible for the death of a "black carpetbagger" when it turned out that forebear's sister – and his direct ancestor – was the mother of the carpetbagger's offspring. Wouldn't Pierre be surprised. And surprised too, shocked actually, when he realized that the fiancé sitting next to him that day at lunch when he went on about his lineage – and who he'd recently discarded because of hers – was related to him.

Chapter Seventy-One

Get Off It

Another misbegotten Bancroft infant? Impossible, Louise told Mrs. Bohr. This tendency toward loose sex wasn't believable. That Lizzie was Albert's daughter from an alliance with a seventeen-year-old was too much. And then that Lizzie, years later, brought into the world an illegitimate son named Byron? About as believable as those rumors about Einstein running around having affairs.

Yet, the proof was there and Mrs. Bohr had been generous in sharing it. And now, Louise found herself ringing the doorbell on Pierre's rear gallery. As on that other day, the day she'd given him the lowdown on her deception, she was again ready to throw light on an inside story. As well, to give him a little of his own medicine. Not to gloat exactly. Well, maybe a little. At least she wasn't as nervous as last time. In truth, not nervous at all.

She gazed around. Everything was familiar, yet different. Nothing as perfect as she remembered. There was an unfortunate odor suggesting rotting shellfish from a heap of newspapers next to the garbage can. And the grass was shaggy. And though the pink azaleas were in bloom, there were no tulips. In their place were weeds. Of course, Pierre being no gardener, tulips were out of the question unless he had someone to fuss with them. Last year –

"What do *you* want?" he spat, eyes fiery as he opened the door.

"I've got some news for you," she responded, holding back an impish grin.

He braced himself on the door frame, more in than out, and the swimming pool off the rear gallery reflected shimmery waves on his glowering, beard-stubbled face. "Seems like you just love coming around with juicy tidbits," he snarled.

"I suppose you're right," she answered calmly. "It's a little different this time, though. The news this time has to do with you."

"Me, huh." He tittered softly. "It's hard to find much dirt about me. If you think some cockeyed story Celeste's been spreading about child support fits the bill, I'd advise you to –"

"There's no cockeyed story from Celeste. And if you're not meeting child support obligations it's no business of mine. The news this time has to do with those boxes you donated to the historical society and what your good friend Mrs. Bohr found in them."

He shrugged. "Tell her to shove it up – "

"No need to be offensive, Pierre." She was getting a little worried he might slam the door in her face, and decided that laying bare her news in a speedy manner would be best. "What Mrs. Bohr found," she went on, "was a photograph and medal that prove without doubt that – "

"Wind Bag Bohr! After me again." His lips formed an unconvincing smile. "Nothing she does will ever spook me."

"Oh no?" Louise had over the past couple days thought about this conversation many times, like a child anticipating that moment when she'd prove to her parents that she was tougher than they may have thought. Now, at last, the moment of proof with Pierre having arrived, she felt like her plan for this moment hadn't been good enough. Her barnburner of a revelation needed some kind of dramatic lead-in, and she didn't have one. All she had was the simple statement, "You and I both are descendants of Albert Bancroft," which, leaving her lips, sounded as ordinary as a comment on the weather.

Pierre's response was more in keeping with the drama she'd imagined. "My God, woman, what's gotten into you?" he squealed. "You're losing your marbles." Following his words came a burst of wild laughter so delirious she could see every tooth in his mouth and smell every drop of the red wine that stained it. "Oh dear," he said finally, tears running down his cheeks as he wiped at them with his fists, "I had no clue how crazy you'd gotten. This thing about my great, great . . . whatever she was to me . . . my antecedent, Olivia? That refined lady was happily married with two gorgeous – and very white – kids. I've seen pictures."

"You're right, I'm sure. But before she got married, in her early years, she was the paramour of Albert Bancroft. And that's how it happens that this disgusting blood coursing in my veins also coursed in Lizzie Bancroft's, who was the daughter of Olivia – "

"Get off it," he snapped, as though grasping what was coming next.

" – the daughter of Olivia Nicholas and Albert Bancroft."

His recoil was the most carefully suppressed and quickly checked she'd ever seen, but it was an authentic flinch, one that on the spot switched to a vigorous rubbing of the right eye. "And you expect me to even consider this shit you're spouting?"

"It might be worth your while to at least give it some thought, being it indicates that even the lofty Nicholas pedigree is not without African linkage. And – " She simply had to add a few words she knew would rile him even more. " – maybe instead of bragging about some criminal relative named David Nicholas and his role in Albert Bancroft's death next time you donate a box of memorabilia, you might take care to be sure, even if that box comes from a lowly female relative of little importance that . . . " She couldn't come up with the right words. " . . . it doesn't catch you with your pants down."

The veins in his neck stood out as he backed into the house and slammed the door.

Chapter Seventy-Two

Filthy Blood

His one-time fiance's bombshell was both revolting and improbable. How anyone, even one as schizo as Louise, dared come around with fiction like that was just plain stupefying. And to present it as though it were honest-to-God truth was ridiculous. As was asking a man of his education, caliber, background to believe it. But Louise was Louise, after all, and she had a penchant for lying. To her it was likely just another story. Whether it was legitimate or not made little difference. Nor would it make any difference to Queen Bee Bohr, the only one he knew who gave a damn about Albert Bancroft and who, seeking revenge for the home construction baloney, was open to this kind of smear. In which case Louise, already unbalanced and looking for something to take the sting out of his rejection, joined right in. That being the case – two crazy broads with vendettas – was there any reason to give credence to the story and go back to the museum to check out the boxes? Hardly. Better to forget it. Hard to do, being the claim was so revolting. But best to try.

And that's what Pierre did until the stormy day he got a letter from Louise that said she just wanted to give him the facts. Which were: a picture of a baby that was a dead ringer for Albert as well as one of Albert's war medals had turned up in Olivia Nicholas's boxes, as well as some nonsense about matching handwriting. None of which much mattered. Yes, Olivia had been a Nicholas, but not one that counted. If she'd counted, he wouldn't have given the boxes away. And as far as the other part, the filthy blood? By the time he'd come into the world, that blood was likely so diluted that, if tested today, his body wouldn't show a trace.

Chapter Seventy-Three

A Fine Idea

Not a cloud in sight. A hint of breeze. The air cool and dry. A mockingbird on a bare branch of the swamp maple near the garage singing every song he knew. It was the beginning of a beautiful day and, if weather held, one that would end the same way. Toward evening Fred hoped to be out on the course at Sugar Lake.

He pulled out onto the river road, moving to the side so that a van, coming up fast, could pass. Being it was Fat Tuesday and there was little going on at work – nearly everyone down in New Orleans at Mardi Gras parades – he had all the time in the world to once again take in what he'd grown to love. Tin-roofed cottages, handmade fences, sugar cane kettles – there was just no place like this neighborhood he now called home. Sure, there were drawbacks, like the oil refineries and chemical plants and, for that matter, grain facilities. But knock his bread and butter? Locals did enough of that already with their complaints about emissions and dust and waste. And the press didn't help either. Lately, though, bad press had turned good, at least toward Welbourne Grain and the few who supported the cause. Public sentiment had turned too. And the amazing thing about it was that he, Fred Bohr, was the one to thank for the turnaround. Fred Bohr, who as a kid had hoped to make the world a better place but who since then had become a little jaded. Of course he had to give Margaret some credit too. She'd urged him on in the first place.

Urged? Too mild. What she'd really done was coerce. It was after dinner one night, when during "Crossfire" he was faithfully flossing his teeth, that she really started in about Learning House, that venture to help train construction workers that he'd never fully endorsed.

"These drib-drab contributions I'm getting aren't going to get Pierre's workers any training anywhere," she said. "The way things are going, those people will never escape his greedy iron fist. If, that is, anyone's even hiring Pierre anymore."

"Well, you knew it wasn't gonna be easy." Aware that she liked complete attention while speaking, he turned down the television and resumed flossing.

"But I didn't know how tight people could be. I mean, they're cheaper than me." She gave him one of her canny smiles. "So, you know what?" Smile having vanished, she looked away, then back. "I've decided to give up on donation jars and door-to-door. I'm going for the gold."

"As in – ?"

"Big contributions. Like the one your company made."

"From?"

"Who else? Businesses along the river road."

"Good luck."

"Good luck to you."

As he remembered, it took a moment for him to digest her words. But when he did, he stopped sliding the waxed string up and down between his lower teeth and answered with a bit of bite. Quite a bit. "I'm not doing it."

She looked like he'd surprised her with a punch to the gut. "But why not? You're the one with influence. If you'd ask some of those muckamucks, we'd probably get a lot more contributions. Major ones."

"I will not go begging."

"It's not begging. It's a tradeoff. You said it yourself. The people in those houses neighboring the elevator have stopped complaining about grain dust, and all because your donation to the Learning House project got written up in the *Lasserre Parish Sentinel*. Don't you see? You bought goodwill."

"So now you're an authority on that too?" The comment had slipped out. And at that moment hadn't seemed unusually cutting. Maybe a little sarcastic. Nothing more.

But Margaret saw it in a different light and in an instant changed from supplicating and pliant to obstinate and determined. And stayed that way. A week later she was still meeting his clarifications and apologies with frigid shrugs. She wasn't going to let it pass.

"Why can't you forgive and forget?" he'd asked. "Why take personally what wasn't meant that way? I wasn't mocking your good intentions. I didn't mean it as a putdown either. Really, I'm sincerely sorry if I hurt your feelings."

Still she remained cool. Asking forgiveness obviously wasn't the key.

So what was? What could he do to show he respected both her and her efforts? Words had no impact. Actions spoke louder than words, as his mother had always said. But he could think of only one action that would mend the rift. It was to go out and, like a Girl Scout minus cookies, beg. A terrifying prospect. One he simply couldn't accept. There had to be an easier way.

Days later, however, he still hadn't come up with it.

And that's what led to that terrifying prospect of solicitation on behalf of The Learning House turning into miserable reality. He had no alternative. If, that is, he were to return his marriage to its previous state of passable harmony.

So now came the really hard part – choosing the unlucky joe he would hit up for a contribution. It was going to be a most stressful mission, this singling out, and all because there was no one in the river road business community that he felt like taking a chance on alienating. The group was a bunch of ordinary guys who just seemed to want to get along. He considered most of them friends. Even Delbert Atwater of Shimer Chemical was okay if you didn't spend too much time with him. Otherwise, his way of looking down his aquiline nose at just about everything and everyone was a real put-off.

A put-off that in this case might not matter, though. A response in the negative would be just fine. At least then Margaret would be forced to admit he'd done his best. Or whatever. At this point he couldn't determine if she'd gotten mad because he'd been sarcastic or cutting or obstinate, and all he could hope was that she'd find it in that impenetrable heart of hers to let it pass.

So who would it be? There were those fellows he couldn't bear turning off, some of them golf buddies, and then there was Atwater. The price of losing the buddies? Costly not only to that cooperative spirit that meant so much, but to those friendships that had taken time to nurture. The price of alienating Atwater? Honestly, he wasn't even sure at the moment if Atwater liked him.

And with that, he placed the Shimer exec's name at the head of his "To Do" list.

It was on the following Wednesday that, having set up the meeting earlier in the week, Fred sat down to lunch with this fellow he'd never much cared for and exchanged stilted chitchat until their food arrived. Then, just as Atwater elegantly placed a portion of tomato wedge between his wrinkled, supercilious lips, Fred began his solicitation.

Which led to exactly what he'd expected. Atwater's faded hazel eyes narrowed and as his mouth worked away, obviously with an urgency to swallow what prevented him from verbally expressing displeasure, Fred felt himself wince. Here it comes, he thought, expecting the worst. Or, hard to conceive but true, the best: he'd be able to tell Margaret he'd made the effort and failed.

So what did the big kahuna say after patting his lips with his napkin? His response was an uncomplicated, "Now that is a fine idea. And you say your company has already made a donation?"

"In fact it was written up in the paper a few weeks ago." Beside a ping of complete astonishment, Fred was feeling an immediate affinity with the former obstructionist.

"Hmm. Sorry I missed it. You know, I've been out of the country." He rolled his tongue behind his lips and gently nibbled a found morsel. "You know, this is so ironic. Back in my hometown in Oklahoma we had a tremendously successful program much like you're suggesting. Amazingly, we called ours Learning House too. There was an article about it in the magazine our church publishes." His creased fingers played with an equally creased earlobe. He seemed to be thinking. "I bet you're Methodist," he said, meeting Fred's eyes.

"No, but the woman organizing the program is."

"Ah." His expression went soft and he stared out the window. "My wife, who died in August —" His voice unsteady now. " – was one of the organizers of Learning House in our town." He swallowed, turned back. "So if you're looking for a proponent of the cause, you sure picked the right man. That aside, it's just the sort of thing Shimer Chemical has been looking for. Something to improve image. This reputation we industries along the river road between New Orleans and Baton Rouge have of turning the area into a cancer alley makes it awfully hard to do business down here."

Two days later, when a generous check from Shimer Chemical came in the mail, Fred was still marveling at his luck. Sometimes, not very often, but on occasion, it seemed things fell into place in a most fortuitous way. Not only had he unwittingly chosen to approach a man predisposed to supporting the cause, he'd chosen one who as a member of the local Rotary – and soon-to-be president – also promised that charitable group's involvement, and in a big way.

Chapter Seventy-Four

The Gathering

Everything was perfect. Daylight savings time. Gorgeous evening. Strains of Saint-Saens organ symphony softly wafting from the outside speakers, just loud enough for Margaret to feel the usual tingle as the Finale began and the organ broke in like a burst from heaven. A breeze rippled the fronds of the windmill palms at the far end of the deck. Dragonflies, blue and iridescent, landed and took off from the clear plastic rafts in the shimmery pool. A lustrous hummingbird hovered at the pot of orange honeysuckle near the iron fence in the rear. And the table was beautiful, with a yellow cloth, an old-fashioned bouquet, and trays of finger sandwiches, mushrooms stuffed with breadcrumbs and herbs, and chocolate-covered strawberries Margaret had driven all the way to Jefferson Parish to pick up the day before. There was a pitcher of lemonade for the kids too.

It was a compatible group, and more compatible as the evening wore on and the wine flowed. There was talk about everything from the charming home to how things were going at the old racetrack to what was happening with the Learning House project to – once Cedro and his skinny little friend loosened up – Little League plans for the summer.

The gathering wasn't big. Seven adults, three children. Ten, including Fred and herself. Not an insignificant group, though. Among them were Margaret's best friends.

There was Alma, in a skirt for a change, and a blouse with a collar that hung like spaniels' ears. She'd taken to chewing both Wrigley's Spearmint and fingernails since giving up smoking, she said, holding out her hand to expose fingertips raw as rare beef.

There was Sharlene, in the same green dress she'd worn to dinner at the apartment. She'd asked if her daughter Gina could bring a friend and it looked to Margaret, watching the three as they stood next to the table, like they were confused as to what Gina and that friend were going to do now they were at the party. "You want to meet the animals?" Margaret asked the girls, motioning them to the rear bedroom where Wolfgang and Carol were holed up. Once the girls were settled in front of the television, one with the cat in her lap and the other patting Wolfgang while he breathed his hot, smelly breath in her face, Margaret returned to the pool area and Sharlene, ushering her over to where Cedro and Bradley were listening to Fred tell about the three-legged dog he'd had as a kid in Minnesota.

There was Delbert Atwater, too, with his flushed cheeks and bald head and superior demeanor. Margaret would always be grateful to him for saving the Learning House project. Tonight he seemed to be the only one really loving Saint-Saens. At the moment he was deep in conversation with Louise who, in understated but skimpy simplicity, looked lovelier than ever. "No, not Portuguese," Margaret heard her say. "Actually, African-American. I'm a descendant of Albert Bancroft. Don't know if you've heard of him. He . . . . "

About the Author

In 1986, when she and her husband moved to a small community on the River Road in Louisiana, Susan was enthralled with the idea of living amidst beautiful antebellum homes across from where a steamboat had once docked in order to bring ashore performers to entertain the isolated residents. When, later, Susan found out that an African-American doctor killed in one of the last duels in Louisiana had lived on her property, she was even more enthralled, deciding then and there that, with time on her hands, she'd spend it writing a factual account of this historic duel. Not so quick, she soon had to tell herself. With her search for relevant materials turning up nothing conclusive as to the reason for the duel and its peculiar circumstances, she had to change tack. Her story, still based on what she knew of the duel, would be fictional.

So began Susan's writing career. Up to that point, she'd made little use of her English/Journalism degree. She'd been a church organist, piano accompanist for the Suzuki violin program at the University of Minnesota, and – at least to her mind – the consummate wife and mother. But when she found herself in what she considered the "boondocks" of South Louisiana, she turned a page.

Now that page is many pages, and has taken the form of a genealogical mystery set in the late twentieth century. Having spent hours researching the unfortunate doctor and his family at Louisiana State University and libraries and courthouses between Baton Rouge and New Orleans, and even at the National Archives in Washington D.C., Susan felt she had material to work with. Having at the same time experienced the bitter pill of dislocation and, with it, insight into people and situations she'd never experienced before, she had the building blocks of her novel.

The story is based on how secrets past and present haunt goings-on of the moment. Racism, displacement, the plight of the disadvantaged – subjects that had previously held little interest for her – began to enter the picture as Susan plotted a narrative based on what she both did and didn't know about the duel as well as what she would soon know of the misery of dealing with a bigoted and corrupt home builder. A gambling husband, a star-crossed painter from Cuba, and, most importantly, the beautiful passing African-American descendant of the duelist round out the fictional picture.

All of it the upshot of one aging empty-nester starting life anew in rural Louisiana.

www.ingramcontent.com/pod-product-compliance
Lightning Source LLC
Chambersburg PA
CBHW070820190726
48292CB00006B/2059